PASSION'S SPELL

"Richard." Serena raised her head to look up at him with shadowed green eyes. "Just tell me . . . you're willing to try. Tell me I'm not alone in believing we're more than Master and Apprentice. Tell me that what I feel isn't wrong."

He lifted one hand to cup her cheek, his thumb stroking over satiny skin and lightly brushing the curve of her lower lip. Had he always known her eyes were bottomless? He thought he could lose himself in them, a terrifying, seductive notion. "What do you feel, Serena?" he asked, his voice hushed.

Her long lashes quivered a bit, not veiling her brilliant eyes but betraying a pang of vulnerability, and her mouth twisted a little in painful self-mockery. "I . . . oh, hell, you have to know exactly what I feel. It's not like I can hide it from you—"

He bent his head and touched her lips with his. It was a careful, tentative kiss, very gentle and so fleeting that when it ended Serena looked as if she wasn't certain it had happened at all. "Tell me," he murmured.

"I love you," she whispered. "I've always loved you. And I've always been afraid you'd send me away if you knew."

"I would have. Once, I would have." He was bending his head again as he spoke, covering her mouth this time with more certainty and a sudden hunger. . . .

THE WIZARD OF SEATTLE

Kay Hooper

BANTAM BOOKS

New York · London · Toronto

Sydney · Auckland

THE WIZARD OF SEATTLE
A Bantam Fanfare Book / June 1993

FANFARE and the portrayal of a boxed "ff" are trademarks of
Bantam Books, a division of Bantam Doubleday Dell Publishing
Group, Inc.

ISBN 0-553-28999-3

Published simultaneously in the United States and Canada

Bantam Books are published by Bantam Books, a division of Bantam
Doubleday Dell Publishing Group, Inc. Its trademark, consisting of the
words "Bantam Books" and the portrayal of a rooster, is Registered in
U.S. Patent and Trademark Office and in other countries. Marca Reg-
istrada. Bantam Books, 1540 Broadway, New York, New York 10036.

PRINTED IN THE UNITED STATES OF AMERICA
RAD   0 9 8 7 6 5 4

This book is for my editor, Nita Taublib, because of her enthusiasm, her honesty, and the sneaky tactics she uses to get me to return phone calls.

This book is for my agent, Eileen Fallon, because she never yells at me, even when I deserve to be yelled at, and because we can talk about anything—even politics.

And this book is for my friend Catherine Coulter, because of something she said in San Diego.

THE
WIZARD
— OF —
SEATTLE

PROLOGUE

Atlantia—Past

It was near midnight, but the sky remained a deep and pulsing blood red, as if a dying sun lingered long past its time. Directly above the village, above the miles-across natural amphitheater formed by the tall mountains that ringed the valley, the very air was alive with energy, crawling and crackling softly. The small cottages of the village were dark and silent, huddled in among themselves.

If anyone heard the girl, no one answered her cries.

She did not scream hysterically, nor was there any note of hope in her calls for aid. Her wide blue eyes lifted often to the shifting sky that could be glimpsed between the trees, but she spared no glance behind her, where the sounds of pursuit grew louder. After a time she saved her breath for running, knowing only too well that she could expect no help from the villagers.

"Where'd she go?"

"I saw her—"

"There! Quick, cut her off!"

Harsh voices. Three of them. Ruthless male voices containing no pity, no mercy, no emotion save furious urgency.

With the instinct of a hunted animal, she evaded their trap, choosing the thickest part of the forest and ignoring the thorns that ripped and tore her white robe as she ran. The sounds of pursuit dimmed, the forest echoing with ghostly epithets no less savage for the distance between them and the desperately fleeing girl.

The stabbing ache in her side forced her to halt when she was less than halfway across the valley. She leaned against a squat and gnarled tree and stretched her right hand up to the sky, as if beseeching some nameless, faceless god to help her. Her only answer came when her feeble energies were turned back on her fiercely by the unforgiving night of Atlantia; there was a flash of dim, grim light and a searing pain in her hand that jerked a moan from her lips. She brought the hand to her breast and cradled it there with her left one, not bothering to look at the new blister that had been added to the others.

At night in the valley, all were powerless.

Especially the women.

Over the sounds of her labored breathing, she could hear her pursuers, closer now, on her scent like a pack of ravenous wolves. They were not wizards. Unlike her, they were not enervated by the heavy pressure of energies lashing in the sky above or unable to use the natural strengths of their bodies and minds. They were not exhausted, or lost, or alone.

And they were not afraid of her. Not now. Not at night.

She pushed herself away from the tree and stumbled on, so weakened now by her useless attempts at defense that she knew she would never reach the slope of the mountain looming ahead.

They wouldn't kill her, she knew, at least not deliberately. Even in this valley, where she was powerless, they would not dare to take her life. She almost wished they would, for what they intended to do to her would destroy her slowly and in agony. The power she could not use to defend herself would be stolen from her by their greed and lust.

Or so they believed.

She slowed her pace simply because she could no longer run, but continued to make her way through the forest, trying to move silently through the thick undergrowth. She held her seared and blistered hand to her side in an effort to ease the pain in both. She was so tired. So weak. Sanctuary was too far away; the slopes of the mountain ahead seemed more distant with every step she took.

Her terror and hatred, rising from the depths of her soul like some black thing alive and on the wing, blinded her. Her strength almost gone, she plunged through a thicket of brambles, into a shaft of brilliant moonlight—and into the brutal embrace of her hunters.

Two of them grabbed her by the arms, stretching her limbs out from her sides and holding them immobile as if, even now, they half feared her power. They were strong, their work-roughened hands grasping her arms with a force that nearly broke bones. These were farmers, she realized dimly, men who worked exhausting hours to tear crops from the capricious soil of Atlantia. And all three were still young enough to hope for something better.

"Hey, boys, we caught ourselves a wizard," a third one said with a laugh, approaching her with a caution that suggested both eagerness and wariness.

"Don't do this." She felt the rough bark of a tree against her back, and pain stabbed her shoulders as her arms were nearly pulled from their sockets. She didn't bother to deny her powers, knowing it would make no difference even if they believed her. And they wouldn't believe her, for she bore the unmistakable sign of a female wizard of Atlantia.

The two men holding her were silent but for their heavy breathing; the third stood before her and looked slowly, insolently, from her wildly tangled hair to the delicate, scratched ankles below the hem of her torn white robe.

"Haughty bitch," he muttered. "Strutting around in the daylight with your nose in the air like you own the world. Not so proud now, are you?"

Terror, rage, and aching despair welled up inside

Roxanne like a tide of anguish. She couldn't stop this! They would never listen to reason, and they certainly feared no punishment for what they were about to do. She was helpless against them, powerless, without any defense at all. No matter what she said or did, they would be on her like animals, rutting out of hate and ambition and fear and lust. And she couldn't stop them.

Men. Even women of power were ultimately helpless against them. These valley men who hunted at night with their brutal hands and frightened lust, eager to vent their hate and greed and frustration on vulnerable females. Those male wizards with their lordly palaces high in the mountains and their lies and schemes and arrogance, enacting laws expressly designed to torment and degrade both the women of power they feared and the valley women who served as the vessels for their pleasures and their sons.

With a choked sound she spat in his face.

He stood motionless for an instant, as if he feared her saliva might contain some terrible magic that would melt his flesh. Then a hoarse growl erupted from his throat, and he slapped her, with the full strength of his arm behind the blow. It rocked her head back against the tree; blackness swam before her eyes, and nausea churned in her stomach. As if from a great distance, she heard hollow, echoing, booming voices.

"Bitch! Make sure she can't move."

"You gonna plow her standing up?"

"Just hold her."

Nearly unconscious, Roxanne moaned as the pull on her arms sent spasms of agony through her shoulders and back. She felt the touch of fingers, cold and clammy as they fumbled against the base of her neck, and then there was a sharp tearing sound and the rush of air as her robe and shift were ripped open from neckline to hem. She tried to struggle, but her movements were only weak twitches. Fighting to hold the blackness at bay, she shook her head to clear it and looked up into the feral, feverish eyes of the man.

He was tearing at his own clothing, yanking his trousers open and shoving them down, his lust further inflamed by the sight of her slender body. He half stumbled and lurched closer, his meaty hands grasping and clawing at her naked flesh.

Roxanne made a last desperate bid for freedom, ordering her drained muscles to offer up what strength they had left. But the effort was little more than a jerk, and cost her almost unimaginable pain as the men tightened their grip on her arms.

"Hold her," the one pawing her grunted as he reached a hand down to guide himself. "Hold her—"

She didn't have the strength to fight, the breath to scream, or the will to die. The tears she might have shed were burned dry by her hatred before they could escape her eyes. She stared over his shoulder at tiny distant lights high on the highest mountain, and tried to detach her mind from the agony and degradation of what he was doing to her.

They were laughing. The other two, the ones holding her, were laughing and fondling themselves with their free hands, waiting for their turn. They would take turns with her all night, using her again and again until dawn stole their courage and sent them slinking away from what would be left of her.

She couldn't . . . couldn't . . . Something inside her snapped, and the pain was gone. She didn't feel anything at all. Or hear anything. Or see anything.

Tremayne drew his cloak about him to protect against the chill of the night air, and leaned against the balustrade. Far below, the valley was spread out in the peculiar flickering darkness of an Atlantia night; up here atop the tallest of the seven mountains that ringed the valley, the air was clear and sharp. Sound carried well up here.

Especially some sounds.

He tried to close his mind to what was happening at the other end of the terrace, not so much disturbed as disgusted. His "uncle" Varian—the title was actually one of respect, since their familial connection was distant—was entertaining his favorite concubine, a plump village girl of perhaps eighteen who had already borne him four sons and who was eagerly at work to accept a fifth into her womb. Varian tended to get sons on his women; his favoritism toward the improbably named Virginia stemmed more from her energetic lustiness than her fertility.

They were rutting now on a pile of cushions at the opposite end of the terrace, some sixty feet from Tremayne, and he knew it would not disturb his uncle at all if he went over and pulled up a chair to watch; Varian, upon occasion, enjoyed performing for an audience—usually made up of his sons.

Tremayne, however, was no voyeur. He would have much preferred to go inside, but knew only too well that his "cousins" were engaged in activities similar to those of their sire. He doubted he could find an empty room.

So, closing his ears to the sighs and moans coming from that end of the terrace, he gazed out over the valley and let his thoughts wander. They were disjointed, as thoughts often are, skipping across his mind like stones on a pond. Occasionally one would drop and cause ripples that circled outward.

The lady. No, don't think of her. Think of something that won't drive you mad. Your father sent you back here to Atlantia to find out why the earthquakes have worsened, why the tides are erratic, and why even across the sea the flickering clouds above this continent are visible. All the wizards outside Atlantia are worried—and now you know why.

Yes, he knew why. Because here on this isolated island continent, ambition and greed had run rampant. An old civilization was splintering, the population teetering on the brink of extinction, the very ground beneath them shuddering in the first throes of death.

The Master wizards here saw themselves as gods. Especially Varian.

After being in this house for several months, Tremayne had come to the conclusion that Varian was a glutton, his appetites insatiable. He was a glutton for food, but since he was also a glutton for sex, perhaps he needed the energy. He was a glutton for power. He was obsessed with the determination to rule Atlantia, whatever the cost—and his frantic begetting of sons on every powerless female capable of bearing them was only one of the strands of his web.

Varian, Tremayne had realized, intended quite literally to people the wizard population with his offspring and eventually crowd out all other male wizards. He was confident of his ability to control his sons—with some justification, Tremayne thought—and equally scornful of the other Master wizards' less energetic reproductive abilities. As for the female wizards, he was plotting even now to find a way to destroy their Sanctuary and them.

He'd steal their powers if he could—and he hasn't given up the idea of that yet. He hates and fears them, but he can't help wondering. . . . It's all that's forbidden to him, taking a woman of power into his bed. One day his lust may overcome even his fear of vulnerability, and he'll risk his life to satisfy his urges.

Somewhat grimly Tremayne wondered if Varian had considered the fact that by slaughtering their female infants and busily using the available powerless women as broodmares, he and his male offspring were steadily destroying the balance of the population. Probably not. Though there was a certain cunning in his nature, Varian's appetites overwhelmed any rational overview of the future. His obsessions were blind, deaf, and mute.

"Alone again? God rot you, Tremayne, it isn't natural for a man your age to ignore bitches the way you do!"

Tremayne glanced briefly aside to find his uncle, stark naked despite the chill of the air, staring at him with a frown.

"Didn't you take a fancy to that black-haired bitch who was twitching her teats at you during supper?" Varian asked, leaning an elbow on the balustrade as he looked at the younger man.

Tremayne had once objected to his uncle's degrading terms for women—powerless women were bitches to him, and female wizards were whores—but Varian had only laughed at him. Having always considered himself rough-mannered, Tremayne knew that here in his uncle's house, and perhaps in Atlantia itself, he was by comparison a veritable gentleman.

"No," he said finally, his voice even. "She was very pretty, but I won't bed a child half my age."

Varian looked surprised. "A child? Fifteen's a bitch all filled out and haired over. Why, I got a boy on her . . . let's see, must be a year ago. You have to get 'em while they're fresh, man, not dried up and stretched out of shape."

For a brief moment Tremayne felt curiously detached. He was, he realized, listening to a Master wizard, probably the most powerful one in the world, and this supposed giant had absolutely nothing on his mind except breeding. Varian was barely forty, just ten years older than Tremayne. He had more than sixty of his sons in residence (those deemed too young to be sexually active occupied a house nearby), triple that number of girls and women in various stages of being impregnated, a home that was a virtual palace, and any luxury he could wish quite literally his for a snap of his fingers.

Tremayne imagined Varian and his offspring breeding like rabbits for another thirty years, and into his mind crept the clear, cold awareness that they would have to be stopped. Somehow. Before Atlantia broke under the weight.

"You worry me, Tremayne," Varian said.

Tremayne looked at him, not for the first time grateful that his own considerable abilities shielded his thoughts from even a Master wizard. "Would it ease your mind if I told you I kept a mistress in Sanctuary?" he asked dryly.

Varian's frown cleared, though the twist of his full lips indicated scorn for a man who could be satisfied with only one woman. "I suppose that's where you were all afternoon?"

"Yes," Tremayne answered, not lying. He *had* been in Sanctuary, though there was no mistress; if Varian dared show his face in the city, he would realize that the laws there prohibited any male wizard from so much as touching a female, with or without power, unless she was his legal wife. And since none of the male wizards in Atlantia had ever married, all the women of Sanctuary were completely off-limits to them. But few males of power ventured inside the walls of Sanctuary, and few atop these mountains knew or cared what laws prevailed there.

Tremayne knew the laws well. He had spent much of his time these last months exploring the city, taking extreme care to give no offense and wearing the mark of power without either shame or arrogance. He had learned a great deal.

Varian shook his head almost pityingly. "You're too damned choosy, Tremayne, that's your trouble. And a fool to keep your bitch in the city. Her place is here, warming your bed. Is she breeding yet?"

"No," Tremayne replied. Again no lie. She was not pregnant, the woman he wanted; at least she showed no sign of it. And he had hardly gotten close enough to be responsible if she were. She had proven elusive; he hadn't been able to find her since that brief meeting more than a week ago that had struck him with such numbing force, he still felt shock when he thought about it.

"My Lord?" Ginny's voice was almost a wail, bereft.

"She's ready for another ride," Varian said to his house guest with a wide smile, and turned away to stride back along the terrace.

Tremayne didn't linger to hear the noisy coupling. He descended through the gardens rather than returning to the house. It would be dawn before he reached the valley floor, but he was restless and, more than anything, had to get away from his uncle's house.

Thoughts of the lady pushed every other aside, and he felt again that strange, wrenching shock inside himself. He didn't know if she was a wizard or powerless; their meeting had so affected him that he had been blind to even that most basic of questions. He knew only that he wanted her. She had been slight and rather fragile, but not childlike; hers had been the ripening body of a young woman. Golden hair escaping the net into which she had carelessly bundled it, wide blue eyes in a heart-shaped, delicately lovely face. The grace of a young doe. The innate wariness of a woman of Atlantia.

He didn't know who she was. Or what she was. But he knew he had to find her.

It was past dawn when Tremayne reached the valley floor and took the road to Sanctuary. The Curtain was dispersing as the first rays of the morning sun reached over the mountaintops. And it had been many long hours of torment since Roxanne's final, hopeless cry had echoed through the forest beside the road. If he glanced to the left, he might see something like a pile of soiled laundry against the base of a tree no more than thirty feet away.

He didn't look.

Seattle—1984

It was his home. She knew that, although where her certainty came from was a mystery to her. Like the inner tug that had drawn her across the country to find him, the knowledge seemed instinctive, beyond words or reason. She didn't even know his name. But she knew what he was. He was what she wanted to be, needed to be, what all her instincts insisted she had to be, and only he could teach her what she needed to learn.

Until this moment she had never doubted that he would accept her as his pupil. At sixteen she was passing through that stage of development experienced by humans twice in their lifetimes, a stage marked by total self-absorption and the unshakable certainty that the entire universe revolves around oneself. It occurred in infancy and in adolescence, but rarely ever again, unless one was utterly unconscious of reality. Those traits had given her the confidence she had needed to cross the country alone with no more than a ragged backpack and a few dollars.

But they deserted her now, as she stood at the wrought-iron gates and stared up at the secluded old Victorian house. The rain beat down on her, and lightning flashed in the stormy sky, illuminating the turrets and gables of the house; there were few lighted windows, and those were dim rather than welcoming.

It *looked* like the home of a wizard.

She almost ran, abruptly conscious of her aloneness. But then she squared her thin shoulders, shoved open the gate, and walked steadily to the front door. Ignoring the bell, she used the brass knocker to rap sharply. The knocker was fashioned in the shape of an owl, the creature that symbolized wisdom, a familiar of wizards throughout fiction.

She didn't know about fact.

Her hand was shaking, and she gave it a fierce frown as she rapped the knocker once more against the solid door. She barely had time to release the knocker before the door was pulled open.

Tall and physically powerful, he had slightly shaggy raven hair and black eyes that burned with an inner fire. For long moments he surveyed the dripping, ragged girl on his doorstep with lofty disdain, while all of her determination melted away to nothing. Then he caught her collar with one elegant hand, much as he might have grasped a stray cat, and yanked her into the well-lit entrance hall. He studied her with daunting sternness.

What he saw was an almost painfully thin girl who looked much younger than her sixteen years. Her threadbare clothing was soaked; her short, tangled hair was so wet that only a hint of its normal vibrant red color was apparent; and her small face, all angles and seemingly filled with huge eyes, was white and pinched. She was no more attractive than a stray mongrel pup.

"Well?"

The vast poise of sixteen years deserted the girl as he barked the one word in her ear. She gulped. "I . . . I want to be a wizard," she managed finally, defiantly.

"Why?"

She was soaked to the skin, tired and hungry, and she possessed a temper that had more than once gotten her into trouble. Her green eyes snapping, she glared up into his handsome, expressionless face, and her voice lost all its timidity.

"I *will* be a wizard! If you won't teach me, I'll find

someone who will. I can summon fire already—a little—and I can *feel* the power inside me. All I need is a teacher, and I'll be great one day—"

He lifted her clear off the floor and shook her briefly, effortlessly, inducing silence with no magic at all. "The first lesson an Apprentice must learn," he told her calmly, "is to never—ever—shout at a Master."

He casually released her, conjured a bundle of clothing out of thin air, and handed it to her. Then he waved a hand negligently and sent her floating up the dark stairs toward a bathroom.

And so it began.

PART ONE

Seattle

ONE

"Ten bucks says you can't do it."

Serena Smyth lifted an eyebrow at her friend, her catlike green eyes alight with amusement. "You're on."

It was one of many bets between the two young women since they had met in high school years before, lighthearted and, as usual, challenging Serena's uncanny ability to get information, or anything else she wanted, from a man.

Jane Riley, an attractive and vivacious brunet, giggled, but then suddenly looked nervous. "I don't know. Maybe this isn't such a good idea. Serena, Jeremy Kane uses his column to trash anybody he hates, and since that model broke up with him, he hates every woman still alive and breathing. There's no way he'll dance with you, let alone spill the beans about the grant. And if he realizes you're just after information, next week's column will make you look like the whore of Babylon."

"He'll never guess what I'm after," Serena retorted confidently.

"Oh, no? Look, friend, we both know he's virtually pickled after years of drinking, but he *was* a crackerjack

investigative reporter once upon a time, and some of
the old instincts might still be there."

Serena shrugged. With the frankness that often startled people because her appearance made them believe
she was too elegant and haughty to ever speak bluntly,
she said, "I don't think he could find his butt with both
hands and a flashlight."

Jane, knowing her friend rather well, began to regret
her own impulsive challenge. "Serena, why don't we
just forget the bet this time? If you go and do something crazy, Richard will never forgive me."

"Forgive you? Don't be silly, he knows me too well
to ever blame anyone else for my tricks. Besides, you
know you're dying to find out if Seth gets the grant."

Jane couldn't deny that. Seth Westcott was her live-in
lover, an artist with a difficult temperament, and Jane
knew their cluttered loft would be much more peaceful
if she could tell him that the fifty-thousand-dollar grant
from Kane's newspaper was going to be his. More
peaceful for a while, at least.

But she hesitated, mostly because of Serena's uncle
and onetime guardian, with whom her friend still lived
here in Seattle. Richard Merlin had always made Jane
feel just the tiniest bit uneasy, though she couldn't have
said exactly why, since he'd always been perfectly pleasant to her. It might have been his dramatic appearance;
his slightly shaggy black hair, austere, rather classical
bone structure, and startling black eyes gave him the
appearance of a man who might have been anything
from a poet or maestro of the symphony—to a serial
killer.

In actuality, he was a businessman, involved in various
real estate ventures, and both well known and highly respected in the city. A rather ordinary kind of career, certainly, and he had never done anything to call undue
attention to himself or any of his actions. But Jane still
felt curiously in awe of him, and it always made her
nervous when Serena cheerfully did something they
both knew her uncle would not be happy about.

Shaking her head, Jane said, "Of course I want to

know if Seth gets the grant, but I'd rather not see your name in bold print in Kane's column."

"Oh, that'll never happen." Serena spoke absently, her attention elsewhere as she scanned the well-dressed crowd. The occasion was a dinner-dance charity benefit, and since the charity was a good one, the crowd was happy to be here. Both the food and the band were first-rate, and the party was being held in a hotel ballroom, so none of the guests felt the automatic constraint that came with being in someone's home.

The huge room was very noisy.

Serena finally found what she'd been looking for: Richard's tall form on the other side of the room. He was talking to the mayor, his attention firmly engaged, and was unlikely to notice what she was up to.

"If you're so sure Richard won't care what you're going to do," Jane said suspiciously, "then why did you check first to make sure he was across the room?"

Serena rose to her feet, leaving her wrap over the back of the chair and her evening purse on the table. She was a bit above average height and slender, but by no means thin. In fact, she could have earned a healthy income posing for the centerfold of any men's magazine, and the backless emerald green evening gown she was wearing displayed that eye-catching figure to advantage.

The gown also set off her bright red hair, currently swept up in an elaborate French twist, her translucent complexion, and her vivid green eyes. She was a beautiful woman, her features exquisite and deceptively haughty, and a considerable intelligence made her able to hold her own in most any situation.

Smiling, she looked down at her friend and said, "I never said he wouldn't care. I just said he wouldn't blame you."

Watching her friend move gracefully among the tables toward her intended target, Jane felt a brief, craven impulse to find Seth in the crowd and announce that she wanted to go home. But he'd be suspicious, and she'd have to confess she had dared Serena to do something dangerous. Again.

It had been fun during their teenage years, because Serena had accepted even the wildest dares and because peculiar things always seemed to happen when she did.

Like the time Jane had dared her to approach the famous rock star who'd been performing in Seattle. Serena had gotten past the guards at the stage door with incredible ease, emerging in triumph ten minutes later with an autograph. She had been wearing a stage pass, impossible to buy or fake, and had only laughed when Jane had demanded to know how she'd gotten it.

Later Jane had heard an odd story. The sprinkler system backstage had been acting up just when Serena had been there, going on and off in different areas randomly, drenching equipment and driving everybody nuts.

Serena, of course, had come out perfectly dry.

And there had been another occasion Jane had never forgotten. A mutual friend had taken the two girls out on a fishing boat, and he had bemoaned the fact that the small family fishing businesses such as his were a dying breed; they simply couldn't compete with the huge commercial operations. He was on the verge of going under financially, he had confided, and during this particular week the catch had been truly abysmal.

Jane had happened to look at Serena just then, and she'd been struck by her friend's expression. Gazing out over the water, Serena had chewed her bottom lip in a characteristically indecisive gesture and then, looking both guilty and pleased, had nodded to herself, her eyes very bright.

There had been no opportunity to ask her friend what was going on, because their host had begun to haul his nets in. To his obvious shock, the catch was the best of the season, incredibly good; the boat rode low in the water with the weight of the fish. It seemed his luck had turned. In fact, after that day he had only to cast out his nets to be rewarded by all the fish he could handle.

Jane had never asked Serena about that, just as she'd never asked her about a few other peculiar things, such as why light bulbs had an odd tendency to blow out near her and computers often went haywire, or why she couldn't wear a wristwatch (they went crazy or simply died on her), or why the weather always seemed to be good when she wanted it to be. Jane simply accepted the good fortune of Serena's friends and privately decided that she was three parts witch.

But she was nervous about this bet, and watched anxiously as Serena reached Jeremy Kane's table. The newspaperman had been drinking steadily all evening, and had more than once gotten so loud that those at nearby tables couldn't help overhearing him as he caustically held forth on a number of subjects. But he hadn't left his table even once to dance.

Jane saw her friend lean down to speak to Kane, but she didn't get the chance to observe his reaction, because her own date returned to their table just then.

"Sorry to be so long, honey," Seth said as he sat down beside her. "Thompson's wife had to tell me in great detail how she wanted her portrait to look." He was a tall, very thin man with average looks and deceptively mild brown eyes, and possessed only two unusual physical characteristics. His voice was so beautiful, it was nearly hypnotic; and his hands were incredibly graceful and expressive.

Jane had no trouble in fixing her attention on Seth; she was absolutely crazy about the man. "Megan Thompson? If she has any sense, she'd just ask you to make her look like somebody else."

Seth grinned at her. "Meow."

"She has mismatched eyes," Jane insisted. "Besides that, her ears are set too low, and she has dark roots."

Leaning back away from her in exaggerated caution, Seth said, "Whew—what's with you? If I didn't know better, I'd say you were jealous. But I do know better, so I has to be something else."

"I just wish you didn't have to take commissions from people like that," Jane muttered.

Seth frowned suddenly. "I know that's the way you feel, Janie, but it isn't what's bugging you now. You look guilty as hell. What've you done?"

A sudden burst of laughter that was audible even over

the music drew Jane's attention, and she saw Serena dancing quite gracefully in the arms of Jeremy Kane, even though he was indisputably drunk and loudly amused about something.

"What's Serena doing with Kane?" Seth wanted to know.

"Dancing, obviously."

"Smartass. You know damned well what I meant by that. It's bad enough that the man's a mean drunk, he also happens to write a syndicated column that's nothing less than a weekly character assassination. Serena's got no business anywhere around that son of a bitch."

Since Seth had seen his character assassinated in Kane's column some years previously, his bitterness was understandable.

Jane cleared her throat and tried not to look even more guilty. "Well, Kane's on the committee handing out that grant, you know."

Seth closed his eyes briefly and shook his head. "You dared her to go pump him for info, didn't you?"

"I didn't mean to, it just slipped out. Seth, do you think maybe you should go get her?"

"Why?" he asked, surprised.

"If she's in over her head—"

With a short laugh Seth said, "Janie, you ought to know your friend better than that. With the possible exceptions of Richard and myself, Serena can wrap any man in the room around her little finger—including Jeremy Kane, drunk or sober."

"Then why'd you say she had no business anywhere around him?" Jane asked, a bit indignant.

"Because it's true. I don't doubt she'll get whatever she's after from him, but she may be opening Pandora's box to do it. In case you haven't noticed, almost every curious eye in the room is on them. After the little stunt she pulled with that actor last year, her reputation isn't exactly the greatest. Flirting with Jeremy Kane won't help."

Ever loyal, Jane said, "I still say it wasn't Serena's fault that guy fell for her and made a fool of himself.

What was she supposed to do when his publicist kept slyly hinting there'd soon be wedding bells?"

"She might have just waited until it all blew over," Seth noted dryly. "But, no, not our Serena. She had to take matters into her own hands. Calling a press conference to announce in no uncertain terms how hilarious she found the very idea of marrying the poor guy wasn't exactly subtle."

Jane started to respond, but changed her mind. Though she'd never said so to either Serena or Seth, Jane had the odd idea that some, if not all, of Serena's very public "affairs" during the past few years had been nothing more than a whole lot of smoke disguising little or no fire. As if she had quite deliberately painted the portrait of a woman who enjoyed men without getting serious about any of them.

That press conference, for instance—Jane found it completely out of character. Serena was a private woman, yet she had deliberately sought out public attention and had presented herself as, at best, a woman careless with both her good name and the feelings of others. It was a wildly inaccurate characterization, as any of her friends would have attested, yet Serena had seemingly cultivated it.

For some reason known only to herself, Serena coolly and methodically sacrificed her reputation in order to protect something more important to her.

That was the feeling Jane had, but as close as they were, Jane had never challenged her friend on that point. Serena had a way of laughingly, but quite firmly, discouraging questions about topics she preferred not to discuss, and her love life was definitely hands off even to her best friend. Yet Jane wouldn't have been terribly surprised if Serena had confessed to being a virgin; there was a look of innocence in those bright green eyes, something unawakened, untouched.

Probably what attracted men so wildly, Jane had decided.

"Look at that," Seth was saying disgustedly. "She practically had to pour him into his chair. Huh. She has muscle under that lovely skin."

Jane wasn't dismayed or made jealous by the remark; she had learned a long time ago that Seth's appreciation of other women was aesthetic and impersonal.

"D'you think she'd sit for me?" he asked absently as he watched Serena coming toward them. That this sudden interest in Serena had come about because she had surprised him was characteristic of him. He generally preferred to paint people he didn't know rather than those he did, claiming that foreknowledge of a subject clouded his artistic perception.

"Only if you appeal to her sense of self-discovery, not her vanity," Jane advised. "Tell her you can show her something about herself she can't see in a mirror, and I'd bet she wouldn't hesitate to sit for you."

Seth nodded slightly and rose to hold Serena's chair for her, but when he spoke, it wasn't to entice her to pose for him. "It would serve you right if he drooled all down your neck," he said severely.

With a low laugh Serena said, "Well, he didn't. I'll have a slight bruise on the rear where he pinched me, but otherwise he was almost a perfect gentleman." Then she lifted an eyebrow at Jane. "You owe me ten bucks."

"What did he say?" Jane asked, forgetting everything but her eagerness to know about the grant.

Serena looked at Seth with a smile. "Congratulations."

His thin face lit up, but he shook his head. "How much faith should you place in the word of a drunk?"

"Very little," Serena agreed. "Which is why I'm glad he has the rough draft of the announcement in his pocket. The grant's yours, kiddo."

"I'm gonna go find some champagne," Seth said delightedly. He kissed Serena's cheek, then strode off in search of a bottle to celebrate his good fortune.

Jane had a streak of uncompromising logic in her nature, and that made itself apparent when she asked, "Why would he have a draft of the announcement in his pocket? It won't be made until next week."

"I don't know," Serena said, totally unconcerned. "But he has."

"And how did you find it, pull it out, and read it while you were dancing without making Kane just a tad suspicious?" Jane wanted to know.

Serena widened her eyes innocently. "Isn't it a good thing he's so drunk, he never even noticed?"

Jane didn't completely buy the answer, but as with so many of Serena's answers, she found herself accepting it against her better judgment. She did want to ask if Serena was sure Kane wouldn't figure out what she'd been after once he eventually sobered up, but Seth came bounding back to their table just then with champagne, and she let the subject drop.

Serena didn't drink often, so perhaps the champagne went to her head. At least, that was her defense later.

It had all started innocently enough with the bet. Kane had been ridiculously simple to manage while they were dancing, drunkenly talking about how he'd written the draft of the announcement awarding the grant. It had been easy—once she'd gotten the address of his apartment out of him—to send for the paper and have it appear in Kane's pocket.

That trick was so elementary, she'd been able to do it before she hit her teens.

Having brought the announcement to Kane, she'd had only to put her hand over his breast pocket to know what it said. And once she'd poured Kane back into his chair, it had seemed only humane to put him to sleep so he wouldn't spend the rest of the evening offending people and pickling his liver.

She should have stopped there. Actually, what she should have done was skip the champagne, because it always made her reckless. But she had to toast Seth's good fortune and share Jane's happiness, and one thing led to another. . . .

It was nothing *major*, she assured herself at various points throughout the evening. Just simple little things that hardly mattered. Besides that, a lot of these people were her friends, and friends helped each other.

So when one friend, while dancing with her, complained of having lost a treasured heirloom ring the day before, she sort of found it for him and placed it in his pocket—and hoped he'd check the pockets before he took the tuxedo to be cleaned. And when another friend talked to her about a very important business meeting she dreaded attending on Monday, Serena gave her a small gift of confidence.

Several other friends received modest gifts, as well, ranging from a boost of willpower to help a smoker kick the habit to the deft manipulation of a virus to keep another friend from becoming ill in the coming week.

Healing was by no means Serena's strong suit. In fact, it had only recently been introduced into her potpourri of skills, and she had mastered just the rudiments. So the practice couldn't hurt, she thought.

By eleven-thirty that evening Serena had consumed three glasses of champagne and had bestowed a number of "gifts." She was standing alone near the bar, and was just about to send another little present winging across the room when a hand closed gently but firmly around her upraised wrist.

"No, Serena."

The hand, large and long-fingered, was a powerful hand, a beautiful hand, and quite distinct. She would have known it anywhere.

She lifted her gaze to the man's face, making her eyes wide and guileless. "No?"

"No." His voice was deep, calm, resonant. A voice that made people sit up straighter and listen to whatever he had to say. "I believe you've done quite enough for one night."

"I didn't do anything *major*, Richard," she protested.

Richard Merlin shook his head slightly, his lean, broodingly handsome face holding a touch of wryness. "No, of course not. You never do. They're playing a waltz, Serena. Dance with me."

Her wrist still held captive, Serena followed him out onto the dance floor, a bit amused that he hadn't waited for her response. But then, why would he? He hadn't asked—he'd commanded. As usual. Given their relationship, it wasn't surprising, but Serena bore the seemingly high-handed attitude only because she knew very well Richard intended no domination of her personality when he commanded.

Both skilled and graceful, they danced well together and made a striking couple. It was rare they appeared as a couple at any social function; both usually brought dates to this kind of event. In fact, their public relationship as uncle and niece was so solid, few had ever questioned it—and those few were merely vaguely skeptical without being truly suspicious.

"I really didn't do anything significant," Serena insisted as they danced.

"Serena, how many times must I tell you that *everything* is significant? Every action, no matter how minor, could have unimaginable consequences." The statement held the sound of a litany, often repeated, patient and unwavering.

She rolled her eyes. "Yeah, right, I know. Because the powerless people might notice, and they'd probably see us as a threat to them. And then it'd be the Salem witch hunts all over again, except that they'd use psychologists and scientists to try to dissect and denounce us instead of priests with dunking stools, thumbscrews, and the rack."

He looked down at her for several beats, then said, "How much have you had to drink?"

"More than usual," she admitted cheerfully. "Seth wanted to celebrate, and he kept filling my champagne glass. I could hardly say no."

Merlin nodded. "Now I understand why you were dancing with Jeremy Kane earlier—to find out about the grant. I gather it will be awarded to Seth?"

"Yes, isn't it great?"

"He deserves it. But did you have to pick a man like Kane from whom to get the information, Serena?"

"There was nobody else here who's on the committee," she explained ingenuously.

Merlin's mouth twitched slightly, but his expression remained forbidding. "It's never wise to tempt the fates, and ensnaring a newspaper reporter, even a drunk, is asking for trouble. How did you do it?"

She answered readily. "He said he'd typed up the

rough draft of an announcement about the grant and left it at his apartment, so I just sent for it to come to his pocket."

"And did you also send it back where it came from?"

Serena shook her head guiltily. "No, I . . . I forgot. I was so excited about Seth winning. . . ." She turned her head to search the room. "But I left him at his table, so—"

"He's gone." Merlin sighed. "Guests who pass out at these functions are usually discreetly removed and sent home in a cab; Kane was carried out an hour ago."

"Oh." She cleared her throat. "Well, still, it won't matter. He was so drunk, he'll never be sure he didn't stick the announcement in his pocket himself."

"I hope you're right," Merlin murmured.

A bit unsettled by his frown, Serena said, "Richard, Kane's a long way from the reporter he used to be. He hasn't broken a story in fifteen years; I doubt he'd recognize one if it stood in front of him waving its arms. There's no way he'll get suspicious of me, I promise you."

"I hope you're right," Merlin repeated.

The music changed smoothly just then, from a waltz to a much slower and more intimate beat. It enticed the dancers to move closer and speak in murmurs. The lights in the huge room, already fairly low, dimmed even more.

Merlin automatically shifted his hold on Serena, drawing her a bit closer as their steps slowed. No observer was likely to have mistaken them for lovers even then, but their nearness made Serena struggle inwardly not to tense in his arms. She tried to avoid situations such as this one, maintaining their necessary charade in public by treating Richard exactly as a niece would treat the uncle who had virtually raised her, with affection and the gentle mockery that came with it.

She was usually successful.

Now she spoke quickly to keep her mind off the sensation of his hand at the small of her back, and his body too close to hers.

"I'm surprised Kane's the one you're worried about, actually. I did a few other things tonight, you know."

"Yes, I know," Merlin replied dryly. "Remind me to keep you away from champagne from now on. I'll remind myself to keep a closer eye on you."

It was Serena's turn to frown. "I don't like the sound of that at all. I'm not a child anymore, Richard."

He didn't meet her eyes, but gazed past her, and when he spoke, there was an odd note in his voice she couldn't define. "Yes, I know that, as well. But you still lack control. Self-control, perhaps."

She felt ridiculously sulky. "I just wanted to help my friends. What's wrong with that?"

The childishness of her words and tone drew his gaze back to her face, and he smiled. "In the general scheme of things, nothing at all. But you can't help everyone, Serena. Besides that, people are meant to solve their own problems, to use their own abilities, skills, and intelligence. I've tried to teach you that. I've tried to make you understand that we can't cure the ills of the world."

Serena knew she still looked petulant; she could feel how far her bottom lip was sticking out. But she was honestly perplexed. "I don't see why we can't *try*. I mean, what's so awful about me finding a lost ring for Thomas, or . . . or boosting Maggie's confidence before a big meeting, or fixing it so that Chris doesn't get the flu next week?"

Only the last part of the demand prompted Merlin's concern. "The flu? Serena, you aren't ready to heal yet."

"I didn't do anything major," she repeated for what seemed like the hundredth time this evening. "And it wasn't really healing, since he isn't sick yet. I just made the virus inert, that's all."

Looking stern, Merlin said, "You must promise me to never again attempt any kind of healing until I say you're ready. It's the most complex skill you'll ever learn, and demands a great deal more knowledge of human biology than you have yet."

Sobered by his grave tone, she nodded. "All right, I promise."

He relaxed visibly. Though she was a sometimes difficult pupil, Serena's word was as good as gold.

"But what if I've already screwed up?" she went on, worried now. "I might have given poor Chris the bubonic plague or something even worse."

"I doubt it. But I'll check him before we leave, just to make sure."

The band finished with a flourish then, and they went back to their table. Seth and Jane had disappeared, undoubtedly to celebrate further their good fortune, and Serena felt a stab of pure envy. Even with all the occasional hassles and confusions, their lives seemed so simple to her, and their relationship was so clear—and normal.

She wondered, not for the first time, if her friends could even begin to imagine how different her life was.

"I see Chris near the door," Merlin said, draping Serena's glittery evening shawl around her shoulders. As she turned to face him, he added slowly, "I don't think . . ." He went very still, his black eyes almost glowing, they were so intense.

The look was familiar to Serena, but each time she saw it she felt respect and wonder and a great deal more, because at such times the incredible power in him was literally tangible. She stood gazing up at him, waiting, unaware that her heart was in her eyes for that brief moment, and that anyone who saw would have known a truth she had spent a great deal of effort to obscure.

Anyone would have known her secret—except the man she was looking at.

Merlin relaxed, then looked down at her. His eyes were still vibrant, though they no longer radiated so much of his inner power. "Chris is fine, Serena. You *did* turn the virus inert."

She drew a quick breath. "Good. You had me worried there for a while. I sure won't forget my promise, you can bet on that."

He took her arm and began steering her toward an exit. "No, I'm sure you won't."

Serena looked up at him with curiosity as they wended their way from the ballroom and toward the front of the hotel. She kept her voice low and chose her words carefully, conscious of the other departing guests all around them. "You've never asked me to promise not to . . . um . . . practice what you've taught me. The way I did tonight. Why not?"

Merlin didn't answer, not until the valet had delivered his car and they were on their way home. Concentrating on the rain-slick streets as he handled the big Lincoln, he said slowly, "How could I ask you to promise you'd never use any of your powers without my approval? It would be like asking a young bird to promise not to fly. But I *can* insist that you learn the dangers of flying, along with the necessary skills needed to fly well. And I can do my best to guide you through the hazards."

Serena didn't respond to that out loud, but she thought about his words all the way home. Perhaps the effects of the champagne were wearing off, but in any case she felt decidedly guilty about her indiscriminate use of her powers.

The old Victorian house welcomed them with a number of lamps left burning. Most of its rooms were decorated with style and simplicity and were hardly different from any of the neighboring houses. The rooms that *were* different were kept locked whenever they had guests, and not even Merlin's longtime housekeeper was encouraged to enter them.

Merlin strode toward one of those rooms as soon as they entered the house. His study. "We should work tomorrow," he said to Serena, loosening his tie as he paused at the door and looked at her.

Answering the implicit question, she said, "I don't have any plans for the weekend, so that's fine."

"Good. I'll see you in the morning then."

Serena said, "Good night," but found herself addressing the closing door of his study. She stood there for several moments, slowly removing her shawl. The house was very quiet.

It wasn't unusual for Merlin to shut himself in the study and work far into the night, especially during recent months. Since his "normal" life and business occupied a great deal of his time during the day, his real life's work had to be scheduled for odd hours, weekends, holidays, and vacations.

After nine years Serena no longer questioned his dedication, his strength, or his stamina. Whatever time and effort it took for Richard Patrick Merlin to make his unusual life succeed, he was prepared to give it. And then some. So he bought, sold, and developed real estate during the day, and with all his free time he worked to perfect his art.

It said much for his skills in both areas of his life that he had attained the level of Master wizard, the highest level possible, years before. In fact, long before Serena had come to study with him. At the same time, he had achieved a high degree of respect and esteem within the powerless community of Seattle.

None of whose citizens had any idea that an ancient art was practiced in their midst.

Serena gazed at the closed door for a few moments more, then went up the stairs to her bedroom. She undressed and changed for bed, took her makeup off and her hair down. She turned on the television to catch the late news, but paid little attention to the program as she moved restlessly around.

How much longer could she go on? The simple answer was—as long as necessary. Like Merlin, she grudged no time or effort in her quest to become a Master wizard; that had been her ambition from earliest childhood. But unlike him, she was constantly distracted and disturbed by . . . other matters.

Other matters. How laughably inadequate that phrase was, she reflected somewhat bitterly.

His powers set him apart from most men, and Serena thought her knowledge of his difference made him often seem somewhat remote, even with her. At least she hoped that was it.

He was the most powerful wizard to walk the face of modern-day earth, and that had to be a kind of burden even as it was an accomplishment matched by very few in all of history. Serena had long wanted to ask him if it *was* a burden, but she had always hesitated. She had, over the years, learned not to pry, not to ask personal questions. It was useless in any case; what Merlin chose not to answer, he simply ignored.

And so, wholly occupied with perfecting his art and passing the knowledge on to her, his Apprentice, he rarely, if ever, saw her as a woman. At best she was a young student with a great deal to learn, at worst a bothersome child.

Serena had learned to live with that, or thought she had. Nights like this one made her doubt it. There was a strong part of her, intensifying year by year, that demanded she make Merlin see her as the woman she was, and that part often let itself be known. But each time it happened, she sensed something in him she didn't understand, something she couldn't put a name to and was frightened by.

She had felt it in him tonight, so briefly, when she had reminded him she was no longer a child. And, as usual, she had reacted immediately and out of sheer instinct to right things between them once again. She'd felt driven to retreat, to reclaim childhood or at least a childish mood, to make him forget that he had glimpsed a woman.

The moment always passed, and with it that indefinable tension she felt in him. But more and more, Serena was left frustrated and bewildered, angry at him for some failing she couldn't understand or even describe clearly to herself.

What *was* it? Was it something in Richard, as she sensed—or something in herself?

In the nine years of her apprenticeship, she had come to know him probably as well as anyone could. Publicly he had been her uncle and guardian; privately he'd been much more. He had been her parent, brother, teacher, companion, her harshest critic, and her best friend.

She had, at sixteen, fallen wildly in love with him. A

natural enough thing to happen. That he seemed unaware of her feelings had puzzled her, but she had eventually come to understand that his ignorance stemmed
from the same reason he had so instantly accepted a
ragged, hungry, rain-soaked sixteen-year-old orphan as
his pupil.

Her mind was completely shielded from him.

In time Serena was sincerely grateful for that innate
protection. Merlin often knew what she was thinking
for the simple reason that she tended to blurt out her
thoughts, but he couldn't read her mind. And aside
from the benefits of hiding her childish fantasies from
him, she also learned to respect the shield itself, for she
discovered through Merlin's absent remarks on the subject that few living souls could hide their thoughts and
feelings from a Master wizard. It was a sign of great potential power, and not to be taken lightly.

But if her shield hid from him the chaotic emotions
he evoked in her, it did nothing to help her cope with
them. And because of that failing of his—that lacking,
that missing something that made him refuse to see her
as a woman—she had the added burden of feeling in
limbo, suspended in some bewildering emotional pur-
gatory between woman and child.

So Serena returned to the question once again. How
much longer could she go on? The pressure was building inside her; she could feel it. She thought he felt it,
too; his occasional business trips out of town had been
more frequent with every passing year, and she had to
believe the trips had something to do with the increasing tension that lay just under the tranquil surface of
their lives.

If he had not been so often remote, especially in recent months, she might have gathered courage and
brought up the subject. But he had been.

She couldn't risk it. What she feared most was being
sent away, being banished from his life. He was capable
of such a merciless act, she thought, given a good
enough reason. Though he had never been cruel to her
and she had seen no evidence of it, she sensed a streak

of ruthlessness in him—perhaps the price he paid for the incredible power he wielded.

Serena was too familiar with the scope of that power to have any wish to put her fate to the test. She wasn't that desperate, not yet. But time was running out. The pressure was building, and something had to give.

Still ignoring the television that was now broadcasting some old movie with melodramatic music, Serena went to one of the windows and stared out. She felt very much alone, and oddly afraid.

It was raining again.

TWO

The blinding flash of pink, purple, and blue sparks was wrong, all wrong, and Serena winced even before the deep voice, coming from a dark corner of the room, could reprimand her.

"You aren't *concentrating*."

"I'm sorry, Master." The proper humility, apology, and respect were present in her voice, but all were belied by the wry amusement shining in her vivid green eyes. In deference to him she was obedient to the long-standing rules governing the behavior of an Apprentice wizard—but only in this workroom. And only when he was teaching her.

From the very beginning she had refused to assume any kind of subservient manner, and Merlin had been wise enough not to insist on many of the ancient and decidedly outdated customs between Master and Apprentice.

"*Why* aren't you concentrating?" He emerged from the shadows where he'd been observing and stepped into the candlelight, showing her the lean, handsome face and brooding dark eyes of her Master wizard.

"I just have a lot on my mind, I guess. The party last night, for instance," she explained, gesturing idly with one hand and jumping in surprise when a thread of white-hot energy arced from her index finger to ignite a nearby lampshade.

Merlin hastily waved a hand, and both watched as water appeared out of thin air to douse the tiny fire. The Master turned to his Apprentice in exasperation, and Serena spoke quickly.

"I didn't mean to do it."

"That," Merlin said witheringly, "is the whole point."

Gazing in admiration at the dripping lampshade, Serena ignored the point. "Why won't you teach me to summon water? I can summon fire so easily, it's only logical that I should learn to put out my mistakes."

Ignoring the request, Merlin said, "Stop saying *summon*, as if the elements are lurking about just waiting to be called to heel."

Serena blinked. "I thought they were."

"I know. But they aren't."

"Then . . ."

A brief spasm of frustration crossed Merlin's face. "Serena, I can't seem to get it through your head that wizards *create*. This is what sets us apart from witches, warlocks, sorcerers, and the other practitioners of . . . magic." The definition was wholly unwilling; Merlin hated putting labels on anything, particularly his art. "We create. We do not need to harness existing elements. We are not limited to that."

"All right. So teach me to create water."

"No."

Serena sighed with regret and unsnapped the Velcro fasteners of her long, black Apprentice's robe. Sweeping it out behind her, she sank down on one of the cushions scattered over the floor and contemplated her jean-clad legs. "I suppose you have a reason?"

Merlin, wearing his midnight blue Master's robe, moved about the dim room, blowing out their working candles and turning on several lamps. Their workroom, tucked up on the third floor underneath the rafters of the house, was always dark owing to the fact that the small, narrow windows were always shuttered. So even though it was the middle of the day, some artificial light was necessary.

The candles were used during work for two simple reasons: they provided a more organic light; and the energy expended during the practice of the wizard's art, particularly when the wizard was an Apprentice and lacked perfect control, tended to cause any nearby light bulbs to burst. In fact, those energies tended to play havoc with *anything* electrical, which was one of the reasons Merlin had chosen this attic room in which to teach Serena; it was as far as possible from most of the modern appliances in the house.

"Yes," Merlin said in answer to her question. "My reason is a vivid memory of what happened the first time I allowed you to try and create fire."

Her lips twitched, and Serena sent him a look from beneath her lashes. "That was years ago. I was just a rank beginner in those days. And besides, you put the fire out before it could do any serious damage."

"True. However, I doubt my ability to hold back the floodwaters of your enthusiastic creation."

Merlin unfastened his long robe and hung it over a stand in one corner of the room. Like Serena, he wore beneath it jeans and a sweater, which revealed a tall, broad-shouldered form that held the considerable strength of well-defined muscles as well as might from less-obvious sources. Serena couldn't help watching him, her expressive eyes still guarded by lowered lashes.

Though he might have been any age and looked to be about thirty-five, he was certainly in his prime. Still, Serena would not have dared to guess how many years—or lifetimes—he had put behind him. In response to a long-ago childish question, he had said with a grimace that he was quite mortal. She hadn't believed it then, and wasn't sure she did now.

He was a compelling man physically, attractive to women of all ages. The young ones found his face exciting, and the older ones imagined tragedy in his black eyes and thought he needed taking care of.

Serena knew better.

"I wouldn't create a flood," she assured him. "Maybe a little waterfall, but not a flood."

Merlin gave her a look and opened his mouth to respond, but before he could say a word, the bulb in the lamp nearest Serena exploded with a pop. Only the shade kept her from being pelted with shards of glass.

"Serena, turn it *off*."

"I know, I know." She closed her eyes and concentrated on corralling her wayward energies, drawing them in, tamping them down, erecting a kind of barrier inside herself to hold them in. It was something that tended to happen after a lesson, this "spillover" of her energies, particularly when her concentration was erratic.

Merlin had repeatedly tried to teach her that there was indeed a "switch," that she would someday be able to "turn off" her energies—something he had perfected long ago—but it was one skill Serena had failed to master.

She had, however, learned to restrain and cloak her energies well enough that she usually didn't explode light bulbs or cause other electrical problems merely by walking past.

Merlin, alert in case she needed his instruction, waited until she relaxed and opened her eyes, signaling her success. He went to get a replacement bulb from a well-stocked closet. Serena watched him dispense with the broken pieces of the exploded bulb with a flick of his finger, then screw the replacement into the socket.

She couldn't help smiling, reflecting silently that wizards were strange creatures, an odd mixture of ancient and modern. At least he was, and she seemed to be, as well. They used their powers in a peculiar patchwork of ways, often for the sake of convenience and yet in no recognizable pattern.

Serena herself had made up her bed with a sweep of her hand this morning, not because she was lazy or in the habit of doing it, but because she'd overslept and was in a hurry.

Physical gestures were not necessary to spell-casting, Serena had been surprised—and a bit disappointed—to learn; but the motions of the hands *did* tend to help focus concentration and were generally used, unless the wizard was in public or had some other reason for wishing to be inconspicuous. In any case Serena liked the ancient gestures.

They made her feel like a wizard.

As the new light bulb glowed to life, Merlin said almost absently, "Your powers are growing."

She knew they were; she could feel it.

"Which makes it all the more vital that you learn to find the switch, Serena," he continued, facing her again with a slight frown. "This spillover of energies—"

"I know, it's a waste and a danger," she recited.

Merlin's frown deepened, but he shook his head a little in the traditional reluctant acceptance of teachers everywhere when they recognize a lack of attention in their pupils. He glanced at his watch—unlike Serena, he could wear one, and did, even though one of his many talents was a constant and perfect awareness of time.

"It's almost noon; you wanted to break?"

"Yes." Serena got up, shrugged out of her robe, and hung it near his. "Lunch. Rachel left a casserole for us, and I put it in the oven before we started this morning."

Merlin tended to forget about unimportant things like eating when his mind was occupied with his work, but between them, Serena and their housekeeper kept most meals on a fairly regular schedule. Rachel came in daily except weekends, and kept the freezer well stocked with quick and easy-to-prepare meals for the days Richard and Serena were on their own.

It was up to Serena to make sure they observed regular meal times on weekends, and since she was almost always hungry, she rarely needed reminders herself. One delightful bonus of being a wizard, she had realized long ago, was an unusually high metabolic rate; expending as much energy as they did, both she and Merlin could eat anything they pleased, and tended to require more calories than normal people just to maintain their weights.

"Are you going out tonight?" she asked him as they descended the stairs.

"Yes. Dinner and a concert with Lenore Todd. How about you?" His tone was casual.

"No. I'm going to stay blamelessly at home tonight and study that manual of incantations you added to my reading list," she replied lightly.

"Study but don't practice," he reminded her more or less automatically.

Serena didn't say *I know* again, contenting herself with a nod. She was tired of saying it. She had been warned so often about not practicing new skills without Merlin's being present that it was beginning to annoy her. He just couldn't stop treating her like a child, she thought.

It didn't help that she had felt a stab of jealousy about his date, even though she *knew* that he dated for the same reason she did—to maintain a normal appearance for friends, neighbors, and the rest of the society in which they lived. The importance of that appearance, made up of normal jobs and regular social activities and all the other trappings of an ordinary life-style, was something Merlin had explained to Serena when she had first come to study with him and they had created the fiction of blood relation and guardianship.

Serena had long ago come to the conclusion that her Master wizard was too obsessed with his art to be concerned with lesser pursuits. Besides, since so much of his energy was focused and quite literally expended on perfecting that art, there was undoubtedly little left over for women and sex.

That was what she had told herself at sixteen, and his habits over the years seemed to bear out that deduction. If he had affairs, there was certainly no sign of them, and since he tended to date women who were in Seattle only temporarily—for business or pleasure—gossip could only speculate on his prowess as a lover.

Serena refused to speculate. As an adoring teenager, she had convinced herself that he was a monk with his mind on a much higher plane, and nothing had happened to destroy that creation.

So there was no reason for her to feel jealous about Lenore Todd. The woman would be in Seattle only a week or so for an environmental seminar, according to what Merlin had told Serena when he'd met her a few days ago. He always told Serena about the women he dated, because she always asked, and there was always an indifferent note in his voice when he answered.

Serena listened for that indifference. And heard it this time. But the increasing tension and frustration she felt made it difficult for her to be reassured.

Though her turbulent emotions had made the previous night a rather miserable one, she had managed to sleep, and today she had managed—more or less—to assume her usual relaxed attitude toward Merlin. It was getting harder, though, for her to act as if nothing had changed, as if she were still that obsessed child who had crossed a country to find him, wanting nothing in life except to be a wizard.

Because something *had* changed. In Serena. Her determination to become a Master wizard had not lessened, but she had grown up these last years, and she had come to the realization that there was much more to life. To her life, anyway. She was a wizard, yes, but she was also a woman, even if Merlin couldn't see that was true.

And it was getting very difficult for her to fight the resentment she felt every time he treated her like a child.

It was nearly noon on Saturday when Jeremy Kane fell off his couch. He struggled up, using the cluttered coffee table to lever himself back onto the cushions, and sat there for several minutes with his head in his hands. It was a familiar pose, his dizziness a familiar sensation, and he waited grimly for his head to stop spinning.

When it eventually did, he got up slowly and made his way into the narrow alley kitchen of his apartment. Mixing tomato juice and a few other ingredients, he made his usual pick-me-up and drank it down, then fixed another and carried the glass back into his cramped and messy living room.

He sat down on the couch again and pulled his loosened tie off, fumbled for the remote, and turned the television on. He switched to CNN out of habit, just in case anything interesting had happened in the world while he had been passed out. It took him three tries to wrestle his jacket off, and the sound of paper caught his attention even as he wondered at the unusual brevity of his hangover.

The dizziness had faded almost instantly, the nausea he usually felt was totally absent, and his mouth didn't feel or taste like the bottom of a bird cage. Even though his pick-me-up was good, it wasn't *that* good.

"What the hell?" he muttered, bothered, as always, by anything out of the ordinary. Even his voice sounded better than it had any right to, only a little raspy. Then he pulled the neatly folded paper from the inside pocket of his tuxedo jacket, unfolded it, and stared at it.

It was his rough draft of the announcement awarding the newspaper's grant. When he had gone to the party last night, he had left the draft in his old manual typewriter, he was sure. Looking across the room to his small desk, he could clearly see the top of the typewriter even over the usual clutter of newspapers, magazines, an empty pizza box, two cracked mugs half filled with cold coffee and cigarette butts, and the remains of a two-day-old microwavable dinner.

There was no paper in the machine.

Kane might have been a drunk, and he might have lost or squandered most of the raw talent that had made him a nationally recognized name at the tender age of twenty-five nearly two decades before, but he was not a stupid man, and he did not doubt either the evidence of his eyes or his memory—neither of which had ever failed him. And he had never drawn a blank after a night of drinking, even on those frequent occasions when any merciful God would have spared him the memories.

So he remembered the previous evening, and the only unusual thing he could call to mind was that Serena Smyth had asked him to dance. She had never done that before, even though they had been intro-

duced years ago, and though he saw her at many of the
high-ticket social and charity events in Seattle.

She had asked him to dance. And while they danced,
she had sweetly encouraged him to talk about himself
and what he'd been doing lately—a sneaky tactic if he'd
ever seen one. She had even casually asked the address
of his apartment, he recalled, which had made him
grow an inch or two and had filled his head with something besides brains.

And then . . . And then he had a vague memory of
leaning heavily on her as he staggered back to his chair,
and falling into the sweet blackness of unconsciousness.

Had Serena brought him home? Why on earth would
she? Just to get her hands on this announcement? There
didn't seem to be any other reason. She certainly hadn't
stripped him, had her way with him, and then put his
clothes back on before leaving. He would have remembered that even if he'd been nearly dead.

No; it had to be the announcement. But why? She
was friendly with Seth Westcott and his girlfriend, Kane
knew that well enough, but it didn't seem likely she'd
go to so much trouble just to find out what would be
announced in a few days. And if she *had* brought him
home to get an early peek at the announcement, then
what would possess her to remove the draft from his
typewriter and leave it in his jacket pocket—where he
could hardly fail to find it?

Jeremy Kane didn't like puzzles, and though his instincts might have dulled over the years, he could still
recognize something that didn't make sense. He also
had so little going on in his life that even a minor mystery was a welcome thing—though that was something
he didn't like to think about. So he decided it wouldn't
hurt to find out more than he already knew about Miss
Serena Smyth.

He placed a call to a private investigator in Seattle
who owed him a few favors, and was lucky enough to
catch the man in his office on a Saturday afternoon.

"Taylor, I need a favor," he announced without pre-
amble.

Brad Taylor groaned. "I'm not gonna dig up any

more dirt on politicians for you, Kane," he said quickly. "I'm sick of wading through the muck."

"This is no politician, believe me. She's sort of a society deb, near as I can figure. If you find even a few little bones in her closet, I'd be surprised. And don't forget how much you owe me, Taylor."

"Okay, okay. What do you need?"

"Everything you can find out about this woman. Her name is Serena Smyth." He spelled it briskly, then added, on impulse. "And whatever you can find out about this guy she lives with, supposedly her uncle . . ."

Following an afternoon's work, Serena took advantage of Merlin's absence on Saturday evening to relax her guard somewhat, which was a relief. Since she never minded being alone, the quiet of the big house didn't bother her, and she was perfectly happy fixing herself a light dinner, taking a long bath, and then curling up on her bed with the television turned low and a big, very old leather-bound volume of incantations open before her.

She was tempted to practice a few of the more interesting spells, but contented herself with memorizing those she especially wanted to remember. After all, you never knew when you had to tame the wildest animal or turn an enemy into a toad.

The book was so fascinating that Serena passed a pleasant evening, and since she was tired by the long day of honing her abilities, she went to bed before midnight—and long before Merlin came home.

The next day was virtually a repeat of Saturday, with lessons in the attic workroom in the morning, a break for lunch, and then more lessons in the afternoon. Nothing out of the ordinary happened until they were eating supper early that evening, at the kitchen table rather than in the more formal dining room, since it was just the two of them.

Serena brought up the subject, having come across at least three incantations regarding the control of weaker minds in her studies the previous night.

"I thought you told me that mind control was beyond our capabilities, that we could only do fairly simple things—boost willpower or self-confidence or induce sleep, but never truly control the mind of someone else."

"Gray's *Spells and Incantations*?" Merlin said, naming the book she had studied.

"Uh-huh. According to him, it's fairly easy to control another mind, especially a weaker one. But he seems to have his doubts about making people do something that's completely against their core morality. Sort of like the limitations people believe about hypnosis, I guess."

Merlin nodded and said, "I did tell you we could never completely control another mind, which is quite true. *Momentary* control is possible, at best, but it's almost always imperfect. The human mind is too complex to be fully controlled. And it's a dangerous device to use without great care."

"Is that why you haven't taught me?"

A bit dryly Merlin said, "Alphabetically, *mind control* comes after *invisibility*, which is what we were working on yesterday and today."

Unwilling to let him get away with that, Serena said, "You called it *vanishing*, and so did my manual, which puts me near the end of the alphabet—and well past *M* or *C*."

Merlin sighed, giving up the attempt to placate her. "It's a difficult device, Serena, and I just don't think you're ready yet." He often used the word *device* when referring to a spell or incantation; it was another way he had of avoiding magical terms for their art.

She looked down, pushing creamed corn around on her plate and feeling annoyed. It was easy for her to get annoyed these days, and knowing her irritation stemmed from other things did nothing to lessen it. "Yeah, I'm not ready for anything challenging, according to you."

"You couldn't vanish," he murmured.

Serena didn't look at him. He sounded amused, and if she looked at him and saw him smiling, she would either say something she'd undoubtedly be sorry for later or throw her corn at him, she decided mutinously. "It was my first lesson," she said. "Give a girl a chance."

After a moment of silence he spoke in a very conversational tone. "Can you read my mind, Serena?"

She did look up then, startled out of her funk. "I don't know. I've never tried." Oddly enough, she really hadn't.

"Do so."

Obediently, Serena put down her fork, folded her hands in her lap and closed her eyes, and rather hesitantly sent her mind wandering. She fully expected to find herself blocked by Merlin's mental shields; just as her powers guarded her thoughts from even a Master wizard, so would his screen his mind from her probing. At least that was what she expected.

She felt nothing for a moment, but then, as if a curtain blocking her mind's eye were suddenly swept aside, she saw herself. Sitting. Eyes closed, face calm. And she felt a peculiar, unfamiliar spring-coiled vitality in her lean body. A different weight distribution. A consciousness of muscle and sinew and incredible, living power contained by a strong, masterful, and confident hand. Her eyes widened, but they weren't hers somehow. There was surprise, yet it wasn't hers, either. There was a feeling of being enclosed in a strong, warm embrace, and seeing through black eyes. . . .

Get out, Serena.

Steely. Polite.

Hastily, she climbed back into her own body, confused. What on earth had she done? Her eyes—her own eyes—opened slowly, cautiously. He was watching her with an intent, searching stare, and despite his composed expression, she had the notion that he was deeply shaken.

"What . . . what did I do?" she asked uncertainly.

"You didn't read my mind. You were *in* my mind. Inside my head, my consciousness."

She blinked. He didn't sound angry, only thoughtful. Apparently his shield would allow her in, and even allow her to sense some of his emotions, while still protecting his thoughts. "I was? Did you . . . um . . . could you . . ."

"Read your thoughts? No. As always. I merely felt your presence, curious and—" He broke off and looked away from her, leaving the rest unsaid. "Interesting," he murmured finally.

Serena tried and failed to read his expression, but she had that feeling again, the perception of a sudden withdrawal in him. She had surprised him, somehow unsettled him, and as usual he was pulling away, closing himself off from her as if she posed some kind of threat.

She was positive that if she were to try now to read his mind, she would find no way in at all.

She wanted to confront him right then and there, to tell him she felt his remoteness, and to demand to know what caused these swift, silent retreats of his. Had she somehow reminded him she was no longer a child, or was she entirely wrong about that being the cause of his withdrawal? *What's wrong with me? What am I doing to make you go all cool and distant?*

But she didn't confront him. Instead, as always, she instinctively tried to find some cautious path back to the comfortable and familiar relationship they had established over the years.

In a light, wry tone she said, "If you were trying to make a point, you succeeded. Obviously I'm not ready for any kind of mind skill."

"One step at a time, Serena."

She didn't wince because she had her features under control, but the aloofness in his deep voice cut her like a knife. Holding her own voice as steady and light as before, she said, "And patience is a virtue, I know. Well, I'll just concentrate on vanishing until I've mastered that."

Merlin rose to carry his plate to the sink. "A good idea. But no more studies tonight, I think. Don't you have an early meeting tomorrow?"

Serena's "normal" job was as an assistant office manager at an engineering firm, which she found pleasant enough but not especially challenging. She could have been a part of Merlin's real estate business—he had left it up to her—but she had reluctantly decided to avoid the appearance of being always in his company.

"Yes, at eight," she answered.

He nodded and said, "There's some work I should finish up in my study tonight." Then, rather abruptly, he added, "I have to go out of town for a day or two, probably tomorrow or Tuesday. Will you be all right?"

"Of course." It wasn't unusual for him to go out of town, and as far as she knew, he always went alone. Serena had asked only once where he went; he had ignored the question, and she had never asked again. She could only assume he had business of some kind, or that, perhaps, his trips concerned activities known only to Master wizards.

"Good. I'll see you in the morning, Serena."

"Yes." She remained there at the table, reminding herself steadily that his remoteness would likely be gone by morning. Or, at the very latest, when he returned from his trip. Then things would be back to normal between them.

After a while she got up and carried her plate to the sink. She straightened up the kitchen, then went to her room. It was far too early for sleep, but Serena got ready for bed anyway, and curled up with the book of incantations once again. But this time the book failed to hold her attention—until she idly looked for some reference to what she had experienced in the attempt to read Merlin's mind.

Nothing. As far as Gray's *Spells and Incantations* was concerned, inhabiting the mind of another individual didn't seem possible. There was no spell, and no mention whatsoever of the trick, which left Serena puzzled and uneasy. Was that why Merlin had been upset? Because she had inadvertently done something objectionable or unique?

Serena fully intended to ask him about that, but when she went down to breakfast early the next morning, he had already gone.

"He said he'd be at the office for a few hours, and then off on one of his trips," Rachel said placidly. Middle-aged and utterly unflappable, she had been

Merlin's housekeeper for years; exactly how many she never said, and she'd only smiled when Serena had asked her bluntly.

"He said it would just be overnight," Rachel continued, "to expect him tomorrow evening, probably in time for supper. Did he tell you?"

"Yes. But he wasn't specific about when he'd return."

"I imagine he didn't know for sure himself last night," the housekeeper offered tranquilly as she set Serena's breakfast in front of her.

"No, I guess not," Serena responded a bit hollowly. She couldn't help thinking that Merlin *had* known, that he had decided on this trip simply because his mental and emotional withdrawal from her hadn't allowed him enough distance. And she still didn't know what she had done wrong. . . .

His fingers touched her breasts, stroking soft skin and teasing the hard pink nipples. The swollen weight filled his hands as he lifted and kneaded, and when she moaned and arched her back, he lowered his mouth to her flesh. She tasted faintly of salt, but more of woman, a taste that aroused him further and yet drew a hazy curtain across his mind. He stopped thinking. He felt. He felt his own body, taut and pulsing with desire, the blood hot in his veins. He felt her body, soft and warm and willing. His mouth toyed with the beaded texture of her nipple, sucking as if commanded by instinct. He felt her hand on him, stroking slowly, her touch hungry and assured. Her moans and sighs filled his ears, and the heat of her need rose until her flesh burned. His hand slid down her rippling belly to cup her, fingers probing her swollen wetness, testing her readiness. The tension inside him coiled more tightly, making his body ache, until he couldn't stand to wait another moment. He spread her legs, positioning himself between them. Her hand guided him eagerly, and the hot, slick tightness of her sheath surrounded him. He sank his flesh into hers, feeling her legs close strongly about his hips. Expertly, lustfully, she met his thrusts, undulating beneath him, her female body the cradle all men returned to. The heat between them built until it was a fever raging out of control, until his body was gripped by the inescapable, inexorable drive for release and pounded frantically inside her. Then, at last, the heat and tension drained from him in a rush, and he heaved at the intense pleasure of pouring himself into her. . . .

Serena sat bolt upright in bed, gasping. In shock, she stared across the darkened room for a moment, then hurriedly leaned over and turned on the lamp on the nightstand. Blinking in the light, she held her hands up and stared at them, reassuring herself that they were hers, still slender and pale and tipped with neat oval nails.

They were hers. She was here and unchanged. Awake. Aware. Herself again.

She could still feel the alien sensations, still see the powerful bronzed hands against paler, softer skin, and still feel sensations her body was incapable of experiencing simply because she was female, not male—

And then she realized.

"Dear God . . . Richard," she whispered.

She had been inside his mind, somehow, in his head just like before, and he had been with another woman. He had been having sex with another woman. Serena had felt what he felt, from the sensual enjoyment of soft female flesh under his touch to the ultimate draining pleasure of orgasm. *She had felt what he felt.*

She drew her knees up and hugged them, feeling tears burning her eyes and nausea churning in her stomach. Another woman. He had a woman somewhere, and she wasn't new because there had been a sense of familiarity in him, a certain knowledge. He knew this woman. Her skin was familiar, her taste, her desire. His body knew hers.

Even Master wizards, it seemed, had appetites just like other men.

Serena felt a wave of emotions so powerful, she could endure them only in silent anguish. Her thoughts were tangled and fierce and raw. Not a monk, no, hardly a monk. In fact, it appeared he was quite a proficient lover, judging by the woman's response to him.

On her nightstand the lamp's bulb burst with a violent sound, but she neither heard it nor noticed the return of darkness to the room.

So he was just a man after all, damn him, a man who got horny like other men and went to some slut who'd spread her legs for him. And often. His trips "out of town" were more frequent these last years. Oh, horny indeed . . .

Unnoticed by Serena, her television set flickered to life, madly scanned through all the channels, and then died with a sound as apologetic as a muffled cough.

Damn him. What'd he do, keep a mistress? Some pretty, pampered blond—she had been blond, naturally—with empty, hot eyes who wore slinky nightgowns and crotchless panties, and moaned like a bitch in heat? Was there only one? Or had he bedded a succession of women over the years, keeping his reputation here in Seattle all nice and tidy while he satisfied his appetites elsewhere?

Serena heard a little sound and was dimly shocked to realize it came from her throat. It sounded like that of an animal in pain, some tortured creature hunkered down in the dark as it waited helplessly to find out if it would live or die. She didn't realize that she was rocking gently. She didn't see her alarm clock flash a series of red numbers before going dark, or notice that her stereo system was spitting out tape from a cassette.

Only when the overhead light suddenly exploded was Serena jarred from her misery. With a tremendous effort she struggled to control herself.

"Concentrate," she whispered. "Concentrate. Find the switch." And for the first time, perhaps spurred on by her urgent need to control what she felt, she did find it. Her wayward energies stopped swirling all around her and were instantly drawn into some part of her she'd never recognized before, where they were completely and safely contained, held there in waiting without constant effort from her.

Moving stiffly, feeling exhausted, Serena got out of

bed and moved cautiously across the room to her closet, trying to avoid the shards of glass sprinkled over the rug and the polished wood floor. There were extra light bulbs on the closet shelf, and she took one to replace the one from her nightstand lamp. It was difficult to unscrew the burst bulb, but she managed; she didn't trust herself to flick all the shattered pieces out of existence with her powers, not when she'd come so close to losing control entirely.

When the lamp was burning again, she got a broom and dustpan and cleaned up all the bits of glass. A slow survey of the room revealed what else she had destroyed, and she shivered a little at the evidence of just how dangerous unfocused power could be.

Ironically, she couldn't repair what she had wrecked, not by using the powers that had destroyed. Because she didn't understand the technology of television or radio or even clocks, it simply wasn't possible for her to focus her powers to fix what was broken. It would be like the blind trying to put together by touch alone something they couldn't even recognize enough to define.

To create or control anything, it was first necessary to understand its very elements, its basic structure, and how it functioned. How many times had Merlin told her that? Twenty times? A hundred?

Serena sat down on her bed, still feeling drained. But not numb; that mercy wasn't granted to her. The switch she had found to contain her energies could do nothing to erase the memory of Richard with another woman.

It hurt. She couldn't believe how much it hurt. All these years she had convinced herself that she was the only woman in his life who mattered, and now she knew that wasn't true. He didn't belong only to her. He didn't belong to her at all. He really didn't see her as a woman—or, if he did, she obviously held absolutely no attraction for him.

The pain was worse, knowing that.

Dawn had lightened the windows by the time Serena tried to go back to sleep. But she couldn't. She lay beneath the covers, staring up at the ceiling, feeling older than she had ever felt before. There was no limbo now, no sense of being suspended between woman and child; Serena knew she could never again be a child, not even to protect herself.

The question was, How was that going to alter her relationship with Merlin? Could she pretend there was nothing different? No. Could she even bear to look at him without crying out her pain and rage? Probably not. How would he react when she made her feelings plain, with disgust or pity? That was certainly possible. Would her raw emotion drive him even farther away from her? Or was he, even now, planning to banish her from his life completely?

Because he knew. He knew what she had discovered in the dark watches of the night.

Just before her own shock had wrenched her free of his mind, Serena had felt for a split second *his* shock as he sensed and recognized her presence intruding on that intensely private act.

He knew. He knew she had been there.

It was another part of her pain, the discomfiting guilt and shame of having been, however unintentionally, a voyeur. She had a memory now that she would never forget, but it was his, not hers. She'd stolen it from him. . . . And of all the things they both had to face when he came home, that one was likely to be the most difficult of all.

The only certainty Serena could find in any of it was the knowledge that nothing would ever be the same again.

THREE

Tuesday was a very unsettling day for Serena. Preferring to keep busy, she went to work as usual, despite her shortage of sleep. But she couldn't keep her thoughts off Merlin and what had happened the night before. Still, she had years of practice in maintaining a normal facade, and that enabled her to get through the day without disgracing herself by bursting into tears or snapping at everyone she encountered.

At least the "switch" she had finally discovered remained firmly off, which kept her inner turmoil from manifesting itself in another dangerous release of unfocused energies. For that she was grateful.

But a bad day was made immeasurably worse when she found Jeremy Kane waiting in the lobby of her office building.

"Hello, Kane." Everyone who knew him, even women, called the reporter by his last name.

"Serena." He was smiling. "If you have a few minutes, I'd like to talk to you. There's a coffee shop just across the street. Shall we?"

His manner was less abrupt than usual, and all her instincts went on alert. She didn't like his uncharacteristically pleasant smile, and there was a gleam in his eyes that made her want to hold on tight to her purse. But Serena knew she had taken a risk on Friday night, and if there was going to be fallout, she intended to deal with it herself.

The last thing she needed right now was an I-told-you-so from Merlin.

Besides that, she was curious about what the reporter had in mind, so she willingly accompanied him into the coffee shop. They were shown to a booth in a corner, fairly private in the less-than-crowded shop, and Kane talked desultorily about the weather (overcast, as usual), politics (screwed up, as usual), and the latest best-seller (his name wasn't on the cover, so he hated it) until their coffee came.

"What's on your mind, Kane?" Serena asked after the waitress left. Ordinarily she would have let him get around to it in his own time, but she wanted to hurry home and see if Merlin had returned.

Kane sipped his coffee for a moment, pale blue eyes fixed on her face. He wasn't a bad-looking man, but the wear and tear of nearly twenty years of a downhill slide was stamped into his features, lending them an oddly blurred, indistinct appearance that was a bit unsettling.

"Did you take me` back to my apartment Friday night, Serena? After our dance?" he asked finally in a very casual tone.

As she assumed an expression of surprise, her mind worked very swiftly, examining the question and recalling every one of her own actions. Of course she knew why he was asking: because he had most likely found the draft of the announcement in his pocket and, obviously remembering she'd been with him before he passed out, had concluded that she was somehow responsible. The most logical answer, naturally, was that she had accompanied or followed him home and had, for some reason, left the paper in his pocket for him to find.

"Why would I have done something like that?" she asked in a puzzled voice.

"Never answer a question with a question."

"No, I didn't take you back to your apartment. I repeat, why would I? A dance is one thing, Kane, but we certainly don't know each other *that* well."

He didn't lose his smile. "Why *did* you ask me to dance, by the way? I'm hardly your type."

Gently, Serena said, "Somebody dared me to, Kane. Sorry about that, but I've never been able to resist a dare."

"And did this somebody also dare you to ask me what my address was while we danced?"

So he remembered that, too, dammit. "Your address," she replied, "is in the phone book. I looked it up months ago when I was chairing that committee and needed a speaker. Don't you remember?"

Judging by his tightened lips and narrowed eyes, it appeared he had forgotten that. So had she, as a matter of fact, until just now.

Going on the offensive, Serena shook her head and said, "I don't know what you're after, Kane, but if this is the way you react after a woman asks you to dance, it's no wonder you don't get invited very often."

He ignored the latter part of her statement. "What I'm after? Answers, Serena. I'm a very curious man. I'd like to know, for instance, just who you are. You certainly weren't born Serena *Smyth*—that much I've found out. I believe you took the name, legally, at sixteen. That was after you came to Seattle, of course, and moved in with Richard Merlin."

She allowed one of her eyebrows to climb in mild amusement. "You make a perfectly innocent and commonplace act sound criminal, Kane. So I changed my name—big deal. If you must know, after my drunken father wrapped his car around a telephone pole when I was six and made me an orphan, I was passed from relative to relative for ten years. That was when I ran away."

"To Merlin," he said in a silky tone.

Serena ignored the tone. "To Richard. I decided to change my name, since I was old enough and since I wanted nothing further to do with any of my other relatives."

"Other relatives? So you still claim he's an uncle?"

She smiled. "No, he's actually some kind of third cousin. But calling him an uncle simplifies matters. Are you planning a story for the tabloids, Kane? One of those juicy headlines like, 'Uncle and Niece in Incestuous Relationship'? Why don't you just write that I'm going to have Elvis's baby? Or an alien's, maybe."

He flushed an ugly red. "I think the society page would be interested in the story," he said tightly. "Wouldn't all your tight-assed friends just love to know the real relationship between you and Merlin?"

Serena couldn't help it; she giggled. "Sorry, Kane, but you seem to have lost track of what really matters to people these days. Do you think you're the first to suspect Richard and I are lovers? Don't be ridiculous; those rumors pop up about once every year or so, as regular as clockwork, until something else comes along to stir up interest." Because she made very sure to distract anyone who suspected the relationship was in any way unusual.

"Can you deny it?" he snapped.

She looked him straight in the eye and replied with a calmness that was far more convincing than histrionics would have been. "Of course I deny it. Richard has been a lot of things to me, but never my lover."

"Maybe not," Kane insisted, "but there's something screwy in your relationship. What name *were* you born with, Serena? The court documents are sealed, oddly enough."

"Oddly? You know, for an investigative reporter, you seem to have a blind spot regarding facts. I was a minor; of course the court documents are sealed. The name I was born with is no longer mine, and is certainly none of your business. As for my *screwy* relationships—with Richard or anybody else—they also are none of your business."

"I'll find out what I want to know," he warned her softly. "Sooner or later I'll find a way through all the walls I keep hitting in Merlin's background. And it's just a matter of time until I figure out all your secrets. There's a story here somewhere, Serena. I can smell it."

Serena slid out of the booth and smiled pleasantly at

him. She had kept her cool easily until he mentioned a search into Merlin's background, and then she had felt a surge of anger mixed with worry. That was all she needed, to have unintentionally put this story-hungry reporter onto Merlin's trail.

"The only story here concerns a desperate search for lost glory, Kane," she said. "And it's a bit pathetic, you know. If you can't find something a hell of a lot more important than us, then it's no wonder you've fallen so far. Thanks for the coffee, and don't get up."

She walked away without a backward glance, which was a pity. If she had looked back, she might have seen the look of obstinacy on his face. And it might have warned her.

Serena got home to find that Merlin had not yet returned. She changed out of her business suit and into slacks and a sweater, went into the kitchen long enough to say hello to Rachel and fix herself a glass of iced tea, then wandered back to the entrance hall. Merlin's study opened into this foyer, and Serena headed toward it, intending to look for another of the books on her reading list.

Two feet from the door she suddenly stopped as though she'd run into a wall.

The study was always locked except when he was in it, but Merlin had never barred the room to his Apprentice. The lock was easy for her to undo, since it was intended only to keep out Rachel and any visitor to the house who might find the contents of the room a bit odd. But the door was blocked now by something a great deal stronger than the impotent man-made lock. And no Apprentice wizard could breach that barrier.

After several moments Serena retreated to the stairs and sat down on the third tread, staring toward that solid oak portal and feeling more than a little shaken. How long had he been doing this? Certainly not always; several times she had entered his study while he was away, looking for a book or scroll or something else she needed. When had she last gone into the room when he was absent?

Months ago, she remembered. She had undone the lock easily and automatically, and there had been nothing else to keep her out of the room.

She set her half-finished glass of tea beside her and hugged her upraised knees as she continued gazing at the forbidden door. Why? Why had he shut her out? Was this just another sign of his withdrawal from her, or was there something else going on, something he hadn't told her about? Something he didn't trust her to know?

No matter what the answers were, the questions had sown even more seeds of anxiety and fear in Serena. Coupled with the pain and fury of what she had discovered in the night, this new sign of trouble between her and Merlin made her emotional state so turbulent, she couldn't even think straight. She could only sit there on the stairs and wait, the confused emotions simmering, until he came home.

When he finally opened the front door almost an hour later, she didn't move or greet him. She just watched as he set an overnight bag on the floor, shrugged out of his raincoat, and hung it on the coat tree by the door.

His lean face still, the handsome features composed, he turned and looked steadily at her. After a moment he said calmly, "You found the switch."

It didn't surprise her that he knew. He had sensed her power from the first time he'd set eyes on her, so of course he could sense that she was now able to completely contain that power.

Serena rose slowly and stepped down to the bottom of the stairs. "That's not all I found," she said, and she could hear the strained note in her own voice contrasting sharply with his utter self-possession.

Rachel came into the foyer before he could respond. Whether she saw or sensed a problem, all she placidly said was, "You're home. Dinner in half an hour."

"Thank you, Rachel," Merlin said, still looking at Serena.

As the housekeeper retreated to her domain, Serena felt a stab of real panic. It was now, she realized. The confrontation she had shied away from loomed between them. There was no way to stop it now, not for her or for him. And no matter how it ended, their relationship would never again be the same.

"Richard—"

"In the study. Not out here." Leaving his bag there on the floor, Merlin crossed the space to his study door and opened it.

"That's a dandy lock you made," she said as she followed him into the room and closed the door, leaning back against it. She didn't look around at the book-lined walls, or at the very old scrolls placed on several shelves, and she didn't notice that his big desk was unusually cluttered with several opened books and a number of scrolls.

He didn't reply or react to her faintly accusing statement, merely walking to the front of his desk and then turning to face her as he leaned against it and lightly gripped the edge on either side of his hips. Serena wondered vaguely if they both felt the need of support. No, not Merlin, she thought. Surely not Merlin.

"Who is she, Richard?" The question was blurted without tact or grace.

Very quietly, impassively, he replied, "Who she is doesn't concern you, Serena."

Once Serena might have heeded the warning in his tone and backed away from what he clearly had no wish to discuss, but that time was past. Her stormy emotions were clawing at her, demanding an outlet, and she could no more stop her falsely bright, brittle words than she could stop breathing.

"Well, I'm reasonably sure she isn't a wife. A mistress then? She was surely no stranger, I know that."

"You know nothing about it."

"I know it wasn't the first time you were with her. That was obvious. I know what she looks like. Boy, do I know what she looks like. Head to toe."

"You had no right to be there," he said slowly, giving every word a terrible weight.

Stung, she said, "I didn't *try* to be there, dammit. I have no idea how I *got* there. I was asleep, Richard, and so far you haven't taught me a thing about controlling my sleeping mind."

"I will, never fear."

"I'll look forward to that. It wasn't exactly pleasant to find myself in some kind of bordello."

A faint sound came from him, an indrawn breath that was muted evidence of growing strain, and anger flickered in his black eyes. "It was not a bordello."

"No?"

"No. But whatever it was is none of your business. I don't have to justify myself or my actions to you, Serena. Aside from teaching you what you came here to learn from me, I have no obligation to you. None."

She was glad the door behind her lent some support, because she definitely needed it. Every clipped word he uttered stabbed at her. It had been bad enough before, but this was so hurtful, she could hardly breathe. No obligation? And no interest in her, his tone said that, as well.

The nine years they had spent together apparently counted for nothing.

"I see." The words were hardly more than a whisper, and she fought to shore up her composure, to save a bit of her self-respect. "You'll . . . have to forgive me. It seems I'm guilty of presumption, at the very least."

She felt behind her for the door handle, and held on to that for balance as she straightened and turned to leave.

"Serena."

Looking at him right now was impossible, but she went still, waiting.

"I didn't mean that." His voice was low.

She was very much afraid he had meant every word. "No, I needed the reminder," she said as evenly as she could manage. "You're right—your only obligation to me is what I asked for in the beginning, what you agreed to. Anything else is . . . anything else is completely inappropriate. I know that; I've known all along." She told herself fiercely to shut up, to stop making her pain so damned *obvious*.

"Serena, there are things you don't understand.

Things I can't explain to you." His voice was unquestionably strained now. "Some boundaries mustn't be crossed; the penalties are . . . too great. What we are, you and I, is precisely defined. It has to be."

She turned her head slowly and looked at him. Even through her pain she could sense his tension, see it in every line of his body. And there was something leaping at her out of his eyes, some intense emotion she couldn't interpret and that she had never seen before. She didn't completely understand what he was saying, but the gist of it seemed clear enough; the barriers separating them were not to be crossed.

"Yes, of course," she said almost politely, still clinging to the shreds of her dignity. "Everything has to have a clear definition; I know that. Because control is so important when dealing with power. Vital, really. So you're a Master wizard, and I'm your Apprentice. And that's all."

A muscle tightened in his jaw. "Anything else . . . anything more is impossible, Serena."

After a long moment she repeated, "Yes, of course," then added gravely, "I apologize for intruding into your personal life. It won't happen again." Quickly, she slipped from the room, closing the door behind her.

Merlin drew a slow, deep breath, trying to ease the constricted sensation in his chest. It didn't really work, which didn't surprise him; he had been conscious of that odd tightness for a long time now. It had been an ever-present feeling for months at least. Before that it had been an erratic thing, something of which he had been aware only occasionally.

He remembered clearly when he had first felt a hint of the strange sensation. Serena had been with him about three years then, and they had been totally immersed in study most of that time. But he had taken her out to dinner one night, and looking at her across the table, he had been jolted to realize she was wearing lipstick.

Such a small thing, and the sudden squeezing inside his chest had been fleeting, easily forgotten. Until the next time he had glimpsed some sign that the ragged urchin he had taken into his home and his life was becoming a woman. Was, actually, *reveling* in being a woman.

He hadn't lied to her just now, he told himself. There were precise lines dividing Master and Apprentice, and because of the power involved, those boundaries really did have to be respected. Serena knew that, as her words had proven. But he hadn't told her the whole truth, and he had allowed her to believe he was far more emotionally indifferent to her than he was.

Indifferent? Christ, if she only knew . . .

Merlin pushed himself away from the desk and went around behind it, where his chair was pulled back. He didn't sit, but put his hands on the smooth oak of the desk and leaned forward, staring down at an old, old book lying open. Like so many of the books in this room, its fragile parchment pages were hand-lettered in a strange language that would have baffled even the most erudite linguist, but Merlin read it easily because it was the language of his kind.

> *It is forbidden for any Master, or any wizard of any level, to encourage or teach a woman to understand or implement any part or the whole of spells, incantations, or any other tool of the wizard's craft. No wizard of any level may reveal his true nature to a woman at any time without the prior express permission of the Council of Elders. Any wizard encountering a woman of innate power, whether or not she be aware of that power, must instantly report the discovery to the Council. Failure to obey these laws will result in the most severe of penalties, up to and including total banishment and the deprivation of all powers. . . .*

Merlin didn't have to look at the other books and scrolls on his desk, because he had pored over them for many hours already. Without exception, each of them pronounced the same laws in an identical tone of dire warning. The words might have differed slightly from source to source, but there was no ambiguity, no loophole through which to pass. What it all boiled down to was quite simple.

He had broken an ancient law in accepting a woman as his Apprentice—teaching her secretly, without the knowledge of the Council—and with every day that passed he was compounding the original crime.

It had seemed such a foolish law then, when a half-starved and half-drowned girl had turned up on his doorstep, her untapped powers practically radiating from her thin little body in an aura of promise. How could he turn his back on that promise merely because she was female? He couldn't.

He hadn't.

Since wizards tended to isolate themselves, and no other lived in Seattle, he'd had no trouble in keeping his activities secret from the Council and others of his kind, even over the span of nine years. Serena had been so consumed with the desire to learn that she had been unquestioningly obedient to his carefully devised rules, and he had been able to shield her developing abilities so as to escape notice. So far.

But what Merlin had not anticipated were his own confused instincts and emotions. The more Serena matured, the more he found himself overwhelmingly aware of her. She held his total attention with startling ease, no matter what she was doing, with her voice and her grace and the laughter in her green eyes, and even the way she had of charmingly and cleverly manipulating people and her surroundings to suit her—whether or not she used her powers to do it.

Their years together had given them knowledge of each other and a certain familiarity, and of course she had become a beautiful woman, so his notice and interest should have seemed perfectly normal and hardly surprising. And though he couldn't be sure of Serena's feelings any more than he could read her thoughts, he would have to have been blind and stupid not to recognize, even before today, that she saw him as something more than a teacher.

So why was he fighting his own feelings? There was, after all, nothing standing between him and Serena ex-

cept a ponderous ban in some old texts Serena had
never even seen. And since he'd already broken the law,
anything else had to be an insignificant matter of degree. At least that was what he told himself. But what
seemed simple on the surface turned out to be far more
complicated underneath.

He had found himself withdrawing from her time
and time again, feeling a strange and senseless appre-
hension whenever something reminded him she was no
longer a child, that she was a woman only nominally
under his control. The feelings grew stronger and
stronger, the tightness in his chest, the wariness, the in-
explicable urge to be on guard, as if against a threat.

Serena . . . a threat. Why? *Why?*

Her innate power was truly incredible; that was beyond question. She frequently startled him with the
strength of some ability he was in the process of teaching her—as well as an occasional seemingly natural or
unconscious skill that was unknown to him even after a
lifetime's study of his art—but he had no logical reason
to feel apprehensive or threatened by Serena nevertheless.

It had occurred to him only recently that what he felt
was far too powerful to have originated in the simple
breaking of a law, that surely there was little power in
dry words of warning written in ancient books and
scrolls—certainly not enough to cause this turmoil inside him.

No, this was something else, something embedded in
him, inherent to him, to who and what he was, that he
could only sense. It was as if all his deepest instincts recognized a prohibition so vitally important, it was more
like a taboo, a primitive command demanding instant,
wordless obedience. Part of him wanted to obey, struggled to obey, but part of him didn't want to and fought
against it. Since he was a logical man, and since that
command stirred an increasingly stormy conflict he
didn't understand in himself, Merlin had begun searching for the reasons behind the law.

So far he hadn't found them.

Sitting down in his desk chair, Merlin leaned back

and gazed across the room at nothing. How could he explain to Serena what he didn't understand himself? About what he felt and what he recoiled away from feeling. . . . And how could he even begin to tell her that the closed, secret society of wizards she aspired to join wanted nothing to do with her?

"Have you seen today's paper?"

Serena peered at the clock on her nightstand—a replacement for the one she'd zapped—and made a muffled sound of indignation when she realized it wasn't yet seven o'clock. In the morning.

"Jane, do you know what time it is?" she asked into the phone, yawning.

"Of course I know what time it is. You weren't awake? Serena, you're always up by six on a weekday."

Unwilling to explain that she hadn't slept well in the two nights since the confrontation with Merlin on Tuesday, Serena merely said, "I was up late last night. What's this about the paper?"

In a patient tone Jane said, "Thursday is when Kane's column runs, remember?"

Serena thought about it. "Yeah, I remember. So what? Did he call me the whore of Babylon?" She wasn't very interested; since most of her concentration and emotional energy had been taken up with the urgent need to act as if nothing out of the ordinary had happened between her and Merlin whenever he was present, she had completely forgotten that Kane might have decided to make trouble for her.

"Let me put it this way. If at all possible, you'd better hide the relevant section of the paper before Richard sees it."

Pushing herself up in bed, Serena frowned. "Did Kane attack Richard?" she demanded fiercely.

"Well, he certainly didn't nominate him for citizen of the month, but Richard is not going to like the publicity, and I doubt he'll be terribly pleased at the stuff printed about you—even if none of it's new. Really, Serena, just get to the paper and read it, okay? And call me later."

Serena hung up the phone on her way out of bed. She was in such a hurry that she used her powers to get ready for work in three seconds flat, going from a nightgown to a businesslike skirt and sweater between her bed (which made itself up as soon as she left it) and the door. It always felt a bit unsettling to have shoes appear on her feet while she was walking, especially high heels, but she adjusted and hurried from her bedroom after a quick glance to make sure the shoes matched. At least twice, hurrying like today, she had ended up with a weird combination.

Merlin's bedroom was down the hall, and the closed door didn't tell her whether or not he was up.

They hadn't talked, beyond what was absolutely necessary and then with distant courtesy, since Tuesday. He had spent his evenings in the house closeted in his study, so she had seen him only at meals. As she went quickly down the stairs, she could only hope that a late night of work, or whatever he was doing in his study these days, had kept him in bed past his usual time. Both of them tended to rise early, usually before six A.M., as Jane had noted.

The front door was still latched, and Serena breathed a sigh of relief when she opened it to find the morning's newspaper lying on the porch. Rachel always entered the house through the kitchen door in the mornings, and so the newspaper was brought in by whoever happened to come downstairs first.

Pushing the door shut, she rifled quickly through the sections until she found the one that always held Kane's column.

"Looking for something, Serena?"

Swearing silently, she replied in a light tone, "The life-style section. You know I always read my horoscope in the morning."

"And you know it's meaningless," Merlin said as he joined her in the foyer.

"It amuses me." Serena shrugged, then handed the remainder of the newspaper to Merlin and followed him toward the kitchen, from which came the smell of frying bacon. She would have much preferred to steal away somewhere private to read Kane's column, but didn't want to do anything that appeared suspicious.

She sat down across from him at the table, casually greeted Rachel, and sipped her coffee before unfolding her part of the paper. She forced herself to turn the pages without haste, but had to struggle not to stiffen in silent fury when she saw the title of Kane's column.

"Uncle and Niece . . . ?"

Thinly disguised as one of those Meet a Couple of Our Leading Citizen commentaries (which would fool no one; Kane's articles were eagerly read because he invariably trashed somebody), the piece was actually not as bad as Serena had feared, and certainly not as bad as it might have been. Obviously Kane knew better than to go over the line and risk libel. Other than with the title, he didn't even make implications about Serena and Merlin's true relationship, in fact—perhaps because her scornful charge that he would resort to "tabloid journalism" had touched him on the raw.

Nothing he said about Serena in the article bothered her in the slightest, especially since most of the details of her various relationships had already been made public. He didn't refer to her as the whore of Babylon, though the picture he painted wasn't far off the mark.

But what Kane *had* done with his malicious article was focus a spotlight on Merlin, as well as Serena, which was the kind of unwelcome publicity the wizard had always studiously avoided. And he must have battered his way through a few of those walls he'd mentioned, because he had unearthed several hitherto unpublished facts about Richard Merlin's background. Facts that surprised Serena and pointed out to her how very little she actually knew about Richard.

His father, for instance, was a judge in Chicago. Mother deceased for a number of years, her death caused by some accident. No siblings. Merlin had attended Harvard University, earning a degree in political science "at an unusually young age." Never married or engaged, he had lived briefly in Boston after college, then had moved to Seattle almost fifteen years ago. From all appearances—and no doubt to Kane's immense disgust—he seemed to have led a blameless, fairly unremarkable life.

Deliberately unremarkable, Serena thought shrewdly. After all, the best way to escape undue notice was to lead an outwardly bland existence with no unusual highs or lows.

"What is it?"

She looked up with a start to find Merlin watching her. "What's what?"

"Your horoscope. Isn't that what you're reading so intently? What fascinates you so much?"

Looking into those unreadable, impenetrable black eyes, Serena suddenly knew it was useless to try to keep him ignorant of the article. He was, after all, Merlin. Trying to keep something hidden from a Master wizard—especially *this* one—was rather like trying to hide a storm from radar.

With a sigh she said, "It's going to be a bad day."

"According to the stars?" He held her gaze steadily. "Serena, despite your newfound ability to contain your energies, I can certainly see and almost hear your distress. What's happened?"

She glanced around, realizing only then that they were alone; Rachel had apparently left the kitchen some time ago. Serena hadn't even touched her breakfast, which was rapidly growing cold. No wonder he had noticed her preoccupation; she *never* ignored meals.

Looking back at Merlin, she tried to think of some way of cushioning the blow, but finally blurted, "I didn't know your father was a judge."

He frowned. Instead of responding to her statement, he held out a hand for the section of the newspaper she'd been reading, and Serena gave it to him.

"It's not so bad," she offered as she watched him read the article. "Kane could have done a lot worse. I know you hate publicity of any kind, but he didn't say anything bad about you. And all that stuff about me is old news. I guess I could have tried to stop him, but he didn't seem to know anything for certain when he talked to me—"

"When he talked to you?" Merlin raised his eyes from the paper. "At the party?"

"No." She cleared her throat, unnerved by the mask-like hardness of his face. "It was later. He sort of cornered me leaving work, and—"

"Serena, why the hell didn't you tell me?"

Merlin swore rarely, and she'd never heard his voice sound so harsh. She didn't know what was so wrong about the article, but there was no doubt he was seriously upset. She knew then that she should have told him about Kane's interest while he could have done something to stop or at least deflect the man.

"I . . . I just forgot about it," she explained.

"Forgot?"

His disbelief touched a nerve, and Serena felt herself stiffen. A bit tautly she said, "It was on Tuesday. You may remember I had a lot on my mind Tuesday."

He leaned back in his chair slowly, still gazing at her with grim eyes, the newspaper lying on the table before him, his plate pushed to the side.

Serena's instincts told her to keep her mouth shut until he calmed down, but this hadn't been her best week, and she needed to let off a little steam. Being Serena, she opened every valve.

Recklessly, she said, "If you're so worried about the damned article, zap it out of the paper. Of course there'll be a rather large blank place, but you can probably fill it with a farm report or something."

"And am I supposed to *zap* it out of the mind of everyone who's already read it?"

"Why not? I may be no good at mind control, but I'll bet you're terrific at it. Aren't you? It certainly can't be beyond the powers of a Master wizard to create a little amnesia here and there."

"Kane's column," Merlin said evenly, "is syndicated in a hundred newspapers across the country."

"Including one in Chicago, I'll bet. That's it, isn't it? You don't want His Honor to know you're living with a woman he knows damned well isn't your niece."

Ignoring that, Merlin said, "I can hardly influence

the minds of a few million people. I'm not all-powerful, Serena, and certainly not infallible."

"I know." She suddenly wanted to cry.

His anger drained away as quickly as hers had, and Merlin looked at her with instant awareness. They were both remembering a blond woman and an all-too-human act, and this time it was Serena who looked away first.

"Sorry I didn't warn you about Kane," she said. "It's obviously a little late to worry about closing the barn door, since the horse is on its way and there doesn't seem to be much we can do about it. Anyway, the article certainly could have been worse, so we're lucky there. And maybe whoever it is you don't want reading it won't."

Merlin didn't say anything for a moment, and when he did speak, his voice was still a bit rough. "Serena, don't judge me before you know all the facts."

Her gaze returned to his face, the green eyes guarded. "Sure. You just tell me when I have them, okay?"

He couldn't blame her for the frustration she clearly felt, nor could he make it easier on her by disclosing a few of those necessary facts. There was far too much he didn't understand himself, and his own emotions were making it more difficult for him to see the situation clearly.

All he could do was try to keep everything, including Serena, under control until he found the answers for which he'd been searching.

Serena pushed back her chair and left the table, every taut line of her body expressing her vexation with him. Merlin rose, as well, and followed her out into the foyer, intending to say something that would allow them to part for the day on fairly amiable terms. He didn't like being at odds with Serena; it made him feel uncharacteristically morose and had a tendency to cause the rest of his day to be miserable.

But before he could say anything, the phone on the hall table rang.

She was getting her raincoat from the tree by the

front door, so Merlin answered. And even though he'd been half prepared for it from the moment he had read Kane's article, the matter-of-fact voice on the other end of the line nonetheless caught him by surprise.

"Merlin, this is Jordan."

Unconsciously, Merlin gazed straight at Serena. "Hello, Jordan. How have you been?"

Ignoring the pleasantry, the other man said, "How soon can you get here?"

An interesting question, Merlin reflected. He could, of course, "get there" instantly, and both of them knew it. But the appearance and demands of his normal life made instantaneous transportation an extremely rare thing, used only during the direst of emergencies.

"I can clear my desk by lunchtime," he said.

"Good. Take the first available flight after noon. I'll meet you at the airport."

"I'll be there." Merlin listened to the dial tone for a moment, then cradled the receiver. He was still looking at Serena. She had put on her raincoat but hadn't left the house because his stare and his end of the conversation had caught her attention. So much so, in fact, that she seemed to forget she'd been mad at him.

"Be there?" Her voice was hesitant, as if she wasn't sure she wanted to hear the answer.

Merlin started to tell her he was going out of town for a day or so, but the memory of what had happened last time forced him to be much more specific. "A meeting of the Council of Elders has been called," he said. "I've been asked to attend." Asked? He'd damned well been ordered.

Serena took a step toward him, still hesitant but probably alerted by some tone in his voice. "Have you done something wrong?"

A bit dryly Merlin replied, "You could say that, yes."

FOUR

Wizards were born with finite degrees of power, some high and some low. No amount of learning could increase that inherent level of force; instruction and knowledge could only perfect the control, the mastery of what was innately possessed. Merlin was on the high end of that scale, one of the extraordinarily rare beings born with almost unlimited potential.

Jordan was at the low end of the scale.

He was almost as tall as Merlin, but lacked the other man's power in almost every respect. Jordan was fair, thin, pale-eyed, soft-voiced. Born with so little ability that he barely qualified as a wizard, he might have grown to resent those farther up the evolutionary scale than himself; instead, he had chosen to put his stronger talents of organization and efficiency to good use, and so served as a kind of administrative manager for the Council of Elders.

He met Merlin at O'Hare Airport, his cool Nordic looks and placid voice an island of tranquillity in a sea of bustling humanity, and led the way briskly to the dark, inconspicuous Lincoln he had left in a no-parking zone. Naturally there was no ticket.

Merlin sat in the front beside Jordan, unwilling to

give the appearance of being chauffeured, even though he was. He disliked ceremony and avoided it whenever possible. Especially whenever he was in the company of other wizards.

It was just after six o'clock, and since it was late autumn, it was both dark and chilly outside. A gloomy omen, Merlin thought, and instantly chided himself for the superstition.

"Where's the meeting?" he asked, even though he was fairly sure he already knew.

Jordan didn't turn his attention from the road. "The judge's house, as usual," he replied.

Merlin glanced at his driver, wondering idly and not for the first time why Jordan referred to the Council members by their positions or titles in the "real" world rather than their names. A mania for secrecy perhaps? If so, it was no wonder. The six men he served had in common a secret that would have rocked this technically advanced and cynical world if it had been made public.

The news wouldn't have done wizards much good, either. Though Serena had been flippant when she had described another Salem witch hunt, the truth was that the discovery of wizards in their midst could certainly have the powerless population of the world both frightened and up in arms.

Hardly something anyone wanted to happen.

The remainder of the drive out of the city and into the suburbs was spent in silence. Almost an hour after leaving the airport, Jordan turned the big car into the driveway of a secluded mansion. The gates opened to admit them, and moments later the car drew to a stop near the bottom of wide brick steps leading to a front door.

"They're already waiting for you in the study," Jordan said as the two men got out of the car. "I'll see that your bag is taken up to your room."

In the short time it took Merlin to mount the steps, the massive front door opened to reveal a soberly dressed elderly man, the very image of an old-world butler.

"Good evening, sir."

"Charles." He shrugged out of his coat and handed it to the butler, then half consciously straightened his tie and shot his cuffs. Not because he was vain, but because a neat appearance was essential. A meeting of the Council of Elders demanded the semiformality of a suit; Merlin, at a much younger age, had once shown up in jeans, and it had been two years before he'd been allowed to forget that breach.

He wasn't nervous, but he did pause in the foyer for a moment to collect himself.

"The study, sir."

"Yes. Thank you, Charles."

With a deliberate tread Merlin crossed the seeming acres of polished marble floor to the big double doors of the study. He knocked once, purely as a matter of form, and entered the room.

It was quite a room. Sixty feet long and forty wide with a fifteen-foot ceiling, it held two fireplaces large enough to roast whole steers without crowding, a row of enormous Palladian windows, floor-to-ceiling bookshelves on either side of both fireplaces, and a marble floor. A huge, very old and beautiful Persian rug lay beneath the long table and dozen chairs placed squarely in the center of the room, and two chandeliers were suspended above the table. The remainder of the room was furnished with groups of chairs and small tables and reading lamps scattered about as if to invite intimate conversation, but nothing would ever make that room appear cozy.

It practically echoed.

The six men who made up the Council of Elders were seated at the end of the table opposite the door. The judge was at the head; on his right were a senator, a financier, and a diplomat; on his left were a world-famous actor and a scientist. All the men were middle-aged to elderly, with the scientist being the oldest, and all possessed that indefinable look of powerful, successful men. Which they were.

They were the eldest practicing wizards—hence their name. Though from various parts of the world, they all spoke English so well, their national origins weren't obvious. Each had been selected for his position on the Council by an ancient process that clearly and precisely determined the necessary qualities of wisdom and leadership, and which allowed absolutely no chance that personal ambition could influence results.

Though all were powerful men and powerful wizards, only two had achieved the level of Master wizard. That distinction was rare because it meant, by definition, an individual with total mastery over his powers, and that demanded a strength of will so great, few were able to attain it. In actuality, fewer than one-tenth of one percent of all the wizards who had ever lived had been able to reach that stature.

And even among that exceptional company, Merlin stood out as a unique being, because no wizard in all of history had achieved the level of Master at so young an age.

Which, at the moment, mattered not one iota. The Council of Elders was grim, individually and collectively, and all they saw before them was a wizard who had broken the law.

Merlin walked to his end of the table and sat down. He was wary but not unduly nervous; this wasn't the first time he had been caught in some rebellion—he and the Council seldom saw eye to eye on even minor matters—and he had every expectation of being able to defend himself. He folded his hands on the table and waited, knowing from experience that he could shape his defense only after he had heard whatever they had to say.

It wasn't long in coming.

The judge, his expression dispassionate and his voice flat, said, "Is she a woman of power?"

"She is." Hiding Serena's existence from these men for nine years was one thing, but Merlin wasn't about to lie to them now. Defiance could be explained and perhaps understood; stupidity was something else entirely. He felt as well as heard the Council's collective indrawn breath, and realized that each man had hoped he would tell them it wasn't true.

The actor, his trained voice particularly effective in the huge room, said, "You know the law. How do you justify breaking it?"

Merlin's previous offenses had been relatively minor. This time, as he studied the somber faces at the other end of the long table, he realized there was nothing minor about his latest infraction. And the power of the Council was nothing to underestimate. If the Elders felt his offense warranted it, they could destroy him. So he gave himself a moment to think before answering, and when he spoke, he kept his voice calm and reasonable.

"It's a senseless law, and I could find no reason for it. Why should I turn away from the potential Serena represents simply because she's female?"

Merlin felt a slight ripple in the room, as if every man present had shuddered inwardly. They were nervous, all of them, tense to the point of being stiff. The reaction baffled him—and yet some part of him *understood*.

The diplomat, his voice unusually quavery, said, "It's forbidden to teach any woman. Forbidden for any woman to even *know* about us. You must stop."

"Why?" He looked at each of them in turn. "Someone tell me *why* it's forbidden."

"It's the law," the scientist said, as if stating an incontrovertible and absolute truth in his universe.

"It's a bad law," Merlin snapped, beginning to lose his composure in the face of their inflexible conviction. He had the odd feeling that no one at the table was listening to him, that they wouldn't—or couldn't—hear any part of his defense. "We're hardly rich enough in power to be so eager to squander it," he added more quietly.

The senator's voice was grave. "You're obviously too close to the subject to be able to see it clearly—"

"Her. See *her* clearly. The subject is a woman, Senator. And I see her clearly enough."

Several of the men began to speak at once, their voices high and agitated, and the judge held up a hand for silence. Gazing unwaveringly at Merlin, he spoke in a steady voice.

"We've lived by our laws for thousands of years, and

in all that time no law has ever been renounced by a practicing wizard: You must not be the first. Our ancestors devised the laws because they saw an overwhelming need for us to control our powers, not *be* controlled by them. If we're to survive as a race, we must all respect and obey the rules we live by."

"Except this one," Merlin retorted. "It's a *senseless* law. Why should learning be denied to a female born with power? Why do you—all of you—see that as a threat? Why are you afraid of Serena?"

Very softly the judge said, "Why are you?"

Merlin stared down the table into a pair of eyes as black as his own. "I'm not afraid of her." Despite his effort, his voice lacked conviction.

"No? I think you are. Apprehensive at least. Can you honestly say you haven't felt yourself drawing away from her? That you haven't felt wariness, an uneasiness, a sense almost of panic as she has matured in her abilities and as a woman?"

Of all the Council, only the judge had married—only he had even lived with a woman, for that matter—so he was really the only one who could have imagined what Merlin might feel toward his Apprentice. Unfortunately, though that might have made him an ally, Merlin knew better. The judge had been married to a powerless woman, not an Apprentice wizard, and while that was frowned upon and discouraged, it was not forbidden.

"Whatever I've felt is beside the point," Merlin said at last.

"Hardly," the judge said. "It is the point. That a woman is forbidden to know our craft isn't simply a moldy old law written in ancient books; it's written in *us*. Stamped in the deepest part of us. And *we must obey*."

"You must stop teaching the woman," the actor said inexorably.

"It's the law," the scientist agreed.

"Be reasonable," the financier begged. "Stop this before it's too late. Don't force us to do it."

Merlin stiffened, his gaze again flying to the head of

the table. There was a long silence, and then the judge sighed.

"According to the newspaper article, she's lived with you for years. How many?"

"Nine."

"Then she's barely into the training?"

Merlin hesitated, then shrugged. "I accelerated in several areas because of her innate power." Again there was that odd ripple through the room, and this time the men sat back in their chairs or moved restlessly.

"But her control *is* imperfect?" the judge demanded.

"Yes. But she's young and she did begin the training later than usual. I have every reason to believe she can one day achieve the level of Master."

If Merlin had hoped that his clear vote of confidence in Serena's potential might persuade the Council, he knew instantly that he'd been wrong. To a man, the faces across the table actually paled, and even the judge, normally impassive, was clearly appalled.

"It must stop," the diplomat whispered.

"There's no time to be lost," the actor said nervously.

Quietly the judge asked, "We're agreed, then?"

Without exception, the Council members nodded, looking away from Merlin. The judge nodded, as well, then stared down the table at his son and spoke heavily.

"The Council has decided. This woman must be rendered powerless. Because she is female and not yet in full control of her abilities, it will be possible for you to strip her of all levels of power."

"What?" Merlin whispered.

The judge went on as if nothing extraordinary had been said. "The process is an ancient one, not commonly known, requiring several weeks to complete. I'll give you the reference material before you return to Seattle. The woman will not be harmed by this, merely rendered powerless."

"Merely." Merlin's voice was still hardly louder than a whisper. "Merely rendered powerless."

"It's the only way," the senator told Merlin. "The

law must be obeyed. We have no choice. Don't you see that?"

The judge again waved a hand for silence. "The decision of the Council is final. Your punishment for breaking the law will be determined at a later time; the severity of that penalty will depend on your obedience now. You will render this woman powerless."

"Or?" Merlin asked flatly. They were all staring at him with shuttered eyes and impassive faces, and in that moment he thought he could hate them.

"Or we will do it," the judge replied calmly. "And you'll pay a very high price for disobeying the Council."

Ironically, Merlin was the most powerful wizard in the room in terms of raw force, and all of them knew it. But the simple fact was that he was under their control—not because he wanted to be, but because he *had* to be. No society of powerful beings could exist without a governing body; for wizards that body was the Council, and their decisions *were* final.

If he disobeyed, the punishment could be anything from the curtailing of his freedom to the reduction or even total removal of his powers.

That last would literally kill him, but it had been done more than once in the history of wizards when an individual had committed an unpardonable offense. It was not something he could fight with any possibility of success; power against power simply canceled itself out. So if the Council voted to take his powers and he struggled against it, there would be two dead wizards instead of one. Himself . . . and the Elder closest to him in raw force, the natural choice to be the one to seize his powers: his father.

They had him in a neat, bitterly effective vise, and he knew it. If he obeyed the Council, Serena would be stripped of her powers, and no matter how little the process harmed her physically, Merlin knew she would be destroyed by it. If he disobeyed the Council and they voted on the ultimate punishment for him—which was highly likely—he would be destroyed, and Serena's powers would be stolen from her anyway.

Merlin didn't realize the meeting was over until he

felt a hand on his shoulder and looked up to see the judge standing beside his chair. The others had gone.

"Come into the den," the judge said.

Merlin rose and followed the older man across the hall to a smaller and much more intimate room of the big house. The fireplace in here boasted a roaring fire, and Merlin was drawn to it instantly. He felt cold. He stood at the hearth, watching the leaping flames.

"Have you slept with her?"

Merlin stirred impatiently but didn't answer.

"Have you slept with her?"

"No, of course not." He turned then and stared at the still handsome, white-haired man who was sitting a few feet away from him. "She was a child when she came to me—and that's the way I saw her."

"What about now?"

Merlin hesitated, images from recent years flashing through his mind. Serena in a clingy evening gown dancing gracefully; her long legs bared by shorts as she worked in the garden in summer; regal and beautiful in her Apprentice's robe, green eyes flashing with humor and challenge. . . .

Almost inaudibly Eric Merlin said, "I see she's no child to you now."

"Isn't that my business?"

His father shook his head. "It would be bad enough if you had told any woman what you are—but a woman of power?"

"I didn't have to tell her what I was. She recognized me the way I recognized her." Merlin kept his voice calm. "The way beings of power have always known each other. She knew what I was, and she knew I could teach her. She was drawn across three thousand miles to find me."

The judge frowned. "Then her instincts are strong. But it makes no difference. There is no place in your life for a woman of power, you know that. There's no place in our *world* for her."

"I can't take her powers away from her."

"You must."

"I can't!" Merlin turned back to the fire, and his

voice was as fierce as the flames when he went on. "Can't you see what you're asking me to do? It would destroy her. A wizard isn't something Serena wants to become, it's what she *is*, as much a part of her as the blood in her veins. Taking her powers would be like . . . like taking the wings of a bird or the fins of a fish. She'll die."

"If the process is successful, she won't remember that she ever possessed any power out of the ordinary."

"I don't believe that. It will kill her as surely as the loss of my powers would kill me, or the loss of yours would kill you. But suppose it's true—what happens if the process isn't successful? You don't have to tell me. She'll die. I say she'll die no matter what."

"You're being unnecessarily pessimistic."

Merlin laughed harshly. "Am I? Well, let's examine this from a more general viewpoint, shall we? How many wizards are born in this modern world? How many never realize what they're meant to be?"

"Richard—"

"You know the ones I'm talking about. The ones who take photographs with their minds, and bend spoons on television talk shows, and are studied in laboratories, wasting their powers because we didn't notice they were there until too late and now no one can tell them what they really are."

"There have always been some who didn't recognize their abilities, but—"

Merlin turned back toward his father, and another bleak laugh escaped him. "Some? And what of the ones who'll never be born, Dad, what about them?"

The elder Merlin shifted a bit in his chair. "Wizards are born in every generation. You know that."

"Fewer and fewer of us. Especially since we're all discouraged from producing offspring of our own. I must say, I'm glad you disobeyed that particular law."

"It isn't a law," his father said instantly. "And I had the permission of the Council to marry." He hadn't been a member of the Council then, nearly forty years before.

"But we *are* discouraged from siring children, who would certainly inherit powers as I inherited yours."

"You were born with far more than I could give you. One of the chosen few with almost unlimited power. Your equal hasn't been seen in a thousand years."

Unimpressed by the tribute, Merlin said, "And could such a wizard as I have been born to powerless people?"

"I don't know. Probably not."

Merlin shook his head. "Then don't you see how rare and valuable someone like Serena is—male or female? She *was* born to powerless parents. An 'accidental' addition to our race. The only way we're to generate, it seems. Why is that, Dad? Why must we survive as a species only by chance?"

Again the older man stirred in his chair. "I can only tell you what you already know. Enough wizards are born by chance to ensure our survival as a race without the risks we run in producing our own offspring. According to the most ancient of our writings, our ancestors believed that sons bred dangerous ambition."

"What about daughters?"

"There's no mention of daughters in the writings, except to note that wizards must never sire them."

. . . must never sire them . . .

Given their genetic material, which was identical in all meaningful respects to that of powerless men, wizards were as likely as any other group of randomly selected men to sire female offspring as well as males, Merlin knew. Daughters must have been born somewhere along the way, and the offspring of a wizard was *always* born with some degree of power.

Staring at his father, Merlin had a sudden chilly intuition that any female child sired by a wizard, no matter how healthy, had not survived long. For the first time in his life, he felt a pang of aversion for what he was.

Slowly he said, "So sons are feared because they breed ambition, and daughters are never to be born at all—or at least never to long survive their birth. I'm somewhat surprised I was allowed to survive."

His father stiffened. "What are you accusing me of, Richard? There was never any question of abortion or infanticide, if that's what you're thinking. We may be discouraged from having sex with any woman who isn't unquestionably barren, and we're certainly discouraged from marrying, but when it *does* happen that a son results from such a union, we're civilized about it."

"Civilized," Merlin said. "How nice."

"Your sarcasm is uncalled for. The point is that I wasn't searching for a wife when I met your mother. You know that. But there's an exception to every rule. She was . . . a remarkable woman."

"A woman who knew what you were."

"Yes, but she was powerless. I would never have given in to my feelings if she had been anything else. The very idea is unthinkable. Richard, sit down."

After a moment Merlin sat down across from his father in a matching chair, and sighed. "Maybe Serena's an exception. Have you considered that possibility? She has so much power, Dad, so much potential."

"Can you read her thoughts?"

Merlin shook his head. He wasn't about to confess that Serena had an absolutely unprecedented ability to slip into his consciousness; that had shocked him to his bones, and he had no doubt it would horrify his father.

"Is that why you accepted her when she came to you? Because you couldn't read her thoughts?"

"That, and the power I could feel in her. It honestly didn't occur to me that I was doing anything seriously wrong. I barely remembered the law."

"Until she got older?"

Merlin sat forward, his elbows on his knees, and stared at his father. "Yes. Until she got older. What does it mean? As a child Serena was no threat; as a woman she is. Yes, she makes me feel uneasy, wary sometimes—but why? She would never harm anyone. Least of all me."

After a moment the judge shook his head. "I don't know why. Why the law exists, what prompted it, or why we feel it so deeply. Our writings are ancient, but I've never found any reference to the creation of the law. All I know is that there must be no female wizards. And that we must never trust any woman."

"You trusted Mother," Merlin said.

The judge looked at his son, and there was an old, old pain in his eyes. "No. I didn't."

Merlin was only dimly aware that he had risen to his feet. "She lived with you for twenty years," he said slowly. "Bore you a son. And she kept your secret. How could you not trust her?"

"She asked me the same thing. Over and over again she asked me. I never could give her an answer." The judge hesitated, then went on softly. "She asked me that night, and when I had no answer for her, she rushed out of here in tears. An hour later her car crashed into a wall."

"Are you telling me—"

"I'm telling you that . . . accident . . . shouldn't have happened. That's all I'm saying. That's all I can ever know."

Merlin turned away from his father to stare into the bright heat of the fire. Suicide? Dear God, had his mother killed herself? Clearly his father believed it, or at least believed it was possible. Was that the price she had paid for loving a wizard?

"Richard, you can't blame me for being what I am. Any more than I can blame myself."

"Why couldn't you trust her?" he demanded harshly, not looking at his father because he didn't know if he could.

"It's not in me to trust a woman, just like it isn't in you."

"I don't believe that."

"You'd better. For your own sanity if nothing else, you'd better. You *feel* it's true even if you don't *think* it is, and that kind of conflict will tear you apart. Go back to Seattle, Richard, and take her powers away as gently as you can. And then send her out of your life before both of you are destroyed by this."

"I can't."

"Yes, you can. You have to. Because you don't have a choice."

Serena was not, by nature, a patient woman. So it was very difficult for her to hang on to what little tolerance she had when Merlin returned on Friday afternoon and shut himself in his study. Since she was at work when he got home, she didn't even see him.

"He said he's not to be disturbed. For any reason," Rachel informed Serena when she came home.

"He has to eat," Serena objected.

"That's your problem, at least until Monday," Rachel said, a gleam of amusement in her eyes as she put on her coat and picked up her umbrella. "Dinner's in the oven, but I've a feeling you'll be eating alone tonight."

To Serena's frustration, the housekeeper was correct. Merlin's study was barred to her—just as it had been once before. The door was unlocked, she knew that, but he wasn't going to allow anybody to cross the threshold until he was ready.

That weekend turned out to be the longest one of Serena's life. Reluctant to leave the house until she found out what had happened at the meeting of the Council—a group about which she was intensely curious simply because Merlin had told her very little about them—she occupied herself as best she could with her studies.

On Saturday afternoon she canceled a planned shopping trip with Jane. By Saturday night she found herself sitting on the stairs gazing at that closed door with what she didn't realize was so much intensity that she actually started in surprise when she felt the barrier vanish.

Hesitantly she crossed the foyer and knocked softly on the door.

"Serena." The acknowledgment was unmuffled by the thick oak of the door.

She opened the door and went into the study. Lighting kept the room from being too dark, but the study was still overpowering, filled with the ancient writings of a mighty race. The tall shelves, normally bursting with age-darkened heavy volumes written in odd scripts and ancient scrolls dust-dry and fragile, now showed gaps among the old books. Volumes were stacked, open and closed, on the floor, piled on the desk, and overflowed two chairs.

In the chair behind his cluttered desk, Merlin sat in an apparently relaxed position, his hands clasped together on the parchment pages of the book open before him. He was gazing across the room at her, impassive.

He looked tired, the sharpened planes of his face telling of too many long hours of study without food or sleep. His deep-set black eyes burned with the inner energy that was always a part of him, but there was something else, something even more vibrant than she was accustomed to seeing radiating from him.

"It's been more than twenty-four hours," she offered.

He was mildly surprised. "Oh? I hadn't realized."

"You have to eat."

"Do I?"

She blinked. "Don't you?"

With a sudden, slightly rueful smile, Merlin said, "Of course I do. But I'm not hungry right now. Sit down, Serena. We have to talk."

Those four little words were enough to make her feel extremely apprehensive, and his smile didn't reassure her a bit, but she removed several books from the chair nearest his desk and sat down.

Master and Apprentice, that's all we are. Master and Apprentice. There can't be anything else.

With forced lightness she asked, "How was the Council meeting?"

"Difficult." Without elaborating, Merlin abruptly changed the subject. "Do you trust me?" he asked her.

"Of course." Her answer was instant, unthinking, and she felt an odd jolt when he seemed to wince. Was her answer unexpected, or simply unwelcome? She didn't know. His features smoothed out quickly, and his voice was calm when he went on.

"Good. Because I'm going to have to ask you to hold on to that trust with both hands."

She eyed him warily. "Why? Are you going to do something to make me doubt I can trust you?"

"I hope not," he murmured, then shook his head a bit. "Serena, I can't explain everything just yet. I know you're tired of hearing that, but please try to be patient.

I have my reasons, and they're good ones. You have to trust me on that point."

"All right," she said, slowly and reluctantly—but he definitely had her interest. Since she did trust him, it didn't seem too much to ask. For the moment.

"Thank you. If it helps, I believe you won't have too many questions left by the time we get back."

"Back? Where are we going?"

He looked down at the book lying open on his desk. "We're going through a gate, Serena. A gate into time."

That surprised her so much that she could only stare at him when he went on somewhat broodingly.

"We'll have to be careful. Our presence alone could have unimaginable consequences. To change the past is to change the present. And the future."

Serena was trying to fathom the undercurrents she could barely sense in him. It was as if he had severed some tie, burned his bridges behind him, and that unnerved her. How much was she to take on faith? Everything? Or could she ask questions? Uncertain on that point, she opted for a simple statement. "You haven't taught me about time travel."

"Of all our abilities, it's the most dangerous." His gaze turned to her, still brooding. "It's also forbidden without the approval of the Council."

"Do we . . . have its approval?"

Merlin shook his head.

All Serena knew of the Council of Elders was that it was the ultimate authority among wizards. Merlin hadn't told her much more than that. But it was enough to make her feel a little chilled just then.

She attempted a laugh that didn't quite come off. "You, Richard, breaking a rule?"

His mouth twisted oddly. "If I had not broken another . . . Well, never mind that now. I'll deal with the Council, if need be, when we return."

"This is very important," she realized.

"Very."

"Why?" She wasn't sure he would answer.

Merlin hesitated. "The less you know about the specifics, the better our chances of success."

"Really?" She couldn't help doubting that.

"Really, Serena. I'll take an oath if you like, but I hope you won't need that from me. The truth is I honestly believe that for you to know everything *at this point* is to invite potential disaster."

The sincerity in his voice convinced Serena he meant what he said. It was frustrating, but she had to trust that he knew what he was doing. "All right. What can you tell me?"

Merlin obviously chose his words carefully. "I believe that something went wrong in our past."

"Our past?"

"The past of wizards. I can't be sure, since it was so long ago and most of the records haven't survived— either because of the passage of time or because they were deliberately destroyed. All I am certain of is that we must go back and try to understand what happened."

She frowned. "And change it?"

Again he hesitated. "I don't know. That decision can only be made when we have more information. If we make a mistake—change too much or the wrong thing—we could destroy our present."

Serena felt another chill. "If we did that—made a mistake in the past, I mean—then couldn't we go back again and just fix the mistake?"

Merlin shook his head. "Not even a wizard can exist twice in the same time and place. Paradox: the bane of time travel. Once we go back, then we *were* there."

"Yes, but . . ." Serena chewed on her bottom lip as she tried to figure that out.

Patiently Merlin said, "There are two paradoxes in time travel. The first is our inability to alter our individual lives—our personal time lines—in any way whatsoever. Any change, however minor, affects who and what we became; that, in turn, affects our reason for going back in the first place."

Serena blinked. "Um . . . I'm confused."

He smiled briefly. "All right, then consider the example today's thinkers like to offer when they say time travel is impossible. Suppose you build a time machine, and it takes you back along your personal time line—

which is, in effect, the direct line of your ancestry. You encounter your father years before your own conception. Either directly or merely by your presence, you influence events in his life, and he dies."

She waited, then said, "And so?"

"And so it isn't possible. If your father dies before your conception, then you are never born to build a time machine and travel back in time. Paradox."

That example worked. Serena nodded slowly. "I get it. We can't do anything that would directly affect our own present, because it would change too much for us to be able to go back."

"Close enough," Merlin murmured.

"But you said there were two kinds of paradoxes. What's the second one?"

"In a sense the second is much simpler. Once we go back, we were there. What do you suppose would happen, Serena, if you went back to the same place a second time and came face-to-face with yourself?"

She shivered. "That's eerie."

"It's also dangerous. The theory is that a duplication of self occupying the same place and time would fracture that time line. Destroy it—or unalterably change what must be."

Serena cleared her throat. "So what would happen to me in that case? Both of me?"

"I can only offer you another theoretical answer. In theory, there would be, from that point on, two separate Serenas in two separate—and probably quite different—time lines. Alternate lives, alternate futures, and both of you would be diminished."

"Yuk." She stared at him. "I don't like the sound of that at all."

"I should hope not."

"So we only go back once."

"We could go back to an earlier or later time, or another place in the same time, but we aren't allowed the luxury of repeating our actions until we're satisfied with them." He looked at her steadily. "It's a one-shot deal, Serena. We have to get it right the first time."

FIVE

After a moment she said, "But how can we go back into the past of wizards? Won't that affect our present?"

"Not yours or mine, no, at least not directly. I've traced our ancestries back as far as possible, and neither of our personal time lines in any way touches Atlantis."

Serena leaned forward slowly in her chair, reaching out for the edge of the desk as if for support. "Atlantis? The lost continent? That's where we're going?"

"Yes." A frown tugged at his brows, and he said almost to himself, "Still a risk if we change anything, unless there were no survivors. And if there were no survivors, how could what happened there have changed the history of wizards?"

A little numb, she murmured, "Another paradox?"

Merlin stopped scowling and shrugged. "Perhaps. But there must have been survivors. At least one. Someone had to tell the others what happened there. Someone had to know what had gone wrong, or else why would they have felt so strongly that they made the law—and made it so inviolate."

"What law?"

He looked at her for a long moment, then shook his

head a little. "The point is that someone must have survived the destruction of Atlantis, and because of that person's beliefs or experiences, a decision was made that altered the society of wizards. That's the only possible answer."

Aware that her question hadn't been answered, but assuming it was because she had strayed into the part of all this he didn't want her to know about, Serena merely said, "Are you sure it was only one person?"

"I'm not sure of anything. My guess is that there couldn't have been more than a few survivors. Atlantis was too remote, and travel too difficult in those days, for it to be very likely that many escaped."

"Surely they had time to plan their escape. Wouldn't there have been some kind of warning? I mean, the whole continent vanished. Even if it sank all at once, wouldn't the people have realized long before it actually happened that they were heading for disaster?"

Merlin shrugged again. "It's difficult to say. I doubt the continent existed in calm for years and then simply disappeared one day; there must have been earthquakes, volcanic activity—something. But that may have been going on for so long that the people simply accepted it as normal. Or they may have been trapped there with no way of escape. Or, even more likely, they may not have realized that their whole world could vanish so completely. Look at the people today who build houses and businesses along earthquake fault lines, Serena; they may know the risks intellectually, but do you honestly think they really face the knowledge that one day it could all be gone?"

"I see what you mean. So the people of Atlantis might have gone blindly to their fate. But at least one escaped."

"I believe that must have happened. Atlantis was so cut off from the other civilizations in the world that no one could have known for certain what happened there unless they were told by a witness."

"Were there a lot of wizards then?" Serena asked curiously.

"More than today—relative to the population at

least. And those in Atlantis were probably in some sort of control over their society."

"I thought wizards didn't do that."

"Not now, and not for a long time. But then . . . who knows? Power has a way of corrupting, and at that time there weren't many other ways to be powerful. There was no worldwide society as there is today, no technology, only crude weapons. Though they were primitive by our standards, wizards must have stood head and shoulders above most others in terms of power."

Thinking of the romantic stories she knew of wizards, Serena said, "How were they primitive? I mean, look at some of the things your namesake did."

Merlin half closed his eyes in a pained expression. "Fiction, Serena. I've *told* you."

In a small, wistful voice, she said, "No King Arthur?"

He hesitated, then sighed. "I wouldn't go that far. But reality—if it was reality—can never measure up to legend. If there was a Merlin then, and if he was great, it was mostly by comparison to those around him." Taking note of her dejected air, he decided to abandon the subject of Arthurian legend. "Serena, the wizards of Atlantis are probably first graders in relation to us. They're still learning to read and tell time and count without using their fingers."

She brightened just a bit and, using the same yard-stick, said, "If they're first graders, where are you?"

"Working on my doctorate," he said promptly.

She wasn't sure she wanted to hear the answer, but asked anyway. "And me?"

He was silent and reflective long enough to make her nervous, but then said judiciously, "A few credits away from your baccalaureate, I'd say."

Surprised and a bit flattered, she said, "I thought you'd say I was still in high school."

"You're still a long way from final graduation," he reminded her.

Serena nodded with a stab at meekness, but she was quite pleased by his assessment of her progress. One thing she did know about wizards was that it required a good many years of study to achieve the highest levels of the craft; she had gotten a late start, so if she had done as well as he said, she had every right to be proud of herself.

"In any case," Merlin went on, "we should certainly be able to hold our own with even the most powerful wizard of Atlantis."

Yanked from her self-congratulation, Serena felt a little shiver of unease. "You say that as if you expect us to land in the middle of a battle."

Merlin glanced down at the book before him again, then looked at her seriously. "I don't know what we're going to land in the middle of, but I'm expecting the worst. We should both expect the worst. The continent vanished, Serena; whatever happened there can't be good."

"That makes sense." She took a deep breath. "Okay. So what happens next?"

"First I have to teach you to completely shield your powers. After that I'll build the gate."

Somewhat confused, Serena said, "Shield my powers? You mean, from another wizard? I thought I could already do that."

"No. You shield your thoughts, but the fact that you possess power would be obvious to any other wizard who came near you. I must teach you to project a powerless facade so that no one, not even a Master wizard, will suspect you to be anything other than completely powerless."

"Why?" she asked slowly.

He looked at her for a long moment, as if considering whether to answer her, then said, "I have a hunch that it would be . . . more difficult for us to travel together if both of us are obvious wizards. But whether I'm right about that or not, it's still a prudent step to take. With your powers hidden from other wizards, we have an ace up our sleeve—*and* present a less-threatening appearance to those we encounter."

Serena chewed on her bottom lip for a moment, then said, "It won't *really* affect me, will it? I mean, I'll still be able to use my powers if I need to?"

With that uneasy question, she reassured Merlin that he had made the right decision in electing not to tell her why they had to go back in time. If Serena had any idea that he could steal her powers from her, she would never be able to trust him—and he had a strong feeling her trust was needed.

"Of course you will," he replied calmly. "What I'll teach you to do will be rather like putting on a mask. You'll be able to see and hear clearly, and the mask will remain in place until you reach up and take it off. As long as you wear it, your powers—your true identity—will be hidden behind it. But only hidden. Not changed in any way."

Serena relaxed, not even aware until then that she had tensed. "That doesn't sound so bad. Will it take me long to learn?"

"A few days, I think. And a day at least for me to build the gate. You have a week's vacation left, don't you?"

She nodded. "Yeah. Owen won't be happy if I suddenly take off this coming week without warning," she said, referring to her boss, "but everything's caught up, so he really doesn't have an argument. I gather that's the idea? That I should start my vacation beginning tomorrow?"

"The sooner we get started, the better. I can close the office for the week and give Rachel the time off so we won't be disturbed at all."

"What'll we tell people? When we leave, I mean."

Merlin shook his head. "We won't tell them anything, because no one will ever know we even left the house. I'll set the gate to return us within minutes, no matter how long we spend in Atlantis."

Serena had to think about that for a moment, but then nodded. "We'll be in the past, so time won't advance in the present—right?"

"Right."

"So how much time *will* we spend in Atlantis? Relative time, I mean?"

Once again Merlin glanced down at the opened book on his desk before he replied. "If we're to be successful,

I believe we have to be there at the end—or as close as possible. A month before the destruction, I think. That should give us enough time to observe and understand the society."

"You know exactly when it happened?"

He nodded. "Yes—another reason why I suspect there was at least one witness. The account of Atlantis's final hours is extremely detailed and seems to have been written from a ship at sea."

She looked curiously at the book lying open before him, but since it was upside down from her viewpoint, she was unable to see much. "That account?"

"This account," he confirmed with a slight nod.

"That isn't one of your books," she noted. From ancient times Apprentice wizards had been required, as part of their training, to hand-copy (with exquisite penmanship, no less) a complete set of spellbooks from their Master's library. This was required not only for the discipline gained in the long process of carefully copying the books, but also because spellbooks were never translated or printed.

Since Serena was in the process of copying her own set of spellbooks (only those in which she had completed her training), she could recognize all of Merlin's, and all the reference books in his library, as well; the book on his desk was something else. It looked very, very old, and she had the feeling that despite all her training and learning, she wouldn't have been able to read the enigmatic script.

"No," Merlin said, replying to her comment. "It was given to me, recently, by my own Master."

She hesitated, but since the topic didn't seem to be taboo, she said, "I never thought, but of course you would have had to be apprenticed to a Master when you were a child."

"In my case, the Master was my father." With a slight smile he added, "A difficult undertaking for both of us. Wizard or powerless, fathers and sons always seem to be at odds."

"He was a difficult taskmaster?"

"Not so much that as a . . . difference in personalities and temperament."

"You must take after your mother then," Serena ventured.

Merlin's face closed down instantly, as if a curtain had dropped. "Yes, I suppose I do."

"I'm sorry. I didn't mean to—"

He shook his head abruptly to cut off her apology. "Never mind. We wandered from the point. This account of the destruction of Atlantis is very detailed, obviously from an eyewitness who was at sea. So there must have been at least one survivor."

Serena realized she had touched a nerve in her comment about his mother, but she had no idea why. Nor could she probe for an answer; his shuttered eyes made that clear. All she could do was follow his lead.

She was relieved to find a humorous angle in her own thoughts, and that relief was audible in her voice. "It just occurred to me that since the nonwizard world has no idea about some of this stuff, any powerless historian would just love to get his hands on your books."

Merlin smiled slightly. "They wouldn't be able to read a word."

"True." Serena thought for a moment, and found a genuine worry to distract her from everything else. "Something else occurs to me. Since we'll be in Atlantis just when everything's about to hit the fan—you will be able to get us out of there in a hurry, won't you?"

"If we're near the gate, certainly."

She stared at him. "If we're near it? You mean it's a fixed gate?"

Returning her stare, Merlin said, "Well, I don't propose to carry it around in my pocket."

"That's not what I meant, and you know it. If we happen to get stuck away from the gate just when we need it, wouldn't you be able to make another? A spur-of-the-moment escape hatch, so to speak?"

"No. One gate causes a small rip in the space-time continuum, which is dangerous enough; a second gate could create a crosscurrent and make it impossible for either doorway to be closed. We don't want that to happen."

"I guess not." Serena frowned. "So there really *is* a space-time continuum?"

"Of course."

"Oh. I thought the science fiction writers made that up."

"So do they."

Serena laughed, and realized only then that in the surprise of Merlin's announcement about their forthcoming trip, she had completely forgotten the tension between them. It felt more like old times, talking to him like this without difficulty, as if no trouble had sprung up between them.

Remembering, of course, brought all the emotions and stress back to mind, and even as Serena heard her laugh trail off, she saw Merlin's smile fade, as well. The tension hadn't vanished, it had merely been ignored for a while.

Would she really have all her questions answered by the time they returned from Atlantis? Even the painful ones—like the identity of his blond bedmate? Would this trip be a panacea for their strained relationship, or would it only make matters worse between them?"

"Serena . . ."

She looked at him, at the awareness in his eyes, and wondered despairingly if she had forever lost her ability to keep her feelings hidden from him. It seemed so.

Carefully neutral, she said, "So you want to get started first thing tomorrow?"

He nodded slowly in reply, but said, "Serena, what we have to do is going to be difficult enough without—"

She couldn't let him finish that, and got up even as she spoke briskly. "I know. Look, neither of us has eaten supper, so why don't I go and see what Rachel left for us?"

"Fine."

When he was alone again in the study, Merlin gazed broodingly down at the open book on his desk, trying to forget the naked moment with Serena. He was able to push it aside, if only because there were so many other things to think about.

Odd the twists and turns fate pursued. If his father had not given him this book, the "reference material" that contained the procedure to take Serena's powers, he would never have found what he had searched for all these months. It wasn't an answer, but it was definitely a beginning.

The book seemed to have been written long after Atlantis's destruction and long after the law forbidding women to become wizards had been created. But in the section of the book detailing the extended and elaborate procedure used to render a female powerless (Merlin refused even to read the actual procedure), there were numerous vague references to "the dark times" and allusions to some dreadful cataclysm.

As the judge had said, there was nothing specific in this book about the reasons for the law, but the use of the word *cataclysm* had struck Merlin forcibly. How many true cataclysms had there been in all of history? Not many, really, given the span of time. And in the history of *wizards*, none was claimed to have had any meaningful effect on their society.

Yet in this same book, in another section dealing with the historical accuracy of certain events, was an old account of the destruction of Atlantis, clearly written by an eyewitness who had been, of course, a wizard. (The doings of powerless beings were detailed by their own books.) Though the account was concise and detailed, it was not dispassionate; there was anger and bitterness and pain in every word. And after the bald details of what a continent looked like as it wrenched itself apart and sank into the ocean, there was one line that had made Merlin's heart suddenly beat faster.

We mustn't let it happen to us.

A great deal of meaning could be inferred from that brief statement. "It" had to be the destruction of the continent; and "us" had to be the other wizards, the ones who had lived, then, primarily in Europe. The implication was that the eyewitness had been a visitor to Atlantis. And the statement was a strong indication that the wizards of Atlantis had somehow caused their own destruction.

Speculation, certainly, but possible.

It had taken hours of searching through his library for Merlin to find any other information about Atlantis, and what he did find was sketchy. The society there had seemed to be one of great promise, its people strong and healthy, their land fertile, and their community vigorous. There were definitely wizards among the powerless; Merlin couldn't find out how many because whole passages in several of his books and scrolls were completely illegible, and nothing he tried had any effect.

As if the information had been deliberately destroyed.

Still, there was enough to convince Merlin he was on the right track. Common sense told him that the taboos against women must have resulted from some immense traumatic event (a good definition of a cataclysm, he thought, would be the destruction of an entire continent), and it was surely no coincidence that much of the information regarding Atlantis was as elusive as that regarding female wizards.

From that deduction it was only natural to consider going back in time to find out what had happened.

It wouldn't be the first instance of time travel for Merlin, so the actual journey didn't disturb him—even without the permission of the Council. He wasn't even unduly alarmed at the prospect of landing on a continent about which he knew next to nothing except that it was about to vanish under the sea. His worries were more complicated.

What tormented him the most was Serena, and what he would have to do to her if the past held nothing to help him. He would have to destroy her. To see the astonishing trust in her eyes turn to horror and fear . . . and pain.

Merlin tried to shake off the thoughts; there was no use worrying until he knew whether or not the past offered anything helpful. But he couldn't stop thinking about Serena; he'd never been able to do that. Not since she'd grown up.

Was he being reckless as well as irrational in taking her with him into the past? There was no real reason for that course of action, after all. He had certainly never needed help, and given the tension between them, her presence was likely to cause more strain than he wanted or needed to deal with. There was no reason at all for her to accompany him.

Was there?

He'd been sitting here at the desk for hours with that question in his mind, and had come to a decision only when Serena walked into the study. It might have been because he was a fair man and this certainly concerned her; it might have been because he had a hunch that this time he *would* need help—her help—to attempt to understand what had gone wrong in the society of wizards.

Might have been, but wasn't.

Ever since he had talked with his father, Merlin had been struggling to cope with the painful knowledge that the older wizard had not trusted his wife of twenty years, despite her fidelity, trust, and devotion, and that she might have killed herself because of it. That, more than anything else, revealed to Merlin just how tragic and unnatural was the wizards' reflexive wariness and mistrust of women.

When Serena had walked into the study, he had looked at her and had felt the disturbing jumble of emotions that had become painfully familiar these days—and his father's words had echoed inside his head. *There is no place in your life for a woman of power. . . . It's not in me to trust a woman, just like it isn't in you. . . . You feel it's true even if you don't think it is, and that kind of conflict will tear you apart.*

His deepest instincts were at war with his intellect, and Serena, innocent and unsuspecting, was in the middle of that battle. If there was something in Atlantis that would help resolve his conflict, Merlin intended to find it, and he wanted Serena to be with him when he did. In the end his decision to take her with him was just that simple.

As it turned out, both Serena and Merlin had to go to their offices early on Monday to arrange to take the remainder of the week off, so they decided at breakfast to begin getting ready for their forthcoming trip in the early afternoon.

Serena met Jane for lunch, mostly because she knew her friend was sincerely worried about her. Their broken shopping date on Saturday, as well as Serena's recent preoccupation, had convinced the lively brunet that Kane's column had caused all kinds of problems, and it required Serena's best efforts to convince her otherwise.

After soothing her friend, she returned home to find the house deserted. Rachel had gone, and Merlin apparently hadn't gotten home yet. Serena changed into jeans and then, on impulse, went downstairs to his study. The door wasn't barred, which was something of a relief for more reasons than one.

What she wanted were a few answers. She didn't know if she could find anything Merlin wanted to keep from her, but she had to try because she had the uneasy feeling that what he was doing—his apparent dispute with the Council of Elders and his flouting of their authority in his decision to travel through time without permission—was somehow her fault.

Besides that, there was simply too much curiosity in her nature to allow a puzzle to continue unchallenged.

For the first time, Serena entered Merlin's study with her mind and senses deliberately wide open—and as soon as she crossed the threshold, she felt breathless. She realized that her own strong mental shields had always blocked whatever energies were contained in the ancient writings—but she felt them now.

Not a negative force, the sense she had was of sheer power, muted and dormant. She leaned back against the doorjamb and half closed her eyes, cautiously probing. And at the extreme edge of her awareness, she almost heard soft whisperings of a hundred, a thousand voices.

The languages were varied, but all were obscure and contained Latin phrases and strange words that belonged to no language mankind had ever known. Or had ever heard, even when it had been spoken.

Her veiled gaze traveled slowly around the room, sliding over books and scrolls, then stopped. She pushed herself away from the door and walked to the shelves between two windows. A particular book, oversize and so old that the leather had been worn almost to nothing, seemed to pull at her. She had never noticed this book before. It wasn't the one that had lain open on his desk; that book was not in the room.

Damn him—he knew her too well.

She got the other book down, the one that seemed to tug at her senses. Handling it carefully, she carried it to Merlin's desk; then holding it balanced on its spine, she allowed the book to open where it would.

A glance showed Serena that the language was totally alien to her, and she wasted no time in trying to decipher the unfamiliar symbols. But there was a full-page illustration on the righthand side, a stark, black-and-white drawing. It was faded by time so that little of it was even identifiable to her. She thought it represented a terrible conflict; bright jagged lines like lightning bolts seemed to be emanating from some kind of structure, and framed by what looked like a lighted window, two human figures struggled.

Serena touched the drawing and almost instantly drew her fingers back. She felt unsettled, strangely anxious and almost afraid. It was a primitive fear, like something rustling in a dark corner of her mind.

Bad. The simple word of a child, yet it encompassed what Serena felt about the drawing.

Unwilling to look through the rest of the book, she closed it and returned it to the shelf. That was when she saw the box. It lay on a higher shelf and was built of some glossy dark wood, every inch of which was carved with strange symbols. She'd never seen it before, even though she had been in this room often over the years.

Had she missed it until now because her senses had never been open? Was the strange box one of the things

in a wizard's world that had no substance until it was
seen? She lifted it down; it was about two feet long, eight
inches wide, and eight inches deep. It was heavy, and she
could see no seam, no hinge or lid of any kind.

She carried it to the desk and set it down, then studied the box intently. The symbols were vaguely familiar
to her, and she thought she might have seen them somewhere else, in a different combination, perhaps in one of
Merlin's spellbooks. She felt along the edges of the box
very carefully with just the tips of her fingers, but could
still distinguish no seam or opening of any kind.

"Damn," she muttered.

"Ever heard of Pandora's box?"

With a guilty start she looked up to find Merlin leaning against the doorjamb, his arms crossed over his
chest. He didn't look angry—but then, she hadn't had
much luck in interpreting his expressions lately, so she
couldn't be sure.

Sighing, she said, "Yes, I've heard of it. Sorry, I
didn't mean to snoop. Well, I did, actually, but I
shouldn't have, so I'm sorry."

Merlin inclined his head slightly, as if accepting the
apology, but his eyes were speculative. "Open the box,
Serena."

She started to say she could see no way to open it,
but then she realized. If there was no apparent seam, no
hinges or handles or obvious lock, then clearly it was
meant to be opened by less-conventional means.

This was not something Serena had been taught to
do. And since she hadn't been able to open the study
door when Merlin had barred it, she wasn't at all sure
she would have much luck with the sealed box. But
given his permission and urged on by her own curiosity,
she gave it her best shot.

Without actually touching the wood, she glided her
fingers along the edges very slowly, allowing her senses
to probe. She could feel something inside the box,
something that radiated the warmth of power, and her
fascination grew. She focused her concentration even
more, using her energies to delicately explore the box.
Searching . . . searching . . .

The lid of the box silently lifted.

Serena caught her breath, staring. Inside, cradled on a bed of black silk, lay the most curious-looking thing she had ever seen in her life. It was a staff about twenty inches long and made of carved wood that was heavily inlaid with gold and crusted with numerous jewels. At one end, obviously the top, was a large round crystal, polished to a flawless finish and about the size of a man's fist. Below the crystal, a narrow band of gold encircled the staff, and below that were diamond-shaped bits of inlaid gold, each set with a marquise diamond of several karats.

The handgrip, about halfway down the staff, was made of brushed gold; immediately above and below the grip was a heavy ridge of large rubies encircling the staff, the stones a brilliant scarlet. Below the handgrip, the staff began to narrow, finishing almost at a point. Along the lower section were three inlaid bands of gold, each set with several radiant sapphires.

Serena understood the significance of the various stones. The crystal was the most obvious; from ancient times it had been used by wizards, seers, and other beings of power to divine the future. Diamonds were known as the "king-gems" and symbolized fearlessness and invincibility, as well as conferring superior strength, fortitude, and courage on one who possessed them. Rubies symbolized command, nobility, and lordship, as well as vengeance. Sapphires, particularly blue ones, represented wisdom, high and magnanimous thoughts, and vigilance.

Gold, in the society of wizards, denoted absolute truth—and absolute power.

Tearing her eyes away from the incredibly beautiful staff, Serena looked across the room at Merlin and almost whispered, "What is it?"

For a moment he didn't move or answer, merely looking back at her with a slight frown and narrowed eyes. But then he left the open doorway and came to the desk, halting to the left of Serena so that no more than a foot of space separated them.

He wasn't looking at her now, but at the staff. With

his left hand he lifted it from its box, holding it horizontally, then turning his wrist so that the staff came upright, the crystal at the top gleaming and every gem catching the light and reflecting it in white, red, and blue fire. The gold handgrip fit his hand perfectly.

"The staff of a Master wizard," Merlin said slowly. "Made by his hand, without power. The stones have to be gathered from all over the world, and the gold has to be mined. Everything borrowed from the earth, from the wood of the staff to the crystal crowning it."

Serena turned her head to stare up at him. "You made it? Without any of your powers?"

He met her gaze, his own grave. "With my powers, it would have been easy. But the final step from Advanced wizard to Master is the learning of a very simple lesson. Nothing should be too easy, Serena. We can never forget that we were meant to work at life."

Gazing into his black eyes, she felt . . . caught. Had they been this close before? Yes, when they danced. But dances were public, and this felt very, very private.

"If you made it without power," she managed to say, "then why can I feel power emanating from it?"

"What you feel is my power." He spoke as quietly as she had, his low voice a little husky. "The staff is a conduit, channeling and focusing energies. In ancient times, it was used like a wand to direct the current of a wizard's energy in a specific direction; now it's more a symbol. But a Master's staff always absorbs and holds a part of his power. A part of himself."

From the corner of her eye, Serena caught movement and realized that he was returning the staff to its box, but she couldn't take her eyes off his face. She had the curious idea that she had never looked at him before.

Merlin half turned toward her and lifted one hand as if to touch her. But then his face changed subtly and he was moving away from her, around to the other side of the desk. Serena was left feeling bereft, struggling silently against the urge to reach out to him or say his name—anything to recapture that instant of closeness.

But she knew it was gone, gone because he had

pushed it away. Gone because there were boundaries they weren't supposed to cross, that was what he'd said.

Serena drew a breath. "Do you want me to put the box back on the shelf?"

"No, leave it." He was opening one of several books on the big desk, frowning down at it. "We'll need the copy of Gray's *Spells and Incantations*. Could you get it, please?"

"Yes, of course." She left the study without another word. Obviously he wanted to be alone for a couple of minutes, she decided. Not a bad idea; she could use a little time to pull herself together.

When she'd gone, Merlin looked after her for a moment and then turned his gaze to the staff in its box. The lid of the box closed silently when he directed it to, and it returned to the shelf where Serena had found it.

He sat down in the chair behind the desk and drew a deep breath. This time the tightness in his chest didn't ease at all. Once again Serena had jarred him with an unprecedented ability. Only a Master wizard could open the box containing his staff, and her ability to open his had caught him completely off guard despite his invitation for her to do it.

What else could she do? Three times now she had gotten closer to him than anyone ever had, twice inside his very consciousness and now this.

The urge to protect himself was almost overwhelming, and his struggle to master that instinctive alarm was a fierce inner battle. In the end all he could do was reach a truce with the primitive emotions Serena had awakened inside him—a momentary peace, but no resolution.

It was enough, he thought as he heard Serena's light step on the stairs. It would have to be enough.

"It doesn't look like a gate," Serena said, contemplating one corner of Merlin's study.

The corner did indeed look quite innocent on this Friday morning, with nothing to mark its importance except for a very slight shimmer in the air—like heat radiating off pavement on a summer's day—which seemed to hold the shape of an arch.

"Why that corner?" she asked. "I mean, why not one of the other corners?"

Merlin leaned back against his desk, one hand resting lightly on the box containing his staff, and shook his head. "We're about to journey back in time to a lost continent—a lost *world*—and you're worried about why I chose a particular corner among four of them in which to build the gate?"

Serena sighed. "Okay, so I'm nervous. I've never traveled through time before. What do I expect?"

"It won't be like stepping through a doorway," he told her. "There will be a period of . . . unusual sensation. Darkness probably, and sounds."

She didn't have the nerve to question him for more specifics. "Oh."

Merlin smiled slightly, but went on in the same matter-of-fact tone. "I've set the gate to help us blend into our surroundings once we reach Atlantis. We'll hear the people there speak in English, and they'll hear us respond to them in their own language; that way, if the language is completely unfamiliar to us, we won't be at a disadvantage. And our clothing will be whatever is suitable."

Serena looked down at her sweater and jeans. "Suitable? What if they're nudists?"

"Then we'll be naked."

She wasn't particularly shy, but found that idea appalling. "I hope you aren't serious."

Still smiling faintly, Merlin said, "Serena, communal nudity isn't at all likely. In fact, you'll no doubt think they wear far too many clothes—especially since you'll presumably be in some kind of skirt."

She winced. "Great. Something guaranteed to get in my way for sure. Can't I keep my jeans and call it a new style?"

"No."

She watched him pick up the box containing his staff and tuck it underneath one arm, and felt a wave of panic. They were going. They were really going, right now. "Um . . . are you sure I'm ready for this?"

"Certain. Your mask of powerlessness is perfect, Serena. No wizard we encounter will be able to sense anything else."

"Maybe, but I could always use another lesson. For instance, I'm not quite sure—"

"Serena."

She looked at him, then drew a breath. "All right. I'm as ready as I'll ever be, I guess."

He held out his free hand to her, and when she took it, twined their fingers together securely. "Hold on," he instructed.

That was something Serena didn't need to be told. She wasn't about to let go of him. The reality of what they were about to do had hit her only last night when she was supposed to be resting for the trip, and now only her trust in Merlin enabled her to walk to the gate beside him.

They paused for an instant, their glances meeting briefly, green eyes and black both holding glimmers of wariness and uncertainty—and then stepped through the gate together.

She knew the village men had finally left her even though there was no respite from the pain they had inflicted. It washed over her in glittering white-hot waves, causing her muscles to jerk feebly in a response far beyond her control. But her mind was clear and calm, her thoughts almost peaceful and detached from the pain of her poor, tortured body.

She was dying. Roxanne knew that, but it didn't seem to matter very much to her. She wished idly that they hadn't left her naked, but the coldness of the ground beneath her no longer disturbed her, and she fancied she could feel the first warmth of the rising sun and sense its light.

She heard a faint sound and, untroubled and vaguely curious, considered what it might be. Footsteps? Perhaps. Coming toward her, she thought. It was morning now, and the village men wouldn't hurt her anymore. Couldn't hurt her anymore.

No one in Atlantia could hurt her now.

PART TWO

Atlantia

SIX

It was like stepping into total darkness with no idea if you would find solid ground beneath your feet or only miles of air. Serena could feel Merlin's hand gripping hers, but nothing else. There was a whistling sound like wind rushing by, yet she felt no sensation of its passing, and there were colors she couldn't see. It seemed to last a long time, or maybe it was only seconds. Then, with jarring abruptness, her foot touched something hard, night sounds flooded her ears, and there was light.

She realized that she was breathing in a jerky rhythm, that her heart was pounding. "You didn't warn me," she muttered, blinking because her eyes were tearing.

"I've never gone this far before," Merlin replied, his own voice a little breathless.

Neither of them moved for several moments, both concentrating on catching breath and balance, adjusting to an atmosphere that felt thickened, humid, and chilly and held a faint smell like sulfur. Their body weight seemed greater, and they had the skin-prickling perception of energy in the very air around them.

"God, it's like an alien planet," Serena murmured as her senses began coping. "Are you sure it isn't?"

"I'm sure," Merlin replied. "We're in Atlantis."

They were standing on a rocky slope above an enormous valley. Mountains, like the one they stood upon, encircled the valley completely, their high peaks jagged and inhospitable in the gray light just after dawn. The trees Serena could see nearby were peculiar, usually tall and spindly with sparse growth; in the valley below, the distant trees appeared to be squat and gnarled, with scant but very large leaves that seemed to glow dully.

There were two visible lakes, the larger one toward the northeast part of the valley and the smaller one at the west end, and half a dozen streams. There were numerous ravines and gullies cutting jagged rips in the valley floor, and there were ridges of raw earth like the hideous scars of lethal wounds twisting among the forests and fields.

An odd, mistlike haze hung over the valley, but the fog was unlike any she had ever seen in her life. It was dynamic, shifting and swirling with threads of luminescence like something pulsing with life. It *was* alive; she could feel the energy of it.

Even as she stared, enthralled and intuitively wary of it, the first rays of the sun found their way between the peaks to the east, and the mist seemed to thin and begin dispersing as soon as the light hit it. Even its energy appeared to diminish, as if stolen by the sun.

"What is that?" she asked Merlin nervously.

"I don't know. It is—or was—made up of energy, but I've never seen or felt anything like it."

"Me, neither." Serena realized she was still clinging to his hand, and hastily released it. That was when she noticed that they were in clothing quite different from what they normally wore in their time.

Merlin's outfit suited him rather well, she thought. Black trousers tucked into knee-high black boots and a black shirt with a laced and open neckline made him look even taller and more powerful than he was, as well as explicitly masculine. The long, robelike coat with its standup collar and full sleeves was a light brown, almost gold color, worn open and unbelted, and gave him a regal air.

Serena's outfit, on the other hand, made her feel rather like a medieval peasant girl. She was also in a long, robelike garment with a square neckline and full sleeves, but except for the white sleeves, hers was dark green, loosely belted at the waist, and worn over a white shift. There were flimsy brown slippers on her feet, and her long hair hung down her back in a single neat braid—which was how she often wore it.

"Oh, brother," she muttered.

"I did warn you it would probably be a skirt," Merlin pointed out dryly.

"Yeah, but I hoped you were wrong." She moved just a bit, trying to adjust to the heavy and rough-textured material of the clothing, and felt suddenly self-conscious when she realized that the shift was her sole undergarment. No bra and panties for the women of Atlantis, obviously. Of course, that also meant there'd be no panty hose, which was a merciful thing, and at least she wasn't burdened with a corset or some other instrument of fashionable torture that had been inflicted upon women at various points in history.

She looked at Merlin just in time to see the box he carried vanish, and realized he had sent it into limbo until he needed it or else found a safe place to leave it. He'd had to carry it with him through the gate, naturally.

"What if all the Master wizards here carry their staffs?" she asked him, wondering for the first time how many Master wizards there would be here.

"Then I'll carry mine," he replied calmly. "When we know for sure." He looked around slowly, taking note of their surroundings rather than searching for a particular thing, and Serena decided she'd better do the same.

Behind them a rocky face jutted out from the slope, and a smooth expanse of granite shimmered very faintly to indicate the presence of the gate. Serena noted at least three landmarks in the area—a twisted tree, a rock formation bearing the distinct shape of an elephant, and the orientation of the peak above them in relation to the rising sun—and fixed the location carefully in her mind. They were at the south end of the valley and nearly halfway up this mountain; it was something to remember. If there was a need to return to the gate quickly, she wanted to be able to find it.

Having done that, she looked back over the valley, not even sure what she was looking for until she heard her own question. "Where are the people?"

Merlin was looking down into the valley. Much of it was forested, but here and there were clearings and meadows, as well as patches of cultivated land, their boundaries too neat to be natural, and at the base of the mountain they stood upon was the faint trace of a dirt road that seemed to encircle the valley. Throughout as much of the valley as they could see clearly, there were no other visible roads, merely indistinct paths.

"There are some people in a village in that direction," he replied, pointing to the west. "But not many for a valley this size. Maybe a hundred men and women. Almost no children. All powerless, I think." He frowned as he continued to stare toward the west.

"What?" Serena could have opened her senses, but she was a bit wary of doing so until she felt more secure behind her innocent mask of powerlessness. Besides, Merlin could absorb twice the information she could glean for herself.

He shook his head. "I don't know. There's something wrong there. I can't quite bring it into focus."

"Maybe when we get closer," she offered.

"You're probably right." He turned his gaze away from the west, scanning the remainder of the valley. Far to the east, barely visible now as the sunlight streamed into the valley, something at the base of another mountain caught his attention. "A city," he said.

Serena looked, as well, and felt a jolt of excitement mixed with uneasiness. The city was too far away for her to be able to see clearly, but one fact was evident. "It's a walled city, isn't it?"

"Yes, I think so. And the gates appear to be closed."

"Then they're afraid of something . . . out here?"

"A reasonable assumption." Merlin scanned the valley again, frowning. "But it isn't clear what that might be. I'm not sensing any dangerous animals. In fact, except for birds, insects, a few small rabbits, and the like, I don't sense any animals, not even livestock."

That didn't strike Serena as particularly strange, mostly because she was simply worried about why anyone would build a walled city. "Could the people in the city be afraid of wizards, do you think?"

Merlin gazed toward the city, obviously probing. After a moment a muscle tightened in his jaw and he looked down at her. "I think more than half the people in the city are wizards. A few hundred people, certainly not more. Maybe some children, though not many. And there's something else. As near as I can tell, it's a city populated almost entirely by women, with very few men—and the men are all powerless."

Bewildered, Serena said, "Where are the male wizards?"

His dark gaze swept the valley again, then turned upward to probe the mountains. "In the mountains, high up on the peaks. They're all around us, Serena, encircling the valley. I can feel them. More of them than the women. Some of them are quite powerful. I can't tell if there are women or children; the energies of the males is acting like a screen."

"Wait a minute. The male wizards are up here in the mountains, the female wizards are in that walled city with some powerless women and men, and the rest of the powerless people, as far as we can tell, are in the village? What kind of segregated society is this?"

"One we have to understand," Merlin told her. "And we don't have a lot of time. Just a month, thirty days."

The reminder made Serena more uneasy. "That sounded like a lot of time back in Seattle, but it doesn't now."

"I know." Merlin looked thoughtful for a moment, then gestured slightly, and packs appeared on their backs. "We'd better get started. We're travelers, Serena, visitors here in Atlantis. Our customs are a bit different, so we're curious about the society here—remember that when you ask questions of anyone."

"Works for me." She adjusted the light pack and added, "What's in this, anyway?"

"A change of clothing, the minimum any traveler should have. Anything else we need along the way, we can create—or I can. You shouldn't use your powers unless absolutely necessary, at least until we figure out what's going on here."

"All right. So where do we start? Up here with the male wizards, or down there with the rest?"

"Down in the valley, I think. We'll head toward the city, but not by the road; I'd rather not be that visible until we know something about this place and its people."

Serena nodded and followed Merlin as he began picking his way down the rocky slope. She kept close to him, but studied her surroundings warily as she tried to get a sense of the place. The air still felt heavy to her, even though the sunlight was chasing away the chill, and she was grateful that the mist that had hung over the valley was almost gone, because it had made her feel uneasy.

It took nearly an hour for them to reach the valley floor, and by then Serena was fascinated. Along the way they had seen weird flowers growing from odd places—at least three different ones from solid rock—and the strangest trees, bushes, and other plants growing in assorted shapes and sizes and colors, a few of them also in odd places.

In the valley the vast majority of the trees were squat and gnarled, just as Serena had thought, with meager broad leaves gleaming dully. Most of them were green, but no fewer than half a dozen trees she saw had leaves of odd shades, such as red and blue; the effect was more grotesque and unsettling than attractive. There were bushes, pathetically stunted, twisted things, and an incredible number of uprooted or simply broken trees, some dead and others dying.

Down here it really did look like an alien planet. And for all its bizarre, fascinating strangeness, it was an ugly place, as ghastly as an open wound.

When they paused, Serena looked down at a four-inch-wide crack in the hard-packed dirt that zigzagged across the road and on into the forest as far as she could see, and she murmured, "So much for the popular lovely image of Atlantis as paradise; this place is beginning to look more like somebody's idea of hell."

The words were barely out of her mouth when the ground beneath them shuddered and heaved. Serena would have fallen if Merlin hadn't caught her arms. For what seemed like minutes, she held on to him and tried to keep her balance, hearing the crash of trees and boulders and the indescribable sound of the very earth writhing in torment.

Then, as abruptly as it had begun, the quake ended. Silence was absolute for a full minute, and then a few birds cheeped and sang tentatively.

"It's over," Merlin said. "For now, at least. Are you all right?"

"That's a loaded question." Serena adjusted her pack when he released her arms, and tried to conjure a smile as she looked up at him. "My first earthquake. To be honest, I didn't like it much. There'll be more, won't there?"

He nodded. "And probably worse as we get closer to the end. We should always be on guard, and try to stay away from the more dangerous areas, where there could be rock slides, for instance, or falling trees."

"Yeah." She was staring down at the crack in the road, which was now a couple of inches wider. She swallowed hard. "I'd rather not become a permanent part of the lost continent."

Merlin took her hand in his. "Come on. We'll move off the road but keep it in sight for a while."

Serena was more than willing to move; that crack in the earth unnerved her. And she was grateful for his reassuring grasp, though she dared not say anything about it. Not so much because she didn't want Merlin to know she was jittery, but because she didn't want to call undue attention to the contact between them. As he had said, what they had to do here would be difficult enough without . . . that.

The sun was well up now, so they had no trouble seeing when they moved into the forest. But even without darkness the forest evoked a creepy feeling, Serena decided, eyeing the distorted, stunted trees and listening to bird sounds—she thought they were bird sounds, anyway—that were alien to her ears. It was impossible to adjust completely to the strangeness of the surroundings, she decided, because everything that was odd affected the senses in an overwhelmingly primitive way.

This place looked strange, sounded strange, smelled strange, and definitely felt strange.

Merlin stopped suddenly, and Serena followed suit, her wandering mind recalled to more pressing concerns when she saw that they were about to have their first contact with the citizens of this alien place. Powerless citizens. Serena could sense no power at all emanating from them, but she sensed in them a great deal of brute strength.

The men, three of them, approached after a momentary hesitation when they first saw the strangers. Their eyes were fixed on Merlin; as far as Serena could see, not once did any of the three even glance at her. But she didn't really think about that because she was so busy staring herself. At them. And the fine hairs on the nape of her neck were stirring in a primitive response to what she saw.

Now she knew what "wrongness" Merlin had sensed earlier.

"May we be of service, My Lord?" the first asked in a courteous and deferential tone as they halted before Merlin and Serena. The man had to look up quite a ways to meet the Master wizard's black eyes.

Merlin didn't react visibly to the men, nor did he correct or question the assumption of his rank, and when he replied, his tone was uncharacteristically careless, even arrogant. "No, I think not."

Still respectful, the same man said, "You are a stranger to Atlantia?" It was more of a statement than a question.

"Yes, though I don't see why that should concern you," Merlin replied, bored.

The man ducked his head slightly, as if in apology,

but his eyes remained on Merlin's face. "No offense was intended, My Lord. We see few strangers here these days, and I merely wished to be of service. If you should be interested in trading or selling your property, I'm sure I could arrange a viewing with the Mountain Lords."

"My property?"

"The woman, My Lord. Her coloring makes her rare. She *is* your concubine?"

That caught Serena's attention. "I—" she began indignantly, only to be silenced when Merlin's hand squeezed hers in warning. The man still hadn't looked at her.

"She is mine," Merlin replied calmly.

"The Mountain Lords are always greatly interested in powerless women, My Lord, particularly when they possess rare coloring and have not yet been affected by the Curtain. My Lord Varian, especially, would pay any price for her."

Serena, still struggling with shock and incensed by the assumption that she was any man's property— *concubine*, for God's sake!—tried to make sense of the man's words. The "Mountain Lords" had to be the male wizards, she decided, but what in hell was the "Curtain"?

"I have no desire to be rid of her," Merlin told the man, his tone still bored.

The man inclined his head. "If you should change your mind, My Lord, I can be found in the village to the west. My name is Payne."

"I'll remember that. Good day."

"My Lord." Payne inclined his head again and half bowed, his two companions did likewise, and the three men strode off toward their village.

Putting aside, for the moment, her outrage at being called a concubine, Serena said, "Richard, what the hell's happened here? Did you *see* them? They looked like . . . like Neanderthals. As if they'd regressed physically. Is that possible?"

Merlin gazed after the men, frowning. "Neanderthals . . . yes, they did resemble ancient man. Sloping forehead, overhanging brow, jutting jaw. Much shorter than modern man, heavily muscled, conspicuously hairy."

With a shudder Serena said, "They made my skin crawl. Even *before* Payne offered to sell me for you."

"They were definitely hostile, despite Payne's so-polite tone," Merlin said, looking down at her. "His respect and courtesy were no more real than his smile. He was afraid of me, afraid and resentful, I think. I was recognized instantly as a wizard, and he just as quickly assumed you were powerless. Why? They had no power and shouldn't have been able to sense mine."

Serena pulled her hand gently from his and took a couple of steps to sit on a fallen tree. She was trying to think, fighting to overcome the aversion she'd felt toward the three men. "Well, if all the powerless men here look like them, and the wizards *don't*, it would be easy to see the difference."

"True. But if their women, the powerless women, also look like throwbacks to the Ice Age, then why did he assume you were powerless?"

"The women must not look like them." She frowned. "We aren't *in* the Ice Age, right? I mean, those men don't look the way men are supposed to look whenever we are?"

Merlin untangled the question silently, then shrugged. "No, we aren't in the Ice Age; we haven't traveled seventy thousand years back in time. The men of this time *should* look very much like modern man in most respects. A few inches shorter, on the average, but they should certainly not look like Neanderthals."

"Is it possible they've regressed?"

Merlin shook his head slowly. "I think not. Neanderthals died out; we aren't directly descended from them. But I suppose these people here might have . . . mutated."

"What could have caused it?"

He joined her on the fallen tree, still frowning. "Mutations sometimes occur during the duplication of DNA. Or if DNA is damaged by X rays or some chemicals. Or—" He looked up suddenly, through the sparse leaves above them at the pale blue sky. "Or, perhaps, the energy spillover of generations of wizards."

Remembering the weird fog they had first glimpsed hanging over the valley, Serena shivered again. The mist had been alive with energy, crawling with it. "You mean, the wizards caused those men to look like that?"

"It's possible," Merlin replied thoughtfully. "Even likely. Electrical energy affects the human body in various ways. It could have caused a mutation. Once a gene has mutated, the new form duplicates as faithfully as the original. And a mutation that occurs in a sex cell can be transmitted from generation to generation. In this case, there would have been a whole series of mutations happening over time."

"But we agreed the women must look fairly normal, more like me. If we're assuming only the males are affected—" Serena broke off as an idea hit her. "The mutations affected only the Y chromosome?"

"If only the males are affected, it has to be the Y chromosome," Merlin agreed. "It's been proven that many abnormally aggressive men have double Y chromosomes; the men we've seen could fit that profile even to an exaggeratedly brutish physical appearance—that could be the mutation. Or the Y chromosome could have simply been damaged by generations of exposure to unrestrained, unfocused energies. Over time the physical appearance could have been altered by internal changes. They could have evolved into what we've seen."

He gazed around them at the gnarled trees and other bizarre vegetation, and added softly, "It might once have been a paradise, Serena, a long time ago. But now almost everything has been twisted and stunted."

She didn't say anything for several moments, but then stirred slightly and sighed. "Payne said that the Mountain Lords were interested in powerless women who hadn't yet been affected by the Curtain. Do you suppose he was talking about that weird mist we saw hanging over the valley before the sun rose?"

"Could be. It could be that the energy expended by all the wizards is somehow trapped over the valley each night, making it even more likely that the people would be affected."

"Including the women. From what he said, the women *have* been affected—but probably not in the way they look, because he assumed I was powerless." Serena sighed again. "It's like trying to put together a jigsaw puzzle when you don't know what the picture is supposed to look like."

"We don't know enough," Merlin agreed. "Still—not bad for our first couple of hours."

"I guess. Didn't Payne call this place Atlantia? Did history get the name wrong?"

"Proper names are often altered by the passage of time and imperfect translations. If we say Atlantis, they'll hear the name they're accustomed to hearing, so it doesn't really matter. Nothing to worry about, Serena."

Serena stood up when he did and, as she adjusted her pack, said somewhat grimly, "I'll tell you one thing. If the women here are no more than concubines, *that* is something to worry about. I'm going to have a hard time keeping my mouth shut."

He smiled slightly. "Try, please. At least until we have a better idea of what's going on. In the meantime, I'm afraid you'll have to resign yourself."

She looked away from his gaze, feeling a bit unnerved. So she was to play the part of his concubine? Lovely. Just lovely. This place really *was* turning into somebody's idea of hell.

It was nearly an hour later when Serena saw what she first took to be a pile of discarded clothing at the base of a tree near the edge of the forest. They were moving in that general direction, heading back toward the road that would lead them to the city, and her first thought was that somebody had tired of carrying laundry and had simply abandoned it.

"Look," she said to Merlin, nodding toward the tree. "I guess somebody didn't want to carry—" She broke off, frowning, and her steps quickened. "Richard, that isn't just a pile of clothing . . . is it?"

He didn't answer, because he didn't have to. Within seconds they were both kneeling on the ground, pushing aside dirty and stained tatters of cloth to find what was underneath.

"Oh, my God," Serena whispered, helping Merlin gently turn the girl over.

Her blond hair was matted and filthy, her face so swollen and discolored, it was impossible to guess whether her features were delicate or coarse. She was horribly bruised and bloody, her pale skin marked with deep lacerations that were unmistakable evidence of deliberate torture. There was hardly a place on her naked body that had escaped the awful abuse, and it was obvious she had been repeatedly and brutally raped.

"Is she alive?" Serena asked unsteadily.

Merlin nodded, his fingers grasping one of the girl's fragile wrists. "Barely. But she won't be for long."

The girl moaned, a thin sound of agony.

"We have to help her."

He looked at Serena, his eyes compassionate in a face of masklike self-control. "Serena—"

She shook her head, unwilling to hear whatever objections he had. Her voice was fierce. "We have to help her. I don't know enough to heal her, but you can. We can't leave her to suffer like this. Please, Richard. Please."

It might have been because it was the first time he had ever heard her plead, or it might have been his own pity for the dying girl, but in any case Merlin found he couldn't just turn his back and walk away.

He shrugged out of his pack and leaned over the girl. He placed his left hand gently over her forehead to remove her pain and induce a deep sleep, then moved the right to hover over her body. Slowly, pausing at each injury, his hand moved inches above her skin.

Serena watched, overwhelmed by his ability and skill even in her anxiety for the girl. As his healing energies touched the girl's poor wounded body, she was slowly, painlessly made whole again. Broken bones knit together, straightening her limbs. The burns on her fingers and hands were healed. The terrible bruises faded away to nothing. Rips and tears in her flesh sealed themselves, leaving only faint pink scars that would, Serena knew, be gone within hours.

Merlin's face tightened as his hand hovered over the girl's lower body, and he was still for a long time, concentrating his power there. The girl had suffered severe internal injuries, Serena realized, sickened by the thought of what she must have gone through.

Finally he sat back on his heels, gazing down at the girl. She was unmarked now, her flesh pale and smooth from her peaceful, lovely face to her delicate feet. She was obviously very young, probably not yet out of her teens, not so much frail as fragile. Merlin lifted his hand from her forehead and made a slight gesture over her, and the girl's clothing, clean and repaired, covered her nakedness.

Looking at Serena, he said, "She'll sleep for a few hours."

Unguarded because she wasn't thinking about hiding anything from him, too much of her heart shining through her eyes, Serena said, "Thank you, Richard."

Something flared in the depths of his black eyes, and for a moment it seemed he leaned toward her. But then he was rising to his feet, expressionless. "You do realize I might have changed history just now," he said conversationally.

Serena blinked. "But you said she was dying."

"Exactly."

"Then she couldn't have been the witness. I mean, if she died the first time—"

"Serena, every life touches other lives, sometimes in very dramatic ways. Her death may have been a direct factor in whatever happened here. Her survival could change everything, even in our time."

After a moment Serena shook her head. "I don't care. We couldn't just let her die."

Very gently Merlin said, "They're all going to die, don't you remember?"

She hadn't remembered, and the reminder was a shock. Of course, the entire continent was destroyed.

They were fairly certain that one person survived, but maybe only one. . . .

Serena looked down at the peacefully sleeping girl and said, "At least she has a few more weeks now. That might matter to her, you know, it might make a difference. Maybe helping her to live is the single thing we should have done to fix whatever went wrong here." Her eyes raised to meet his. "That could be right, couldn't it?"

Unable to resist the appeal in those green eyes, Merlin nodded slowly. It could be true, after all. This girl's survival might be the sole occurrence that would mend the future society of wizards.

Or destroy it utterly.

"We might as well make camp," he said finally, accepting that it was too late to worry about it. "She'll sleep most of the day, and we should spend the night here. Tomorrow we can go on to the city."

"All right," Serena said. But before he could turn away, she added quietly. "This girl . . . she's a wizard. I can feel her power."

"Yes," Merlin agreed, "she's a wizard. And she apparently couldn't use her powers to protect herself. You'd better keep that in mind, Serena. We'd both better."

By midafternoon their camp was in place in a small clearing near where they had found the girl. A fairly wide stream curved around behind them, a deep ravine was on their right, and a fairly dense section of the forest was in front and to the left of the clearing.

Like any experienced woodsman, Merlin had chosen a place that would be difficult for anyone to approach without giving them warning, and provided the natural protection of the ravine and the stream.

"Why?" Serena asked when she realized.

"Because I'd rather be cautious," he replied. "Because we have a walled city to the east, a city apparently designed to keep something or someone out. And because we found a nearly dead wizard who, for some reason, couldn't use her powers to save herself."

It made sense to Serena, and she didn't question him

further. And she didn't object when he made their camp look more primitive than it needed to, with two lean-to's made of branches and foliage for shelter, and a small fire to provide warmth. He had at least bowed to her request and conjured blankets that only *looked* primitive; they would insulate against the night chill far better than would the local variety.

The girl he had healed was sleeping peacefully under one of the lean-to's, lying on a bed of thick moss covered with one blanket while another was tucked around her. She hadn't stirred since they had moved her to the camp.

Merlin had conjured a pot of stew for their lunch, amusing Serena because she'd never known him to cook anything before—with or without his powers. She enjoyed the stew, eating with her usual appetite, and complimented him so solemnly that she actually got a laugh out of him.

"Why don't you go check on the patient," he said, taking her empty bowl away from her. "By now she might need food worse than she needs sleep."

Serena nodded and got up from the broad tree stump she'd been using as a seat. She shook out her skirts and sighed. "Damn this outfit. It weighs a ton and feels like burlap."

Merlin glanced over at her and then made a slight gesture, just a flick of his fingers.

Immediately most of Serena's discomfort disappeared. She felt inside the neckline of the shift and, surprised and grateful, said, "You lined it with silk. Thanks."

"My pleasure." He was sitting on a fallen log near the fire, poking a stick into the flames, and didn't look at her.

Serena hesitated, feeling oddly reluctant to walk away from him right then. "Um . . . I meant to ask you before. When you healed the girl, did you take away any of her memory?"

He frowned as he stared into the fire. "Strictly speaking, no. She'll remember what happened to her, but it will be as if it happened months ago; the sharpest edges will be blunted, less painful and traumatic." He turned his head and met Serena's gaze. "She needs to remember. We're all shaped by our experiences, positive and negative."

Nodding slightly, Serena said, "I suppose so. She'll be grateful to you."

"Will she?" Merlin looked back at the fire "I wonder. Men hurt her; I'm a man."

"But you healed her."

He shrugged. "Maybe that will count for something. But don't expect her to feel the way you do about it, Serena. I'm a stranger to her—and from the looks of this society, men and women seem to have problems relating to each other."

Serena thought he was undoubtedly right about that. If the male wizards kept powerless concubines whom they bought, sold, and traded like property, and the female wizards lived, for the most part, in a city protected by a wall, then there were definite problems here.

She crossed the few feet of clearing to the lean-to, which was quite roomy, and knelt beside their patient. Almost immediately, she knew that the girl was awake, though she appeared to be still deeply asleep. How long had she been awake? Had she heard anything they didn't want her to hear?

Serena hesitated, then said softly, "You must be hungry by now, aren't you? I know you're awake. Won't you at least look at me—and tell me your name?"

After a long moment the girl's eyes opened and focused on Serena's face. They were wide, blue, and shadowed, and her voice was innately gentle and very wary when she said, "I'm Roxanne. Who are you?"

"My name is Serena."

Roxanne turned her head just slightly and flicked a tense glance toward the fire and Merlin. "And . . . him?"

"His name is Merlin," Serena answered, keeping her voice soft. "He helped you."

"He's a wizard," Roxanne said.

"Yes."

"Then he wouldn't have helped me." Her voice held absolute conviction.

Serena frowned slightly. "He did help you, Roxanne. I watched him heal your injuries."

Slowly Roxanne pushed herself into a sitting position, her wary gaze leaving Merlin—who hadn't moved or reacted in any way to what was happening in the lean-to even though he had certainly heard their voices—and studying Serena no less warily. The blanket fell to her waist, and she looked down at her clean, untorn clothing. She lifted one hand to her hair, finding it clean and in a neat braid down her back like Serena's. Slender fingers probed her face, and a look of confusion tightened her features.

"I was dying," she whispered. "I know I was. They had used me and left me to die. No one could have saved me, not even a Master wizard."

Serena remembered then that Merlin had said the wizards of Atlantis were less advanced than their modern counterparts, and thought quickly for a plausible explanation. "We're visitors here. Where we come from, Merlin is renowned as a gifted healer. He's devoted much study to the art of healing."

Roxanne seemed to accept that, but her eyes were still distrustful and puzzled when she stared at Serena. "You're powerless. Are you his concubine?"

Finding a compromise between a label she refused to wear and the complicated truth, Serena said, "I'm . . . his companion. Look, why don't I get you something to eat, all right? You must be hungry."

"Thank you," Roxanne said quietly.

Serena eased away and returned to the fire, where the remainder of their stew was being kept warm on a flat rock close to the flames.

"My companion?" Merlin murmured.

Ladling stew into a bowl, Serena shot him a glance and kept her own voice low. "Like you said, we're strangers here. Just because everybody we meet assumes I'm your property doesn't mean I have to accept it. *Companion* is a nice, neutral word, and I much prefer it to *concubine*."

"I'll keep that in mind. But there's something you should keep in mind, Serena. In their language the word *companion* may not be neutral at all."

Unnerved by that possibility, Serena carried the bowl of stew and a spoon back to Roxanne. Along with everything else, now she had to worry about how her words translated. Great. She frequently got into trouble with English; what kinds of linguistic pits yawned at her feet now?

She knelt and handed the food to Roxanne, returning the girl's guarded look with a touch of wariness herself. "Do you live in the city?" she asked.

After tasting the stew tentatively, Roxanne obviously found her appetite and began eating, but she didn't take her eyes off Serena. "Yes . . . Sanctuary."

"Sanctuary? That's what it's called?" It seemed a fitting name for a walled city, Serena thought.

"Yes. Where are you from?"

Serena hesitated, but then opted for the truth. Why not, after all? No one here could possibly recognize the name—and besides, it probably translated as so much gibberish. "It's a city called Seattle."

"I've never heard of that. It's across the ocean?"

"Yes, far away. We—Merlin and I—wanted to see a bit more of the world."

Roxanne's delicate lips twisted. "And you came to Atlantia?"

"It seemed a good idea at the time," Serena murmured. "Your customs are no doubt different from ours, and it's always interesting to encounter a different culture."

After a wary glance toward Merlin, Roxanne said, "*He* may find Atlantia to his liking. Men, especially wizards, have the best of things here. But you may wish you had not left your Seattle."

"Why?"

"Because women are ultimately powerless here. Even wizards like me. What happened to me in the night happens to many women, thanks to the *Mountain Lords*." Her voice dripped contempt and hatred when she named the male wizards, the emotions so strong that Serena leaned back.

"The male wizards? They . . . hurt you last night?"

Roxanne offered a painful smile. "If you mean were they the ones who rutted like animals between my legs, no. Village men—powerless men—did that. For all their arrogance, no male wizard would dare attempt to take his pleasure with a woman of power."

Baffled, Serena said, "Why not?"

"Because she would kill him, of course," Roxanne replied a bit impatiently. "We may be lesser in power compared to most of them, but any female wizard who is taken against her will is quite capable of destroying even the mightiest male. It's the one time we're able to defeat them."

Serena knew she looked as confused as she felt. "I don't understand this. *Powerless* men hurt you last night?"

"Yes."

"And you couldn't fight them? Couldn't stop them?"

"No, of course not. It was night"

"What does that have to do with it?"

Roxanne looked briefly confused herself, but then her frown cleared. "It must be different in Seattle, as it once was here. Now we are unable to use our powers at night. From sunset to sunrise the Curtain makes all in the valley powerless."

SEVEN

The lean-to was on the right and slightly behind Merlin, far enough away that the girl wouldn't feel unduly threatened by his presence, Merlin thought, but close enough so that he could hear every word spoken there.

What he heard was hardly reassuring, but he listened nonetheless.

It was nearly an hour later when Serena returned to the fire, her face a bit drawn. She was carrying Roxanne's empty bowl, and set it near the fire absently before she sat down on the stump she had earlier used for a seat.

"She's asleep again. It seemed to hit her all at once."

Merlin nodded. "Delayed shock. The next time she wakes, I doubt she'll seem so calm."

"I wondered about that. She seemed . . . almost detached about what had happened to her."

"Waking to find herself uninjured and with her memory of what had happened to her somewhat distant, she wasn't forced to deal with the trauma immediately. Since we were here, strangers, she was able to concentrate on us. Explaining some of the traits of this place kept her mind off herself. It was a healthy enough response."

"But temporary?"

"She'll have to deal with what happened to her sooner or later."

Serena was silent for a moment, then said, "Is that coffee you're drinking? Do they have coffee here?"

"Yes, it is coffee, and no, they don't have it here. I'm cheating." Merlin gazed broodingly into his mug. "Would you like some?"

"Please."

He conjured a mug of coffee for Serena—fixed with cream and sugar, the way she always drank it—directly into her grasp without even looking at her.

"I'm always impressed when you do that," she murmured.

Merlin felt too unsettled to respond to her light tone. Instead he said, "At least now we know why Roxanne was unable to defend herself against her attackers."

"I suppose it's useless to hope we won't be affected the way they are," Serena ventured.

"Probably. If this *Curtain* does indeed reflect energy at the wizard who tries to use it, we're vulnerable to it as well."

Serena spoke slowly. "She said it also drains them. That it depletes more than their excess energy. If that's so, men like those three we met could overpower even the strongest wizard during the night. So why haven't they? I mean, if the powerless men resent wizards as strongly as you felt with those three, then why don't they get together one night and—"

Merlin shook his head. "It isn't that simple, I think. The male wizards live high in the mountains, remember? I very much doubt that many of them venture down here often, if at all, and never once the sun sets. Judging by what we saw this morning, the Curtain blankets only the valley. In the mountains the wizards are above it, and probably beyond its effects."

"Then why don't the women move up there?" Serena's voice was a bit tense. "The female wizards, like Roxanne. It doesn't seem to have occurred to her—and the answer is so simple. Why do they remain down here, where their powers are drained night after night? Where they're vulnerable?"

Merlin turned his head slowly and looked at her strained features. He had hoped they could avoid talking about this until there was more information, until he found some painless way of dealing with it, but Roxanne's matter-of-fact words were undoubtedly echoing in Serena's mind just the way they were resounding in his.

... no male wizard would dare attempt to take his pleasure with a woman of power.... she would kill him....

That was what Serena wanted to talk about, he knew. Roxanne had drawn an ugly picture of the battle going on between male and female wizards with a few brief but stark sentences, and that was so alien to what Serena knew of wizards that it was deeply troubling to her.

How much time did he have before she figured out why they were here? Not much, Merlin thought. She was a highly intelligent woman, and even now her mind must be filled with a jumble of impressions and speculations.

But he still didn't want to cope with this right now. Roxanne's intense hatred of the male wizards had shaken him very much, because it told him just how ominous the situation was. And his own reaction to the knowledge of a city filled with women of power was just as troubling. Even now he was struggling against the negative feelings.

"Richard?"

Returning his gaze to the mug in his hands, Merlin said unemotionally, "You heard Roxanne. The males are more powerful. The mountains must be their strongholds; so far they've apparently been able to keep the women down here in the valley."

"But why?"

Because female wizards are capable of destroying males—if only when they are taken against their will? Did this hate and mistrust come about because too many females were raped and too many males paid for the crime with their lives?

"I don't know why," he said evenly. "Any answer I could offer would be sheer speculation."

"Then speculate." Serena nearly snapped out the words.

"On the basis of what?" His tone was a bit snappy as well. "We've encountered three village men and one traumatized female wizard—hardly a representative sampling of the population. Roxanne's hatred for the male wizards may be more unique than she's led us to believe; those three men could have been mutant individuals rather than the norm; and the male wizards may have taken to the mountains simply to escape the Curtain *or* combative females. I—we—just don't know enough yet even to speculate, Serena."

She drew an audible breath. "You asked me to trust you, to accept this little trip of ours without posing too many questions, and I agreed to that. But I didn't agree to stop thinking, Richard."

Merlin heard something in her voice he'd never heard before, not hostility but something very close, and he found it both disturbing and painful. For all her occasional arguments and minor defiances through the years, Serena had never been in any way antagonistic toward him. Was it only because of Roxanne's bitter words, or did the very atmosphere of Atlantis kindle suspicion in everyone exposed to it?

He turned his head slowly and looked at her. She was clearly as tense as she sounded, as tense as he felt himself, and he knew he had to tread carefully. "I never asked you to stop thinking," he said quietly.

"Then don't ask me not to think about all this."

"Think what you like, Serena. But be careful in drawing conclusions. Remember your own analogy? This place *is* like a jigsaw puzzle; we won't know what the picture is until we have all the pieces assembled."

After a long moment she looked away from his steady gaze. Her features were still a bit strained, but her eyes were not so much wary now as uneasy. "The sun's going down. We . . . aren't going to transport up into the mountains to get away from the Curtain, are we?"

"To understand this place, we should experience as much as possible. Even the Curtain. And until we see one of the wizards here transport, it's one ability we won't be using. They may not believe they can fly any more than the powerless people of this time believe they can."

"Then I have a suggestion," she said. "Before the sun goes down, maybe you should conjure up a couple of guns."

Merlin shook his head reluctantly. "Cheating with coffee or blankets is one thing; we can't bring devices from our time into this world, even to protect ourselves. The risk of changing the future is too great."

She didn't argue with him; she didn't even seem surprised by what he said. She simply looked at him and said, "In that case I think I'll go and find myself a couple of really big, heavy sticks."

"That might be a very good idea," he conceded.

She felt hideously uncomfortable, Serena decided. The sense of being in an alien place seemed multiplied at night, with the unfamiliar night sounds and the queer faint shudders of the earth beneath her body. She noticed the latter only when she lay down to sleep, those almost imperceptible pulses in the ground that were even more frightening than the earlier earthquake because they were continuous reminders of instability. And the Curtain.

When she had sat near the fire with Merlin just after dark, both of them gazing up at the luminescent mist thickening in the air above the air above the valley and nearly hiding the full moon just on the wane, Serena had managed to feel a bit detached, marveling as the visible spillover of wizards' energies took on a life of its own. But with every passing hour, as the sky darkened to a peculiar blood red and seemed to pulse with energy, she felt more uncomfortable, lethargic and weak, until finally she bade Merlin a quiet good night and went to join the sleeping Roxanne in the larger of the two lean-to's.

She would have preferred to remain with him, to talk about what they had so far learned about Atlantis, but Merlin had made it clear he had no intention of speculating until they had more information. At least that was what he said. Serena knew it wasn't that simple. She didn't have to read his mind to know that he was deeply disturbed by what information they had already, and he had withdrawn from her again, retreating behind his remote mask to keep distance between them.

The truth, Serena thought, was that he didn't want to discuss some of what they'd learned because it cut too close to them and to the tension between them.

Neither of them had actually mentioned what Roxanne had said regarding male and female wizards—that they apparently never engaged in sex together—but Serena couldn't stop thinking about it. . . . *no male wizard would dare attempt to take his pleasure with a woman of power.* Even when there was no force? When it was not merely sex, but lovemaking? Were there no wizards capable of trusting each other enough to mate?

That question troubled Serena more than all the others, causing her to consider her relationship with Merlin in an entirely different light. She knew no wizards other than him in their time; if she *had* known others, would she have seen the same male/female segregation in their society? Was it considered normal even in their time? And was her relationship with Merlin so tense and tentative now for that very reason—because an unthreatening girl child had become a woman he could never trust?

Was the "boundary" he had told her they mustn't cross an uncompromising and ancient line born out of hate and suspicion, created to divide not Master and Apprentice, but male and female wizards?

The questions and thoughts followed Serena into a shallow, restless sleep, the last sight to meet her eyes that of Merlin sitting by the fire, his face turned upward as he studied the shifting, glistening Curtain. When she woke abruptly, the fire had burned out, Merlin was not

visible—probably sleeping in his own lean-to—and
Roxanne lay stiffly beside her.

Serena's instincts told her more than her clouded
senses, and she put a gentle hand on the younger woman's rigid arm. "It's all right," she murmured. "Cry if
you need to. Grieve. Get mad about it. Then you can
really begin to heal."

Roxanne did cry, almost silently but with such intensity that her slender body shuddered beneath the force
of her pain and grief and rage. Serena didn't attempt to
soothe or stop her; she merely provided a willing shoulder and compassionate silence.

Exhausted at last, Roxanne slept, but Serena lay
awake for a long time. She realized she was listening
tensely to the unfamiliar night sounds of Atlantis, that
being reminded of what had happened to Roxanne had
made her nervous and more than a little frightened—
enough so that sleep was not going to come easily.
Packs composed of some of the village men hunted
most nights, Roxanne had told her, hopeful of finding
a careless female wizard who had strayed too far from
Sanctuary and had gotten caught by the night and the
Curtain.

It was all because the male wizards had, long ago,
created the fiction that by possessing a female wizard
sexually, a powerless man could acquire some of her
power.

"Never mind that it isn't true," Roxanne had said
bitterly. "The males made it *seem* true by gifting an occasional rapist with a little bit of power—not enough to
hurt the males, of course. They still do it sometimes,
still reward the rape of a female wizard. So we're all vulnerable at night."

"But the rapists have to live in the daytime, too," Serena had protested. "If a woman is raped, can't she go
after them later, when she can use her powers?"

"If she survives." Roxanne's voice was bleak. "Most
don't. So even though any of the wizards in Sanctuary
would destroy the rapists without hesitation, there's
usually no way of knowing the guilty men. And we
can't destroy them all. . . ."

Serena gazed across their darkened camp, thinking, acutely aware that her body was far weaker than she was accustomed to, that the Curtain had drained her strength even though she hadn't attempted to use her powers. Despite the large branch that she had earlier found and put nearby for defense, the truth was that she was hideously vulnerable to anyone or anything that might attack her.

All her life Serena had been carelessly certain of her strength, her power; it had formed the core of her self-confidence and presence. She had felt vulnerable emotionally, but never physically, and her sense of helplessness now was as alien as this place.

She was afraid and felt very, very alone. Worst of all, the person closest to her was no longer someone she could instinctively and trustingly go to with her fears. Now she hesitated, wary and uncertain.

Because he was a man—and a wizard.

By midway through the following morning, they were no more than a mile from Sanctuary. Roxanne hardly spoke—not at all to Merlin—and kept close to Serena. The fragile blond was pale but controlled; she seemed physically all right, or else was drawing on her wizard's powers, because she had no trouble in walking steadily with the other two.

Still, Merlin called a halt after they'd been traveling for a few hours. He had carefully avoided getting near Roxanne, but it was obvious to Serena that he'd kept an eye on the young wizard and knew she needed rest, even if she wouldn't show it or admit to it.

Serena left Roxanne sitting on a fallen tree and moved a few yards away to join Merlin, who stood on the bank of a wide but shallow stream they would have to cross.

"This water's bad, isn't it?" she asked.

He nodded. "You can smell the sulfur. I'm willing to bet most of the groundwater's no good. The wizards can create fresh water, but I don't know what the villagers do."

Serena started to suggest that maybe the lake near

the village contained drinkable water, but she caught a glimpse of his left hand just then, and all thoughts of water vanished. With a gasp she caught his hand and lifted it between them. His arm tensed as if to draw away from her, but then relaxed.

"What happened?" Cradling his hand in both hers, she stared down at the vicious blisters marking each of his long fingers. Burns, she realized. Then she remembered, and looked up at his face quickly. "Roxanne had burns like these all over her hands when we found her."

Merlin met her gaze, his own calm. "Yes."

"You had to find out, didn't you? You had to try and use your powers last night."

"Of course," he answered matter-of-factly. "We couldn't know for sure that the Curtain would affect us as it does them until I made the attempt."

"So now we know it *does* affect us."

"Yes. And I wouldn't advise you to try. The effects are rather painful."

Serena looked down at his hand again, knowing that the burns must have been much worse when they were first inflicted than what she saw now. Wizards tended to heal from their rare injuries extremely quickly, but not even a Master wizard could heal himself. Merlin had once told Serena he believed that inability was simply another reminder that no mortal being could be all-powerful.

She very gently traced one blister on his index finger with the tip of her thumb, not even conscious of her desire to heal him until the blister began to fade.

"Serena . . ."

"Roxanne can't see what I'm doing."

"That isn't the point."

"Healing the skin is simple," she murmured, touching the blisters one by one and watching them fade away, replaced by healthy skin. "It was the first thing you taught me when I began studying healing."

"You promised not to attempt to heal anything until I said you were ready," he reminded her.

Serena looked at his unblemished skin with satisfaction, then met his eyes innocently. "How can I be expected to keep a promise I won't even make for millennia?"

"You won't be *born* for millennia. Don't split hairs, Serena." But his low voice was amused rather than annoyed.

They were both speaking quietly, aware of Roxanne's presence a few yards away.

"It's still a fact that I can hardly keep a promise I haven't made yet. That isn't logical."

"Logical? Correct me if I'm wrong, but wasn't it you who once said that math wasn't logical?"

She dismissed the memory with a shrug. "Numbers confuse me. But I'm very good with words, you know I am, Richard. And ideas. I may be new to this time travel business, but I think I'm getting the hang of it. And I *know* that promises I made in our time aren't valid here."

His half smile faded a bit. "Even the promise you made to obey me?"

After a moment Serena let go of his hand, rubbing her own down over her thighs in an unconsciously nervous gesture. "Even in our time that promise was reserved for the workroom and my lessons," she reminded him, striving to keep her voice easygoing. "You're my Master as a wizard—not as a man."

Merlin nodded slowly. "I wanted to make sure you remembered that. I haven't forgotten it, Serena. And I won't. No matter what happens here, no matter what ideas and customs these people have, you and I are from a different time. We can't let ourselves be torn apart by what's destroying them."

She gazed up at him, and for the first time since Roxanne had talked about this place and its people, Serena remembered all the years that Merlin had virtually raised her. She owed him a great deal, far more than she would ever be able to repay.

Without his willingness to guide her, she probably would have ended up using her inborn powers simply to survive any way she could. Instead he had given her the first real home of her life and had not only taught her the skills of a wizard, but also provided her with an excellent model of what a decent human being should be.

The recent strain between them, strong and bewildering though it was, had not erased her memories of those times or her awareness of how much she owed Merlin, and she couldn't allow Atlantis to wipe them away, either.

At the very least she owed him her trust—unless and until *he* did something to betray that trust. What other wizards, male or female, did was hardly something for which she could hold him responsible.

Serena drew a breath and nodded. "Point taken. I'll try to remember that what happens here doesn't necessarily have to affect us."

Merlin didn't ask her to explain the qualifier. "Good. Now, I'm going to follow this stream a bit father north and see if there's a better place to cross."

"You could just conjure a bridge."

"I probably will, but I hesitate to use my powers too often until we find out just how much these wizards are capable of."

"That makes sense. I'll stay here with Roxanne." She had taken no more than two steps away when he said her name, and she paused to look back at him.

He lifted his left hand, the thumb brushing over the unmarked fingertips lightly. "Thank you."

"Any time." She went back to join Roxanne, unaware of smiling until the younger woman's openly curious stare made her aware of it. "Is something on your mind?" she asked lightly, sitting down on the fallen tree.

After she'd glanced past Serena to make sure Merlin had gone, Roxanne said slowly, "You two are certainly . . . different."

"In what way?"

"Sometimes you seem very comfortable together, and other times it's almost as if you're strangers. You seem to view each other as equals, and yet you appear willing to follow his lead. I can see now you aren't his concubine, but the way you look at him and the way he looks at you makes it obvious there *is* something between you."

"You're very observant," was all Serena could think to say. The way Merlin looked at her?

Roxanne gazed at her steadily, the wide blue eyes puzzled. "You say you're his companion?"

Serena felt uneasy, remembering what Merlin had said. "Yes, but maybe you'd better tell me what that word means to you."

"What it means? It means a comrade, a friend—"

"That's it," Serena said, relieved.

"—or a mate," Roxanne finished. "But you couldn't be his mate, because male wizards don't have mates."

"Well, I'm not his mate, but why do you say male wizards don't have them? If they have concubines . . ."

Roxanne frowned. "That's different. The males want sons, of course, and they want their pleasure, so they have concubines. But never mates. All they have to give to any female is their seed. Even if they possessed hearts, they could never give them to a woman, not even a powerless woman."

"But a powerless woman couldn't hurt them, could she?"

"Not the way a wizard could—although I suppose she could cut his throat if he trusted her enough to sleep in her bed." The idea seemed an interesting one to Roxanne, her eyes going distant and thoughtful as she considered it silently.

"They don't ever do that? Sleep together in bed?"

With a shrug Roxanne said, "I could hardly know for sure, but according to powerless women who were once concubines, the males always leave the bed once their needs have been satisfied."

"Oh." Trying not to feel appalled—this was *not* her time or her society, Merlin had been right to remind her of that—Serena probed for more information. "You said the male wizards kept concubines partly because they wanted sons; do the mothers raise their children?"

"No, never. Their babes are taken from them immediately after birth. The sons are suckled by older powerless women, and raised by lesser male wizards in a separate house near their fathers' palaces."

Serena shook her head in disbelief. "Those poor women lose their children? God, that's not just cruel—it's inhuman."

Roxanne seemed a bit puzzled by Serena's words, but she merely shrugged. "The males fear their sons' being influenced by any female, so they take care to avoid it."

Realizing only then what she was hearing, Serena frowned. "Wait a minute. Sons. What about the daughters?"

"They are killed at birth," Roxanne replied matter-of-factly.

"What? Just automatically slaughtered because they're female?"

"Yes."

Her thoughts whirling and nausea churning in her stomach, Serena couldn't bring herself to say a single word. It was one thing to tell herself this was not her society, but the knowledge that any society could practice or condone the practice of murdering innocent newborns deemed the "wrong" sex was simply horrifying. And that *wizards* could commit such a dreadful act tore at Serena.

Unaware of the blow she had dealt, Roxanne returned to her original point. "You and Merlin are something out of the ordinary. Aside from your oddity as a pair, he doesn't really behave—so far, at least—like any of the male wizards I've encountered. And you don't act like a powerless woman."

Serena forced herself to respond casually. "How do the powerless women here act?"

"Subservient."

Startled, Serena frowned. "What, all of them?"

"Outside the walls of Sanctuary, yes. In the city, of course, things are different; the powerless women are never threatened or abused, and they seem content—if somewhat simple and pliable. But out here I suppose they've learned that a bowed head is less likely to anger their men."

Serena cleared her throat. "We encountered a few village men when we first arrived, and I can see how the women might have a great deal to fear. The men looked rather brutal, even though one of them was smiling."

"A powerless woman's lot is no better than a wizard's here in Atlantia," Roxanne said broodingly. "If she escapes being taken into the mountains by one of the male wizards, she is still liable to endure a hard and wretched life under the domination of some man who is as likely to knock her unconscious as he is to throw her down and take his pleasure."

Serena shivered.

Noting the reaction, Roxanne reassured her. "As long as you're paired with a male wizard, you have little to fear from the village men, during the day or night. Very few of them would dare touch you even if they caught you out alone. They couldn't gain any power from you, and fear of punishment would be stronger than any desire for brief pleasure. Male wizards have been known to destroy powerless men for such an offense."

"That's all very well, but how would the men know I was Merlin's . . . companion, if they found me when he wasn't around?"

"He hasn't marked you?" Roxanne asked in surprise.

"No. That is, I don't think so. Marked me how?"

Roxanne studied Serena carefully, then shook her head. "I guess I assumed you were marked under your clothes, on a shoulder or your back; some wizards do it that way, although you're far safer if the mark is instantly visible—"

"Roxanne. What kind of mark?"

"*His* mark. Merlin's. Every male wizard chooses how he'll mark his women, and all who belong to him wear the same sign."

"Sign? You mean a symbol of some kind?"

"Yes. For instance, some of the marks I've seen have been in the shape of animals, letters, or birds. One wizard even marks his women with a constellation—tiny stars."

"Which constellation?"

"Orion, I think. Why?"

"Just curious." Serena sighed. "So how will I wear this mark? I mean, is it stamped into my skin?"

"Yes, I suppose. The marks can't be washed off, I know that. They're created in different colors, and worn in different places. Most are here." Roxanne touched the base of her own throat, just below the hollow. "Instantly visible."

Branded for all the world to see. Sighing again, Serena said, "I think I'll wait until we reach the city before I talk to Merlin about these marks. I'd rather not wear a brand until I absolutely have to. Unless . . . will not being marked there, in Sanctuary, matter?"

Roxanne was gazing at her rather curiously, but shook her head in answer. "No. You won't be harmed by anyone in the city. Wizards and powerless women alike are treated with respect."

"That reminds me. . . . When Merlin and I encountered those village men, they knew right away that I was powerless. Was it only because I was traveling with a male wizard, or does some physical sign distinguish a wizard from a powerless woman?"

"Merlin's being a wizard told them, of course, but they probably checked your hands to make sure."

"My hands?" Serena lifted her hands and looked down at them, puzzled.

Roxanne held her hands out near Serena's. "Outwardly a powerless woman looks just like a wizard, except for this. All women of power are born this way in Atlantia, and have been for centuries. It isn't so in Seattle?"

"No, it isn't." Serena hadn't notice anything odd until then, probably because the difference wasn't obvious until all ten fingers were held stretched out. But there was a deviation from the norm. On each hand Roxanne's ring finger was slightly longer than her middle finger.

Before Serena could say anything else, Roxanne murmured, "He's returning," and let her hands fall to her lap. Her face closed down, eyes shuttered.

"Serena?"

She got up and went to meet Merlin by the stream. "No better place to cross?" she asked abstractedly.

"No. What's wrong?"

"Atlantis gets weirder by the minute. We were wondering why those village men assumed I was powerless? Take a look at Roxanne's hands when you get a chance. She says all the female wizards have been born that way for centuries."

"I have already noticed her hands," Merlin told her, "but I assumed it was an individual trait."

"No, just inherent to female wizards here. She said it was the only *outward* difference between wizards and powerless women. God knows what the internal differences are."

Merlin looked at her steadily and, keeping his voice low, said, "Something else has disturbed you."

Part of Serena didn't want to tell him, but a stronger part did. She watched his face carefully when she spoke. "According to Roxanne, one of the reasons the male wizards keep concubines is because they want sons. They murder their female children at birth."

He didn't look surprised, but rather as if she confirmed something he had known or guessed. "I see."

"It's horrible."

"Of course it's horrible." His voice was level. "It's also unnatural, and we have to find out what caused them to adopt such a practice. Another question to be answered, Serena."

She tried to remain calm, but it wasn't easy. "I'm having a hard time looking at it as just another question we have to find the answer to. If even half of what Roxanne's told us about the male wizards is true, they're monstrous—inhuman. That isn't the way wizards are supposed to be." The final sentence was almost whispered.

Merlin hesitated, wanting to assure her that whatever wizards in this time were like, those of their time weren't monsters—but he wasn't sure that was true. Were his father and the other Elders any less monstrous since they were willing to destroy any woman of power, and avoided offspring of their own simply to avert potential problems? And would he himself have not survived infancy if he had been born female?

He reached out slowly, resting his hands on her shoulders and struggling inwardly between two equally strong but conflicting urges. He wanted to pull her into his arms and comfort her, to banish the look of confusion and fear from her vivid eyes. And he wanted to push her away, to turn his back and close her out in order to protect himself.

The fight went on, but he was able to speak in a fairly even voice despite it.

"Serena, you have to remember that this isn't our world, or our time. Whatever these people are doing, it *was done* long before either of us was born. We can't change them. All we can do is try to understand their society and why it developed the way it did. We came here for answers, remember? Even if we decide to take some definitive action, we can't do anything at all until we have the answers we came for."

She didn't move, didn't shrug off his hands or try to pull back from him, but when she lifted her chin and looked him straight in the eye, it was obvious she had endured one shock too many; she wanted the truth, and her words made that clear.

"What answers, Richard? Why did we come here? I have to know."

His hands tightened, feeling the deceptive fragility of delicate bones and a slight build, the warmth of her. The flesh under his thumbs was soft and satiny. He couldn't turn his gaze away from her, seeing beautiful green eyes in a lovely face, bright red hair that was a symbol of passion, and a desirable, sensual body even the bulky clothing of Atlantis could not disguise.

Was every woman so graceful, or only Serena? Was her voice so enticing because it was a siren song, created to lead him to his doom? She drew him . . . and repelled him. He wanted her—Christ, yes, he wanted her, he'd wanted her for years—but at the same time his wariness of her grew so acute, it threatened to drive him mad.

"*Richard.*" Her voice was low and held pain.

Realizing only then what he was doing, Merlin managed to force his hands to relax. "I'm sorry. I didn't mean to hurt you, Serena."

She was pale, and her eyes seemed larger than ever as she stared up at him. "That's the first time you've ever . . ." She drew a quick breath. "Tell me why we're here. I have to know the truth."

"I think . . . you already know," he said reluctantly.

"Because what's happening here *does* affect our time? Is that what we came back to try to change? Because male and female wizards fight and hurt each other even in the twentieth century?"

Merlin hesitated, and his hands tightened on her again, this time gently. "Serena, in the twentieth century there are no female wizards. Except you."

Roxanne watched them and wished she could hear what they were saying. They looked very intense, both of them a little pale and utterly still, as if whatever they were talking about mattered a great deal to them.

She didn't trust Merlin, naturally, but had to admit if only to herself that she owed him her life. Why had he healed her injuries? From all she knew of male wizards, not one would lift a finger to save a female, counting himself lucky that there'd be one less enemy for him to worry about.

Serena might have encouraged him to do it, of course. But, again, Roxanne knew of no male wizard who would pay the least heed to the wishes of any powerless female. If Merlin had indeed healed Roxanne because Serena had asked him to, the rapport between them was certainly out of the ordinary.

And baffling to Roxanne. They traveled together, a very powerful male wizard and a strikingly beautiful woman, both of them obviously in the prime of life and health—and yet she wasn't his concubine? They were companions, Serena had explained, and yet Roxanne saw and sensed an intensity of emotion between them that she could only compare with those of the mated pairs she knew in the city. There was always an underlying wariness between such mates, but also a powerful need that seemed to be beyond reason or understanding. To Roxanne, anyway.

Watching the two by the stream, she wondered what it was they felt. Though he was quite adept at controlling his features, even Merlin seemed to be struggling with emotion, something Roxanne had believed was impossible for a male wizard. Did he actually *care* about Serena? She cared for him, that was plain, but many powerless women Roxanne knew had deluded themselves into believing that the wizards who bedded them felt love, as well as lust. Still, despite her emotions, Serena was hardly subservient to the wizard. She followed him readily, but seemed to do so by her own choice rather than his force or will.

Could such things be the norm in the place where they came from, that Seattle? Were male wizards there capable of kindness, perhaps even of genuine caring?

Roxanne didn't know, couldn't know, but the possibility made a pang of wistfulness dart through her— gone as quickly as it had appeared. Even if there *were* places outside Atlantia where male wizards weren't treacherous and brutal, it could make no difference to Roxanne, because she was trapped here and because she was a wizard.

Unbidden, she remembered her recent encounter with another stranger. He had come to the city— unusual though not unheard of behavior for a male wizard. A young man, he had obeyed the laws without protest and had seemed content to wander about, his occasional questions polite and unthreatening. Handsome, as most of the male wizards were, he had smiled often and once had even laughed out loud. . . .

With an effort Roxanne closed the door on those thoughts. It was, after all, pointless to think of such things. Perhaps she *had* felt something unexpected, even extraordinary, when she had looked up into his clear gray eyes, but it hardly mattered. They were both wizards.

Besides that, Roxanne doubted she would ever be able to feel anything except fear and cold sickness if any man, wizard or powerless, came near her. Her memories of what had happened to her were mercifully clouded, but they haunted her nonetheless. They always would, she knew. Merlin had healed her injuries so well, she bore not a single scar to remind her of the violence of that night; still, she could hardly forget.

In fact, she could be bearing a lasting reminder of the violence done to her. It had occurred to her last night, and though Serena had urged her to grieve and get angry, Roxanne's tears had come from the realization that her rapists' seed might well have taken root in her womb.

If that had indeed happened, Roxanne would be bound by the laws of Sanctuary to bear the child, though she wouldn't be required to rear it herself. Oh, everyone would be sincerely compassionate about what she had suffered, but she would not be allowed to harm herself or the unborn child. In Sanctuary the scarcity of children made abortion punishable by death.

Roxanne's hand crept to her lower belly, and she prayed to every god she didn't believe in to spare her the torment of giving life to the child of a brutal rapist. And even as she prayed, her eyes lifted to scan the mountains ringing the valley, probing for the gleam of palace windows half hidden among trees.

EIGHT

The closer they came to the city, the larger it looked to Serena. The stone wall surrounding it was very high—at least twelve feet—which meant that as they approached, what they mostly saw were rooftops (slate or tile), and what little was visible through the open gate.

Open, but guarded. Four powerless men, armed only with knives at their belts and simple bows, stood impassively on either side of the gate, arms folded. Like the village men Serena and Merlin had first encountered, they were dressed in heavy trousers and laced shirts, but wore no coats. They appeared formidable, since they were carbon copies of the Neanderthal villagers, but it was obvious they weren't the true guards—at least not during the day.

The two women evidently were guards; Serena could sense their power and knew both were wizards. Unlike the men, they carried no visible weapons, but their inner force would undoubtedly make them far more deadly than the males until the night and the Curtain sapped their strength.

Both were as delicately lovely as Roxanne. Like her, they were blond, a couple of inches shorter than Serena, and appeared almost ethereal—fragile rather than frail. There was nothing weak about the way they stood, hands on hips, and watched Roxanne and the newcomers approach.

"Let me speak to them," Roxanne warned her companions quietly. "Strangers are rare here, and a Sentinel's duty is to be suspicious of everything."

A bit hurriedly Serena said, "Is there anything in particular we should know about the city before we go in?"

"Yes." Roxanne glanced at Merlin to include him in what she had to say, but looked directly at Serena. "You'll be cautioned to obey the laws posted just inside the gates, but no one will mention punishment. It's very simple here. The price you pay for breaking any law is banishment from the city—forever. That's true of wizard and powerless alike. However, because of the fear and mistrust between male and female wizards, every male is watched carefully, and if he's caught breaking any one of the laws, he's likely to be attacked and severely injured before the Sentinels can get him out of the city. Remember that."

Merlin nodded slightly to show he understood, even though neither woman was looking at him. Serena had said very little since their brief but intense talk by the stream; finding out that she was the sole female wizard in their time had shaken her badly, and she had pulled away from him almost immediately. Her face had closed down and was still closed, pale, expressionless, and her eyes were unreadable.

He hadn't wanted the conversation to end that way, so abruptly and with so little explained, but it was clear Serena had absorbed all she was able to for the moment. So now they were on the verge of entering a city where it was clear Merlin could be viewed with open suspicion and hate, and where Serena would undoubtedly be forced to digest even more disturbing information about this splintered and doomed society.

How would that affect them both?

Roxanne reached the guards first, the other two halting behind her, and spoke pleasantly to her fellow wizards. "Good afternoon, Nola. Phaedra."

"We thought you lost, Roxanne," Phaedra responded in the same amiable tone. She was the taller of the two guards by an inch or so, and wore a half smile that didn't reach her slate gray eyes. "Two nights away from Sanctuary?"

"I was foolish, and I paid the price for it. If it hadn't been for these strangers, I would have died."

Showing little interest in whatever Roxanne had suffered, Phaedra frowned. "They are a pair?"

"They—travel together. Such things are done where they come from, Phaedra."

Phaedra looked beyond Roxanne at the strangers, particularly Merlin—at whom Nola had been coldly staring during the conversation. Without speaking to Merlin, Phaedra looked at Serena. "You are not bound in any way by him once you enter the city. Do you understand that?"

"Yes."

"If you wish to remain inside the city walls, he cannot compel you to leave. Any claim to ownership he has is meaningless inside Sanctuary."

Serena couldn't let that pass. Quietly she said, "He doesn't own me—in or out of the city."

Phaedra was clearly surprised and not a little disbelieving. "No?"

"No. Where we come from, things are . . . different." Serena wondered miserably if they really were, but managed to keep her voice cool.

"Interesting." Still doubtful but not overly concerned, Phaedra turned her flat, slate gray eyes to Merlin. "Whatever your customs may be, the laws of Sanctuary are clear and strictly enforced. Within these walls you do not command. Do you understand?"

"I understand." Merlin kept his voice calm and neutral.

"Are you prepared to obey the laws of Sanctuary?"

He inclined his head slightly. "I am."

Phaedra turned her head to look questioningly at Nola. "How does he rank?"

"Powerful. A seventh-degree Master."

Serena was a little startled by that, since she hadn't

been aware there were degrees of achievement past the ultimate level of Master. She thought both Roxanne and Phaedra were startled, as well, and wondered how Nola was able to differentiate among amplitudes of power. A specialty, perhaps? It made sense; in primitive cultures an individual's strongest or more distinctive talent was often how he or she was known to others, and frequently determined chores or duties.

If there were wizards with strengths in designated areas, then no wonder Roxanne had accepted Serena's explanation about Merlin's being a gifted healer.

Phaedra was frowning again as she stared at Merlin. "A seventh-degree Master. I know of only two wizards here who have ever achieved so high a degree of power. Why did you come to Atlantia?"

"I'm a traveler, no more," Merlin replied, still neutral. "Atlantis is one stop among many. I have no intention of breaking your laws, or interfering in any way with your society. I give you my word."

Looking sharply at Serena, Phaedra demanded, "Can he be expected to keep his word?"

Serena's slight hesitation went unnoticed by everyone except him. "Yes, he can."

"We shall see." Phaedra shrugged and spoke to Merlin again, coldly. "Make no mistake—no matter how powerful you may be, we in this city have learned to defend ourselves. We will not tolerate any difficulty from you."

"I understand."

"Where is your staff?"

Merlin used one hand to open slightly the left side of his coat, revealing his staff, which was fastened to his belt the way a sword would be worn, with the gleaming crystal uppermost. Only Serena seemed to be aware that the staff had not been there seconds before.

Studying the gem-studded instrument, Phaedra appeared unwillingly impressed by its magnificence and its craftsmanship, but she didn't comment. Instead she said, "No male wizard may pass into the city unless he is willing to bear the mark of power. Is that your choice?"

If he wanted to enter Sanctuary, Merlin thought wryly, then there was obviously no choice to make. He had only an inkling of what this "mark of power" would be, but he answered the question in a dispassionate tone. "Yes, it is."

Nola spoke for only the second time. "Hold out your hand, palm down."

Merlin obeyed, holding his right hand out in front of him, and Nola stretched out her hand without coming any nearer. Watching, Serena felt more than saw Merlin tense as the reddish shadow of an owl etched itself across the back of his hand between wrist and knuckles. It was a highly visible sign.

When it was done, Phaedra spoke again. "Our laws are posted just inside the gates. Study them well. And welcome to Sanctuary."

The two Sentinels stepped aside.

Roxanne immediately led the way past the guards and through the city's gates. She didn't take them down the main road, which wound from the gates through the city, but halted just a few yards inside, where the solid stone wall of a building provided a smooth surface for the laws to be recorded.

"Both of you should study the laws," Roxanne said to Serena. "While you do so, I have a few matters to take care of, including arranging accommodations for you." She paused, then asked diffidently, "Will he be permitted in your house?"

Serena wondered if Roxanne would ever address Merlin directly. "Yes. Will that be a problem?"

Roxanne frowned. "I don't know. I'll have to find out if special permission is required. If you'll wait here, I will return in a few minutes."

Serena looked after her as she headed toward what looked like an official building not far away. Every visible building was very plain and quite solid in appearance, with stone walls and slate or tile roofs. Doors were heavy wood, and windows used a kind of glass that was poorly made, thick, and warped.

From where they stood Serena couldn't see very many people, but those she glimpsed were almost all

women. There were two men, both obviously powerless, standing near or walking with women, the couples
too far away for her to determine if the women were
wizards. And she saw one child, a little girl with carrot-
color hair who was playing with a doll on the steps of
one of the smaller buildings.

It was a very quiet city.

Despite being female, Serena didn't feel very welcome. She could only imagine how Merlin must have
felt.

Turning her head, she looked at the wall and, for an
instant, saw nothing but meaningless symbols. But then
the writing seemed to shimmer faintly, and she found
she could see the laws written neatly in English. Apparently Merlin had considered the possibility that they'd
have to cope with an unfamiliar written, as well as spoken, language.

She began reading, not really surprised to find that
most of them were specifically designed to restrict powerless men and male wizards.

"A city of women indeed," Merlin said quietly.

Serena glanced at him, saw that he was studying the
laws and absently rubbing the back of his right hand
with the fingers of his left, and then returned her gaze
to the tersely written decrees. They were certainly clear,
and quite simple.

No male, wizard or powerless, was allowed to touch
any female in public unless she was his legal wife; in private, physical contact by any unmarried male was allowed only by prior arrangement. (Serena found that
last bit somewhat unsettling.)

Every unmarried male and all male wizards were required to exit the city before the gates were closed one
hour before sunset each day; any discovered in the city
after the curfew would be subject to the most severe
punishment (unnamed).

No unmarried male or male wizard could enter any
private residence without an invitation issued and properly recorded in the presence of at least two witnesses.
(The meticulous caution, Serena thought, was terribly
sad and not a little tragic.)

And no Master wizard, male of female, was permitted to draw his or her staff inside the city walls.

There were a few more laws, most of them a bit more general and applicable to all the citizens of Sanctuary—the usual rules most societies eventually adopted about not stealing or destroying private or public property or hurting other people.

Serena could feel Merlin looking at her. They hadn't spoken directly to each other since that confrontation by the stream, and she was wary of talking to him now. He'd given her so much to think about, and there had been no chance for her to try to work through it all. All she was certain of was that she had never really known him, or the society of wizards she had longed for her entire life to be a part of.

"The law about Master wizards' drawing their staffs," she said finally without looking at him. "Does it mean using the staffs to focus power?"

"I assume so. Serena—"

She cut him off. "There must be quite a few Master wizards here—relative to the population, I mean. When we first came in, I saw a woman with a staff tucked in her belt."

"Yes, I saw her. With so many wizards in the population, I suppose an unusual number are Masters."

"Do you think being a Master wizard means the same thing here that it does in our time?"

Merlin didn't answer immediately, then said, "In substance, although the wizards here obviously have fewer and less-developed abilities."

She nodded, still not looking at him. "That's probably just as well. We're sort of outnumbered."

"Serena—"

Again she cut him off. "According to these laws, you won't be able to stay here in the city for more than a few hours before you'll have to leave. But I should stay, I think. That way I can find out how the people in the city cope with the night, and the Curtain."

"We probably shouldn't separate," he said quietly.

Serena turned to face him, lifting her chin and meeting his eyes directly. "I need some time away from you, Richard. I have a lot to think about. Maybe a few days on my own here in the city will give me the chance to . . ."

"To what? To decide if you still trust me?"

"I don't know. All right? I don't know what I think, or what I feel. I just have to find a quiet place and sit down and try to figure it all out."

"Serena, I have to tell you the rest of it. You can't understand the situation until you know all the facts."

Fiercely she said, "You had every opportunity to give me the facts before we left Seattle, and you refused to do it. Why? Why didn't you tell me then?"

"Because I knew this would happen," he told her. "I knew you'd begin questioning and doubting everything I had taught you or told you about wizards. I knew you'd doubt *me*. Serena, I had hoped we'd be able to observe this society without being affected by it, but I had a hunch it wouldn't be easy—and I wanted at least *one* of us to avoid being torn to pieces by the conflict here. So I didn't tell you any more than I had to. Was that so wrong?"

She didn't know how to answer that, reminding herself that all this must be as difficult for him as it was for her, if not more so. Serena had been virtually ignored—and discounted as mere property—by the men they had encountered, but Merlin had been viewed with open hatred and suspicion by the women. He was being treated as though he were guilty of unnamed but heinous crimes without being given any chance to defend himself. He had even been marked, branded, to make certain others knew what he was.

She glanced down to see that he was still rubbing the mark on the back of his right hand, and murmured, "That hurt, didn't it?"

"Yes, it hurt. Considering that male wizards are obvious from their appearance, I gather the point of the mark is to make us feel like lepers rather than warn the females. And I got the distinct impression that Nola made very sure it hurt."

Serena started to reach for his hand, but Merlin took

a step back. "No, you mustn't touch me on a public street; we can't break any of their laws."

"The law says an unmarried male can't touch a female; it doesn't say anything about the other way around," she reminded him.

"In this case I think it's better to be safe than sorry. Besides, the pain's gone now. I just . . ." He hesitated, then shrugged. "I just don't much care for the way the mark feels."

"How *does* it feel?"

"Heavy. Cold. Obvious." He smiled slightly, a bit wry. "Now I have some idea of how Hester Prynne felt in *The Scarlet Letter*. It isn't a very pleasant thing to be branded a social outcast."

"Especially when you didn't do anything to earn it," Serena agreed. "I'm sorry, Richard, I keep forgetting that. Whatever other wizards do, or have done, I can hardly blame you for their sins. In fact, I think you've probably gone out on a very long limb to avoid being like the others in our time. You weren't supposed to accept me as your Apprentice, were you? That's why you got in trouble with the Council of Elders."

"You . . . deduced that from what's going on here?" he asked slowly.

Serena thought about it. "Partly. You said something had happened to alter the society of wizards; from the looks of things here, it was some kind of struggle between the sexes. And then, when you said I was the only woman to be trained as a wizard in our time . . . It makes sense, that's all. We're here *because* I'm the only female wizard in our time. Aren't we?"

Merlin glanced around and spotted a long wooden bench nearby. "Why don't we go over there and sit down," he suggested. "I'll tell you the rest while we wait for Roxanne to come back."

"I'm not going to like it, am I?"

"No. No, you're not going to like it."

"I thought Merlin would come, as well," Roxanne said as she led the way along the narrow main street of Sanctuary. "I'm sorry I took so long to return, but—"

"It's all right," Serena assured her. "Merlin wanted to explore a bit on his own before he had to leave the city for the night, so he went ahead. I'm going to meet him by the gates tomorrow morning. Are you sure it's all right for me to stay at your house? I mean, I don't want to impose. . . ."

"I'll welcome the company, truly." She hesitated, then added, "Merlin may also enter my house if he wishes; I recorded the invitation properly before witnesses."

Serena regarded the younger wizard soberly. "I think that took a lot of courage, Roxanne. And he'll appreciate your offer as much as I do."

"He saved my life. For that, at least, I owe him the courtesy of admitting him into my home." Her voice was deliberate rather than filled with gratitude, but since she was struggling to overcome the beliefs of a lifetime, it was no wonder she couldn't summon very much enthusiasm.

Serena, struggling with new and complex emotions herself, since she now knew that Merlin could strip her of her powers, managed to sound calm and casual. "He may want to visit your house tomorrow, but if so, it will probably be a brief visit. He's too curious about the city to remain long in one place. Speaking of the city, that building you came out of back there looked like a hospital. Was it?"

Roxanne nodded. "Yes, I wanted to see a Healer immediately to discover if those village men had left me with child."

Shocked, Serena realized she hadn't even considered that possibility. "I'm sorry. I should have asked Merlin to tell you that."

"I wouldn't have believed him," Roxanne answered matter-of-factly. "I would have gone to my own Healer anyway."

"I know it's none of my business, but are you? With child?"

"No, I'm safe," the younger woman said with obvious relief. "And she said . . . that Merlin is indeed an excellent Healer. All my injuries were skillfully repaired."

Serena nodded. "I'll tell him she said so; it's always nice to get a compliment from a peer. And I'm glad you won't have to worry about a pregnancy."

"Yes. It would have been . . . difficult."

To say the least. Serena decided to change the subject. "I've noticed signs above some of the doors—are all the buildings public establishments? For instance, that one on the corner seems to indicate a tailor." She used the word hesitantly and felt relieved when Roxanne nodded.

"Yes, it is. And that one, across the way, is an eating establishment."

"What's used for money here?" Serena asked.

"Money?"

"Um . . . currency? Coin? Legal tender?"

Roxanne's frown cleared. "Ah, I see. We haven't used coin in Atlantia for a long time. There's no need. We simply barter. Some wizards are more adept at creating food, others garments—and still others choose to build new houses or heal."

"Oh. Well, that makes sense, I guess. And the powerless people here? What do they do?"

"Whatever is needed. Whatever they wish "

Serena thought about that as they walked, she looking around curiously. The streets were fairly busy with other people on the move, though still quiet. She saw several apparently powerless women (without the telltale elongated ring finger), and they did indeed look very much like the women of power, though a trifle less fair, and their expressions appeared rather vacant. There were *very* few men, most of whom were with a female wizard, and all of whom were clearly deferential to the women. When the women stood talking to others of their sex, the men waited silently and patiently.

But mostly there were women, almost all slender and rather fragile in appearance, which made them difficult to distinguish as individuals. As far as Serena could see, blonds outnumbered brunets by more than ten to one; the only redhead she had seen was the little girl playing with her doll. The range of ages appeared normal, from elderly women to at least one child, and Serena counted half a dozen obvious pregnancies.

That made her wonder, but before she could frame the question, she noticed something that seemed a bit odd.

"What's going on there?" She nodded toward a small house set apart from those around it. The windows were curtained, which was unusual from what Serena had observed. At each of the house's corners, two women stood talking, occasionally falling silent to gaze intently at the house.

Roxanne looked. "Breeding," she replied.

"What?"

"It's a breeding house. Wizards stand guard outside so that the one wishing to be bred is protected and made to feel safe. She takes her chosen powerless male inside so that he may try to impregnate her." Roxanne frowned slightly. "The males don't perform well unless they have a certain amount of privacy."

"I'm not surprised," Serena said, wondering that Roxanne could speak of this so dispassionately after her own brutal experience. Merlin must indeed have made the trauma seem distant to her. "But why do the women feel a need for protection? The man is powerless, you said, so—"

Roxanne looked at her new friend with something near astonishment. "They're afraid. We're all afraid. Our safety here in the city is very much dependent on our caution. The man who smiles respectfully today and inside these walls may attack any night he chooses."

"But she's safe during the day. It's hours yet until night; surely she isn't afraid now? If she's gone in there to let him get her pregnant, she must feel something for him. Trust, at least. Doesn't she?"

"Here women are never able to trust a man," Roxanne said.

"Then how can she sleep with him?"

"Sleep? Oh, no! If they went to sleep, they could wake in the middle of the night, and then he could hurt her."

Language, Serena reflected, was a tricky thing. So

were euphemisms. "No, I meant . . . have sex. She's having sex with him, and that's such an intimate act. How can she do that without trust?"

"She wants a child. Are such things done differently in Seattle?"

Serena answered the question literally. "Yes. Yes, it's different in Seattle."

Roxanne looked curious, but didn't question. "There are so few children born now in Sanctuary. For a long time there were almost none, because the female wizards were too afraid of men to even attempt to mate. The male wizards increased in number, while we were on the verge of dying out, destroyed by the results of their lies and schemes. Then the laws were written and strictly enforced, which made it possible for female wizards to allow themselves to be impregnated."

Curious, Serena said, "What about the man? He goes in there to . . . um . . . perform, and then he just leaves?"

"When he has succeeded in his task, and a Healer has verified a pregnancy, of course he leaves. He's no longer needed."

"Doesn't he help raise his child?"

"No."

"Then she's using him. What does he get out of the deal?"

Roxanne shrugged. "He probably believes he'll get some of her power, but that's only a myth, as I told you. Most appear to enjoy servicing wizards, even without being empowered. A few of the ones proven to be unusually fertile have chosen to make it their life's work."

Serena stared at her. Career studs? Lovely. "But the laws mention unmarried males, implying the existence of married males here in the city. You said the male wizards didn't marry, but do female wizards?"

"Yes, though rarely. A very few manage to accept a particular man to the extent of allowing him to share her home and her life, and those pairs marry. It was almost unheard of when I was a child, but slightly more common now."

Serena already had an awful lot to think about, but one final question was tormenting her. "Since all the powerless men look . . . well, look so brutal, aren't any of the female wizards afraid their children will be . . . abnormal?"

The question seemed to surprise Roxanne. "The child of a wizard is never born deformed—and always with power, of course." Then she frowned. "But there does seem to be a sickness of some kind. The powerless males who mate with powerless women and live in the village often sire healthy sons, but when they breed here in Sanctuary with female wizards, only their daughters are healthy enough to survive the first few weeks. Our Healers don't understand why, but it's always so."

Serena didn't say a word. But she wondered.

By the time he spotted another male wizard sitting at a small table at what appeared to be a sidewalk cafe near the center of the city, Merlin was more than ready to get off the street. He'd never been particularly concerned about what others thought of him, but running the gauntlet of scores of hostile female stares had made him feel even more like a stranger in a strange land— and definitely detested.

He had no idea if his fellow males would be any more friendly, but approached the table anyway. He was relieved when the other man rose to his feet with a faint but cordial smile.

"A stranger to Atlantia?"

"Yes," Merlin answered, reminding himself that the population was small enough to make strangers obvious.

"Not many of us venture into the city," the other wizard said somewhat wryly. "And the first time tends to be hideously uncomfortable."

"That is putting it mildly. My name is Merlin."

"I'm Tremayne. Join me?"

"Thank you." Merlin sat down across from Tremayne, weighing the other man swiftly. A few years younger than himself, he thought. A couple of inches shorter but well built, with dark hair and gray eyes.

Powerful, but not a Master wizard—though possibly Advanced.

"I'm a virtual stranger here myself," Tremayne said casually. "I've only been in Atlantia a few months—and I don't mind telling you I'm looking forward to my ship returning to take me back home."

Merlin hoped his sudden tension didn't show. "Are you leaving soon?"

"A few weeks. And you?"

"I haven't decided." Could Tremayne be the witness who would record the destruction of Atlantis from a ship at sea? "Do ships call here often?"

Tremayne shook his head. "Never by accident, and rarely by design. It's because there's no harbor, of course, and the reefs are so treacherous. The captain who gave me passage demanded a king's ransom and then refused to return for me as quickly as I wanted. If I had known of the ship carrying you, I probably would have requested passage aboard her."

Merlin smiled. "I'm sorry, I had no idea anyone was so anxious to leave Atlantis, though the captain certainly lost no time in setting sail. He said . . . this place was cursed."

"I don't doubt it. There have been tales for years, and since the skies above Atlantia are often lit with the strange glow of the Curtain, some of those tales have assumed mythic proportions." He hesitated, then added, "That's why I'm here, really. Some of the wizards outside this continent are growing concerned by what they hear of Atlantia."

"And you've been asked to report to them?"

"Well, to my father. He's on the Council of Elders." Tremayne looked at Merlin curiously. "Are you from Europa?"

Long before the "civilized" world had dubbed the land north of the Mediterranean Sea *Europe*, the world-wide society of wizards had named the area *Europa*. There had been more wizards in that area than anywhere else in the world, though they had certainly not been confined there.

Replying to Tremayne's question, Merlin said, "No, I

come from a land far to the west. It's called Seattle. I doubt you've heard of it." Like Serena, Merlin saw no point in not sticking as closely to the truth as possible.

"It isn't familiar, but I'm afraid I can hardly be termed a world traveler. If my family hadn't been able to claim a distant kinsman in Atlantia, I wouldn't have come here."

"Kinsman?"

Tremayne pointed toward the south and to the very mountain where Merlin and Serena had arrived via the gate. "He has a palace up there. His name is Varian."

Something in the other man's tone told Merlin that Tremayne had little love for his relation. Carefully he said, "I was rather surprised to find this society so segregated—male wizards in the mountains and females down here in the valley."

A bit grim, Tremayne said, "So was I. Of course, there's always been distrust between male and female wizards, but nothing like this. From what I've been able to gather, there were some bloody battles fought here generations ago in a power struggle. The males were stronger and might have won outright, but in the war both sides expended too much unfocused energy—and the Curtain was created from the spillover. You know about that?"

"Yes. I've felt its effects."

"It probably prevented this from becoming a male-dominated society, and made it a segregated one. The males, being more powerful, were able to create and defend strongholds in the mountains, keeping the females down here, where every night saw them weakened and vulnerable." Tremayne shrugged. "If it hadn't been for Antonia . . ."

"Antonia?"

"Yes. She organized the females and built this city." He nodded toward the northeastern section of the city, where one building rose above those around it. "She lives there, looking down on what she built. They call her Leader."

"So she's responsible for the laws that prevail here?" Merlin asked.

"More or less. I've never met her—or even seen her, for that matter—but I'm willing to bet she's probably the most intelligent person in Atlantia. She built this city under the very noses of the male wizards, and not one of them realized what it would mean to them."

"What did it mean to them?"

"A stalemate. With all the female wizards gathered here in one place, they were able to defend themselves effectively even though they were outnumbered. The males stayed away at night because they didn't want their own powers diminished by the Curtain. During the day it was hardly safe; the females had a nasty habit of ambushing any male they saw, and Antonia had taught them to concentrate on damaging the males' most vulnerable area, the groin."

Merlin winced, but said, "That sounds like a very convincing strategy. I assume the males got the point?"

"Oh, yes. Most of them decided, quite logically, that fighting the females—at least openly—wasn't worth the risk. They were ahead in the battles, after all, especially since the powerless males of the village had developed the practice of systematically raping and killing so many female wizards at night in the valley."

"But Sanctuary gave the females a safe place," Merlin said. "The powerless males didn't dare scale the walls even at night because they were so outnumbered."

Tremayne nodded. "So things were relatively calm for some time. But then the male wizards began to realize that Antonia was attempting to correct the unbalanced population. She was encouraging the female wizards to bear children even if they didn't want to marry, and her laws made it possible for breeding to take place with little threat to the females."

"Ironic. She built this city to shut out the males, wizard and powerless alike, and then had to admit some of them in order to repopulate. What did the male wizards do?"

"They began breeding like rabbits," Tremayne said flatly. "Seducing powerless women and taking them to the mountains in a concerted effort to breed more male wizards. They slaughter their female children at birth."

"Yes, I heard that," Merlin said. "Monstrous." Serena's word, and she'd been right.

"It's also incredibly shortsighted," Tremayne pointed out, his expression still grim. "With the female wizards using powerless men, and the male wizards using powerless women, there is almost no marrying or mating of powerless couples. And when they do manage to couple, their unions produce few offspring—probably because of the effects of the Curtain. Which means that *their* population is now shrinking."

Slowly Merlin said, "Eventually there'll be no powerless people at all in Atlantis. Only wizards."

"And male and female wizards fear and detest each other far too deeply to mate. There may be a few generations still to be born, but after that . . ."

Merlin knew only too well that Atlantis would not survive long enough to reach that point, but this new information made the inevitability of their doom even more pitiable.

"Even the land's being torn apart," Tremayne muttered as if to himself, his gray eyes lifting to scan the buildings and, beyond Sanctuary's walls, the mountains. "They tell me the ravines in the valley weren't there ten years ago, but now a new one opens up every few days. The earthquakes are worse, the plant life is stunted, and most of the animals died out long ago."

"A dying place."

Tremayne nodded, his gaze returning to Merlin's face. "I believe that's exactly what it is, and I don't know if anything can prevent the death. I think it may be too late for Atlantia."

The note of bitterness and helpless rage Merlin heard in the other man's voice was very close to the emotions evident in the written account of the final hours of Atlantis, and he thought Tremayne was quite probably the author of that narrative. The wizard across the table from him might well be the only survivor of what was to come. But there was no way to be sure.

Before Merlin could respond to what Tremayne had said, the sound of a bell rang out over the city, three tones, clear and sharp.

"Our summons," Tremayne said, getting to his feet. "Every unmarried male is being called to exit the city."

Merlin rose, as well, and fell into step with the younger man as they left the cafe and headed down the street. "Are you going to return to your kinsman's . . . palace?"

"No, not today. I've been looking for someone here in the city, and I think I'll come in again tomorrow. We are permitted to camp outside the walls as long as it's within sight of the guards. You're welcome to share my fire."

"Thank you, I think I will." *Was* Tremayne the wizard who would report the destruction here to the Council of Elders? And if so, what could Merlin do to change that report without risking the possibility of making the situation in his time even worse than it already was?

"He's invited me to visit his kinsman," Merlin told Serena as they stood a few yards inside the city gates early the next morning. "Apparently Varian is the most powerful male wizard here, a Master."

She had been briefly introduced to Tremayne when the two wizards had entered the city. Tremayne hadn't questioned the introduction of Serena as Merlin's "companion"; though he had been obviously puzzled by the term, he was apparently too courteous to ask awkward questions. He had left the two of them alone, continuing into the city after arranging to meet Merlin later at the cafe where they had been the previous day.

Serena nodded. "Then you should certainly go. We'll probably learn more if we split up, and there isn't a lot of time to waste. I'll be all right here. Roxanne is . . . very informative."

Merlin studied her face, wishing it didn't seem so unresponsive. He could hardly blame her for withdrawing from him, especially after he had confessed that he'd been ordered by the Council to take away her powers, but it hurt nonetheless. She had said she trusted him; didn't she know he could never deliberately hurt her?

Or had her confidence in him been shaken by what he had told her—and by this place?

Christ, was she afraid of him now?

"I think Tremayne might be the witness," he told her, keeping his voice matter-of-fact. "There's no way to be certain, of course, but the more time I spend with him, the better able I'll be to reach a judgment about that."

"And then?"

He shook his head. "I don't know, Serena. If Tremayne is the witness, it seems to me that our best chance of changing what will happen to the society of wizards in the future is to somehow change his report to the Council. To convince him that male and female wizards *can* coexist peacefully, that what happened here doesn't have to happen in the rest of the world."

Serena gazed up at him, remembering what he had told her yesterday, what he had explained about the society of wizards in their own time.

There have been no females trained as wizards for many long centuries. After what happened here, the more powerful male wizards outside Atlantis destroyed the females in some kind of violent purge. And after that the Council made it our most inviolate law that no woman should be instructed in our arts. Ever. The Council enforces that law with an iron fist. They don't even remember why, but the very concept of any woman with our abilities terrifies them.

Them.

Quietly she said, "How can you convince him we can coexist peacefully when you don't really believe it yourself?"

"Serena, I've risked everything I am to change that." His black eyes were suddenly naked. "Everything. At least give me credit for trying. I've been fighting my deepest instincts since I looked across a table one night and saw a woman instead of a child."

She hadn't expected him to admit that, and it shook her. "At least now I know why sometimes you'd go all cool and distant. I never knew before. I . . . I thought there was something wrong with me."

He lifted a hand as if to touch her, but then must have remembered the laws of Sanctuary. His mouth tightened as his hand fell to his side. "No, there was nothing wrong with you. And I didn't really know what was wrong with me until I had to face the Council."

Serena tried to hold her voice steady, but it shook with the intensity of her chaotic emotions. "Knowing what's wrong doesn't seem to help very much, does it? I know you've never tried to hurt me, but now I know you could if you wanted to. You could destroy me with a simple wave of your hand. And knowing that scares the hell out of me."

"I would never deliberately hurt you, Serena," he said. "No matter what happens here, that won't change. Even if I have to fight the entire Council of Elders, I won't take your powers."

"But you could. You have the ability to take from me something I cherish. Something I need to survive. I'd die without my powers. You know that, don't you?"

A muscle leaped in his jaw as Merlin nodded. "Yes, I know that."

Serena nodded in turn, her eyes never leaving his. "So how should I feel about that? Frightened? Worried? A hell of a lot more vulnerable than I was yesterday?"

"I won't hurt you."

"I want to believe that. But how can I be sure? How can you? You can't even let yourself trust me. And I know . . . there's a part of you that can't even bear to touch me."

"Serena—"

She shook her head to cut him off. "Like I said, knowing what's wrong doesn't help. You go along with Tremayne and try to convince him. Maybe somewhere along the way you'll convince yourself."

He knew she was right in the essence of what she was saying; until they got past the tangle of emotions that came of facing barriers neither of them had created, it simply wasn't possible to find a solution.

"All right. I may be gone several days, I don't know. After what happened to Roxanne, I hope you'll agree to stay close to the city."

Serena nodded, but then said, "Just in case I happen to get caught outside the gates when the sun goes down, maybe you'd better mark me so those village Neanderthals won't dare bother me." Her voice was unemotional. "The mark should be here." She touched the base of her throat, just below the hollow.

Merlin knew what she meant, because Tremayne had told him of the common practice. Evenly he said, "For the sake of your safety, I'll do it, but it doesn't *mean* anything, Serena."

She glanced down at the mark of power on the back of his right hand, then shrugged. "Just don't make it a pentagram, that's all I ask."

It was up to him to choose a symbol. Merlin didn't stop to think, he just looked at the spot and marked her.

Serena had been aware of no sensation, but she knew the instant it was done. And she felt . . . peculiar. Still wary and confused and more than a little frightened, yet at the same time conscious of a fragile and tenuous connection between them that hadn't been there before. Was the mark meaningless? No. It told everyone in Atlantis that she belonged to Merlin, and even if it was done as a ruse, there was something so damned *primitive* about being tagged with a mark of possession.

"Thanks," she said dryly.

He looked at her intently. "Serena . . . be careful."

"Yeah. You, too."

"I'll see you in a few days."

"I'll be here."

It wasn't until nearly an hour after that stiff leave-taking that Serena caught sight of her distorted reflection in the thick glass of a window, and saw the mark he had given her. It stood out clearly against her creamy flesh, its outline precise and perfect, its color a rich scarlet, and she had no doubt at all that no other wizard of Atlantis would have used the symbol.

That was probably why he had chosen it, of course. He had marked her with a heart.

NINE

Tremayne had almost given up hope of finding her, but shortly after he left Merlin talking to his companion (whatever that meant) near the gates of the city, he turned a corner off the main street and saw the woman who had haunted his thoughts for so long.

She was standing on the bottom step outside the front door of a house. A small girl with red hair was hopping up and down excitedly in front of her, while the fair-haired young woman held a doll in her hands.

She was a wizard, Tremayne realized as he slowly approached the two. She was neatly repairing damage to the doll, injuries apparently inflicted when the child, also a wizard, had practiced using her own powers.

"There, Kerry," the woman said, handing the doll back to its owner. "Now, try to remember what your Teacher taught you about conjuring. Never practice on any object that means a great deal to you, not until you're more confident." Her voice was gentle, but also firm.

"I didn't mean to practice on Chloe, Roxanne—it just sort of happened," Kerry explained, cradling her restored doll happily.

Roxanne. Her name seemed to run through Tremayne's body like wine, making his heart beat faster and his breath catch in the back of his throat. Though he was still several steps away from her; he thought he could smell the sun-washed scent of her pale hair and sweet fragrance of her skin.

She's a wizard. But it didn't matter. Right then, nothing mattered except his overwhelming need to . . . what? To touch her? No, that was forbidden here, and besides, he wanted something more than that, something deeper. He wanted to . . . make a connection with her, *forge* a connection, to somehow bind her to him.

"Kerry, why don't you run over to Dara's house and play now," Roxanne suggested slowly. She was very still suddenly, and Tremayne knew she was aware of his presence.

But the little girl had seen him, and her eyes widened uneasily as she stared at him.

He stopped no more than two steps from them and smiled at the child. "Hello, Kerry."

Never having spoken to a male wizard in her entire life, Kerry seemed at a loss, torn between natural childish curiosity and the wariness drummed into her by her elders. "Hello. Who're you?" she demanded finally.

"My name is Tremayne. I'm a visitor in Atlantia." He thought it was very important to make that distinction; he wanted Roxanne to know he was not one of the Mountain Lords, who had so tormented the female wizards here. She wasn't looking at him, but he knew she was listening.

"Where do you come from?" Kerry asked. She had also never spoken to anyone born outside Atlantia.

"A place called Europa. It's across the sea."

"I've never seen the sea," she told him somewhat indignantly. "They won't let us cross over the mountains, and that's where the sea is. Does the sea have a Curtain?"

"No," he told her gently. "Only Atlantia has a Curtain."

The child's wide blue eyes lifted toward the mountains, and she said wistfully, "I'd like to live in a place that didn't have a Curtain. I don't like the way it makes me feel at night." Then she looked back at Tremayne and frowned. "I guess you heard her say I'm Kerry. And she's Roxanne."

"I'm most pleased to meet you, Kerry. Roxanne."

Tilting her head to one side, Kerry said, "You sounded funny when you said Roxanne's name. And you looked funny. Does your tummy hurt?"

Tremayne cleared his throat, not surprised that the child had interpreted what she saw and sensed as pain; it was a fairly accurate assessment. "No, Kerry, I'm fine. Do you . . . live around here?"

"Over there," she replied, nodding toward across the street. "My mommy died when I was born, so I live with Felice. But Felice is trying to have a baby. She goes to the breeding house almost every day, so Roxanne looks after me sometimes. She's my very best friend. She lives here."

Roxanne spoke for the first time since Tremayne had introduced himself, her voice low. "Kerry, I want you to go and play with Dara now. I'll come and get you for lunch."

"All right, Roxanne." The child started to back away, her bright eyes fixed on Tremayne. "You'll come back, won't you? An' tell me more about the sea?"

"Of course I will, Kerry."

"You shouldn't have told her that," Roxanne said as Kerry disappeared around the corner and out of sight.

"Why not?" Tremayne knew his voice was husky, but he couldn't seem to control it. He wished Roxanne would look at him, wished it so fiercely that it hurt. "I'll tell her anything she wants to know about the sea."

"So she can long for what she can never have?"

He took a step closer so that he was standing directly in front of her but with a careful distance between them. "I'm sorry—that was thoughtless of me."

"Thoughtless, or deliberately cruel?" She didn't raise her eyes from their contemplation of the middle of his chest.

Tremayne drew a breath and spoke evenly. "After what I've seen in Atlantia, I can't blame you for disbelief and suspicion; all I can do is tell you that I'm not like the male wizards here."

She met his eyes finally, her blue ones as turbulent as the sea during a storm. "No?"

"No. I . . . I've been searching for you since the day I first saw you. I wanted to talk to you, to know your name. That day, the day you looked up at me, I felt something I'd never felt before, and I saw it in your eyes—"

"Wariness," she said.

"No, it was something else."

"It couldn't have been." Her voice was growing strained. "You're a wizard. I'm a wizard. There can be nothing else between us."

"I think you're wrong. I *know* you're wrong. Roxanne, I'm no boy to be deceived by hopeless fantasies—"

"No," she cut him off flatly. "You're a wizard. Wherever you're from and whatever you call yourself, we both know that your kind has the power here. At night you can escape above the Curtain. You can escape Atlantia. You have no reason to be afraid."

Tremayne wanted so badly to touch her, but he dared not; he knew he was under observation, probably from at least one of the windows on the street, because that was the way of Sanctuary, and he knew that if he broke any of their laws, he'd be lucky to get out of the city with his life. All he could do to sway her was to use his words, his voice, his intensity.

"You're wrong, Roxanne, when you say I have no reason to be afraid. This valley scares the hell out of me, because the very earth groans of power misused and hatred and violence. Do you think I find it pleasant to walk the streets of Sanctuary knowing I'm loathed?" He held up his right hand, the back toward her, and the mark of power was an ugly red against his tanned flesh. "If I were like those of the mountains, bent on conquering, do you really think I would allow myself to wear a mark of shame?"

"It isn't—"

"Of course it is." He let his hand fall to his side.

"Roxanne, if you haven't realized yet that the society within these walls is as unnatural as the one high in the mountains, then it's time you did."

"And whose fault is it?" she demanded. "Who started the war that destroyed the Old City and scattered the women of power throughout the valley? Who made the powerless men believe they had only to rape a female wizard to gain her power? Who steals powerless women to be their concubines and slaughters their female children?"

"Not I," he said quietly.

That stopped her, but only for an instant. "Perhaps not. Perhaps outside Atlantia things are different. I—I hear that's so. But it doesn't matter."

"Yes, it does matter, Roxanne, because knowing there's a possibility that the society of wizards is different outside Atlantia should tell you there's another possibility—that male wizards are different, too. I'm not your enemy. I could never be your enemy."

"You can never be anything else."

"I have to be. There isn't much time for me to make you believe I speak the truth, because I'm due to leave Atlantia in a few weeks, but I have to find some way of convincing you I'm not your enemy."

She shook her head a little helplessly. "I don't know what you want of me."

Tremayne spoke slowly and carefully, trying to weigh each word. "What I want . . . is anything and everything you'll give me, Roxanne. I knew that the instant I laid eyes on you."

Through stiff lips she said, "I know one thing of the male wizards outside Atlantia. They're mad. *You're* mad. If you want a concubine, go steal some unfortunate powerless woman to satisfy your needs."

"I don't want a concubine." He hesitated, but the sense he had of time slipping from his grasp made him uncharacteristically terse and utterly graceless. "I want a mate."

Shock wiped the color from her face and made her eyes huge with incredulity. "You are mad," she whispered, and without another word she backed away from him, turned, and went into the house, closing the door with a thud.

Tremayne stood there for a moment, silently cursing himself. He glanced up and down the street. It looked deserted, but he could feel eyes on him. If he pounded on the door or, God forbid, tried to get in, he wouldn't last two minutes.

After coming to that realization, he marked the location of the house in his mind and then walked away, automatically heading for the cafe and his meeting with Merlin. He had invited the Master wizard to meet Varian, which meant he'd be in the mountains for the next few days. And away from Roxanne.

His natural impatience urged him to change those plans, to remain in or near Sanctuary and seize every opportunity to see her again, talk to her again. But the voice of reason prevailed eventually. If he tried to persuade her now, he would be fighting her instinctive shock; far better to give her a few days to think about what he'd said. She would see the sense in his contention that he was different from the male wizards she had known.

Surely she would. . . .

An early-morning rain tapped on the roof tiles as Antonia stood gazing out the window of her study. It was possible to see almost all of Sanctuary from here, a sight she enjoyed. She preferred this view to the others her house offered, and because of that she left the window without glass. Since the Curtain invariably warped glass, it was simpler to do without than to have to replace her windowpanes every morning.

"Excuse me, Leader."

Antonia turned to find one of her best—but least imaginative—agents in the doorway awaiting permission to enter. "Come in, Dorcas. You have a report today?"

Dorcas went to stand near the desk in the center of the room. "Yes, Leader. The woman called Serena is most often in the company of Roxanne. She no longer asks so many questions as she did the first day or two, but she continues to explore the city and watch our activities intently."

"Anything more suspicious?"

"No ... but she does not behave like a powerless woman—or like a concubine, though she bears the mark of the wizard of Seattle, the one called Merlin."

"Perhaps the powerless women of Seattle behave differently. After all, we've long known that the Curtain has affected powerless women here, making them docile and simple-minded. If Seattle has no Curtain, then the women there might well be drastically unlike ours."

"Perhaps."

"What does Roxanne say?"

"She says the pair is unusual, nothing more. There may be a question of loyalty."

Antonia looked slightly surprised. "Roxanne's loyalty?"

"She knows more than she is willing to say, Leader."

"Is that a proven fact?"

Dorcas stiffened. "My impression, Leader."

"As good as a proven fact then."

Pleased, Dorcas relaxed. "Thank you, Leader."

Antonia turned to gaze out of the window once more, but continued to speak to her agent. "I would like to know more of this Seattle, but I am not yet ready to summon the woman Serena. Keep her under observation as long as she's within the city walls, but don't make it obvious."

"Yes, Leader."

"What of the wizard Merlin?"

"I spoke to the Healer who examined Roxanne. If Roxanne described her injuries accurately, then Merlin's skill as a Healer is far beyond our abilities."

That brought Antonia around to face her agent, her strange, pale eyes brilliant. "Is the Healer certain of this?"

"Yes, Leader. She reports that she would be unable to duplicate his success."

"What else?" Antonia demanded sharply.

"Very little, I'm afraid, Leader. He has spent the last several days in Varian's palace, so we have been unable to observe him. He was unthreatening enough the short time he spent in Sanctuary."

After a moment Antonia turned back to the window. Her voice was calm again when she said, "When he returns to the city, watch him. And report to me immediately."

Dorcas knew a dismissal when she heard one. "Yes, Leader."

Alone again, Antonia gazed down upon the city she had created. *Merlin* . . . Was he the one she had waited for so long, the one who would show her the way to triumph?

Some time later she left the window and went into the adjoining room, which was her bedchamber. There was a mirror hanging on the wall by the door, which Antonia automatically cleared of the flaws left by the Curtain during the previous night. When the polished oval was unblemished again, she studied her reflection, turning her head this way and that.

Flawless. She might easily be mistaken for a woman half her age, no more than twenty or so. Her red hair was still bright and rich in color, her skin creamy, her pale blue eyes vivid. And her figure was excellent, slender but seductive.

Satisfied, Antonia crossed the room and sat down at a small table. She removed the black cloth draping her crystal, softly recited the appropriate spell, and gazed fixedly into the bright sphere as colors began to swirl. . . .

"I'm trained to please, My Lord," the girl cooed, her hand reaching for him.

Merlin caught her wrist and gently forced her grasping fingers away from the front of his trousers. She was very young and wore only one of the thin white shifts Varian permitted his concubines to wear. But her body was ripe, and the rounded belly proclaimed her to be several months with child.

Not that Merlin was surprised by that; Varian didn't permit any of his women to seek out other males unless they were first impregnated by him.

He looked down at her, searching her eyes for signs of thoughts or emotions. The moonlight was strong enough up here for him to see her clearly. But, just as he had found in every other powerless woman Varian had claimed for a concubine, there was nothing in this one's pale blue eyes. *Nothing.* They were as shiny and lifeless as those of a porcelain doll. She stood there, her wrist held in his grasp, a vacuous little smile curving her lips as she waited for him to release her ... or take her ... or kill her.

He didn't think it would matter to her.

Quietly he said, "No, thank you—Lasca, isn't it?"

"Yes, My Lord. Have I displeased you?" Her voice was soft and sweet. She was still smiling.

"No, Lasca. I'm simply not in the mood for ... company tonight." He released her wrist.

As the girl wandered away, Tremayne came out onto the terrace and joined Merlin. "Lasca had a go at you?" he murmured.

Merlin nodded and leaned his elbows on the balustrade as he gazed down at the valley. The Curtain lay heavily below, shimmering from time to time with pulses of energy. He glanced at Tremayne. "Tell me, are all the powerless women here like Lasca? So ... simple?"

"You mean so empty?" Tremayne gazed out over the valley. "To varying degrees, yes. The innocent ones, the ones my kinsmen and the other wizards haven't yet seduced, don't wander around looking for someone to bed them, they're merely docile and vacant. But these ... well, you've seen how they've behaved these last few days—and nights."

"Yes." Merlin had lost count of the women—some hardly more than children—he had politely refused. And he'd had to bar the door of his bedchamber after awakening the first night to find a girl named Gaea naked in his bed, her eyes and smile as empty as Lasca's had just been. There was something eerie and not a little horrifying about their vacant sexuality.

They made Merlin think of succubi, lascivious female spirits or demons believed by some to seduce men into lustful intercourse during their sleep. Except that succubi were supposedly so hideous, they *had* to do their seducing while the object of their affections lay sleeping deeply, while the women here were actually quite lovely.

He knew that succubi had more or less been created to explain away the nocturnal emissions most men and adolescent boys experienced, while incubi, the equivalent male demons, had been blamed for the pregnancies of terrified young women who swore they hadn't had carnal knowledge of anyone and so *must* have been possessed in their sleep by lustful demons. But knowing the source of the tales didn't seem to make a difference. In fact, he couldn't help remembering that his own namesake, the great magician and Master wizard Merlin, had supposedly been the offspring of an incubus and a nun.

Merlin startled himself by laughing, which earned him a quick and disconcerted look from Tremayne. Clearing his throat, he said, "Sorry. My mind wandered into a rather ridiculous place. This emptiness of the powerless woman—where do you place the blame for it?"

"It's the Curtain I believe. The men grew ugly and aggressive while their women grew servile and witless."

Merlin glanced at the younger wizard again. They hadn't had much of an opportunity to talk during the past few days, and he took advantage of their being alone on the terrace. "When you look at the rest of what's happened here, the segregation of this society, where do you place the blame?"

"Isn't it obvious? The wizards couldn't live together in a single society. I suppose it hasn't happened elsewhere because we're relatively far-flung and not really a community. Here, with the population so small and isolated, distrust became hate and fear, and that naturally led to turmoil."

How can you convince him we can coexist peacefully when you don't really believe it yourself? Serena had asked.

Carefully Merlin said, "Then perhaps the answer is simply to avoid isolating a group of wizards anywhere."

"Perhaps." Tremayne shrugged, his expression brooding. "The problem seems almost insurmountable once it's taken hold, I know that much. How do you go about changing beliefs so stubborn they might as well have been written in stone?"

After a moment Merlin said, "Tell me to mind my own business if it bothers you to talk about it, but that last question had the ring of personal experience. That person you were looking for in Sanctuary wouldn't by any chance be a female wizard?"

Tremayne glanced around as if to make certain they were still alone. "Yes, she is," he replied, seeming a bit pent-up, as if he badly wanted to tell someone about this. He was looking at Merlin steadily. "Her name is Roxanne."

Given the size of the population and since no one used surnames, Merlin doubted very much that names were repeated. So Tremayne's Roxanne was undoubtedly the girl they had found near death, the girl whose life he had saved—the girl Serena was with even now.

Roxanne, a female wizard; Tremayne, a male wizard who was definitely interested in her. And wizards never mated among themselves.

Merlin was trying to think, to sort through the possibilities. Has his intervention made the situation better or worse? Had Roxanne died, Tremayne would undoubtedly have grieved—but would he have blamed this splintered society for her death? Probably. With Roxanne alive, he had the opportunity to woo her—but would her wretched experiences of men and wizards place her forever beyond his reach? Possibly—and that would certainly leave him embittered about this society. But if Tremayne and Roxanne actually did leave Atlantis as mates and traveled back to Europa together, would their success in overcoming their natural distrust and wariness of each other have the necessary positive effect on the Council of Elders of this time?

Who could know?

Merlin was very tempted to consult his crystal for a glimpse into the future, but it was his belief—obstinate, according to his father—that knowledge of the future interfered with both human will and fate. Even the wisest would find it difficult to make choices and decisions without being influenced if he knew what the outcome was *supposed* to be.

He didn't know if that belief would come back to haunt him, but he was not a man who altered his convictions to suit changing circumstances. Not even during the most unsettled periods of his life had Merlin broken his private vow and gazed into the future for answers.

"You probably think I'm mad," Tremayne muttered after Merlin's silence had stretched into minutes. "*She* thinks I'm mad. And why shouldn't she? Why shouldn't you? I'm beginning to have doubts about it myself."

Merlin shook his head. "No. I don't think you're mad, but I do think you've chosen a difficult path. Perhaps even more so than you realize."

"What do you mean?"

The first intervention had been accidental, Merlin reminded himself; he hadn't really stopped to consider the possible consequences of his saving Roxanne's life, at least not until it was too late to worry about it. But if he went on now, if he did anything at all to help or encourage Tremayne to believe that his desire for a female wizard could be resolved happily, then the intercession would be a deliberate one.

Not only that, but Merlin knew he was running another kind of risk in telling Tremayne what had happened to Roxanne. In most primitive (and many so-called advanced) cultures, the woman was blamed for the crime committed against her, and was almost always afterward considered "spoiled" and completely unacceptable by other men. If Tremayne felt that way, he would certainly turn away from Roxanne, no matter how much he had wanted her.

Merlin had to weigh the possible benefit of Tremayne's knowing what had happened (influencing how he would likely approach a woman who had been so terribly hurt by males) against the risk of his blaming and rejecting her because of what had been done to her. Merlin's instincts told him Tremayne was not stupid, irrational, or insensitive enough to do that, but he couldn't be sure he was right about it.

Christ, he couldn't be sure about *any* of it—and the future was at stake. How much could he risk when there was no way to be certain whether he was right? And if he did take the risk of interfering, was it even possible for him to advocate something that made his own deepest instincts cry out in alarm?

How can you convince him we can coexist peacefully when you don't really believe it yourself?

Because he had to. For the sake of the future, he had to. And for the sake of the terrifyingly fragile bond still connecting him and Serena. These days away from her had convinced him of one thing beyond doubt—that she occupied a place in his life and in himself nothing else would ever be able to fill. He felt half alive without her, incomplete, and their awkward leave-taking had left him with an aching sense of loss.

Lose Serena? The possibility of that stirred in him emotions even stronger and fiercer than those created by an ancient taboo. No, he couldn't lose her. He had to find a way. Not to merely coexist with her, but to tear down the wall primitive fears and mistrusts had raised between them and build a true and lasting bond with her. He needed that, though until this moment he hadn't realized it.

His hesitation lasted only an instant, though it seemed much longer. Turning his thoughts with difficulty away from Serena and obeying his instincts about the other man, Merlin quietly told Tremayne about how he and Serena had found Roxanne that first morning. He didn't go into detail about her condition, but what little he said made it very clear what she had gone through at the hands of powerless rapists.

"I tried to heal more than her body, setting the pain and trauma at a distance for her, but it isn't something she's ever going to forget," he told Tremayne. "Even if she doesn't blame you personally for the situation the male wizards here have created, I doubt that she'll feel very . . . agreeable toward any man."

Tremayne didn't say a word. He was utterly still, apparently gazing out over the valley below as if the view interested him. He didn't even appear to notice when Merlin eased away from him.

With half the length of the terrace between them, Merlin stopped and watched the younger wizard with the wary gaze of a bomb expert handed a ticking package. He saw Tremayne's aura become visible, a shimmering halo that was at first different colors but quickly turned an angry red.

What he was seeing was anger, rage. And Merlin knew better than to intrude while the powerful emotions ran their course. Though Master wizards never displayed their auras, simply because they had learned to control all aspects of their inborn power, lesser wizards sometimes allowed their emotions to overwhelm them. Tremayne's fury over what had happened to Roxanne was perfectly understandable, and Merlin sympathized, but there was nothing he could do to make it easier for the younger man.

He stood by silently, waiting, and when white-hot threads of energy escaped Tremayne's aura like a shower of sparks and rained down on the garden below the terrace, Merlin instantly doused the tiny flames ignited. He was careful not to allow his own energy to touch the younger wizard's, saving them both a nasty jolt, and kept a wary eye turned toward the house because he hoped he wouldn't have to explain this to his host.

After what seemed like a long time but was probably no more than half an hour or so, Tremayne's aura gradually lessened in intensity, the colors fading, until finally it was no longer visible. As silently as he had drawn away, Merlin rejoined Tremayne at the balustrade.

"No wonder she told me I was mad." Tremayne's voice was drained.

Neutral himself, Merlin asked, "Does it change the way you feel about her?"

Tremayne's head snapped around. "If you're asking me if I consider her less than she was—I may be mad, but I'm not a fool. She was a victim of this place and can't be blamed for what happened to her."

"I agree," Merlin said quietly. "But it certainly won't make your task any easier. If, that is, you mean to try and persuade her to go with you when you leave Atlantis."

Tremayne looked shocked for an instant, but then an unsteady laugh escaped him. "I . . . think that is what I was hoping."

"Is it such a startling possibility?"

"Yes—you must know it is. Oh, we don't fight the way wizards here do, but I don't know of a single mated pair of wizards in all of Europa. Not one pair. We mate with powerless; it's always been that way."

Merlin nodded toward the Curtain spread out over the valley. "The way it has been here. And look what's happened. Maybe the blame for all this lies there, in our belief that we can't allow ourselves to be vulnerable—especially to the female of our kind."

"Because they can damage us, even kill us," Tremayne reminded him.

"You and I could kill each other." Merlin turned his head and looked at the younger wizard steadily. "If we became angry enough to use our powers against each other, the likelihood is that we'd both die. But that doesn't stop us from being friends. We're willing to take the risk among males—why not with females? What are we really afraid of?"

Tremayne frowned and spoke slowly. "Because . . . the friendship between male wizards is a fairly casual, unemotional kind of relationship. The one thing we all are, almost by definition, is alone. Wizards have always been separate, unique beings. So much of what we are is inside us, and we study and practice all our lives to harness and control the powers we were born with, including our emotions. We may marry, but when we do, we never give much, if anything, of ourselves. And our children leave their parents at a very young age, just as we did."

"Christ," Merlin muttered.

"What?"

"Nothing. You're right, of course." *And why the hell didn't I see it before now? We* are *solitary creatures, doing our best to control our powers—and our lives. We're closed, guarded, and to reach for intimacy with a woman*

*means more to us than mere vulnerability; it means a loss
of the command with which we center our lives. We learn
at an early age to use what's inside us, to contain and
control, to gaze always inward, not even suspecting that
we can never achieve the perfection we seek simply because
we've locked ourselves away from the ultimate test of our
own humanity. . . .*

Tremayne shrugged wearily. "In that sense what's
happening here isn't so different from the rest of our
world. The wizards here are alone, even if they're surrounded by others. Varian, so frantically begetting sons,
doesn't give anything but his seed. The number of his
sons makes him more powerful, but gather twenty of
them together in one room, and I'll bet he couldn't
name them all. They're no part of him, merely . . .
tools."

"It doesn't have to be that way," Merlin said. "Perhaps it is against our very nature to allow anyone to get
close to us, but we can overcome that. We *have* to.
How can we call ourselves Masters otherwise?"

Tremayne smiled slightly. "You're the Master—I'm
Advanced. But I suppose that's hardly the point. You're
saying we can't be complete as wizards until we *can*
allow someone to get close, because the fear of being
vulnerable is . . . the final flaw in all of us."

"That's exactly what I'm saying." Merlin was abruptly aware of an urgent need to see Serena, to talk to
her. She hadn't been out of his thoughts since he had
left her in the city, but he had managed not to drive
himself crazy struggling with the conflicting emotions
she evoked in him. Now, though still conscious of that
conflict, he at least had some idea of what he was struggling *with*. And why.

"How can you be so sure we can overcome that
flaw?" Tremayne asked soberly. "I don't know anyone
who has."

"Nor do I. But I think both of us had better do our
best to change that."

"Both of us?" Tremayne looked at him curiously.

Merlin hesitated for all of a few seconds, then sighed

and said, "I think I'll tell you about my . . . companion."

He didn't tell the younger wizard everything, of course, but he did confess that Serena was a woman of power (artfully disguised while they traveled together), and he did make it clear that he and Serena were struggling with feelings neither one of them seemed able to easily accept.

Even as he talked, he wondered if these last days had been as difficult for Serena as they had been for him. As painful and disturbing as it was being away from her, he liked even less the uneasy knowledge that she was in a city of women where male wizards were openly loathed and distrusted. Had Serena come to terms with the reason they were here in Atlantis?

And if she had, did she hate him because of it?

Normally Varian was interested in little except bedding his bitches and trying to think of some way he could ultimately triumph over that whore Antonia in her damned city. But when Tremayne returned from one of his frequent visits to the valley with a stranger from someplace called Seattle, a Master wizard named Merlin, Varian's curiosity had stirred.

And that wasn't all. His senses and instincts told him this wizard was unlike any he had ever encountered, and that made him decidedly wary. Merlin was polite and pleasant, but his black eyes were very, very sharp as they gazed about Varian's home, and he showed absolutely no interest in any of the bitches—unnatural, as far as Varian was concerned.

He had a new one in his bed tonight, a ripe young bitch from the village whom he had bought from her father while she was still playing with dolls; it was Varian's favorite tactic to stake his claim long before the other male wizards noticed an available powerless female. The farmer had kept her safe until Varian was ready for her, making sure she came to her Lord's bed a virgin. That had been a few days ago, and he'd spent quite a few hours since breaking her in.

"Oh—My Lord!"

"Do you like that, Mara?"

"Yes . . . please . . ."

Varian always took care to break them in right, devoting his considerable talents to the task of turning a dimwitted but innocent village girl into a dim-witted woman interested in nothing except physical satisfaction. The eagerness he taught them increased his own pleasure. Mara was just reaching that stage after nearly a week; by the time he was finished with her, she'd have his seed rooted in her belly and would spread her legs eagerly for any other male while she was breeding.

They were in her bed this night, and he was teasing her. He hadn't yet undressed, nor had he allowed her to do so; she was wearing a flimsy shift. Lights burned on either side of the huge bed; Varian strongly disliked sex in the dark.

He took her mouth until she was weak and quivering, fondling her breasts through the thin cloth of her shift until they were swollen with hot blood, the nipples stiff. Still dressed, he mounted her. The pressure of his legs had parted hers, and he moved slowly to press his straining groin against the soft notch between her thighs. She moaned raggedly when she felt his hardness, then sighed and whimpered when he rubbed himself between her thighs.

He eased his hips back a bit and slid one hand up her thigh, slowly drawing the skirt of her shift upward. He tugged until the material was bunched around her waist, leaving her naked from there down, and then he settled back against her. He hunched slowly, rubbing himself against her leisurely while he held her wrists above her head on the pillow and gazed down at her flushed, strained face with satisfaction.

She was undulating beneath him, eyes blind as she sought the release her body craved. He licked her parted lips, pleased to find her flesh so hot, she nearly burned him. Ignoring her desperate whimper of anguish, he drew back away from her again, settling onto his heels between her sprawled legs. She was displayed for him, her hard red nipples visible through the sheer material of the shift, the skirt rucked up around her waist, her naked loins lifting and rolling pleadingly.

Perfectly able to control his own lust, Varian smiled at her and made a soothing noise that did absolutely nothing except cause her to groan with the pain of her need. He placed his hands on her white thighs, pushing them wider apart and guiding her knees high, then studied the lewd result. At the front of his trousers, a twitch indicated the impatience of his male parts, but Varian was concentrating on turning her into a mindless broodmare constantly in heat and always eager to be mounted.

He stroked her thighs, gradually sliding his hand up until he touched the pale, silky hair covering her mound. She was incredibly soft, damp, and swollen, and he smiled as he touched that heated womanly core of her.

"My Lord!"

"Do you like that, Mara?"

She groaned wordlessly, her hips lifting as she tried to press herself against his probing fingers. He reached up his free hand to rub her quivering belly and fondle her breasts, still through the shift. His other hand was still very lightly petting her mound, his touch teasing. She shuddered and moaned, her legs spreading wider in an instinctive response to the fullness of her swelling sex.

He glided one finger along the gaping cleft, then very slowly and gently penetrated her. She groaned gutturally, her hands grasping fistfuls of the sheet on either side of her hips, and another shudder shook her slender body as the length of his finger pressed deep within her.

"That's it," he murmured, watching her face as his finger began stroking in her scalding hot, wet depths. "So soft . . . so wet . . . yes, my little bitch. . . ." His thumb found the stiffening nubbin of flesh and rubbed it roughly, and she writhed with a muffled cry.

He could feel her tense striving, see it in her wild eyes. Little whimpering sounds welled up and escaped her trembling lips while her hips undulated furiously to his touch. She tightened even more around his stroking finger and he increased the speed and depth of the thrusts, his gaze intent on her face.

She reached the peak swiftly, writhing, sobbing, the spasms of her pleasure shuddering through her entire body. When she at last went limp, he eased his finger out of her and opened his trousers, freeing his swollen flesh. He mounted her, hooking his arms under her knees and hoisting them high and wide as he seated himself to the hilt in her throbbing sheath.

With utter self-control Varian delayed his own release in order to bring her to the peak again and again. It occurred to him almost idly, as he watched her flushed, sweating face and listened to her moans and cries, that he could never let himself find pleasure until the bitch beneath him was totally caught up in an animalistic frenzy, but he didn't stop to examine the realization. It didn't seem to matter.

When he finally emptied his seed into her writhing body, Varian was pleasantly weary but still not ready for sleep. He rolled off her and undressed himself, then returned to the bed and took her from behind with no preliminaries. Not that Mara noticed anything lacking in the union; by that point she was lost in a kind of sexual rapture.

It was several hours past midnight when Varian felt himself able to sleep. Mara was sprawled across the bed, and he tossed a sheet over her limp body before striding naked from her room and down the hall to his own.

He never slept with a bitch in the same room.

Just before he drifted off to sleep, Varian found his thoughts turning again to the stranger, Merlin, and they made him uneasy, just the way thoughts of his own kinsman, Tremayne, made him uneasy. Neither of them belonged here. But he had nothing to fear from either of them, Varian assured himself.

After all, he was the most powerful wizard of Atlantia.

TEN

Serena tossed the ball to Kerry and winced when it went wide of the mark. "Sorry, kid. I never was much of a pitcher," she called.

Roxanne chuckled as the little girl chased after the ball. "She could bring it back by crooking her finger, but she seldom remembers that."

"Wizards are odd," Serena agreed, not without a touch of irony.

"Um. What's a *pitcher*?"

For a second Serena went blank, but then she remembered—and realized another of her words hadn't translated. Dammit, she couldn't seem to remember to watch what she said!

"It's someone who throws a ball in a game," she replied casually. "I've seen it played it Seattle."

Roxanne nodded solemnly. She had regained all her strength in the days since her attack, and seemed hardly affected by what had happened to her; Merlin had done an excellent job. "It sounds like your Seattle would be a nice place to live."

"Yes. It is." Serena was sitting on a low wall that surrounded a small courtyard between Roxanne's house and the one next to hers, while the younger wizard sat on her front step, repairing—by hand—a torn shift. She had told Serena that she enjoyed sewing, and seldom used her powers to repair clothing.

Kerry returned, the ball clutched in her small hands. "It bounced most of the way to Leader's house!" she scolded.

"I *told* you I couldn't throw straight," Serena reminded her a bit absently, her gaze lifting to study the distant house that was the tallest in Sanctuary.

"Well, I'm not going to run after it again. Roxanne, can I use your sand to try to make a mirror?"

A little amused, Roxanne said, "If you mean the sand in the courtyard, yes. But is my sand so different from anyone else's?"

The child nodded. "It's perfect sand, and Teacher says only perfect sand makes perfect mirrors."

"Very well, but be careful."

Kerry rolled her eyes at the constant adult refrain, then scrambled over the low wall beside Serena and went to select the proper spot for her mirror-making. The one she settled on was several yards away from the two women.

"Teacher says," Serena murmured, still gazing off at the Leader's house. "Can't she create a mirror without sand?"

"No, of course not," Roxanne answered in surprise.

Serena sent her an oblique glance. "But your friend Adina the tailor can create cloth without threads. Calandra makes wonderful soup or sweets from nothing but air. And just yesterday I saw your neighbor Heather conjure enough water for those flowers she's trying to keep alive."

Roxanne frowned slightly. "Mirrors are different. We can no more conjure them than we can living creatures."

Serena heard herself laugh, a low sound that was wry rather than amused. *She* couldn't create a mirror, either, unless she used sand. Nor could Merlin. He had taught her it was because the energies required to create anything from nothing were especially potent, and a mirror conjured that way reflected the energies so fiercely that the mirror always—*always*—shattered into a million pie-ces.

Even using sand, it was difficult, exacting work to create a mirror, and it always had to be done with the mirror facing away. Otherwise the reflection could cause a painful jolt.

As for creating living creatures, that was another abil-ity all wizards lacked even in modern times. They could change one living creature into another—an enemy into a toad, for instance—but they could not create a living being except the same way all humans did—by having children.

"I merely wondered," she said at last, glancing back over her shoulder to make sure Kerry was all right. She was, squatting and carefully smoothing the sand she had chosen into a small oval.

Serena sighed, turning her gaze this time toward the mountains outside the city. Without realizing what she was doing, she lifted one hand and rubbed the little heart—Merlin's mark—at the base of her throat with a finger. What was he doing up there? Varian had a pal-ace, Roxanne had told her; sometimes when the light was right, it was possible to get a glimpse of shining windows or pale marble, a hint of the riches the males enjoyed creating for themselves, but right now she could see nothing.

Was Merlin trying to convince Tremayne that male and female wizards could coexist? Serena didn't know. She had thought about trying to get into his mind as she had twice before, but shied away from the attempt—partly because of the strain between them and partly because she was afraid she would find him in bed with one of the many concubines Varian was reputed to have in his palace.

That possibility hurt her even more than the knowl-edge that Merlin could strip her of her powers and de-stroy her if he wanted to, and it told her something about her own feelings. She was far less afraid of him than of losing him.

"You've been very quiet today," Roxanne observed,

seemingly fixing most of her concentration on the mending in her lap. "Is it—do you miss Merlin?"

"Yes, I do," Serena replied honestly. It was the bald truth. Whatever else she thought or felt about this place and why they were here, one truth she had finally accepted was that Merlin wasn't to blame for any of it. And she missed him desperately; they hadn't been apart for so long in all the years she had lived with him.

She looked at Roxanne, catching a glimpse of something she couldn't quite read in the younger woman's blue eyes; it was a fleeting thing, hidden when the delicate blond returned her attention to her work.

"Perhaps he'll return soon," she suggested colorlessly.

Serena doubted that was a pleasant possibility to her hostess, but didn't comment, and they went on to talk casually of other things—including, when she finished it, Kerry's rather lopsided but functional mirror.

It was very late in the night, actually not long before dawn, when Serena sat up in her bed and used a tinderbox to light the candle on her bedside table. She banked the pillows behind her and leaned back against them, drawing her knees up and wrapping her arms around them. Even inside this solid stone house, the effects of the Curtain were oppressive, and she felt exhausted. Too exhausted to sleep.

One thing she had swiftly noticed about Sanctuary was that only the powerless citizens stirred about in the early mornings; the wizards tended to sleep for several more hours, because they slept so uneasily, if at all, during the dark night. Serena had managed to be up and about every morning before Roxanne, but she had caught herself dozing several times during the warm afternoon hours and knew she was risking an utter collapse if she didn't manage to get some decent sleep.

That thought had barely crossed her dulled mind when there was a soft knock at the door and Roxanne glided into the bedchamber, a ghostly figure in her shift.

"Are you all right, Serena?"

"Did the light disturb you? I'm sorry." Serena strove to keep her voice relaxed.

"No, I was awake." Roxanne came to the bed and eased down near the foot, facing her guest. Her delicate face was pale with the fatigue that gripped all wizards at night in the valley, but her eyes were clear and steady. "It's almost impossible to get any real rest while the Curtain drains us. Isn't it?"

Serena hugged her upraised knees and frowned. Unless her sluggish mind was playing tricks on her, she was fairly sure her friend was asking if she was a wizard. Then Roxanne spoke again, still softly, and the probability became a certainty.

"Do you think I haven't noticed that you're affected just as we are? That the night and the Curtain leave you weary and drained? I don't know what things are like in Seattle, and I'm not sure how you're able to hide your power . . . but you are a wizard, aren't you, Serena?"

Resting her chin on her upraised knees, Serena tried to decide if confession was a good idea and finally gave in because she couldn't think her way out of it. "This isn't fair, you know," she told the younger woman. "You seem to be able to think, and I can't. I suppose it gets a bit easier over time?"

Roxanne drew a deep breath. "Yes, I suppose. Like anything else, one grows accustomed. . . . I—I couldn't believe I was right in what I suspected. You seemed so unlike the powerless women here, far more like us, but that *could* have been because you weren't born here. But then I noticed how tired and listless you were each morning, and I wondered. . . ."

It was Serena's turn to sigh. God, would morning never arrive? "Yeah, Merlin figured he'd covered all the bases, but neither of us expected the Curtain."

"Bases?"

"Sorry." For some reason she seemed to have baseball on the brain, and it hardly translated. "I meant, well, we thought it might be a good idea if only one of us appeared to be a wizard. When you travel as far as we have, you never know what to expect in the way of customs and beliefs, and . . ."

"You're both wizards." Roxanne's eyes were very bright.

"Uh-huh."

"And you're . . . companions?"

Serena glanced toward the window and was relieved to find that dawn had arrived. Just a few more minutes now until the sun came up, and her mind would begin to clear. She looked back at her hostess and tried to concentrate.

What was it? Ah, yes . . . companions.

Frowning slightly, she said, "Merlin and I have been together for a long time, Roxanne, but we aren't lovers—mates—if that's what you're asking. I went to him to learn how to control my powers. He's been my . . . my teacher."

"He never tried to hurt you?"

"Of course not. In fact, we've always been very good friends. Until we came here, I even thought . . . Never mind."

Roxanne leaned forward a bit, her eyes painfully intent. "You thought . . . ?"

Serena felt almost drunk, a little vague and sleepy. And tired. She was very, very tired. She leaned her head back against the rough wooden headboard of the bed, not bothering to try to hide a tiny yawn.

"Oh, I don't know. I used to have these stupid fantasies about him. I knew I was being an idiot, but all the other men I met were always *lacking*. It wasn't just that he was a Master wizard and they weren't wizards at all; it was other things. He was taller than they were even when he *wasn't*. Stronger. He walked like . . . like a king, I guess. His voice was . . . pure magic. And his eyes . . . He has incredible eyes, doesn't he? So black and liquid. Sexy. And that was the laugh, you know, that was the joke on me, because as soon as I grew up and decided I could be pretty sexy myself if I put my mind to it, he just sort of . . . went away."

"What do you mean?"

"He didn't actually go. I mean, he was still teaching me, and we were still living in the same house, and sometimes things were even the way they used to be.

But there was a wall that hadn't been there before. He said . . . there were boundaries we couldn't cross, and I thought he meant between Master and Apprentice, but that wasn't what he meant at all. So we came here, and things are even worse here with those awful male wizards and the Curtain and this walled city—"

A huge yawn suddenly cut into Serena's growing self-pity, and she stared at Roxanne, blinking owlishly. "Oh, God, I'm sorry, but I've got to crash." She slid bonelessly down, pulling the covers up to her nose, and went out like a light.

Holding her head carefully upon her shoulders with one hand, Serena felt her way down the hall to the kitchen, where Roxanne was already sitting at the rough-hewn table. Having been awakened by one of the frequent tremors that shook Atlantis—was it her fourth or fifth earthquake since leaving Seattle?—Serena was feeling disgruntled.

"Good afternoon," the blond offered gravely.

"You couldn't prove it by me." Serena sat down cautiously, and risked letting go of her head. It didn't fall off, which was a nice surprise. Apparently exhaustion had finally caught up with her; she had slept soundly for nearly nine hours, and the aftereffect was rather like a hangover.

Roxanne pushed a heavy mug across the table to her guest. "Drink this. It will help, I promise."

A cautious sip rewarded Serena with a cool, sweet drink that began clearing her head immediately; by the time she set the mug back onto the table a moment later, she felt reasonably human again.

"You took advantage of me," she told her hostess severely. "Unless I dreamed it, you visited me before dawn and forced me to babble like an idiot."

Roxanne was smiling slightly. "I merely asked you a few questions. And you didn't babble."

"I didn't?"

"No. Well, toward the end you may have lost the thread of what you wanted to say, but I would hardly call the result babbling."

Serena winced. "Yeah, right." She cleared her throat. "I seem to remember confessing that I'm a wizard."

"Yes. And now that your mind is clearer, I'm very curious, Serena. How do you hide your powers?"

"A little trick Merlin taught me. I hope you aren't upset about this. It wasn't that I wanted to deceive you, it was just that . . . well, it seemed a good idea at the time."

Roxanne's shoulders lifted and fell in something more than a shrug. "It's just so incredible. A male and female wizard traveling together, not fighting or hurting each other. Is that common in Seattle?"

Serena hesitated, but she couldn't lie to the younger woman any more than she had to. "No, it isn't common—but then, Seattle is hardly a city filled with wizards. Merlin and I are pretty much trying to find our way alone. Or we were, until we came here."

"But you *want* to be together?"

"I want to be with him," Serena answered honestly. "And he's risking quite a lot by being here with me."

"I don't understand."

"It isn't important. All that matters is that Merlin is making an effort to tear down that wall between us. At least I think he is."

"What will happen then?"

For the first time since coming to Atlantis, Serena considered that question. "I . . . I don't really know."

"Will you . . . be mates?"

"I don't know," Serena repeated slowly. "*Can* two wizards be mates? All the years we've been together . . . will that let us trust each other enough to get so close? Can we forget what's going on all around us here? I just don't know."

Roxanne hesitated, then said, "What if Merlin returns from his visit to the mountains more like the male wizards here?"

"That won't happen."

"How can you be so sure? Serena, the male wizards of Atlantia are treated like gods. And you said—you told me he was at Varian's palace. Varian is by far the worst of the Mountain Lords, concerned with nothing except his . . . his gluttony. What if Merlin likes the idea of being godlike?"

Serena didn't hesitate. "He won't. If he had wanted to be treated like a god, he could have made it happen before now." *And after now.* "Believe me, Roxanne."

Solemnly the younger wizard said, "I believe *you* believe it. I just hope you're right."

So did Serena.

"Are you leaving the city for good?" Phaedra asked.

Serena adjusted the pack she carried and smiled pleasantly. It was late the following morning. "No, just for a while. I thought I'd explore the ruins of the Old City I've heard so much about."

The Sentinel glanced at the mark at the base of Serena's throat, and her thin lips curved in a faint smile. "You should be safe enough even at night, but that's by no means certain. I would advise you not to spend the night outside our walls. Unless your *Lord* is with you, of course."

Despite Roxanne's contention that all in Sanctuary were treated with respect, this wasn't the first time Serena had caught a touch of scorn from one of the female wizards. The mark she wore *was* a kind of brand, every bit as degrading as the one the male wizards were forced to wear inside the city. Many of the wizards of Sanctuary seemed to feel that the powerless women marked with the signs of possession were to be condemned for something that was never their fault.

Because she hadn't been marked when she had first walked through these gates, Serena had been treated with respect by the Sentinels; now she was apparently just another powerless woman who had been used by a male wizard.

Serena was tempted, but there was no good reason for her to reveal her own powers to this wizard. Besides that, she had a hunch that keeping the knowledge quiet for a while longer would be for the best. Roxanne had agreed to say nothing, though she'd been obviously puzzled by the request.

Keeping the expression pleasant, Serena said, "I'm quite capable of taking care of myself, Phaedra."

The Sentinel wizard nodded. "Fine. Just remember that we close the gates an hour before sunset. And we don't open them after that, for anyone, until sunrise."

"I'll remember." Serena walked on, past the burned circles on the ground that indicated old and recent campsites where powerless men (and very few male wizards) had spent nights waiting for the gates of the city to open. She moved into the woods toward the northwest, heading for the ruins Roxanne had told her about, the remnants of what had once been the center of culture and society in Atlantis.

No one seemed to remember what it had been called; now it was simply the Old City. It had existed a long, long time ago, when wizards and powerless, male and female, had lived and worked in something like harmony. The population then had consisted mostly of powerless people with a scattering of wizards, and perhaps that had simplified matters and enabled everyone to coexist peacefully.

As she walked steadily through the forest, crossing a narrow stream, working her way around a ridge carefully because she was hampered by the heavy, awkward skirts of an outfit she'd come to despise, Serena thought about that bygone time and wondered what had happened to alter the status quo. No one in Sanctuary had been able to tell her. Probably it had been a gradual change, maybe even over generations. In any case, the result had been the first salvos in the battle between male and female wizards.

It was midafternoon by the time Serena topped a ridge to see what was left of the Old City before her, and the sight froze her. Once, the city must have been huge, far larger than Sanctuary, sprawling out at the northern end of the valley. Now it was tumbled piles of stone and jutting bits of petrified timbers and thin trails that had once been wide thoroughfares.

The increasingly frequent earthquakes of recent times had torn open a ravine like a jagged cut zigzagging in the center of the ruins, and the bizarre plant life of Atlantis had encroached to lend the remains of the city an even more pathetic and ravaged appearance.

Serena made her way down into the ruins cautiously; Roxanne had said that snakes were plentiful, and though none apparently were poisonous, Serena didn't like snakes. She shrugged out of her backpack and hung it over the low branch of a tree barely taller than she was with violet leaves, and then wandered along one of the thin paths threading the ruins.

It was incredibly sad. There were signs that this had once been a thriving culture, far more advanced than the somewhat primitive conditions in Sanctuary. There was evidence of a sophisticated water and sewer system, for instance. The roads seemed to have been laid out with care and logic, unlike the winding and wandering ones of Sanctuary. Bits and pieces of the pottery and stonework that had survived indicated a love of beauty and a high degree of skill.

All that, Serena knew, had been produced by the *powerless* people who had once lived here. How she knew that was quite simple; because any creation of a wizard could always be recognized by another as just that—and nothing here told her it had been conjured by a man or woman of power.

When the female wizards had built their own city, Serena thought, they had made it solid and safe and not very pretty, choosing substance and safety over style. They created water when it was needed, not even bothering to conjure wells that would have probably been destroyed by earthquakes, and they got rid of waste with the same automatic and offhand competence. Since the wizards could also easily create pottery or intricate stonework any time they wanted, they simply tended not to bother.

Serena sat down on a huge flat table of stone that seemed once to have been part of a terrace, and removed a pebble from one of her thin slippers. With the stone gone and her shoe back on, she continued to sit there, looking around her. She learned nothing new from what she saw, but a number of conclusions she'd reached during these last days were reinforced. The major conclusion was inescapable: In their blind struggle for supremacy, the male and female wizards here had literally ruined everything around them.

They had destroyed the powerless people who shared this valley, turning the men into aggressive brutes and the women into virtually mindless doormats. They had destroyed the farm stock that had once flourished; the horses, cattle, and chickens had died out quickly and completely even before the Curtain had formed, exterminated by the energy spillover of battling wizards. The wizards had warped and stunted plant life, contaminated the groundwater, disturbed the very earth beneath them . . . and inadvertently created the Curtain.

Of course, an argument could be offered that they had done all of it inadvertently, not out of the desire to destroy but because they had been ambitious, shortsighted, and self-involved. But that hardly excused them. Of how many races could it be said that they had destroyed a continent?

"A redhead, by God!"

Startled, she jerked her head around to see a tall wizard striding toward her, his coat sweeping out behind him. He reminded her a little bit of Merlin because he was dark and well built; when he got closer, she saw that his lean, handsome face held a subtle stamp of cruelty. And his eyes gleamed flatly, like two lumps of coal.

Serena wasn't frightened, but she was wary. She eased off her stone seat and turned to face him.

Still several feet away, he stopped suddenly, his eyes narrowing as he studied her. Obviously he was momentarily puzzled by her. She didn't have an elongated ring finger, nor did she reveal the power of a wizard, but she was also lacking the blank gaze and subservient manner of powerless women. She looked him straight in the eye, which was hardly something to which he could be accustomed. Then his gaze fixed on the mark at the base of her throat, and he frowned.

"Who owns you, bitch?"

For a full moment Serena was too shocked to be able to utter a word. She had never in her life been called a bitch—not to her face, at any rate—and her response to the word was completely visceral.

"Answer me," he ordered impatiently.

She could feel his power; except for Merlin, she had never met a wizard whose power literally radiated in a palpable aura. But she was too angry to care. "I'm not a female dog *or* a piece of property," she snapped, glaring at him.

He took two large steps toward her and stood little more than an arm's length away, forcing her to look up in order to continue meeting his eyes. He was still frowning, but a little half smile curved his sensual lips at the same time. "The last spirited bitch in these parts died of old age before I was born. Where did you come from?"

"Somewhere else," she said tightly, gritting her teeth to keep from saying something she might regret later. Such as the words that made up the spell to turn an enemy into a toad. Would it work on another wizard? She had no idea, but she was willing to experiment on him.

"I don't recognize that mark," he said. "If your Lord isn't in Atlantia, then—"

"He is," a new voice said calmly.

The wizard turned and eased back from Serena in a clear gesture of giving way as he watched another tall, dark wizard coming toward them. His frown smoothly became a smile. "Merlin. She's yours?"

"Yes, Varian, she is."

"May I make an offer?"

In a polite tone Merlin said, "I couldn't allow you to waste your time. She isn't for sale." He stepped past the other wizard to join Serena, giving her a quick, unreadable look before he faced Varian again.

"Bitches are *always* for sale, Merlin," Varian retorted, still smiling.

"She isn't for sale. Not now. Not ever. And I won't change my mind." Merlin's tone was equally pleasant, but there was a note of steel underneath.

For a moment it seemed Varian would either continue to insist or challenge Merlin in some other way, but finally he inclined his head in an ironic little bow and shrugged. "So be it. You should keep a closer watch on her if you don't want her stolen away from you, my friend. Not all the wizards here are as reasonable as I am about such matters."

"Thank you. I'll remember that," Merlin told him, still cordial.

Varian glanced at Serena again, much in the hungry way some men eyed sleek red sports cars that fired their passions, then said to Merlin, "You're certainly welcome to bring her to my place on your next visit. In the meantime I'll leave you alone with your property. I'm sure that after several days apart, you're eager to lie between her legs again."

Serena felt her mouth drop open as she stared after the departing wizard. She closed it carefully, very conscious of Merlin's silence beside her. And his closeness. After Varian's crude statement, she thought she might be blushing for the first time in her adult life.

In a dispassionate tone Merlin said, "He's the most sexual creature I've ever encountered."

She took a couple of steps away from his side and turned to face him, hoping she didn't look as stiff as she felt. However she might have greeted Merlin after having been separated from him for so long, Varian's presence—and his words—had made her feel emotionally paralyzed. "Yeah, I got that impression. Was he a good host?"

"I didn't see much of him." Merlin was gazing at her steadily. "What I did see, I didn't like."

Serena glanced around them at the dead city, avoiding his scrutiny. She was uncomfortable with Merlin for the first time in her memory. "I know the feeling. Sanctuary is a pretty weird place. It's funny . . . I got a close-up look at the nearest thing I've ever seen to pure sisterhood, and I didn't like it much. Not that the city isn't run capably; it is. And most of the women seem fairly content when they aren't dreading the night. But there's absolutely no mental stimulation at all. Nobody disagrees, because they all think the same on almost every subject. Sometimes they sound like parrots, especially when they blame all their troubles on the male wizards."

"Do you disagree with that?"

Serena crossed her arms beneath her breasts and sighed. "In a way I do. Oh, the males were unquestionably bastards when they encouraged the rape of female wizards and when they refused to allow the females to have at least a mountain of their own to get above the Curtain. And their practices of *owning* powerless women and murdering their female infants hardly qualify them to be members of the human race."

Merlin smiled slightly. "But?"

"But . . . the women in Sanctuary aren't even *trying* to do anything about their situation. They stick close to the city and go on with their lives day to day. If you ask them, they tell you how rotten the males are, but some of them have never spoken to a man—powerless or wizard—in their entire lives. And as far as I could tell, no female wizard has tried to climb one of the mountains in years. I'll bet the male wizards don't even bother to guard them anymore."

"They don't," Merlin confirmed. "According to what Tremayne told me, they haven't had to worry about that in ten years or more."

Serena shook her head. "That figures. I asked one of the women why somebody didn't try, and she looked at me like I was crazy. The female wizards don't *think* beyond what they've been told, never questioning, never even considering that it might be possible to find a way to coexist with the males. Even though it was done here once."

"Yes, I know. I heard about this city from Tremayne."

"Is that why you're here?"

He nodded. "I wanted to take a look at it before I returned to Sanctuary, and when I saw Varian, I decided to follow him. He hadn't said anything about coming down to the valley when Tremayne and I left this morning."

"Where's Tremayne?"

"He was going straight to Sanctuary." Merlin hesitated, then said, "He wanted to see Roxanne."

"They *know* each other?"

"She didn't tell you about it?"

"No ..." Serena frowned. "But now that I think about it, if she's interested in Tremayne—in spite of what happened to her *and* all they've tried to drum into her in Sanctuary—that could explain why she asked so many questions about you and me, especially after she figured out I was a wizard." She briefly explained Roxanne's deductions.

"And she seemed most interested in our relationship?"

Since he had asked the question coolly, Serena replied in the most unruffled tone she could manage. "I think so. The fact that we were together in any sense of the word obviously intrigued her, and she specifically asked if you'd ever hurt me."

"I hope you told her I hadn't."

"Of course I did." Serena didn't remind him that he had come close to hurting her here, although she couldn't help remembering it. She hesitated, then added, "I also told her there was a wall between us."

"Is that the way you see it?"

"Don't you? You told me there were boundaries we couldn't cross, and what's happened here makes it obvious what you meant, I think. When you left Sanctuary a few days ago, you didn't believe male and female wizards could coexist. Has something happened to convince you otherwise?"

Merlin looked at her for a moment, then shrugged off his light pack and dropped it beside the flat stone where Serena had sat earlier. He took his coat off, as well, and tossed it over the stone. It was a warm day, but Serena didn't know if he had removed the coat because of that or in a gesture like rolling up his sleeves. He wasn't wearing his staff, and she thought he'd probably sent it into limbo until it was needed for the sake of convenience.

Answering her question obliquely, he said, "I told Tremayne what had happened to Roxanne after it became obvious to me that he was very interested in her. He wants her to go with him when he leaves here."

From that response Serena gathered two things. The first was that Merlin was, for the moment at least, going to ignore how her question related to them personally. The second was that he had decided Tremayne was indeed the witness who would record the destruction of Atlantis for the future society of wizards.

Following his lead, she said, "How did he take it when you told him she was attacked?"

"He was furious enough to want to kill the men who attacked her; that was obvious. I was half afraid he'd blame her, but he didn't. He has an unusually compassionate nature for a man, or wizard, of this time."

"So you really did change history when you saved Roxanne's life, didn't you?"

Merlin shook his head. "There's no way to be sure of that, not until we return to our time. There are so many variables that could affect the outcome. Not the least of which is that Roxanne can still reject Tremayne, which would certainly leave him bitter and very likely to give his father and the other Elders on the Council of this time a negative report on what's happened here."

"What if she doesn't reject him?"

"If she doesn't reject him . . . if they're able to overcome the beliefs, prejudices, and fears to which they've both been exposed for most of their lives and create a positive relationship for themselves, then his report would probably be far less harsh and certainly wouldn't advise so drastic a step as destroying all women of power. If she leaves Atlantis with him, the future of our kind is likely to be very different."

"But we can't know for sure until we step back through the gate."

"No, we can't."

Serena thought about it for a moment. "Do you think we should do anything else to try and change the future? I mean, have you decided that the best chance of changing what's wrong in our present without screwing up everything else in our time is to help

Tremayne and Roxanne overcome their doubts and wariness so they can leave here together?"

"It makes sense, I think. One person—if it's the right one, that is—can make a small but very critical decision that changes everything. I believe Tremayne is honest and fair-minded enough to be that voice."

"So you told him about Roxanne's being attacked, and he went rushing right over to comfort her?"

Ignoring her mild sarcasm, he said, "I told him about Roxanne. And I told him that even though it's against our very nature to allow anyone—*anyone*—to get close to us, we have to overcome that flaw."

"We?"

"Serena, I don't have all the answers. I can't tell you that the past few days resolved all my doubts or changed me in some fundamental way."

"But?" A dull ache between her shoulder blades told Serena she was standing too stiffly, too tensely, but she couldn't seem to make herself relax. This was too important, too vital to her happiness.

Merlin spoke slowly, as if feeling his way through a mine field. "But seeing what happened here, seeing the waste of lives and energies, the destruction of the powerless people and the death of Atlantis . . . I know I don't want any part of me to come from the wizards here, what they were and what they did. I know I don't want to be so closed and guarded that there's no room in my life for anyone else. No room for you. I don't want there to be any walls between us, Serena. Or boundaries we're afraid to cross. I know that."

ELEVEN

"Does knowing make a difference?" Serena kept her voice matter-of-fact with an effort. "You still don't trust me. I can feel it."

"Do you trust me? Now, after knowing why we're here and what I'm capable of doing to you? You were afraid of me a few days ago, Serena—are you now?"

She wanted to back off, to fence with words and avoid the emotions clawing inside her because they were so painful and disturbing, but she fought against the urge. All around them lay a ruined city, a doomed society, and a dying land; she was no more willing than Merlin to allow herself to be poisoned by what was happening here.

"Not afraid," she denied at last. "But wary. And I do trust you, Richard, in so many ways . . . just not in all the unthinking ways I used to trust you."

Merlin was a little surprised that it hurt so much to hear her say that. "I see."

"I wonder if you do. You didn't answer me; does knowing make a difference? Maybe you don't want to be closed and guarded . . . but you *are*. Maybe this place and what's happening here sickens you, but you still see and feel the boundaries created by what happened here millennia before you were born. I'm a woman and a wizard—and all your instincts tell you that's wrong, unnatural, something to loathe and fear. We both know that. And knowing it doesn't change a damned thing."

He drew a short breath and let it out, wishing she weren't right. "What do you want me to say, Serena?"

She took a jerky step toward him, her arms still crossed defensively. "It isn't enough to define the problem. Change it, Richard. Fix it. Heal the wound the way you healed Roxanne's, the way you mended my broken wrist when I was sixteen." Completely beyond her ability to halt it, a hot tear slipped from the corner of one eye and trickled down her cheek. "Make it all right again, please," she whispered.

Merlin slowly closed the distance between them and pulled her into his arms. He didn't think about what he was doing even to realize he'd never done it before; all he knew was that her aching plea almost broke his heart. It reached inside him, past all the stubborn boundaries, deeper than instinct, and touched a part of him intended by all the beliefs and laws of his kind to lie forever dormant.

In all his life no one had ever looked at him as Serena did, expecting only the best from him and believing he was capable of near perfection. Her confidence in him had often disconcerted him and more than once had given him a sleepless night; and when he had fallen from the pedestal on which she had placed him, the landing had been brutal. Yet, even after he had disillusioned her by behaving as an all too human male, and even after she'd been frightened by the knowledge that he could destroy her, she still possessed an innocent and touching faith in his ability to repair whatever was broken in her life.

And, Christ, he didn't want to destroy that. . . .

He held her close, his head bent and his cheek pressed to her silky hair. "I wish it was that easy," he told her reluctantly in a low, husky voice. "But a wizard's power can't heal his own wounds, correct his own flaws; you know that. What's wrong with me can't be fixed by me with a simple spell or a wave of my staff, no matter how much I want it to happen."

"Then let me try to heal you." Her arms crept around his waist as her tense body relaxed against him, and her cheek rubbed gently just above his heart. "Give me a chance to try, please. Let me be close to you. Let me in, Richard."

It occurred to him as he held her that their only chance might well be Serena's virtually untried ability to heal. Though his intellect would allow him to consider the possibility of their being involved as a man and woman, the taboo stamped in his very genes set up a potent emotional conflict he had little chance of winning—not without years of struggle. In any case the end would likely be meaningless because he was sure Serena would have left him by then.

If he could overcome his mistrust now to the point of allowing her close to him, then perhaps she *could* correct the flaws and wounds his ancestors had inflicted on him and in so doing make him whole. Perhaps . . .

But could he allow her close? She was close to him now, warm against him, soft and yet strong, the scent of her hair and skin going to his head like fine wine. Had they been this close before? No. Not this close. And the urge to comfort was changing into something far more elemental.

The banked desire he had felt for years flared up inside him, and the instant he admitted to himself that he wanted her, he could feel something in him trying to draw back, to pull away from her almost in horror, attempting to close itself off in safety. The instinctive withdrawal was overwhelming, but he struggled against it, trying to master the clamorings of a taboo he wanted no part of.

She was Serena, for nine years a central part of his life, and there was nothing wrong with how he felt about her, he told that wary part of himself fiercely. Nothing. She was no danger to him, no threat. She took nothing away from him, didn't make him less than he was; she added to his life, to himself. He had risked everything to come back in time because he couldn't bear to hurt her, to lose her, and surely the seeds of trust could be found in that. . . .

"Richard." She raised her head to look up at him with shadowed green eyes. "Just tell me you're willing to try. Tell me I'm not alone in believing we're more than Master and Apprentice. Tell me that what I feel isn't wrong."

He lifted one hand to cup her cheek, his thumb stroking satiny skin and slightly brushing the curve of her lower lip. Had he always known her eyes were bottomless? He thought he could lose himself in them, a terrifying, seductive notion. "What do you feel, Serena?" he asked, his voice hushed.

Her long lashes quivered a bit, not veiling her brilliant eyes but betraying a pang of vulnerability, and her mouth twisted a little in painful self-mockery. "I . . . oh, hell, you have to know exactly what I feel. It's not like I can hide it from you even if you *can't* read my mind—"

Merlin bent his head and touched her lips with his. It was a careful, tentative kiss, very gentle and so fleeting that when it ended, Serena looked as if she wasn't certain it had happened at all. "Tell me," he murmured.

It took a tremendous effort for Serena to stop staring at his mouth, but when she met the liquid blackness of his eyes, it was like being kissed again—this time with all the heat and intensity she could see burning in him. Beyond any ability to lie or evade the subject, she whispered, "I love you. I've always loved you. And I've always been afraid you'd send me away if you knew. . . ."

"I would have. Once I would have." He was bending his head again as he spoke, covering her mouth this time with more certainty and a sudden hunger.

Serena was instantly caught up in the almost shocking whirl of sensations. His mouth, smooth and cool against hers, then warming, hardening as hers opened to him eagerly. His body, unyielding and powerful, muscles solid under her touch, his heart like a drum against her. The aching of her breasts longing for his touch, and the hollow feeling of wanting deep inside her. The tremors rippling through her and the faint shudders with which his body answered. The burning she could feel, a surging heat in him and in her that was a stunningly powerful need.

For the first time in her life, Serena felt the sharp, mindless compulsion of her body's urgent passion. She had thought herself rather cool, uninterested in and unmoved by the desire of men who had wanted her, but Merlin's desire ignited her own as a torch lit dry timber. She wanted him so wildly, so desperately, that to think of anything except satisfying her desire required incredible effort.

She made the effort because she had to. Even as she responded eagerly to his passion, Serena fought the compulsion to melt against him, to give herself up completely to the astonishing need spiraling inside her; a new voice of wisdom in her head warned that this was only a first step for them. The conflict inside Merlin was far from over; even now, in this moment of closeness, she could feel something in him trying to pull away or push her away. The fact that he could hold her and kiss her with passion was definite evidence of his struggle, but not of his triumph over it.

We have to be careful. God, we have to be so careful. If we move too fast . . .

Every instinct Serena could lay claim to insisted that if they gave in to this suddenly unleashed, intense desire for each other and became lovers before the conflict inside him had been resolved, the price they would pay would be incalculable pain. She would have to bear the devastating knowledge that he could offer her nothing of himself wholeheartedly, and he would find himself bound forever by the heavy, anguished links of a chain his ancestors had forged out of fear.

She didn't think about how he had responded to her admission of love, simply because she had expected nothing else from him. He was literally incapable of loving her in return, at least for now, and she knew it. Only time would tell if it would ever be possible.

Though it took every ounce of willpower and resolve she could command, she managed to control her desire for him, and she knew he could feel her restraint. When he raised his head at last, she struggled to listen to the wise voice in her head rather than the clamoring demands of her body, and smiled up at him a little wryly. "I really didn't hide it very well, did I?" she asked him huskily.

"I didn't know." His voice was a little hoarse, and his liquid eyes were burning like black fire.

"Maybe you just didn't want to know."

"Maybe." He smiled down at her, but there was a sharpened look of strain and tension in his lean face. His hand had slid underneath the weight of her netted hair when he kissed her, and now his fingers stroked her sensitive nape almost compulsively. "If I had known, it would have forced me to do something I didn't want to do."

"Send me away?"

Merlin nodded. "I wouldn't have had a choice. Not then. Not back in Seattle with things the way they were."

Serena managed another smile. "Then I'm very glad you didn't know. At least now we have a chance. Don't we?"

"I hope so. Serena, I can't lie to you. I—"

She reached up and touched his mouth gently, stopping him. "It's all right. I don't want lies, Richard, only the truth. As long as you're honest with me, I can bear whatever happens." Touching him was like becoming addicted to a powerful drug, she realized, forcing herself to take her hands off him and move half a step back.

"I don't want to let go of you," he murmured, one hand on her shoulder and the other still curved around her neck.

The husky note of longing in his deep voice almost yanked her back against him, but Serena managed to hang on to her resolve somehow. "The sun'll go down in a couple of hours," she reminded him a bit unsteadily. "If we're going to stay in the valley, we should make camp before the Curtain falls."

Merlin hesitated, then glanced up at the nearest mountain. "We have time to get up there, and I can hide our presence from whatever male wizards live on that mountain. By now you must need a break from the Curtain."

"It has made life uncomfortable," Serena admitted with forced lightness.

"Then we'll spend the night up there."

"Good." When his hands left her reluctantly, Serena added somewhat dryly, "You can tell me about that blond."

"What blond?"

She accepted his puzzlement as genuine, but had no intention of allowing the subject to drop—not when it had hovered in the back of her mind despite everything that had happened since. "The blond you were with the night my mind decided to inhabit yours," she reminded him.

"Oh. That blond."

Confronted with the incident a second time, Merlin didn't stiffen or take refuge in offended anger, as he had the first time, back in Seattle. Instead he seemed to Serena definitely uncomfortable and a bit defensive, and he settled his shoulders in an odd motion, as if bracing himself against some anticipated blow.

"You didn't think I had forgotten?"

Merlin smiled suddenly and turned away to retrieve his coat and backpack. "No, I didn't think that. You've always had a talent for remembering—even what it would have suited me better for you to forget."

Serena watched him shrug into the coat and thought again how regal it made him look. "All things considered," she said, "I think I have a right to ask. Now."

He looked at her seriously. "Yes, you do. Let's get up above the level of the Curtain and make camp for the night, and I'll tell you all about it. Fair enough?"

Nodding, Serena said, "Fair enough." She could only hope that his answer was bearable, especially after her claim that the truth was something she could stand.

From his position on what had once been the wide terrace of a large private home in the Old City, Varian watched the couple gather their things and start winding their way through the ruins heading north. Shielded from their awareness by distance and his ability to hide himself, he had watched them throughout what appeared to be a tense discussion that had culminated in a curiously restrained yet obviously intense embrace.

Surprised when nothing but kisses came of the interlude, Varian frowned. They were an odd couple and no mistake. If *he* had been days away from his only concubine and had not eased himself with any other bitch during that time, he certainly would have ridden her within moments of returning to her. Merlin's control, though admirable, seemed somewhat excessive.

And where were they off to now? The northern mountain was inhabited by a number of male wizards, though it belonged chiefly to Justin, Sinclair, and Linus—none of whom was observant enough to take note of strangers on their property unless a red flag was waved in their faces. Varian didn't doubt the wizard of Seattle and his concubine would be able to spend the night undisturbed on the mountain.

Varian looked toward the setting sun and calculated that the Curtain was no more than a couple of hours away. So *that* was why Merlin had postponed a more lustful reunion with his bitch; he wanted to get above the Curtain, where a full night of passion was possible. The logic was clear, and Merlin's deferral of sex was much more understandable to Varian once he reached that conclusion.

He didn't follow the couple, but leaned against the remains of what had once been a fine balustrade and stared after them broodingly. A redhead. Even more, a beautiful redhead with spirit, her body as strong as it was ripe and her green eyes full of life and intelligence. Her coloring and striking beauty were certainly rare enough to invite comment, but that vibrancy was even more singular, and it had ignited a smoldering fire in his loins. He wanted her.

Merlin said she wasn't for sale, and he'd made it plain he meant it, so Varian didn't even consider the possibility of changing the other wizard's mind. No, he would have to deal with the matter a little less directly and simply take what he wanted by trickery—or thievery. It wouldn't be the first time Varian had stolen a desired concubine from under the very nose of her Lord.

But his wariness of Merlin had, if anything, increased after their brief and civilized skirmish over ownership of the redheaded bitch. There was iron in the younger wizard, and Varian sensed that Merlin's reserve of power was far greater than he was willing to reveal. So he would have to be very careful and clever if he was to be successful in carrying the redhead off to his own mountain and the stronghold of his palace—where Merlin would not dare to come after her, not if he valued his life.

There were many benefits to having sired so many sons, not the least of which was the protection they provided. Varian had lost several sons over the years when they had stepped between their father and his enemies just as dutiful sons should—and if Merlin was rash enough to come after his redhead, he would have to fight his way through as many of Varian's sons as were required to destroy him.

Varian glanced at the setting sun and briefly debated. When he began moving through the ruins, it wasn't toward the south and his own mountain, but toward the north.

"So it *was* a bordello," Serena said.

"I didn't say that."

"Oh, no?" Serena leaned against the log that provided a backrest for her and gazed across their small fire at Merlin. "Maybe you have another word for it. You described a house where carefully selected women— barren, powerless, and apparently a little dense, since they never ask awkward questions—are kept in comparative luxury and paid a generous fee for the sole purpose of servicing the men who occasionally visit the house."

After a long silence Merlin sighed. "All right, it's a bordello. But that isn't how I thought of it."

Shrewdly Serena said, "I get the feeling you didn't think very much about it at all."

"I didn't." He shrugged, gazing into the fire. "It was simply part of being a wizard, Serena, a practice as traditional and matter-of-fact in my life as spell-casting or conjuring. It simply wasn't one of the things in my life that required thought."

Keeping her voice neutral with some difficulty, Serena said, "So your ancestors didn't demand celibacy as a law despite their fear of women of power and their wariness of powerless women. They simply arranged matters so that you all could have sex when you wanted it with the least threatening women they could find."

"Males have rarely accepted celibacy as a way of life. You know that. Only religion seems a historically acceptable reason to forgo sex, and the jury's still out on just how successful that's been." Merlin shrugged. "My ancestors were afraid, but clearly not so terrified that they elected to go without one of life's pleasures. So, as you say, they arranged matters to provide reasonable access to 'safe' women. The practice is virtually the same now as it was in ancient times. There are . . . houses scattered all over the world."

"Where's the one you go to?"

He raised his eyes to meet hers across the flames. "Northern California."

"So far from Seattle? I'm surprised you haven't made more convenient arrangements."

"Serena, I'm sorry this upsets you, but you *did* ask. I'm trying to be honest about it."

He was right, and Serena knew it. She got a grip on the painful emotions and struggled to keep the hurt and dismay out of her voice. "Yes, I know. Forgive me, it's just . . . it sounds so damned cold-blooded."

Evenly Merlin said, "Knowing what I do now, I agree, but until we came here, I had no idea where or why the practice had originated among wizards because I never questioned it. Try to understand how I was raised, please. I was taught to always be in control, to waste as little energy as possible on unnecessary emotions and needless complications. To take care of my physical needs as efficiently as possible *in the way that had always been accomplished*."

It was chilling to hear him explain what sounded like a horrible upbringing, and Serena had to remind herself that there were prices, as well as rewards, for being a wizard. "So it seemed normal to you to travel to northern California whenever you needed sex and spend a few hours with some woman you knew only in the biblical sense."

"So normal I never thought twice about it. At least . . ." He hesitated, then continued quietly. "These last years my visits to the house became less and less . . . satisfying even as they became more frequent. Sex had always been no more than a physical release, never touching my emotions and hardly causing a ripple in my life, but lately even that was a fleeting pleasure that did little to drain the tension I felt."

"Why was that?" Serena was trying hard to match his dispassionate tone.

"I didn't know why, not then. Not until that night, when your consciousness slipped into mine. I felt your shock and your pain, and it forced me to think about what I was doing."

"I'm glad something positive came out of it," she muttered almost to herself. "I practically wrecked my room when I came back to myself."

"You always were very . . . intense in your emotions, Serena. Maybe that was why your feelings affected me so profoundly that night. You made me realize the wrongness of what I was doing. Not the act itself, but the fact that I was having sex with another woman . . . when you were the one I really wanted."

"You hid it very well," she managed. "Before then— and when you came home after that night."

"I had to. Everything inside me insisted it was wrong for me to feel anything for you, especially desire."

Serena pulled her gaze from his intent one and looked out over the valley. The Curtain was a glimmering blanket lying heavily over the dark valley below, and she gratefully drew a deep breath of the clear, crisp air. It was a relief to escape the smothering nightly exhaustion she had endured in Sanctuary.

"Have I answered all your questions, Serena?"

"About the blond? I suppose." She didn't look at him. "You really didn't feel anything for her, did you? Or for the others over the years."

"No."

"I almost wish you had."

"I know."

Serena looked at him finally, finding his firelit face drawn and grim. She could feel his tension, and he still had that braced stiffness of a man awaiting a blow of some kind. Hesitantly but truthfully she said, "Sometimes I had the sense there was something lacking in you, something missing, but I didn't want to believe it."

"Now you know it's true." Merlin's brief smile didn't touch his eyes. "God forgive me, I never felt very much about anyone in my life until you came along. I even treated both my parents with the distant courtesy of strangers. Perhaps I can one day make amends with my father—if he permits it, of course, and he probably won't—but I'll never have the chance to tell my mother how sorry I am that I wasn't a better son."

Serena got to her feet and went around the fire to kneel beside him. She felt a bit diffident, but since he seemed willing to talk, she had to take advantage of the opportunity. The only way she could get close to him was to make the attempt. "This isolation you're describing—it's more than a taboo against women, isn't it?"

Recalling his discussion with Tremayne, Merlin nodded. He turned slightly to face Serena, wishing she didn't look so alluring in the firelight. Just the sight of her caught at his breathing and made his heart beat faster. It was difficult to think, especially when he remembered so vividly how her erotic lips felt under his, but he wasn't willing to do anything to risk disturbing this interlude of honesty.

"Wizards have always been solitary creatures, holding others at a distance emotionally. In our time it's especially true; all the other wizards I know are nearly emotionless, and I . . . I'm not much better." He shrugged. "Perhaps it's because power is such a dangerous thing and ours can escape us if we aren't careful, or because so much of what we are is inside us and has to be controlled so strictly. Whatever the reason, our inward gaze makes it all but impossible to reach out to others. And when we do, the contact tends to be very shallow, casual, and more than a little dispassionate."

Frowning, she said, "We never see ourselves clearly, but I don't think I'm like that. Am I?"

"No, you aren't. You reach out to others easily and often, Serena; that's obvious from the number of friends you have in Seattle."

"Then why am I different? I'm a wizard, too."

"Judging by what we've observed here, being a woman may have something to do with it. The female wizards here seem more able to accept friendships and are less wary with each other than the males I've encountered." He remembered Varian's seemingly endless number of sons, all of whom had displayed loyalty to, and fear of, their father but had clearly viewed one another with a strong suspicion despite being related by blood. *There* was a revolt just waiting for the right moment, Merlin thought, then brushed the memory aside to concentrate on answering Serena's question.

"But I believe there's another reason, as well. The first sixteen years of your life weren't influenced by the formal, rigid training that I and most other wizards of our time were expected to endure. By the time you came to me, much of your personality was already set, unaffected by ancient laws or beliefs and restrained by nothing except your innate self-control."

He smiled slightly. "You were like a breath of fresh air in my life, Serena. You were willing to work hard and wanted with every fiber of your being to be a wizard—yet at the same time you had no intention of being *only* a wizard. You questioned the rules and turned many of the ancient customs upside down, and generally maddened me. However emotionless I'd been trained to be, my composure was attacked on all sides by your intensity and enthusiasm."

She couldn't help smiling back at him. "Should I apologize for that?"

"No." Seriously he added, "It will no doubt take you longer to reach your full potential as a wizard than it would have if you had begun the training as a child, but in the end you'll be a much better wizard than I am in many ways. You have the gift of humanity, Serena, and that's something no amount of learning or training can produce."

She wanted to cry suddenly, but managed to sniff back the tendency. Seeing Merlin in this new and definitely more vulnerable light was both unnerving and moving; he knew there was something lacking in him, something she possessed in abundance, and he was willing to be honest about that with her. She hadn't dared to hope he would let her in like this. Before she could speak, he went on quietly.

"If you hadn't come into my life, I would probably never have noticed anything missing. But you did. And while I tried to teach you how to be a wizard, you taught me about things I hadn't even realized I needed to know."

What could she say to that? A bit unsteadily she murmured, "I usually felt terribly ignorant and frustrated when I couldn't do the things that seemed to come so easy to you."

"I know." He reached over and touched her cheek lightly, just a fleeting contact, and the hard, firelit planes and angles of his face seemed to soften. "But if you only knew how astonishing you've always seemed to me. Serena, you're impatient and emotional and sometimes wildly erratic, and you haven't been in training even half your life—yet your accomplishments are nothing short of incredible. You're going to be a Master wizard, probably seventh degree, and if it takes you a little longer to achieve that level, the difference will be that when you get there, you'll be complete. Whole. With nothing lacking."

Serena drew a breath, surprised by the tribute. "I never knew what you thought about my abilities."

"No. I kept my beliefs to myself. If you had known, you would have tried to use them against me."

She started to object, but her indignation was short-lived. "I probably would have at that," she admitted somewhat ruefully. "It always was hell trying to get my way when you were opposed to something I wanted to do."

"If it's any comfort, your attempts were always charming rather than petulant, and I consider it a character-building exercise that I was able to withstand you."

His dry tone made her laugh, but it was a brief sound of amusement. All during the conversation she had been trying to figure out what was wrong. He was being astonishingly open and honest with her, which definitely gave her hope, and yet he was still restrained—not guarded exactly, but as if he was waiting for something unpleasant to happen. Serena was almost sure it wasn't because he had to fight to make himself drop his guard with her. This was something else.

"Richard, what's the matter? I mean, I'm glad we can be so honest with each other finally, but . . . what is it you *aren't* telling me? Why are you so tense?"

He turned his head to gaze into the fire, avoiding her eyes, and countered her question with careful words of his own. "Down in the ruins I felt you pull back, and I could see the restraint in your eyes. The reluctance. Then you asked about the blond as if she'd been on your mind all along, and it seemed to me you were horrified by what you heard when I answered your questions. So I can't help wondering if . . . anything . . . has changed for you."

"Did you think it would?"

"It crossed my mind." His lips twisted slightly, and he continued to gaze into the fire.

Serena stared at his profile, aware that his tension was greater now. But he had surprised her, and it took her a moment or so to find her voice. "Do you really believe love is so fragile? Richard, if finding out you have the ability to take away my powers wasn't enough to change how I feel about you, how could anything else do it?"

He looked at her finally, and his face was still, unexpressive. But there was a hint, just a hint, of vulnerability in his eyes.

Instinctively she reached out, taking one of his hands in both of hers because she needed to touch him. "When you explained who that blond woman was, what I mostly felt was jealousy," she admitted. "That's how I've felt about her all along. Finding out she's a . . . a paid bedmate didn't really change that." She paused, then added deliberately, "Of course, if you go back to her, I'll cut your liver out."

Merlin smiled slightly. "Will you?"

"Yes. Or do my best to turn you into a toad. And we won't even discuss what I'll do to *her*. Remember those intense emotions of mine."

His long fingers twined with hers. "Thanks for the warning."

"Don't mention it." Serena kept her voice grave. "As for what happened in the ruins, I pulled back—*very* reluctantly—because I thought we were rushing things a bit. And because you were still struggling against that damned taboo."

"You felt that?"

She lifted his hand quickly and brushed her lips across his knuckles in a fleeting caress. "I could almost see it. Richard, what we need isn't more time—we've had plenty of that in every sense of the word—but more understanding of each other, and more willingness to be honest like this. If we become lovers before we're ready to be, I think it'll destroy us both."

He nodded. "You're saying that what we're really lacking is trust, aren't you? At least . . . trust on my part."

Serena hesitated, but only briefly. "In all trust lies the possibility of betrayal. We put ourselves at risk when we care about someone, because we trust them not to hurt us. Not to betray our confidence in them." She took a quick breath and let it out slowly. "For a while—not very long—my trust in you was put to the test. I found out what you *could* do to me, and it was terrifying, especially when I heard so many tales of how brutal the male wizards here were. But it was relatively easy for me to hold on to my trust in you, Richard, because you had never hurt me and because you had gone to the extraordinary lengths of traveling back in time to try and change history so you wouldn't have to take my powers."

"You don't fear I'll betray you?"

"No. But even if I were afraid of that possibility, I'd still trust you. I'd take the risk. I don't have the luxury of doing anything else. A part of falling in love with you is being vulnerable." She hesitated, then added quietly, "Don't you see, Richard? You wouldn't have to take my powers as a wizard to destroy me. You can do that as a man. It wouldn't be hard at all."

In the firelight her green eyes were mysterious pools, dark and bottomless. He thought again of how seductive the notion was of losing himself in them—and this time there was no fear of the idea. He leaned toward her, and her erotic lips were soft and silky and warm under his. He kept his eyes just barely open, and through her lashes he could see the gleam of her eyes.

The kiss was not brief, but it was more tender than passionate, careful and sweet.

When he finally eased back, Merlin tried to control a voice that insisted on emerging huskily. "It would be impossible, Serena. I don't ever want to hurt you. And more than I've ever wanted anything in my life, I want to trust you."

She smiled at him. "Then that's enough for now. We'll find the rest, I know we will."

Merlin hoped she was right; he didn't know how much more of this he could stand. For a man who had been virtually isolated and unemotional for most of his life, he was certainly making up for the lack now.

Serena released his hand reluctantly and said, "I haven't had a decent night's sleep since we got here, so I think I should take advantage of being above the Curtain. If you don't mind . . ."

He gestured slightly, and a comfortable lean-to appeared several feet back from the fire in the shelter of a granite outcropping.

She looked, then returned her gaze to him. "There's only one," she noted neutrally.

"I'm not very sleepy," he told her, wryly conscious of understatement. "If I change my mind, it's easy enough to conjure another or a cushion by the fire. Besides . . . I'm a little apprehensive about Varian. He gave in far too easily, from what I know of him. It wouldn't surprise me if he was somewhere about trying to find you."

Serena had forgotten the other wizard so completely that it took her several moments to remember the acquisitiveness in the eyes that had stripped her naked. "Oh, him," she said finally. "Do you really think he could be watching?"

"No, because I've hidden our camp. If he's near, he won't be able to see us. But I'd rather stay alert for a while just to be sure."

She nodded and climbed to her feet. Then a thought occurred to her, and she gazed down at Merlin with a slight frown. "You said that I'd be a Master wizard one day, and I know that's assuming we *do* change our present and change the attitudes of male wizards in our time—but what about us? When we step back through the gate, won't we be changed, too?"

Merlin shook his head. "No. If we're successful, we will have created a slightly different reality for ourselves, but because we were in *this* time when it happened, we'll remember our lives as we lived them."

"What about other people? The other wizards in our time, let's say. If we're successful, *they* will be different, won't they?"

"Yes, very likely, and they may well have different memories than we do. For instance, since the Council will, presumably, have no ban against females to enforce, they won't remember that I was ever called to explain myself on that topic. But that memory still exists for me because I lived through it."

"So . . . we'll retain our own experiences. But will the other wizards have memories of us that we don't? I mean, say they had a wizard gathering for Christmas or something and we came because I wouldn't have been forbidden. Is that possible?"

"Serena—"

"But we won't remember that because we were *here*. So who was there singing 'We Wish You a Merry Christmas' with all the other cheerful wizards? Our doppelgangers? And are those two impostors banished to some weird twilight zone because we return to our proper time?"

"Stop scaring yourself."

Serena heard herself laugh a little. "It's not hard. Please tell me we don't have doubles."

"We don't have doubles. Serena, you and I have been very isolated from other wizards, and I don't see why that would change even if the society of wizards has. You would still have come looking for me when you were sixteen, and since wizards have always learned their craft with a single Master away from others, I would have trained you virtually the way I did. The other wizards won't remember ever seeing you because they *didn't*—though they'll likely know about you."

"Yeah, but—"

"Remember what we discussed before we left Seattle? The theory is, we can't change *our* pasts because if we did, the reasons we had for coming back in time would no longer exist. Paradox. Satisfied?"

"No. I think there's a hole in there somewhere, but I guess we'll find out when we go back to Seattle." She only hoped she didn't have nightmares. She was halfway to the lean-to when another question caught her interest, but she didn't ask until she was comfortably wrapped in blankets against the night chill and turned on her side to gaze toward the fire and Merlin. "Richard?"

"Hmmm?"

"While we're being so honest with each other . . ."

He turned his head toward her, his profile sharply outlined by the leaping flames. "Yes?"

"How old are you?"

A little chuckle escaped him. "Judging by the questions you asked when you first came to me, quite a bit younger than you think. Wizards aren't ageless, though we do tend to live quite a bit longer than our powerless counterparts."

"You didn't answer the question."

"I'm thirty-six, Serena. Now get some rest."

She was smiling. "All right. Good night."

"Good night. Sleep well."

Serena thought she probably would, even if she *did* dream about doppelgangers.

Disgusted, Varian finally conjured himself a warm fire and hunkered down beside it, wrapping his coat around him for added warmth as the chill of the night increased.

God*damn* that Merlin! The younger wizard had somehow managed to elude Varian despite all his efforts, taking his redheaded bitch and going to ground with her somewhere up here. Not that Varian could blame him for being selfish by keeping her to himself, but it was terribly frustrating nevertheless.

He considered making his way to Justin's palace and spending the rest of the night there, but discarded the thought quickly; he was never at ease around other male wizards except in the fortress of his own palace. He also considered conjuring a shelter for himself, but decided against that, as well, because he preferred not to alert Justin to his presence by expending that amount of energy.

So he was condemned to spending an uncomfortably chilly night up here, an indignity he laid at Merlin's door. Still, he felt a certain amount of respect. The wizard of Seattle was clearly both canny and skilled, and he obviously intended to protect his concubine however it was necessary.

Couldn't blame him for that, either, Varian acknowledged silently. One look at that vibrant red hair, luscious, ripe body, and beautiful face, and most any man would be caught even before he got close enough to meet those snapping green eyes and hear her pleasing voice. . . .

He shifted on the hard ground, suddenly uncomfortable as his manly parts swelled and throbbed and protested the constriction of his trousers. God rot the bitch, just the thought of her was enough to have him randy and ready to ride her! He wanted her, and he intended to have her—no matter how vigilantly Merlin protected her.

In the meantime a long and decidedly chilly night lay ahead of him.

It was just after dawn when Serena woke and crawled out of her lean-to. The fire was still burning, and Merlin was asleep on a pallet nearby, his coat wrapped around him and his lean face peaceful. Serena crept close and knelt down, careful not to disturb him. He was incredibly handsome, she thought, admiring the perfection of his strong features. The liquid dark eyes were hidden from her by thick lashes, but even those were sexy in a way she couldn't define.

Compulsively she reached out a hand and very softly touched his tumbled black hair—and her senses nearly went into overload. Soft, thick, a bit damp from the morning dew. Alive under her fingers. All of him was so alive. Even without his intense black eyes radiating power, his strength was obvious. Serena brushed a curl off his wide forehead and wondered if she could heal him.

The vague thoughts coalesced, and her fingers stilled, lightly touching his hair. Could she heal him? He hadn't said no, she remembered. In fact, he hadn't commented at all when she had asked him to let her try.

The problem was, Serena didn't know *how* to try. This wasn't a relatively simple case of healing a burn or mending a broken bone or sealing a tear in the flesh. Nor was it as exacting as the deft manipulation of a virus. This was something almost abstract. Merlin's wound was emotional, maybe even psychic—as that word pertained to the soul. His deepest instincts had been . . . maimed, his natural responses curbed and re-pressed.

There was no way she could repair all that damage; much of it he would simply have to do himself through the natural course of time and positive experience, the way humans had always cured their inner wounds. But perhaps she could make a start, she thought. Drive a gentle wedge to prop open a door—just a small door, carefully chosen.

She tried to focus, tried to single out one thing on which she could concentrate all her ability, and when she found it, she directed a narrow, careful flow of pos-itive energy and healing wishes.

She *wanted* him to heal, wanted it desperately, and that determination infused the brief stream of energy with a strength that made it even more positive.

Was it successful? Serena didn't know. She sat back on her heels at last and gazed down at him, still sleep-ing deeply, his handsome face relaxed. If she had done it, then the door was open now for him to begin trust-ing her; the inclination toward mistrust that had been seared into his instincts would be softened, blurred a bit, more receptive to his intellect's desire to change. A beginning, no more.

If she had done it.

Serena eased up and away from him, still not want-ing to disturb his sleep. But she was wide awake and restless, and the faint gurgle of a nearby stream (cre-ated by one of the wizards on this mountain, Merlin had noted when they'd climbed up here; the fresh wa-ter was undoubtedly careless runoff from some plea-sure pool higher on the mountain) sounded awfully tempting. The bathing facilities in Sanctuary were ad-equate, though hardly inspiring, and the idea of bath-ing under the brightening sky of Atlantis appealed to Serena.

Why not? With a little luck Merlin would wake up and come looking for her, finding her rising up out of the water like . . . like who? Neptune (or Poseidon) was the malegod of the sea, she remembered, but who was the femalegod? Anyway, she'd be rising out of the water like the femalegod of the sea, all naked and wet and tempting and—and she'd probably be draped with the decidedly unattractive freshwater equivalent of seaweed, because that was just her luck. . . .

Smothering a laugh at her own absurd thoughts, Serena went to take a bath.

TWELVE

Tremayne reached Sanctuary in early afternoon after having parted from Merlin at the base of Varian's mountain hours before. He would normally have volunteered to accompany Merlin—more of a stranger here than himself—to the Old City, but after what he had learned of Roxanne's experience, he was anxious to see her, to try to convince her that he had no intention of harming her in any way. Tremayne hadn't needed Merlin's warning to know she was unlikely to put much trust in any male, even less a wizard, but he was determined to do whatever he could to win her trust. And there was so little time before he had to leave. . . .

He was no more than a hundred yards from the gate and approaching from the southwest when he saw Roxanne pass through it, pause to speak briefly to one of the female wizard Sentinels, and then begin walking due west away from the city. She had a small backpack and used a walking stick nearly as tall as she was, around which her fingers whitened tensely when Tremayne approached her quickly.

She halted, knowing they were within view of the gate and that the Sentinels undoubtedly watched. Oddly, she wasn't afraid of the tall male wizard striding toward her, but her heart pounded erratically and she felt very nervous. She hadn't expected to see him. . . . No, that was wrong. She had been expecting him ever since their last encounter, when he had said those incredible, stunning things she hadn't been able to believe. Something inside her had insisted he would return.

Especially after Serena had told her that Tremayne had invited Merlin to meet his distant kinsman Varian. She wondered dimly if only she among all of them felt this strange sense of fate weaving connections like an inescapable web.

Tremayne stopped several feet away and stared at her with a hunger that was alien to everything she knew and yet awoke sensations in her body she instinctively understood, however much they shocked her. For a moment he seemed unsure what to say. When he did speak, his voice was abrupt but not hard or harsh. "What in hell are you doing leaving the city this late in the day?"

Roxanne lifted her chin and fought inwardly to hold her voice steady. "Sanctuary is not a prison."

"I know that." He was impatient now, frowning, but his eyes were still darkened with more primitive feelings. "But it's afternoon now. You could be caught out here when the Curtain falls and be in danger."

"I know I'll be outside the city tonight, it's unavoidable." She didn't know why she was telling him this. "I have to cross the valley."

"The only thing on the other side of the valley is the village."

"Yes. It is."

"Why do you have to go there?"

Her chin lifted another inch, and the blue eyes flashed. "Not that it's any of your business, but my mother lives there."

Was she being truthful? Or had she given herself enough time to heal from what had been done to her and meant now to find the men who had attacked her? Tremayne hesitated, every instinct warning him not to admit to having knowledge of what had happened to her; if she wanted him to know, she would tell him herself. Before he could say anything, she was going on, her voice soft but not at all weak.

"Wherever I choose to go is my own concern. If you'll excuse me, I have a great deal of ground to cover."

She made as if to walk past him, giving him a wide berth, but Tremayne turned with her and fell into step. "I haven't seen the village yet except from a distance."

Roxanne didn't stop walking or look at him, but her fingers tightened around the walking stick. "I don't believe I invited you to accompany me."

"If I waited for that, I've a feeling I should grow old and crotchety before I heard it," he said a bit dryly.

She nearly smiled, but they had reached the forest, and she knew the Sentinels at the gate would soon lose sight of them. Did she really want to be alone in the valley with this male? Even if he seemed different from the other male wizards, a difference that roused strange feelings inside her, and even if Serena and Merlin's odd relationship made such a thing at least imaginable, could she afford the risk?

A part of her wanted to take the risk; but it was impossible, her mind kept insisting. Even if their trip across the valley was peaceful, he was bound to interfere with what she had to do, and the last thing she wanted was to be forced to fight him.

"Roxanne?"

"I don't need your company," she said carefully, refusing to look at him. He was an arm's length away from her side, yet she was overwhelmingly conscious of him, tall and powerful and a *wizard*. She should be afraid of him, yet she wasn't. . . .

"You will when the Curtain falls," he said matter-of-factly. "If I'm with you when any of the village men see you at night, they'll assume you're my concubine."

"I belong to no man," she said, her intense voice so low, it was almost a whisper.

"I know that, Roxanne. But what's the harm of protecting yourself with a bit of deception? Come, allow me to travel with you, please."

"You ask for too much. I don't know you, but I know what you are, and I have no reason to trust that."

Tremayne was silent for several steps, then said, "At night both of us are unable to use our powers in the valley, and during the day you could injure me as easily as I could injure you; I would say the risk you run in trusting me is a lesser danger than the one you face from the village men. I wish only to be with you, Roxanne. Can't you accept that?"

She was silent.

Still Tremayne felt hopeful. She hadn't said no, after all. He kept his voice easy and neutral. "We should be able to cross the valley and return in two or three days, don't you agree?"

After a moment she said, "That is . . . the usual time it takes for the trip."

He managed not to yell in triumph and was even able to speak calmly. "Good. Is your mother expecting you?"

"No, though I usually try to visit every few weeks." Roxanne felt guilty as soon as she spoke, but the feeling didn't prevent her from lying to him.

"You plan to be in the village only during the day, of course."

"Of course."

Tremayne thought about it for a moment, then frowned. "Your mother is powerless?"

"Yes."

He looked quickly at her delicate profile, finding her expression a bit tense but composed. "Then your father is a wizard?"

Guarded blue eyes met his briefly. "Yes," she replied in a flat little voice. "Though, of course, he knows nothing of my existence. If he had known, I would have been killed at birth like all his other female offspring."

Tremayne felt a sudden shock, a peculiar certainty that might have been psychic. "Roxanne . . . who is your father?"

Her smile was filled with a terrible irony. "Your host and kinsman, Tremayne. Varian is my father."

The male guards and female wizard Sentinels were so astonished when Roxanne walked off with a male wizard that they were drawn several steps away from the gate as they looked after the shocking pair. That was how Kerry was able to slip through the gate and out of the city unnoticed.

On her back she carried a small pack that matched Roxanne's, and she walked with a stick that, also like Roxanne's, was nearly as tall as she was. She managed not to giggle and give her presence away as she snuck out behind the guards and Sentinels, but she was so excited, she could hardly bear it, and nearly danced with delight. In all her eight years, she had never been allowed far enough from the city to lose sight of the gate, and then never alone.

She hadn't been sure she could sneak out when Roxanne left, since children were never allowed out alone, but Tremayne's appearance had provided the distraction that had made her escape possible. And it was an even better game to follow Roxanne when she was with that tall male wizard with the smiling eyes and kind voice. He would tell her more about the sea beyond this valley's mountains; she just knew he would.

And Roxanne wouldn't be *too* awful mad, surely. After all, Kerry could take care of herself. She had a good sense of direction, she knew how to conjure something simple to eat if she got hungry, she was real good at conjuring fresh water for drinking and mirrors from sand, in case one became necessary, and she had Chloe in her backpack for company.

She slipped into the woods slightly north of Sanctuary's walls and made sure the trees screened her from sight of anyone standing near the gate, then she turned west in the general direction the other two had taken and marched on happily, wondering where Roxanne was going.

The morning air was a bit chilly even after the sun came up, but to Serena it felt good. Still, after she'd followed the stream a few yards and found a level place on the mountainside with a wide, deep pool suitable for bathing, she murmured a quick spell to warm the water to near body temperature to make the bath more enjoyable.

She stepped out of her slippers, then unbuckled her loose belt and dropped it to the bank. She wrestled the robe up over her head and tossed it aside with a sigh of relief; even though Merlin had lined the garment in silk, it was still the bane of her existence—heavy, shapeless, and making every move she made look and feel awkward. The white shift was better, though not by much; it, too, was shapeless, but it was thin, light, and rather silky to the touch. In Sanctuary she'd gotten used to sleeping in it. She drew it up over her head and dropped the garment to the ground, baring her body completely to the chilly, damp morning air.

The net confining her hair was quickly and easily unfastened and discarded, and Serena shook out the long, fiery tresses, running her fingers through them and briefly massaging her scalp. Then she stepped down into the warm water, wading out slowly to the center of the pool. There the water was just deep enough so that when she sat on a flat rock she absently conjured for a seat, it covered her breasts and nearly her shoulders.

She tipped her head back and splashed water on her hair until it was thoroughly wet, then conjured a dollop of her favorite shampoo. Even as she lathered her hair, she couldn't help smiling as she remembered how puzzled Merlin had been when she had carefully memorized the chemical composition of the shampoo.

"Why do you want to conjure shampoo?" he'd asked.

"I don't. But you never know when I might," she had answered blithely.

He'd only shaken his head when she had also memorized the chemical compositions of various other things, including conditioner, her favorite soap, and selected perfumes and cosmetics, but Serena was definitely grateful now to vanity or whatever other motive had urged her to do so.

She luxuriated in her large bathtub, washing and conditioning her hair, then stood up to soap her body from head to toe. After that she just sat on her rock, her clean hair floating about her in the warm, fragrant water, while she moved her arms languidly through it and looked around at her surroundings.

Even up here it was ugly. The trees were taller than those down in the valley, but they were twisted and bore leaves of weird shapes and colors. There wasn't much grass, just a blue-green moss that was thick and not attractive, and most of the area was rock. The rising sun painted the stone with faint gleams of iridescent color as it touched bits of quartz and mica, but even that didn't improve them very much.

The raw look of the stone reminded her that it probably *was* new, forced up to the surface as Atlantis twitched and heaved in its death throes. She wondered idly if one of the almost-daily earthquakes would open up a fissure to drain her nice bathtub, and grimaced at the thought. It was a necessary but unwelcome reminder of how unstable this place was. All of a sudden she wanted to go back to their camp and Merlin. But before she could get up, she heard a twig snap nearby, and turned her head slowly as the hair on the back of her neck quivered a warning.

"Well, well, well," Varian said, hands on his hips and feet braced wide as he grinned across the water at her. "Did Merlin roll you around in the dirt instead of providing a decent bed, bitch?"

"My name," she said evenly, "is Serena." The strongest reaction she had to this wizard was disgust and anger at being called a bitch.

He bowed slightly, mockingly, and responded in a hatefully soothing voice. "Serena, then. Shall I join you? It's always nice to have someone to wash your back."

"No, thank you. I would as soon share my bath with a herd of muddy cattle, six pigs, three disturbed skunks, and a few poisonous snakes."

His eyebrows went up, and he laughed. "Such an image of depraved and debauched desires, my sweet."

Serena felt her mouth twist in loathing. Naturally he would put a sexual connotation to whatever she said. Merlin had been right; Varian *was* the most amazingly libidinous creature. A bit fiercely she said, "What I meant is that even filthy, stinking, and poisonous animals would be preferable to you. Would you mind leaving now?"

He was smiling. "I'm going to enjoy taming you, Serena, no matter how long it takes. But you needn't fear—I never abuse my bitches. No, you'll be willing, and when you scream out in pleasure as I ride you, you'll be grateful that I decided to mark you as mine."

Silently Serena lifted one hand and pointed to the small, scarlet heart at the base of her throat, which she was constantly aware of.

Varian shrugged dismissively. "Do you think that's going to stop me?" He made a slight and not very graceful gesture with one hand.

The gurgle of moving water became louder, and Serena looked over to find that the narrow place where her pool spilled over this small basin and continued down the mountainside had been opened up, not by an earthquake but by Varian; the water level was sinking rapidly.

For a moment she considered going on with the charade of powerlessness, but Varian's arrogance made her so mad that all she thought about was taking him down a peg or two. So he thought she was virtually helpless, unable to withstand his powers or his supposed skills as a stud? So he thought she was just going to sit here meekly while the draining water left her naked and exposed to his greedy eyes?

Like hell she would.

Her discarded clothing lay on the bank some feet from Varian, but Serena ignored the garments—she was sick of them anyway. Instead she decided it was time to change her appearance.

Of course, being Serena and being mad as hell, she brought about her transformation with a bit of theatrical flair.

It was a relief to rip away the mask Merlin had so carefully taught her to hide her powers behind, and as she gazed across the water at Varian, she had the distinct pleasure of watching his face drain of color as her power became something he could now sense. She smiled at him gently and performed the impressive trick of altering her environment.

Before the sinking water level exposed her breasts, the pool began to churn and bubble. Within seconds a whirlpool circled Serena, the frothy white water easily hiding her body from Varian's stunned gaze. She conjured a few gusts of wind to blow her loose hair about dramatically, and with slow grandeur she rose from the center of the whirlpool perfectly dry and dressed like no other woman in Atlantis.

Fawn-color trousers, tight enough to cling to every curve, were tucked into knee-high boots. A fawn-color vest that snugly shaped her small waist and generous breasts was belted in place over a full-sleeved blouse, which was tightly cuffed at her wrists, and was silky and pale green. Over it all was a rich fur cloak around her shoulders that was loosely fastened by a thin gold chain with a round emerald on either clasp.

While Varian gaped in shock, Serena strolled across the churning water to the bank several feet away from him. (She'd always wanted to walk on water, but had never gotten the chance.) As soon as she touched land, the pool quieted and continued to drain rapidly down the mountain.

Hands on hips, she faced him with a tiny smile.

"A woman of power," he almost whispered.

Serena mocked him with just the sort of half bow he had used earlier. "That's right. Merlin isn't the only wizard of Seattle, you see—so am I."

"No—you're his property—"

"The hell I am. Where we come from, Varian, women don't belong to men—wizard or powerless."

"You bear his mark."

Before Serena could respond, Merlin's quiet voice sounded behind her.

"To protect her, Varian, in case she was caught outside Sanctuary at night."

Serena turned her head and watched Merlin walk toward her. For a moment she forgot everything except the need to sense if her earlier attempt to heal him had been successful. He looked the same, she thought, though perhaps there was less strain in his features and a certain thoughtful quiet in the liquid darkness of his eyes.

But was there an open door to permit him to heal? She couldn't tell.

He reached her side and looked her up and down deliberately. "Nice outfit."

"Thank you. Sorry about dropping the charade without discussing it first, but this . . . this moronic bastard made me crazy."

"I figured he would eventually," Merlin admitted to her in a rather dry tone, and turned his gaze to the still frozen Varian. Politely he told the older wizard, "She is indeed a woman of power, Varian. A female wizard. A rather talented one, as a matter of fact."

"How is it possible you travel together?" Varian asked in a voice that cracked slightly.

Serena waited for Merlin to answer, curious to know how he would. He had been careful when they'd first arrived, only observing, reluctant to do anything else, including providing information unknown to these people. But she had the feeling that he was now perfectly willing to shock Varian, and she didn't blame him one bit.

Lifting an eyebrow, Merlin feigned puzzlement. "Why would it be impossible? Surely you don't believe Atlantis is the center of the universe, governing the rest of the world in all ways, including customs between men and women? No, Varian, outside this twisted little kingdom of yours is an entirely different world. Serena and I travel together because we wish it. We've been together for years."

"She's your concubine?" Varian demanded hoarsely.

Softly Merlin said, "No. My mate."

Already surprised by the out-of-character way he seemed to be taunting the other wizard, Serena nearly gasped at Merlin's words. She had the odd feeling he meant it, that whatever else he said, that statement was truthful, and she didn't dare look up at him, because she was afraid she wouldn't be able to control her expression.

Luckily, Varian was too shocked himself to notice her wonder. He stood stiffly, staring at them, his armor of arrogance certainly dented—if not split wide open—by this living, breathing impossibility even he, in his wildest sexual fantasies, had seldom considered attainable.

If he had stopped to think at all, he never would have risked himself, but he had the confused impression of a threat they represented to his vision of the world, and it was characteristic of him that he struck out to protect himself, roaring in a kind of dumb animal fury.

The stream of energy that shot from his outstretched hand was white-hot and aimed accurately to strike both Serena and Merlin, a target made easier since they were standing so close to each other. Swifter than thought, both of them lifted a hand, acting instinctively and in concert to block and then repel the destructive energy.

What happened then—should not have. Both Merlin and Varian knew that; Serena had no idea, simply because she had never considered what was likely to happen if the energy stream of two wizards—let alone three—collided, and because she had never been called on to defend herself against another wizard.

What happened was visible to all of them in the heartbeats granted them to ponder. The separate energy streams of Merlin and Serena—his white-hot and hers tinted the searing blue of the base of a flame—met scant inches from their outstretched hands and twined together in an almost sensuous motion, forming a single ropelike shaft of living, writhing power. It sliced through Varian's energy stream like the steel hull of a battleship slicing through water, struck him midchest with an audible *craaack*, and knocked him thirty feet down the mountain slope.

He picked himself up, panting and shocked, one hand covering the seared place on his chest, and stared at the pair of wizards, who looked gravely back at him. After several silent moments he drew his coat closed over the burn on his chest, turned, and hurried down the slope away from them.

Serena looked on either side of her and Merlin to find two seared and smoking trees that had taken the brunt of Varian's deflected energy stream, then looked up at Merlin. "What just happened?" she asked hesitantly.

"Positive and negative," Merlin said softly, more to himself than Serena. "That must be it. When they're combined, the energy stream is more powerful . . . much more powerful." He looked down at her. "Serena, Varian has enough raw power that he should have been able to knock either me or you back a step or two at the very least, but he didn't."

"Because there are two of us?"

"No. If two male wizards had stood here and struck out at Varian, *all three* would have gotten a nasty jolt that probably would have broken off the attack. And if it had just been him and me fighting through the first jolt even against our instincts for self-preservation, we would have eventually drained each other, possibly to the death. But if we'd chosen to stop it at any point, neither of us would have been permanently damaged or even left physically scarred by the battle. *Positive energy*, Serena—no matter how many times or ways you combine it, it always cancels itself out."

She frowned up at him. "So what happened with us? Did we knock him off his feet, and obviously hurt him, because we're a pair? Male and female?"

"Positive and negative. And our energy streams were directed together, so they merged."

"You didn't know my energy had a negative charge?" Then she remembered, and answered the question herself. "Of course not, because you've always been so careful that our energy streams never touched during my lessons or whenever one of us was conjuring. Because of the way it always happened with males, you assumed the same danger existed for us."

Merlin nodded. "I should have realized. It explains how male and female wizards are able to harm each other. If it had been just you and Varian here, you in a temper and him scared half out of his wits, both of you could have been badly injured."

"But we weren't alone. You were here. So he got burned—literally—and maybe he'll think twice next time before he barges in on a lady's bath."

With a slight smile Merlin said, "And maybe he'll think about what he's doing here if he knows the outside world is quite a bit different."

Serena looked up at him gravely. "That's why you taunted him? I wondered."

"I shouldn't have done it," he admitted wryly. "I'm not even sure why I did, except . . . it seemed right, somehow. I seemed to know what I should say to him."

"As if . . . you'd already said it?"

Merlin frowned a little. "A sense of déjà vu? Yes, as a matter of fact, that was what I felt."

Had he felt that way because what he'd said to Varian was what he was *supposed* to say? Because their confrontation, like the destruction of this place, had—to Merlin and Serena, anyway—already happened a long time ago?

It had occurred to Serena to wonder if she and Merlin would in some way contribute to the destruction of Atlantis, an unnerving possibility she had promptly put out of her mind. Now it returned, and she had to wonder. Had it been their fate to be a part of the process that destroyed Atlantis? They couldn't be responsible for everything that happened here, Serena knew, because this had been a dying place long before they arrived. But were they perhaps the catalysts, their presence and actions sparking what would become the final upheaval?

Time travel was a tricky thing, its laws elusive and largely theoretical, so how could they know? Perhaps their being here now was a piece of the puzzle, a part of the reason it all happened as it had.

She didn't ask Merlin, because she wasn't at all sure she wanted to hear his answer; sometimes ignorance was indeed a blessed thing. And she didn't ask him something else, though not for the same reason. She didn't ask him why he'd told Varian that she was his mate. Instead she merely suggested that they have breakfast, take another look at the ruins of the Old City, and then head back toward Sanctuary so they could check on the progress of Roxanne and Tremayne.

That was, after all, their best chance at changing the future, which was why they were here.

"Nearly twenty years ago Varian wasn't so careful," Roxanne said with forced composure. "He hadn't yet developed the habit of taking young powerless women up to his palace and keeping them there so he could control his offspring."

Tremayne watched her across the tiny fire. With their late start in leaving Sanctuary, they had gotten less than halfway across the valley before night and the Curtain fell, so they had made camp in the forest. Tremayne had waited until then to ask about her parentage, because he thought she'd be more willing to talk to him with darkness at their backs and the Curtain draining her resistance.

"So Varian . . . encountered your mother in the village?" he said, keeping his voice neutral.

"No, near the Old City, where she'd gone to pick berries. She didn't fight him, even though she didn't like him at all and was more than a little bit afraid of him. It wouldn't have done her much good to fight, and in any case, she was like all the village girls: simple and submissive. She just did as he commanded. He told her he'd come back for her later and take her up to his palace, but he didn't. When she realized she was going to bear his child, she had to leave the village, because she knew her father would beat her; the last thing he needed was another mouth to feed. So she went to Sanctuary."

"The city must have been new then."

"It was. My mother was welcomed, and I was born there. She knew I was born with power, of course, and she thought I should be raised by wizards. So I was." Roxanne was still astonished that she was telling him all this, astonished she was talking to him *at all;* she didn't understand herself, and tried to blame the Curtain for her singular willingness to confide in him, even though she knew that wasn't it.

The frightening truth was, something about this man drew her out of herself and urged her to trust him, and she seemed helpless to fight it.

"She left you there?" His voice was still carefully dispassionate.

"She wasn't comfortable in the city. It was too new, too strange and different for her. She returned to the village, took the beating her father gave her, and went on with her life."

After a moment Tremayne said, "Would it surprise you to learn that there *are* places in this world where women are valued and treated well by their men?"

Knowing that her bitterness had escaped her, Roxanne gazed across the fire at him and wondered what she had heard in his deep voice. Pain? Whatever it was, it unnerved her. "It's getting late," she said, and eased down on her pallet of blankets, wrapping one around her and making sure her walking stick was near—for all the good it would do if they were to be attacked in the night by village men. But she doubted that would happen. Tremayne had been right; his presence made the night safer for her, since it was unlikely that village men would do anything to anger a male wizard.

"Good night, Roxanne. Sleep well."

She didn't bother to remind him that sleeping well was impossible with the Curtain pressing down on them. Instead she half closed her eyes and watched him through her lashes as he sat silently on his side of the fire, until weariness finally sent her into a fitful sleep.

It was just after dawn when she woke, but she didn't move right away. The fire was still burning, and Tremayne was sleeping on a pallet like hers with his coat wrapped around him. His thin face was innocent, with no sign whatsoever of the duplicity, selfishness, or cruelty she had for so long associated with male wizards, and Roxanne felt very odd as she looked at him.

By the time the sun rose and chased away the Curtain, Tremayne was stirring, and she waited until he sat up before she followed suit.

They didn't talk very much, although he made several attempts at conversation. Roxanne was deeply troubled by the strange feelings he roused in her, and she was also thinking about what she intended to do when she reached the village; the result was confusion and uncertainty on both fronts. She didn't object when he conjured a morning meal for them, and excused herself some time later in order to retreat to a nearby stream—one of the few still unspoiled—and perform her morning ablutions.

Since the sun was up, the almost automatic dread of the night was gone, and Roxanne wasn't nervous or wary. After she'd splashed her face, she conjured a bit of material to use for a towel, and was standing there patting her face dry when a heavy body suddenly burst through the undergrowth on the other side of the narrow stream. To her utter shock she found herself face-to-face with her father for the first time in her life.

She recognized Varian only because he had once been pointed out to her by an older female wizard when they had seen him crossing the road some distance from Sanctuary. Roxanne had been able to hide her distress then, but now she knew her mouth was open and her face was undoubtedly ghost white.

"God's blood, another whore!" he snapped, holding his coat about him with one hand as if chilled, even though his eyes were as hot as burning coals.

In that first seemingly eternal moment, as his crude insult stabbed her, Roxanne looked at her father and realized with certainty that she was no part of him. That he was her sire was nothing more than an accident of chance and circumstance; he'd had no part in raising her, had no knowledge of her other than his recognition that she was a woman of power. She was no more like him than she was like her guileless, pliable mother.

It was the most incredible relief.

"I can't escape you whores," he snarled, glaring at her.

"Stay out of the valley." Roxanne was surprised at how cool her voice was.

He half lifted his free hand, fisted as if he wanted to

strike her, but even before Roxanne could brace herself, he jerked the hand back to his side. "Whore!"

She wondered if he had any idea that the insult lost much of its impact with every repetition. "I'm not standing in your way," she pointed out. "In fact, I'd just as soon not be anywhere around you." She would have gone on, but Tremayne spoke as he joined her by the stream.

"I think that's clear enough, Varian. The lady would like you to leave."

Varian's mouth fell open. "You're with her? *She's* the reason you couldn't stay away from the city?"

Tremayne nodded calmly. "She's the reason. By the way, Varian, I won't be returning to the mountain. Thank you very much for your hospitality—and I'll be sure to give my father your regards when I reach home."

Varian didn't seem to hear him. "It isn't possible. By all the gods, *it isn't possible*! No whore of Atlantia would allow one of us near her. . . ."

It was rather fascinating, Tremayne thought, to see his usually arrogant and cocksure kinsman rattled, but he had no intention of prolonging the encounter, because he didn't want to upset Roxanne. She seemed calm, but since this was undoubtedly the first time she'd actually met her father, it had to be difficult for her.

"Varian, even you can't quarrel with the evidence of your own eyes."

They saw his face go still, his eyes narrow as if at a memory, and the hand clutching his coat tightened. "She'll turn on you, Tremayne," he warned hoarsely. "She'll turn her powers on you sooner or later."

"Why would she? I would never do anything to hurt her," Tremayne responded. "Go back to your mountain, Varian, and live your life just as you wish. My life is my own concern."

Varian seemed ready to say something, but finally uttered only a strangled sound of frustration and stalked past them. Roxanne and Tremayne both turned as the older wizard passed, instinctively avoiding having their backs to him. When he was out of sight and hearing, she looked up at Tremayne.

"You didn't tell him who I was," she said gravely.

"No." Tremayne hesitated, then added, "I can't tell how you feel about it, but I know one thing for certain, Roxanne—it doesn't matter who your father is, because who and what you are has nothing to do with him. It doesn't matter any more than it matters that almost everyone around you believes you and I have to hate and fear each other. All that matters is that you make up your own mind—about who you want to be, and about me. Please. That's all I ask."

She nodded slightly, and said, "He's . . . really not very alarming, is he?"

Tremayne smiled. "Well, in terms of power he's formidable, but he often seems rather like a bully trying to get his way. Is that what you mean?"

Roxanne nodded again, this time more definitely, then straightened her shoulders. "It was a bit like coming face-to-face with the monster in your dreams and discovering it was really only shadows on a wall. Nothing. I'm glad I met him. I'm not afraid of him anymore."

"Good," Tremayne said easily. He hadn't planned on any of what had occurred during this hike, but the results more than satisfied him. "Now, if you're ready, we can continue on across the valley."

"I'm ready," Roxanne said.

Kerry hadn't been close enough to hear what went on when the angry male wizard talked to Roxanne and Tremayne, but when they continued, she followed them a bit closer than she had the day before. Chloe was no longer in her backpack; she held the doll tightly as she walked.

Last night hadn't been quite as fun as Kerry had expected. The Curtain felt even worse out here, and there were sounds she didn't know or like. She had wanted to join Tremayne and Roxanne at their camp when it got dark, but it had gradually occurred to her that maybe they *would* be awfully angry at her, and she hadn't been able to summon the nerve to approach them.

Now, following at a safe distance, she chewed on her bottom lip and wished they'd get wherever they were going. If they still hadn't turned back to Sanctuary by tonight, she thought she might be brave enough then to catch up to them—because she *didn't* think she was brave enough to spend another night alone.

It was midafternoon when Merlin and Serena reached the gates of Sanctuary and braved the two Sentinels, Phaedra and Nola, who stared at Serena in astonishment.

"Yes, I'm a wizard," Serena said cheerfully, deciding to cut to the chase. "I hid my powers before because Merlin and I didn't know what the customs were like here. Does either of you have a problem with that?"

"Serena," Merlin murmured.

"Well, everybody seems to think they have a stake in our relationship, and it's beginning to annoy me."

"You two travel together?" Phaedra demanded in a shocked tone.

"If I had a nickel," Serena said with a sigh.

"What?"

"Never mind. Yes, we travel together. Look, you've already marked Merlin, and Roxanne was granted permission to admit him to her house, so—"

"Roxanne left Sanctuary yesterday," Phaedra said flatly.

"With the wizard Tremayne," Nola added.

"No, she didn't leave *with* him," Phaedra corrected scrupulously. "He was approaching Sanctuary when she left, and turned to accompany her."

Serena looked at Merlin. "That sounds hopeful."

"I'd say so."

They left the two uneasy Sentinels at the gate and continued into the city, where the stares they received ranged from covert to open-mouthed. The citizens of Sanctuary had barely grown accustomed to seeing male-female pairs of any kind; a pair consisting of a male and female wizard was a guaranteed traffic stopper, especially since they were the first to walk the streets of Sanctuary. An earthquake distracted attention from them momentarily, but since the city was left standing (Serena doubted a lesser tragedy than full destruction of Sanctuary would have succeeded as a permanent distraction), they were soon the center of attention once again.

"I say we take refuge in Roxanne's house, at least until you have to leave the city," Serena said. "She told me to make myself at home, and nobody here ever locks their doors, so we shouldn't have a problem."

"I agree." Merlin glanced around them as they walked, and added, "Do you realize we've been here two weeks?"

"It feels more like a lifetime." Serena led the way down the appropriate side street to Roxanne's house, and they found the front door unlocked, as expected. The interior was quiet and cool, and when the door was shut behind them, the sense of privacy was so welcome, it was almost overwhelming.

Serena unfastened her cloak and threw it over a chair, and watched as Merlin shrugged out of his coat. "When did you conjure up your staff? When we reached the city?"

He nodded, removing the staff from his belt and laying it gently on top of his coat. "Since Phaedra specifically asked me about it the first time we entered the city, I decided I'd better keep it with me whenever I'm in or near Sanctuary. I wouldn't do it if I felt I had a choice, though; I think the Curtain is distorting the crystal a bit."

"Yeah, Roxanne told me it warps glass and distorts mirrors after a while, so a crystal would be vulnerable. But it'd take years to mar a crystal, wouldn't it?"

"Probably. I just noticed a very slight change in mine, but since I don't use it for prophesy, I'm not going to worry very much about it."

Serena smiled. "You know, if you *did* use it for prophesy, you might be able to tell us how all this is going to turn out."

"That would be cheating."

She couldn't help laughing, and Merlin smiled back

at the slight absurdity of his decision not to look into the future. "You know what I mean. I've explained to you my feelings about using prophesy as a crutch."

"I know, I know."

"We'll see the future when we get there."

"Right. When we step through the gate you made."

Merlin closed his eyes briefly. "Serena, you have an uncanny knack for making me feel like a fool."

She stepped closer and looked up at him with laughing eyes in a solemn face. "That's never my intention, I promise you."

He wanted to be a great deal closer to her, fool or no fool. He wanted to put his arms around her and hold her tight against him, and feel the warm silk of her mouth alive under his. He wanted *her*, more and more with every passing minute, feeling a hunger for her like nothing he'd ever known.

It hadn't been easy to act casual with her since their passionate embrace the day before, but Merlin had done his best because he still felt the conflict inside himself. It wasn't as strong as it had been—he thought he was finally beginning to make some headway in the clash between instinct and reason—but it existed, and he knew she would see or sense it if he touched her the way he wanted to.

He didn't know what he was going to say, but opened his mouth to say it, and before he could utter a word, they heard a sharp knock on the door.

Two female wizards, both Masters and their staffs tucked into their belts, nodded politely to Serena but kept their cold eyes fixed on Merlin. To Merlin the older of the two said in a brusque voice, "Leader wants to see you. Now."

THIRTEEN

Antonia came as a surprise to Merlin. Her power was considerable—he thought she was probably a seventh- or eighth-degree Master; and her temperament seemed, on first impression, oddly low-key for a woman who had single-handedly founded this city and banded the women of power into a defensive alliance.

"Is Seattle a pleasant place?" She was standing at a window, seemingly relaxed and certainly fairly confident, since they were alone in what appeared to be her office and she'd half turned her back to him.

Merlin hadn't been asked to sit, so he stood near her desk and watched her, all his senses probing. "Pleasant enough," he replied mildly. "By the way, do I address you as Leader or Antonia?"

"Whichever you wish. Is Merlin your single name, or do you prefer another?"

"Merlin will do."

She turned her head a bit to study him, a faint smile curving her lips. "Then tell me, Merlin, is it true that your . . . companion . . . Serena is a woman of power?"

He wasn't surprised that she knew; that news must have spread through the city like wildfire. "Yes, it's true. But if you're concerned that our unique relationship might disturb the status quo you've created here, let me reassure you. Serena and I won't be here much longer."

"No?"

"No. It's nearly time for us to leave."

Antonia turned to face him completely, and as she did, Merlin abruptly felt the full force of her power—and her sexuality. The hairs on the back of his neck actually quivered, and it took every ounce of concentration and willpower he had developed over a lifetime's study to enable him to stand there appearing casual.

Her eyes were strange, he decided, studying the pale blue intensity of them. Her hair was vibrant and silky, her skin milk white and flawless. Her lips were red and moist, parted slightly, erotically. Even shrouded in the shapeless garments of Atlantis, her body was ripe, full, more seductive than any other woman's could ever be. Even the way she stood was sexy, and he could almost feel her heat, smell her scent. . . .

His heart thudding and senses swimming, Merlin belatedly realized what she was doing, and it was a shock. He closed his eyes for a moment and concentrated fiercely on erecting barriers against her. She couldn't read his thoughts, he knew, but she was clearly adept at manipulating his emotions and stirring his senses, and he had the distinctly unpleasant sensation of having been violated.

Serena hadn't made him feel that way when she had slipped into his consciousness, and that had actually been a deeper and more personal intrusion. He thought about that fleetingly, accepting it as yet another indication of how right her presence in his life had become. And then he forced himself to think only of blocking Antonia's power.

His heartbeat slowed to normal, and his senses cleared, ending the dizziness. When he opened his eyes, he saw Antonia's lips twisted in a snarl of fury that instantly reverted to the purely female, seductive smile. Her eyes were like pale blue chips of ice.

"You're very powerful," she murmured.

"So are you."

"And very stubborn, I think."

He smiled. "Wizard or not, I prefer some things to happen naturally, without any artificial . . . enhancement."

"And will it happen, do you think? Do you find me desirable, Merlin?"

Merlin began to understand then how his ancestors could have gazed on an angry and powerful female wizard and decided that life would be safer and simpler without the distaff side of their kind. He knew himself to be standing on very uncertain ground; Antonia might not be powerful enough to kill him, but she could most certainly injure him, and no doubt the two Master wizards she had sent for him and who probably waited outside the door even now would be happy to finish him off.

Obviously she had attempted to seduce him with as little wasted effort as possible, choosing to manipulate his emotions and senses until he saw nothing except a woman he had to have. Clearly she either felt none of the fear of the other female wizards or had overcome her feelings far enough to anticipate, with apparent eagerness, sex with a male—and a wizard at that. What he didn't know was why she was so determined that he be her conquest, and why she had made her move so soon after first setting eyes on him. As if it were something she had decided to attempt long before he had walked into the room.

Why? Had her knowledge of his relationship with Serena so piqued her curiosity that she was eager to experiment and chose him because he was a stranger *and* someone she knew to be already predisposed to consider a sexual relationship with a female wizard? Perhaps . . . but he didn't think that was Antonia's only motivation.

"I find you incredibly beautiful," he answered her gravely, honestly. "But I'm committed to Serena." *Odd how easily those words come. Could I have said them even yesterday? Probably not.*

"Are you always so faithful to your . . . companion?" she asked softly.

The voice was sensual, but Merlin kept his attention on those cold eyes. He knew he had to tread very carefully. All the old adages about a woman scorned didn't even begin to describe what could happen when that woman was a wizard.

Thoughtfully he said, "It's so difficult for men and women of power to trust each other. It took Serena and me years, years of knowing each other, before we could try to get close. That's an achievement I could never deliberately sabotage."

"She wouldn't have to know," Antonia suggested.

"Of course she would." Merlin lifted a rueful eyebrow. "She's a wizard. Antonia, I'm very flattered—and a little puzzled. Why me?"

"I could say it was because you're leaving."

"You could. Would it be true?"

"No. I had intended to ask you to stay. As for why, you seemed the best choice. You see, it's only recently that I seriously explored the possibility of joining with a male." Her eyes narrowed slightly as if in thought, and her hands lifted to rest on her hips in a stance more challenging than seductive. "Merlin, Atlantia must be united, and of all the wizards here I'm the one best able to accomplish that."

He saw the change in her manner, but still sensed her sexuality coming off her in waves, intense and hungry. He kept his guard up. Carefully neutral, he said, "That goal is usually a good one for any society. But why do you need me?"

"Because I can't rule the male wizards here, not alone, not without more power. For years I've thought and studied the problem, all the while trying to keep Sanctuary intact to provide all women a safe place for living—and breeding. I've done everything I could to restore the balance of the population of Atlantia."

Merlin had formed a conviction about one aspect of this city, and though he was taking a chance, he was too curious not to ask. "In the mountains the males kill their female children; here, I'm told, male children born with power always weaken and die. The women here seem to blame a baffling fate, but I think the cause is far more . . . practical. Isn't it? Isn't it all a part of your determination to balance the population, no matter what the cost?"

She stiffened. "That is none of your concern," she snapped.

He had his answer. "No, I suppose not. But if that's true, why are you telling me about your intention of ruling Atlantis? Firstly, it's none of my concern, and secondly, my involvement could hardly make a difference. Could it?"

"Yes, it could." Her eyes were still cold, but they were also sharp and eager. "I've seen the future, Merlin. No one else here has the ability of sight, but I have it. I saw you—with me. I saw our powers joined just as our bodies were joined, and together we were invincible. *I saw it.* We were meant to rule Atlantia together."

Merlin chose his words carefully. "You must have somehow misinterpreted what you saw, Antonia, because I have no intention of ruling anything. I am leaving for Seattle with Serena before the next full moon, as I always intended to do."

Her lovely face hardened, and her lips writhed in that snarl of fury. "You spurn me? *Me?*"

"No, I simply decline your generous offer to rule Atlantis. I'm sorry, Antonia, but it was never one of my ambitions to be a king—even with a lovely queen beside me."

For several moments it seemed doubtful that he'd escape this room without feeling her wrath, but Merlin stood his ground, because his instincts told him to do just that. And it seemed his instincts were right, because she finally relaxed and offered him something like a smile.

"Well, since you wouldn't be much good to me unwilling and I can't seem to break through your guard to change that, it seems I have little choice but to accept your refusal."

He bowed slightly, making sure the gesture held no mockery. "Thank you. But I still say you may have misread what you saw. After all, the male wizards are all very similar in build and coloring."

"Yes, perhaps." She was impatient now, a bit imperious as she attempted to regain her lost face. "In any case the matter no longer concerns you. Good day, Merlin."

Since he'd already pushed his luck a couple of times during the interview, he didn't hesitate now in bowing again and promptly leaving the room. As he'd expected, the two female Master wizards were waiting outside to escort him from Antonia's house, though they went only as far as the street, leaving him to find his way back to Roxanne's house alone.

He glanced up to study the sun, calculating he had no more than an hour before he had to leave the city, and quickened his steps. He thought he'd suggest to Serena that they leave the city together and climb the nearest mountain for the night; he could hide their presence from whichever male wizard the land belonged to, after all, and they could return to Sanctuary in the morning to wait for Roxanne and Tremayne.

After the encounter with Antonia, he had the urge to stay away from this place as much as possible.

He was nearly at Roxanne's house when two sudden realizations stopped him in his tracks. The first was that Antonia might have been Serena's older sister, they looked so much alike; the second was that crystal balls had always been used by wizards for prophesy. Always.

Merlin stood there for a full minute, but then continued on his way to Roxanne's house. After all, it wasn't his place to tell Antonia what she obviously hadn't realized—that the Curtain must have distorted her crystal over the years. It wasn't his place to tell her what her own people had obviously neglected to inform her about Serena's so closely resembling her (because she surely would have commented on it if she'd known). And it certainly wasn't his place to suggest that the woman she had recognized as herself in that vision of the future might well be Serena.

"I saw our powers joined just as our bodies were joined, and together we were invincible."

Had Antonia actually seen Merlin and Serena in that

prophesy of a physical coupling and the merging of powerful positive and negative energies?

He pushed the question away, forcing himself to re-examine his decision not to return to Antonia and tell her what he'd realized. The decision felt right. Besides, he'd seen enough to be sure she wouldn't believe him no matter what he told her. In her determination to rule Atlantis, she had blinded herself to everything but her goal, even to the loathsome extent of slyly causing the male children born in Sanctuary to weaken slowly and die, which made her no better than the ambitious males up in the mountains and possibly worse. At least their infanticide was reputedly quick and efficient.

Serena had been right—as an example of sisterhood, this place came up lacking.

Antonia sat before her crystal, staring fixedly into the shimmering depths. And, again, as she had for weeks now, she saw the same scene. The background was only darkness, so she wasn't sure where it took place, but two people lay together, their naked bodies entwined, obviously making love. They were lying on a bed covered with fur, and firelight flickered over their bodies, so there was apparently a hearth nearby. The man was dark, muscled, powerful; the woman slender and yet seductive, her rich red hair spread out like waves of fire, and the aura surrounding them was literally pulsing with their combined power. . . .

Antonia sensed that she was looking at something truly incredible, and it fascinated her. All that power, she thought, and simply due to a sexual alliance! If she had known years ago that her power could combine with a male's, she would have chosen a consort then and saved herself years of a frustrating standoff in which she governed the women while the male wizards bickered and bred like rats.

Striking the table with a clenched fist, Antonia swore softly, intensely. Why had he refused her? *Why?* She wanted to believe his rejection was momentary, that she would find a way to persuade or seduce him, but she wasn't fool enough to indulge in stupid fantasies.

His power was obvious, and when he had slammed the door to shut her out, she had found no possibility of forcing her way back in again.

No, Merlin was stubbornly attached to his Serena. How sweet. The only bright spot Antonia could find was his assertion that they would soon leave Atlantia; given his power and skill, the last thing she wanted was for him to linger long enough that he might be tempted to interfere in her plans—however much he denied an ambition to rule.

But with Merlin gone, what hope had she of finding a powerful male wizard willing to join his body and power to hers—and, of course, to later be commanded by her?

The situation seemed hopeless, but Antonia didn't give up so easily. Instead she covered her crystal with a black cloth and went to her desk, taking from one of the drawers several sheets of parchment. There were written the names of every adult male wizard in Atlantia, with the ones said to be weakest and easiest led at the top. She had devoted much time and effort during the last weeks to the compilation of the list, since she had known only that her lover would be a dark male wizard.

She went to the perfect mirror hanging on the wall of her bedroom and recited a soft spell, then glanced down at her list. Looking back at the mirror, she said, "Show me Selby," and watched as an image swiftly formed. She knew at once he was wrong; this wizard was thin and too pale, not at all like the man she had seen in her crystal.

She cleared the mirror and consulted her list again, knowing it could take her days to work her way through all the names. She couldn't devote all her time to the search, of course, no matter how anxious she was; the city had to be run and its citizens looked after, and that was her responsibility.

But she intended to snatch every moment she could in which to continue her search. She had to find the lover fate was offering to her. Only then could she rule all of Atlantia.

"Show me Wyatt. . . ."

•   •   •

By late afternoon of the second day of their hike, Roxanne and Tremayne had covered very little ground—and she knew it was her fault. The closer they came to the village, the more reluctant she was to continue, partly because she was having doubts about what she meant to do, but mostly because she was—against all odds—enjoying this time with Tremayne.

He seemed perfectly happy to slow their pace to a stroll, and there seemed to be a great deal to talk about. He spoke of his home in Europa, answering her questions with vivid descriptions of a world different from the one to which she was accustomed. And Roxanne found herself listening with a wistfulness she couldn't conceal.

"Is it ugly there, as it is here?" she asked him. "With twisted trees and so much rock—and earthquakes?"

"No, Europa is paradise compared to Atlantia. The trees are tall and straight, the grass grows thick and green, and all the water is pure. As for earthquakes, I've never known one to strike Europa."

"And no Curtain," she murmured.

"No Curtain. It's a beautiful land, Roxanne."

"Male and female wizards don't fight there?"

"No. They *do* tend to avoid each other," he admitted honestly, "but there's no open hostility. What worries me is the notion that the society of Europa could be heading down the same path Atlantia followed. If something isn't done to create a sense of understanding and unity between men and women of power, the entire society of wizards could be doomed."

"Is that why you—"

"No, it isn't." Tremayne's voice was calm. "My feelings for you are entirely personal, Roxanne."

"You don't know me. How could you feel anything for me?"

"I don't know."

That reply startled her so much that she stopped walking and turned to stare at him. "You don't know?"

He was smiling a bit ruefully, but his eyes held that unnerving hunger she had seen before. "It isn't something I can explain or control, you see. It just happened. I looked at you, and something inside me said, 'There she is!' I didn't question it any more than I question that my heart is beating."

After a moment Roxanne turned and kept walking. "You're a very strange man" was all she could manage to say.

Tremayne's only response was to suggest that they find a place to camp for the night. "The village should be no more than an hour or so away, so we can go in first thing in the morning."

Roxanne agreed they should make camp, and by the time darkness and the Curtain fell, they had settled down in the shelter of the trees just east of a ridge. The moon, a bare sliver of light, was briefly visible before the Curtain intensified.

As she made herself comfortable sitting on her side of the campfire, Roxanne noticed that the ground felt warm to the touch, and it made her uneasy. This time of year, the ground never warmed very much even in the sunlight, and here, underneath the trees, it should have remained decidedly chilled. It was another sign of turmoil in the very ground of Atlantia, she realized, like the strong tremor that rocked the valley not long after dark.

Though it didn't seem to damage the area where their camp lay, both Roxanne and Tremayne were disturbed by the quake; it was always unsettling to feel the ground beneath roll and twitch as if it had no more substance than mist. Even after the ground steadied again and the night sounds of the valley had resumed, neither of them felt much like sleeping.

They ate food neither really tasted and talked rather aimlessly for a while, passing the hours. It was near midnight when Tremayne said suddenly, "You can tell me the truth, you know. Or shall I tell you what I think? Your mother would never ask you to risk yourself by crossing the valley at night, would she, Roxanne?"

She was silent, staring at him across the fire.

"Is she even alive?"

"No. She died when I was small."

He sighed softly. "I was hoping you'd tell me yourself, but it appears you aren't going to. So I'll have to confess. I told Merlin how I felt about you, and out of concern for you, he thought I should know about the attack."

"Out of concern for me?" Her voice was brittle.

"Yes. I was so eager for you, I probably would have been impatient and reckless in trying to persuade you I could be trusted—which would have had the opposite effect, as well as quite possibly harming you. Merlin wanted to warn me that you'd been so badly hurt by men, it would take time for you to heal."

He was able to speak calmly only because he had already grappled with his rage and pain at what had been done to her. But he knew that given the chance, he would kill the men who had hurt her. Slowly.

Roxanne looked away from his intent gaze, filled with the oddest combination of emotions. "Do you . . . I'm surprised you still find me . . . acceptable."

"Why would I not?"

"You know very well why."

Tremayne waited patiently until her gaze returned to his, and then he said, "Roxanne, if I could, I would make it so that you had never been hurt in any way by any man. What they did to you was terrible, but it certainly wasn't your fault, and it doesn't change how I feel about you."

She didn't believe him, but didn't protest.

He hadn't expected anything else; she was still too wary. Quietly he said, "You mean to find those men, don't you? To destroy them."

"Yes," she answered flatly.

"Will that give you back whatever you feel you lost?"

"I don't know. All I do know is that I can't live knowing they haven't been punished for what they did to me."

Tremayne was silent for a moment. Did he have any right to tell her what she intended to do was wrong? No, not really, not when he wanted to destroy them himself. He couldn't begin to understand how she felt; perhaps a sense of justice *would* help her to heal completely. But he was very much afraid that killing her rapists would change Roxanne far more deeply and irrevocably than the attack itself.

"Let me do it," he said at last. "Point them out to me, and let me destroy them."

That was the last thing she had expected. "You? But . . . but why?"

Because I want to. "Because you shouldn't do it. If you kill them, they'll always be with you. If I do it, you'll have the satisfaction of knowing they were punished for what they did to you without the blood on your hands. Or your soul."

"What about *your* soul?"

Tremayne never got the chance to answer that, because both of them were frozen by the chilling sound of Kerry's shrieks coming from somewhere in the dark woods to the east.

"Roxanne! Roxanne!"

Their stillness lasted only a second or two. Both of them leaped up and raced off in the direction of the child's hysterical screams. The Curtain provided some light for them to see their way even as it sapped their energy, and both Tremayne and Roxanne were breathless by the time they burst into a clearing.

They saw Kerry struggling in the brutal embrace of two village men, her small face white with terror as they tore at her clothing and began to shove her toward the ground.

Roxanne cried out in anguished protest, and even as she was stretching her hand instinctively toward them, she recognized one of the two men as one of her own attackers. Then everything happened so quickly that afterward she was never sure if her recognition of the man in any way changed what seemed fated to be.

At her side Tremayne stretched out his own hand, despite the danger of the Curtain, his only thought to save the child. The pulsing streams of energy that left his hand and Roxanne's met and twined together, forming one stream. With no interference from the Curtain, the energy obliterated first one of the men and then the other—with no sound at all except the sharp pops of air rushing in to fill the voids left by two bodies that were there one instant . . . and gone the next.

Roxanne rushed to gather Kerry into her arms, holding the sobbing child tightly against her. "It's all right," she murmured. "It's all right."

"I—I just wanted to—to be with you, Roxanne," Kerry wailed, shaking violently. "I didn't mean to do—anything wrong, I p-promise!"

"I know you didn't, sweetheart. It's all right, don't cry. It's over now. You're safe." Roxanne looked at Tremayne as he knelt beside her, both of them only now wondering how and why their power had combined, and how they'd been able to use it despite the Curtain.

Tremayne gazed into Roxanne's wide, darkened eyes for a moment, and then reached out and very gently placed his hand on Kerry's head in a comforting gesture. Roxanne looked at it, large and strong, and remembered how instantly and unhesitatingly he had moved to help the child. Something inside her that had been closed seemed to open up a bit, and she lifted her own hand to cover his.

"It's your fatal charm," Serena said gravely as she followed Merlin up a narrow mountain path.

"I doubt that," he retorted, throwing the words over his shoulder. "What it is, is a power play, pure and simple. Antonia has her own agenda, and my part would have been something like . . . the mate of a black widow spider."

"Yuk. Don't the females—"

"Yes. They do. That's how they got the name."

Serena thought about that as they climbed, then objected. "But she wouldn't kill her mate, would she? Antonia, I mean. A wizard's power dies with him or her, so she'd need her mate alive if it's power she's after. Wouldn't she?"

"How very prosaic you are."

She couldn't help laughing a little, even as she reflected that he must have found the interview with Antonia distinctly unnerving. She was only grateful that he had emerged apparently without having been dragged back into the struggle between his instincts and his intellect; his attitude toward Antonia seemed more to do with the lady's own personality than any prohibition his ancestors had decreed.

"Well," she said finally, "it's true, isn't it? A dead mate wouldn't be much good to Antonia."

"I suppose not. Though I'm sure she has every intention of being the dominant partner in any . . . merger. She's far too ambitious to be willing to share power, despite what she said to me."

The sun went down about then, and the first flickering haze of the Curtain began forming over the valley, but they were high enough to escape the effects. They had chosen a mountain at random and were at the east end of the valley above Sanctuary; they could see the scattered lights of the city, though as the night wore on and the Curtain thickened, those would become less visible.

They were heading for a spot halfway up this mountain, where there appeared to be a clearing. They could have covered the distance far more quickly than they had by simply transporting once out of sight of the gates of Sanctuary, but both enjoyed walking, and they had gotten used to more primitive means of travel in Atlantis.

"I won't know how to drive when we get back," Serena had commented somewhat ruefully. "Has it only been two weeks?"

Now, glancing across the valley, she saw the moon rise between two peaks and shivered slightly. Just a sliver now, but within a few days it would be a quarter, then a half . . . and eventually, in barely two weeks, the moon would be round and full—the final warning of the destruction of Atlantis.

"Serena?"

Realizing she had come to a stop, she turned her back to the valley and quickly caught up with him. "Sorry."

Merlin had stopped to wait for her, and looked down at her with a slight frown. "What's wrong?"

With forced lightness she replied, "I was just thinking how soon the fireworks are due to start around here."

Steadily he said, "It happened a long, long time ago. Try to think of it that way."

As they began climbing again, this time side by side, she said, "I've tried, but I can't help it when that doesn't always work. I think of Roxanne as my friend, you know, and we can't be certain she'll leave here with Tremayne. And then there's little Kerry. . . ."

"Is that the child whose mother was looking for her as we left Roxanne's house?" Merlin asked, trying to distract her thoughts from the coming devastation.

"Um. She's a little imp, always sneaking off and worrying people, according to Roxanne. Between them, she and Felice—who's more of a foster mother, by the way—have their hands full watching Kerry." With a slight grimace Serena added, "I'm not surprised the kid made herself scarce, though; with Roxanne leaving the city yesterday afternoon and Felice preoccupied because she's trying to get pregnant, I imagine Kerry found herself at loose ends. And she's a doer."

"Do you want children?" Merlin startled himself as much as Serena with the question.

"I don't know. Yes, I think so." She cleared her throat. "To be honest, I haven't thought a lot about it. There didn't seem to be much use in it."

They had reached the clearing that was their goal, and Merlin stopped, looking down at Serena. It was getting dark rapidly, but he could still see her lovely, solemn face. "Why not?" he asked her curiously.

"Because I thought you were beyond reach," she answered candidly. "I couldn't see myself getting married or making a baby with anyone else, not when I loved you. So it seemed . . . less painful to just not think about it."

Merlin felt a strange sensation in his chest, as if his heart had turned over. Slowly he said, "You've gone out with dozens of men over the years."

"And you've gone out with dozens of women," she reminded him. "All a part of the social pretense of being just like everyone else instead of wizards." Turning away and shrugging off her backpack, she added dryly, "Of course, *I* didn't have a bordello to go to."

He followed her slowly, grappling with what she seemed to be telling him. As he shrugged out of his backpack, he said a bit absently, "I'm never going to live that down with you, am I?"

"Not on your life. Shall I put the fire here?"

"Yes—and be careful."

"Something *I'll* never be able to live down," she murmured, recalling her youthful attempt to create fire back in Seattle that had nearly resulted in a four-alarm blaze.

The clearing was tucked back several yards away from a sharp cliff overlooking the valley, with trees climbing the slopes. It was as if someone had carved a large step from the mountain. Behind Serena and beginning some feet away was a rock-strewn gradient that eventually grew steeper and became dotted with trees farther up the mountain.

Merlin watched her, critical out of habit because he'd been her teacher for so long.

After dropping her backpack to the ground and pushing the edges of her cloak back over her shoulders, Serena created a small basin in the ground by circling her hand above it, and then prepared to make a campfire. But before she could begin, a deep, angry rumble signaled yet another tremor, and she found herself completely occupied in trying to keep her balance on ground that was suddenly no more solid than quicksand.

It seemed to get darker as the earth heaved and moaned underneath them; even the sliver of moon hid behind scudding clouds. Over the unholy racket of a continent trying to wrench itself apart, Merlin heard a different sound, and he sensed the threat hidden by darkness. Without thought and out of an instinct born of man rather than wizard, he leaped toward Serena.

She clung gratefully to him when Merlin's arms closed about her. She was trying so hard just to keep to her feet that she didn't hear the sharp, angry sounds of stones and boulders plunging down the gradient toward them and only felt the impact of something striking Merlin's body as he shielded her.

That sickening jolt was all either of them needed to remind them of their own abilities, and faster even than thought their combined energies formed a protective aura around them.

Like all the tremors of Atlantis, this one lasted no more than a minute or so, though it seemed much longer. The ground abruptly stopped heaving, and the dreadful groaning of tortured earth became utter silence, disturbed only by the clacking sounds of stone striking stone as the last few rocks cascaded down the mountainside.

"Richard, are you all right?" Serena demanded, easing back just far enough to look up at him. Their protective aura faded away, as it was no longer needed.

"It was just a glancing blow," he said, straightening from the slightly hunched position he had assumed to shield her. The movement made him wince.

"Where did it hit you?"

"I'm fine, I told you."

"Yeah, right." Serena took a step away from him and briskly finished the campfire she'd begun. Then she built a roomy and sturdy lean-to just behind it, with enough space at the front for Merlin to stand up straight, even as she wondered why on earth they both kept sticking to this primitive stuff. Why not a nice little house? With a couple—no, with *one* big bed and a nice bathroom with a sunken tub and maybe a bottle of very good, very old wine. . . .

Merlin barely remembered to throw out a protective screen around the clearing, hiding their presence from any other wizards who might be in the area. The stone, a large one, had struck his upper back just above his right shoulder blade, and though the blow wasn't disabling, it hurt like hell and spread an ache over that shoulder and all the way down his right arm.

He had been injured rarely enough in his life for him to still feel a shock at the vulnerability of his own body. It was a very peculiar feeling. Always before, that sensation had troubled him long after the injury healed, but this time he found himself far more interested in Serena's reaction. He watched her as she conjured, with a rather impatient wave of her hand, a wide, thick pallet for the lean-to, then tossed her cloak over it and came back around the fire to him, frowning.

"Very good," he noted.

"I considered creating a nice little house with all the modern amenities, but figured you wouldn't approve. Stop being a teacher and come sit down," she told him, taking his arm. "I want to see where that rock hit you."

"Serena—" He started to protest, but he found himself led to the shelter and divested of his coat, which she absently folded neatly and then carelessly dropped onto the pallet. Then she reached up to begin briskly unlacing his shirt, and Merlin's amusement faded. She looked very serious, he thought, very competent. But just as he wondered if she was thinking only of his injury, he saw the faint color across her cheekbones and realized she was as aware of him as he was of her.

"You don't have to do this," he murmured. "I mean, if you don't want to."

Her lashes lifted, and fierce green eyes glared at him. "That," she said with emphasis, "was an asinine thing to say."

That was his Serena, he reminded himself ruefully, frank to a fault and completely without guile. "Yes, it was," he admitted.

"Then why did you say it?" She was watching her fingers, which were coping with the lacings of his shirt with far less dexterity than they had only a moment ago.

"Because I felt awkward, I suppose."

"Not . . . not because you didn't want me touching you?"

Merlin didn't answer right away, because he was trying to find the words to tell her how he felt. Then she looked up at him again, and the flash of her eyes seemed to pull the honest response from him. "Christ, no."

She looked startled, then smiled a little. "Good.

Now, why don't you help me get you out of this shirt so I can take a look at your back."

Silently he pulled the tail of his shirt from his pants and, with her help, since his right side had stiffened up a bit, eased the garment off over his head. Then he sat down on the pallet as she directed, half turning to the side so that the firelight illuminated his back.

Serena knelt behind him. "It's a nasty bruise," she murmured, hesitating only an instant before touching him. The ugly reddened stamp of the stone was as large as her two hands, and she could imagine how much it hurt. Without asking his permission, she glided her hand very gently over the bruise and concentrated on healing skin and muscle. The redness slowly faded, and the pain as well, and she felt him relax.

"Thank you," he said. "That's much better. No pain or stiffness at all—"

That was when she leaned forward and pressed her lips to him.

Instantly she felt him react, his muscles tightening in a purely sensual response, and she had the impression he wasn't breathing at all. Her hands stroked upward to shape his shoulders, probing the hardness of bone and sinew and flesh. She rubbed her cheek against him slowly, her eyes half closing.

"Serena . . ." His voice was low, almost harsh.

"You said you didn't mind me touching you," she said softly.

He cleared his throat. "And you said we weren't ready for this."

"That was then," she said. "I think we're ready now. At least ready to try. Don't you?"

Merlin was trying to think, which was virtually impossible, since she ended every sentence by pressing her soft lips to his back. It felt wonderful. Better than wonderful, it was utterly maddening. "You know I want you." He expected to feel that familiar jarring sense of conflict within him, but this time it was no more than a faint uneasiness far in the back of his consciousness.

Serena drew away from him, which made him turn swiftly to stare at her. She slowly unlaced her vest, pulled it off and tossed it aside, then pulled the tail of her green blouse free of her pants.

Without thinking about what he was doing, Merlin got rid of his boots and socks. He couldn't take his eyes off her. She looked oddly demure kneeling there on the fur cloak flung across the pallet, with her fiery hair loose around her shoulders and her expression so solemn, but the firelight danced in her vivid eyes like a pagan invitation, and her slightly parted lips were moist and enticing. While he watched, she dispensed with her boots and socks using wizardry, but began slowly unbuttoning her blouse with her slender fingers.

Merlin moved closer and rose on his knees, grasping her shoulders and drawing her up, as well. Serena felt her hands touch his hard, powerful chest, and then he was pulling her into his arms and hers were around him, and the most incredible sense of relief swept over her. She hadn't been sure. Bravado aside, she hadn't been sure.

But when his mouth closed over hers and she felt the hardness of his body against hers, she was. He was very much with her, she could *feel* it; there was no curtain being drawn in his mind because she was a woman, something to dread and be wary of. And she thought he knew that his need was like hers, emotional as well as physical.

Their bodies, pressed together, strained to be even closer, though they hadn't moved apart long enough to rid themselves of what remained of their clothing. Her fingers clutched at his back, and his swept down her back to curve over her buttocks and bring her lower body tighter against his, while their kiss deepened sharply.

Serena suddenly, fiercely, wanted them both to be naked, and because she wished it, their clothing vanished. She tore her lips from his with a gasp, shocked by the stark sensations of her breasts flattened against his chest and her belly rubbing the swollen hardness of his member as he held her and moved sensuously against her.

His eyes, liquid black, burning, gazed into hers, and it was Serena who tried to struggle against this, not physically but emotionally, all her fears wild in her eyes. For so long she'd thought him beyond reach, and it had been safe to love him, love Merlin, without risk or vulnerability, but now he was Richard, flesh and blood and the heat of need, and it was terrifying to think of giving so much of herself to him. . . .

Merlin could see, as well as feel, her emotions, and her panicked defenselessness made him reach out with an instinct far deeper than any his ancestors had instilled in him.

"Don't, Serena, don't be afraid," he murmured, both his hands lifting to surround her face, his thumbs gently smoothing the hot skin over her cheekbones. "You've been so brave and strong and clearheaded through all of this, even when I gave you so many reasons to hate me. Don't leave me now, please. Fight the way you always have. So stubborn and fierce . . . my Serena . . ."

She caught her breath on a little gasp, and as quickly as it had surged inside her the trepidation was gone. She was left with a necessity that was almost frantic, a hunger for him that held all the intensity of a storm trapped under glass for too long. It felt as if she had wanted him forever.

"Yes," she whispered, all her senses once more focused on the overwhelming contact of their naked bodies.

Merlin kissed her, his mouth urgent, and eased them both down into the softness of the fur-covered pallet. Leaning over her, kissing her again and again, he touched her silken stomach and felt it quiver, then slid his hand slowly up to cup her breast. She jerked and made a little sound, and he raised his head to look down at her. Her eyes were wide and fixed on his face, startled and wondering, color and heat blooming over her cheekbones as his thumb brushed over her nipple.

He kissed her once more, his tongue slipping between her lips to touch and play with hers until she answered the intimate little caresses eagerly. She made another little sound, this one of disappointment, when his mouth left hers to trail over her face. He touched her eyelids and forehead, her cheeks and nose and chin, almost as if he were using his lips to memorize her every feature. Then his mouth moved down her throat, and she felt the shattering sensation of his tongue slowly tracing the little heart with which he had marked her as his.

He was kneading her breast gently, and when his mouth finally reached her nipple and closed over it, she moaned and clutched at his shoulders, her senses nearly drowned by the waves and waves of burning pleasure.

For the first time in his life, Merlin's perceptions of this act were completely unclouded, unaffected by anything except his senses and emotions, and her responses. The hunger inside him was clean and sharp, rising, filling him with a pulsing ache as alive as his beating heart. He had never known desire could be like this, so overpowering, and he gave himself up to it with a joyous sense of freedom and gratitude.

It wasn't simply a female body he needed so badly, but Serena. Her skin was heated silk under his touch, her luminous eyes gleamed up at him with a hunger that matched his, and the little sounds she made touched all his senses with fire. There was something almost familiar about making love to her, as if some deeply buried part of him had always known how it would be.

He caressed her breasts until they swelled and blushed with passion, until she was breathing as quickly as he was, and then he moved his hand down over her quivering belly, his fingers sliding into red curls, parting her to find the soft, hot flesh already throbbing for his touch. She cried out into his mouth and bucked upward in surprise, but he held her securely and stroked her in a steady, quickening rhythm.

Serena was slightly astonished when her thighs parted for him so eagerly, when her hips lifted and moved to his touch, when her body seemed to give itself over to him completely with utter naturalness. But before she could follow the self-preserving instincts all humans shared and try to regain control over herself, it was too late, far too late.

The wash of feelings was vast, tremendous, engulfing

her. Pleasure and heat and a rhythmic pulsing and pleasure, and she heard herself cry out . . . maybe it was his name, because he came to her then, joining their bodies in a merging so stark and powerful and absolute that it felt utterly right. There was pain, but it was fleeting; and when the pleasure returned, she forgot there had ever been anything else. And even in the instant of naked vulnerability when she knew that everything she was lay exposed to him, she was utterly fearless because she loved him.

Merlin couldn't take his eyes off her, drinking in the beauty and mystery of her. She was so giving, so honest in her responses; he could see her every emotion in her eyes. He watched her desire build until it took her beyond herself, until *he* took her beyond herself, saw her wonder and joy. He saw her brief pain and watched her forgive him for causing it. He saw her hunger rise again, this time even more intensely, and he was with her now, completely with her, their bodies moving together with urgent intent, driven toward the release every part of them demanded.

Serena cried out wildly, surging beneath him, her eyes going wide and dazed, and her beautiful features stamped with a profoundly female satisfaction. Her strong inner muscles tightened around him in spasms of pleasure, and Merlin shuddered, groaning, as that shattering caress sent him over the edge.

And even then, even in a moment so primitive and overwhelming that it completely blocked coherent thought, even in that instant of being beyond himself, Merlin whispered her name.

FOURTEEN

He had absently conjured another blanket for them, because neither wanted to move long enough to get under the ones beneath them. Serena's cloak supplied soft and sensuous bedding, and the fire only a couple of feet away provided warmth (since it was a wizard-created fire, it would burn on exactly the same until it was told not to), so they didn't miss being covered until the heat of their bodies ebbed.

Exhausted and wildly happy, Serena lay close beside him as he lay on his back, her head pillowed on his shoulder and her fingers sliding through the thick black hair on his chest and probing the skin beneath. He was so hard, she thought, yet it was a hardness her body and all her senses welcomed eagerly. She felt one of his hands toying with her hair, stroking it and smoothing it over her back, and his other hand came up to where hers was touching his chest. Their fingers twined together.

He hadn't said anything since they had come back to themselves. A little anxious, she closed her eyes and concentrated. It wasn't actually cheating, she assured herself, trying to do what she had managed twice before, because she wouldn't be able to read his thoughts. But if she could perhaps get a sense of his emotions . . .

She saw the front edge of the lean-to and, beyond, the darkness of a sky that was cloudy. She felt that alien sense of a different body with greater muscle and mass, and she felt utter relaxation, and she felt—

You're cheating, Serena.

Startled, she opened her eyes and lifted her head with a jerk to stare down at him. He was smiling. She cleared her throat. "Well. I was curious. Sue me." Before he could do more than lift an eyebrow, she added, "How is it that you can say things to me in your head even though I can't read your thoughts?"

"Because I'm a Master wizard," he replied simply.

"Oh."

"What were you curious about?"

"Now, what do you think?"

The exasperation in her voice made his smile widen, and he reached up his free hand to stroke a wayward tendril of bright hair off her cheek. "I think you're beautiful."

Serena would have protested—if only weakly—that the reply hardly satisfied her curiosity, but his hand slid to her nape and pulled her head down so that he could kiss her quite thoroughly.

"I think you're incredible."

She felt the words murmured against her lips, and almost whimpered in pleasure when the tip of his tongue glided along the sensitive inner surface of her bottom lip.

"And I think I'll never be able to get enough of you, even if I live a long, long time."

"You can have all of me," she murmured, her lips clinging to his and her tongue darting out to answer his maddening little caress. "I want to give you everything."

He kissed her, his mouth fierce, and his eyes burned into hers when she finally raised her head. "If I'd known it would be like this, I would have fought like a demon to have it long ago," he told her, his voice strained with feeling. "To have you. There was an empty place in me, and I didn't even know it."

Serena could feel the heat building in both of them once again, and she decided her curiosity had been satisfied far enough for the moment. Merlin obviously decided the same thing, because he was kissing her again, shifting them until she lay on her back, pushing the blanket off them. Her arms were around him, her fingers probing the muscles of his back, and her mouth was eager under his.

"I don't want to hurt you again," he said against her lips.

"You won't."

Rain woke them hours later, after midnight, the sound almost unfamiliar because it hadn't rained the entire time they'd been in Atlantis. It was a steady rain, not light but not a downpour, and they lay close together watching it.

"Another portent of destruction?" Serena wondered in a hushed voice.

"No," Merlin replied softly, his arms tightening around her. "Just rain."

Serena listened for a while to the soothing sound, wide awake now. They had eaten hours ago, a rather sumptuous meal complete with a bottle of old wine, and then had made love again before falling asleep. She felt rested, and boneless with satisfaction, and she didn't want to move a muscle, because he felt so wonderful against her. They were lying together like spoons, both on their sides as they faced the brightly burning fire and the rain.

He moved slightly, his right hand drawing the blanket up around her shoulders, and she found herself staring at the reddish mark of the owl with which he'd been branded at the gates of Sanctuary. She wanted to try to remove it, but since they were planning to return to the city again, she knew she couldn't. Instead she caught his hand and brought it to her lips.

His fingers twined with hers "What is it?"

"Nothing. Just . . . I hated it when they marked you like that."

"It's all right, Serena."

"Yes. But I hated it."

"How did you feel when I marked you?"

"Strange. Somehow connected to you. I think I needed that when you went up to Varian's palace and we didn't see each other for so long. The more I learned about Sanctuary, the stranger it seemed, and I needed to feel . . . anchored."

"I'm glad it helped you. I can remove it now, if you like."

"No. No, not yet."

He rubbed his chin gently back and forth against her head, silent because he sensed she had another question to ask. Finally, abruptly, she did.

"Why did you mark me with a heart?"

Merlin smiled to himself. "Why are you asking me only now?"

"I don't know. Because there wasn't time before, I suppose. Or because I didn't think about it until now. Why did you, Richard?"

In a musing tone he said, "I used to watch you at parties without your awareness, watch the way people were drawn to you, the way their faces lit up when you smiled at them. And everyone brought their problems to you, because they knew you'd do something to help them. It worried me sometimes, your kind heart. I'd been taught all my life that a wizard was detached, that he couldn't let himself be . . . dragged down by the troubles of those around him, but I watched you, and over the years I realized your heart made you a better wizard."

After a moment she said, "So that was why you marked me with a heart?"

His arms tightened around her. "No. I didn't mark you with your heart, Serena. I marked you with mine. Something you've had for a long time."

Serena didn't move. She didn't even breathe. She didn't dare. She thought this might be as close as he could come to telling her that he loved her, now at least, and her eyes closed briefly as she tried to endure the shattering wave of emotions that washed over her.

With desperate calm she finally said, "You'll accuse me of being prosaic again if I confess that I decided you chose a heart simply because no other male wizard here would have."

"That," he said in a thoughtful tone, "never even crossed my mind. Go to sleep, Serena."

The rain began to come down harder just then, and Serena closed her eyes, smiling, listening to that and feeling his heart beating against her back. Without even realizing she was going to, she drifted off to sleep.

"Where do you suppose Roxanne and Tremayne are?" Serena asked early the next morning. She was standing near the edge of their little clearing, looking down on the valley as the last of the Curtain dispersed in the sunlight.

Merlin came up behind her. "Why don't you reach out and try to find them?" he suggested.

When she'd tried to do that in the past, Serena had never been able to gather anything except vague impressions, but she made the attempt now because she was curious. She closed her eyes, since it helped her to concentrate, and sent her senses winging out over the valley.

Sounds. Bird sounds, she thought. The smell of wet earth and the whiff of sulfur that is always present in the valley. What was that? A hit of motion? No . . . a child's laugh. . . .

Behind her Merlin lifted his hands and put them gently on her shoulders.

Serena gasped and opened her eyes, startled. She could feel Merlin's power spreading through her body, warm and tingling, and an image promptly formed before her eyes. The image wavered as her concentration faltered, but then she focused intensely, and it was as though she were looking at a hologram—three-dimensional, alive—suspended in the air several feet away.

Roxanne and Tremayne were walking slowly, his head

bent attentively toward hers, an expression of shy eagerness on her face as she talked to him. They were holding hands. *Holding hands.* And a little girl rushed up to
them—Kerry—talking rapidly, a doll held in the crook
of her elbow. Tremayne seemed more amused than annoyed by the interruption, and Roxanne's delicate face
softened as she answered the child. Then Tremayne put
his free hand on Kerry's shoulder and they kept walking, and Roxanne turned her head to look up at him so
seriously, talking. . . .

"Damn, doesn't this channel have sound?"

The image vanished instantly.

Merlin took his hands off her shoulders and sighed.

Serena turned to face him, grinning a little. "I know.
I'm such a trial to you."

He bent his head and kissed her. "Yes, but the advan-
tages seem to outweigh the disadvantages."

"*Seem* to?"

"We've only been together nine years, so it's a little
early to be sure," he explained gravely. "As an Apprentice wizard, you have a long way to go."

"Obviously." Thinking about what had happened,
she said, "Your power helped me to see them, right?"

"Yes."

She had several questions about that. "You've never
done such a thing before. Why?"

"Because I didn't know it was possible," he answered
readily. "After what happened with Varian, it was obvious our energy could combine. Something I somehow
doubt my ancestors knew. And after last night . . . well,
I had the idea that either of us could enhance the other's abilities by sharing power."

"Which is what happened. Is that—what we saw—is
that what *you* see when you reach out with your
senses?"

He nodded.

Serena was impressed. "I do have a long way to go.
Alone, all I get are faint impressions."

"Time, Serena. It takes time."

"And I'm impatient, I know."

He kissed her again, then said, "Why don't we start

down now? Tremayne, Roxanne, and Kerry won't reach Sanctuary today, I think, but if we cut across the valley, we should meet up with them before dark."

"Okay. I'm curious to find out what that kid's doing with them."

After leaving the clearing the way they'd found it, they made their way down the mountain, careful of the rain-slick slope, talking idly, not about anything really important. Being lovers, Serena realized happily, had removed barriers and constraints and made them closer, but it hadn't changed the familiarity that came of years together. Being lovers added dimensions and layers and depths. It was wonderful.

They reached the dirt road late in the morning, and before they could even turn toward the west another tremor rumbled through Atlantis. It wasn't a bad one, over in seconds.

"I don't like them," Serena told Merlin in the tone of one who has made a personal discovery.

"No, they aren't pleasant," he agreed.

Serena looked ahead to the dark, dreary forest and said, "I have an idea."

"Which is?"

"Why don't we go just far enough into the forest to be out of sight if anybody happens to be watching, and conjure ourselves a little house or something. Then we can stay there all day, and even tonight, and when Roxanne and Tremayne are close enough early tomorrow morning, we can just pop over." She eyed him hopefully.

In a mild tone he said, "That would be cheating."

"No . . . just taking a little shortcut, is all. Besides, which would you rather do, spend the day walking through that dreadful forest, or spend the day in bed? With me." To make certain he understood his options, she wreathed her arms around his neck and stood on tiptoe to kiss him.

Merlin wrapped both arms around her and lifted her off her feet, an abrupt and intense hunger evident in him. Against her lips he murmured, "Woman, do you plan to use your body to get your way with me from now on?"

"Only when I think it'll work," she confessed.

He shifted his hold on her, cradling her in his arms, and began carrying her toward the forest. "Well, it's working now," he told her ruefully.

Varian prowled the terrace of his palace restlessly. His hand lifted often to touch the place on his chest that had been burned by the two wizards from Seattle, even though it was healing rapidly and scarcely hurt at all now. It wasn't pain he felt at any rate; it was bewilderment and unease, coupled with a growing sense of eagerness and anticipation.

It had to be a portent, he thought, a sign to him. Forty years here without even an instance of power mating power, and yet in a single morning he had encountered not one, but *two* pairs of wizards. First the pair from Seattle, that redheaded whore Serena and Merlin, and then his own crafty kinsman Tremayne and his whore from the city. *Two pairs.*

And it wasn't just the fact of them that disturbed Varian. The two from Seattle . . . their powers had combined. *Combined.* He had never felt anything like the jolt that had sliced through his own energy and knocked him off his feet, and he knew he'd never forget it.

"My Lord . . ."

He looked at one of his concubines as she glided out onto the terrace and smiled at him. He thought her name was Elena. She was very young and ripe to bursting with libidinous juices, and since he'd broken her in right, she was eager for him. She cupped her own breasts and lifted them invitingly, the nipples stiffly visible through the filmy material of her shift.

"My Lord . . . please take me."

He didn't want her.

The thought was so shocking that he waved her away without a word and retreated to the end of the terrace to try to understand what was wrong with him. Why didn't he want her? He had never in his life turned away from a willing bitch, not unless he was exhausted, and he *wasn't*—in fact, he was half hard, partially aroused, but not by Elena.

It occurred to him slowly that he was growing excited by the possibility of taking a woman of power to his bed.

Why not, after all? If Tremayne had managed to do it, then surely he could. He thought of spreading the legs of some haughty whore, her eyes filled with vibrant life like those of Merlin's mate, that Serena, and Varian felt himself twitch urgently.

Of course, he'd have to find a willing one; those whores in the city were reputedly swift to fire off a shift of energy right to a man's groin, which was the last thing Varian wanted. He wondered how Tremayne had avoided that particular fate.

He reached down and fondled himself absently as he gazed out over the valley. A willing whore . . .

"I like that," Roxanne said, eyeing her friend's new outfit.

"What, this old thing?" Serena grinned as Roxanne looked uncertain, and added, "Never mind. I'd be delighted to conjure up something similar for you."

After a moment's thought Roxanne smiled. "No, I don't think so. It suits you, Serena—it wouldn't me."

They were sitting on a fallen tree near the bank of a stream not an hour from Sanctuary, where the two couples and Kerry had met up only minutes before. Merlin and Tremayne were standing several feet away talking, and Kerry was kneeling at the stream washing her doll Chloe's face.

Nodding, Serena said, "So, tell me—if you don't mind, of course—why you left Sanctuary."

Roxanne hesitated, but then confessed her intention of destroying the men who had attacked her. She spoke quietly, telling Serena what had happened when Kerry had followed her and Tremayne away from Sanctuary.

"It was my fault she was put into danger. If I hadn't been so wrapped up in my desire for revenge, I would never have left Sanctuary without making certain there was someone to watch out for Kerry. Felice . . . well, she wants a child of her own, as I told you, and the older Kerry grows, the less Felice is interested. She probably didn't even notice the child was missing—"

"Day before yesterday," Serena said. "Before Merlin and I left Sanctuary, she asked me if I'd seen Kerry. She didn't seem worried, though."

Roxanne sighed. "No, probably not."

"But it was hardly your fault that Kerry sneaked out of the city, Roxanne. I thought the Sentinels were there to keep the kids in, as well as unwanted males out."

"Yes, but Kerry was still my responsibility. And if Tremayne hadn't been with me, those men would have hurt her so terribly, perhaps even killed her—" She swallowed hard. "One of them . . . was one of the men who attacked me."

Serena frowned. "What did you do?"

Roxanne explained what had happened when her power had combined with Tremayne's, and added, "I don't understand it, and neither does Tremayne. The Curtain should have punished us for trying to use power. . . ."

Serena was more interested in another question. "Roxanne, do you trust Tremayne?"

"I—I don't know. Perhaps."

"But the possibility is there?"

"Yes," Roxanne answered honestly. "When he helped me to save Kerry so instantly, without hesitating. I felt . . . I felt I could learn to trust him."

Serena didn't push it. "I see. So, you two saved Kerry and destroyed those two village men, one of whom was one of your attackers. And then? You changed your mind about going after the other two?"

"It didn't seem important anymore. The anger inside me just faded away to nothing."

"You know, I think that's probably a good thing," Serena told the younger wizard. "We have a saying in Seattle—what goes around comes around. The men who hurt you *will* pay for what they did, one way or an-other."

"That's what Tremayne said."

"Obviously a smart man."

Roxanne smiled, then said hesitantly, "You and Merlin seem different. You look so happy, both of you."

"I'm probably lit up like a Christmas tree," Serena reflected, knowing she tended to broadcast every emotion—and she was filled with a delighted tangle of them.

"Like a what?" Roxanne asked, puzzled.

For just a moment Serena thought the saddest part of this place and time was that they hadn't yet begun to celebrate Christmas, but then she brushed the thought away. Stupid, really, when you considered everything else. . . .

"Never mind," she said to Roxanne. "What I mean to say is that Merlin and I have finally found our way past those walls between us."

"You're . . . mates?" Roxanne asked a bit shyly.

"Yes. And I highly recommend the relationship."

Roxanne studied her friend's face for a moment, then said softly, "I envy you, Serena."

Serena looked up to see Merlin and Tremayne coming toward them, and murmured, "Don't miss your chance, Roxanne. Believe me, it's worth the risk."

"Are you ladies ready to go on to Sanctuary?" Merlin asked, taking Serena's hand as she stood up.

"It suits me," Serena replied, smiling at him.

Roxanne was looking at Tremayne. "Yes."

He held out his hand, and she took it.

Antonia stood in her favorite window and gazed down on her city. It was early evening, the quarter moon still visible through the Curtain, and she was feeling too restless to even attempt to go to sleep.

Her agents reported that Merlin and his Serena were seldom apart and appeared quite sickeningly devoted to each other; they obeyed the laws about touching in public, but since they spent most of their time either outside the city gates or else in Roxanne's house, it was simple for them to circumvent the laws. As for Roxanne, it did indeed seem apparent that her loyalties were now divided: the wizard Tremayne had also been granted permission to enter her house during the day.

And Antonia's list of potential consorts was growing short. In fact, there was only one name left, a name she had thus far refused to say out loud to herself, let alone to her mirror. What if he was the one? If so, how ironic that her mortal enemy was to be her mate.

Slowly she went to the mirror on her bedroom wall and stared into the bright surface of it. "Show me Varian," she commanded flatly.

She had seen him before but at a distance—a not uncommon occurrence between male and female wizards—so she had only the vaguest memory of his being dark. Her mirror showed the image of a dark, powerful man in bed with a woman, both of them naked, and Antonia caught her breath. Unlike the prophecy of her crystal, this scene was clear and sharp; she might have been standing over the bed looking down on them.

Unashamed, intensely curious, she watched them, fascinated by what she saw. She knew the mechanics of the act, of course, but she had never thought about how it would look. It was ... rawer than she'd expected, both awkward and graceful. The naked bodies strained apart and came together, glistening with sweat and trembling visibly with exertion. The woman's arms and legs clutched at him as her body accepted his thrusts, and he looked like some savage warrior triumphant, his head thrown back and his hard face a mask of primitive conquest.

Antonia couldn't take her gaze off the scene. Her breathing quickened, and she slowly became aware of the response of her body to what she saw. But before she could feel anything more than the slow tension of arousal, the naked bodies in the mirror convulsed in their release, and the scene faded until her reflection stared back at her with feverish eyes.

Varian. *Varian*.

She knew it was him, knew he was the one she had seen in her crystal. In her future.

Varian was to be her mate.

• • •

As they stood outside the gates of Sanctuary watching Serena and Roxanne say good-bye to each other, Tremayne adjusted his backpack absently and then looked at Merlin. "I know she's going with me partly because she wants to leave Atlantia." He smiled. "But I can bear that. I have a chance now, a chance to earn her love, and that's all any man can ask for."

"What about Kerry?" Merlin asked curiously.

"Why are we taking her with us?" Tremayne looked at the little girl, who was dancing about the two women excitedly. "Several reasons, I suppose. Because Roxanne loves her and feels responsible for her. Because she really doesn't have anyone else, now that Felice is expecting her own child. Because I believe Roxanne will feel less wary of me during the voyage if she has Kerry to care for."

Merlin smiled. "And because you have a soft spot for the child?"

"That, too."

"All excellent reasons."

"I thought so." Tremayne studied the older wizard speculatively. "What of you and Serena? Why don't you come with us?"

"Thank you, but our home lies in another direction. We have to return to Seattle. Our ship will arrive no more than a day or two after yours, I should think. We'll be fine, Tremayne. No matter what happens here, we'll be fine." Merlin changed the subject smoothly. "Will Varian allow you to take Roxanne and Kerry through his mountain pass to the sea?"

Tremayne shrugged. "There won't be a problem. If he even notices us, he'll probably consider himself well rid of us."

Merlin nodded, then looked toward the city. "Did you get any reaction from Antonia?"

"Not really. Roxanne asked for permission to take Kerry from Atlantia, and she said Antonia granted it without question or protest. She's probably relieved we're going; between the four of us, we've definitely shaken up Sanctuary."

"That is certainly true." Merlin offered his hand. "Good luck to all of you, Tremayne."

Shaking hands, the younger wizard said, "Thank you—for everything. I won't forget it."

"Just take care of those ladies of yours. If I've learned anything here, it's that we need women of power. Because without them, we can't be whole."

A few moments later, watching as Tremayne, Roxanne, and little Kerry set off toward Varian's mountain and the pass that would take them to the sea beyond, Serena sniffed and then rubbed her nose fiercely. Merlin put his arm around her.

"Dammit, I swore I wouldn't cry!"

"They'll be all right now," he reminded her.

Serena sniffed again. "I know. That is—are we going to stick around until we're sure they made the ship?"

"It would be prudent, I think. Would you mind spending a few more nights here, Serena?"

"If we can sleep up on one of the mountains the way we have been, of course not. As a matter of fact, I'd just as soon we got started now. I know it's early, but the way people have been staring at us inside the city is really beginning to bother me. Do we have to go back in there?"

"No. Pick a mountain."

She did, and long before nightfall they were comfortably settled halfway up one of the western mountains, having transported there when they were sure no one would be able to observe them.

"Although why it matters, I don't know," Serena commented some time later as she conjured a fire while Merlin took care of the lean-to. "The witnesses are gone. No one left here will get the chance to influence the future, no matter what they see us do."

Merlin knew she was increasingly disturbed by thoughts of the coming cataclysm; he had seen her look to the sky each night, watching broodingly as the moon edged toward full. So when he pulled her down beside him on the pallet inside their lean-to, he tried to make her feel a little better about it.

"Serena, no matter what we might have done, we

couldn't have saved Atlantis. Some things are simply too vast and too complex for mortals to consciously control. Some things really are fated to be."

She hesitated, then said in a small voice, "But were we a part of it? I've been thinking about it, you see, and I can't help wondering. Maybe we changed the future by helping Roxanne and Tremayne, but is that all we did? What if we were always meant to be a part of the process that destroyed this place?"

Merlin couldn't deny the possibility. He hadn't told Serena about Antonia's prophecy, or about his own belief that the Leader had misread what she had seen. But if he was right about that, and right in believing Antonia had no understanding of the trust required for a man and woman of power to mate, then her attempt to do so might well strike the final blow to Atlantis.

"You can't agonize over it, Serena," he said finally. "Neither of us can. Look around you. No matter what we did, when we came here, Atlantis was already dying. The powerless people here, men and women, had mutated and were dying out. The wizards were doomed, as well. It's possible that merely by being here and being what we are, we became a step in the process . . . but that's all. And it happened a long, long time ago."

She looked at him solemnly. "I'll try to remember that. But can we leave as soon as we know Tremayne and Roxanne and Kerry are safely away? I don't want to watch what's going to happen here."

"Of course we can." Merlin bent his head to kiss her, and as always, sharp hunger flared between them. She melted into his arms, and forgot about everything except him and her and the way they made each other feel. . . .

When Varian received the message carried to his palace by a powerless male from the city, his first urge was to burn it without even reading the scroll. But he did read it out of curiosity, and then he wanted to burn it.

Meet with Antonia to discuss the future leadership of Atlantia? Was the whore mad enough to imagine he was that much a fool?

But when the rage faded, Varian considered the matter from another angle. Antonia was, after all, a woman of power. And he'd heard she was still beautiful. He owed it to himself to at least meet her—under the proffered flag of truce, as it were. And if she *was* still beautiful, well, he might just find out what a woman of power was like in bed.

But she suggested they meet in her city, and there was no way he would agree to that. He sent an alternate suggestion back to her, proposing that they meet in the Old City, where he would conjure an appropriate meeting place from the ruins.

Rather to his surprise, she accepted promptly, and they agreed upon an early afternoon three days away.

Serena and Merlin returned to their gate into time just three days before the end. Merlin was certain that Tremayne, Roxanne, and little Kerry had boarded their ship safely and departed from Atlantis. But, of course, they had no way of knowing if the future had indeed been changed by that, not until they passed through the gate into their own time.

"Assuming we were successful in changing the future," Serena said as they stood on the mountain's slope and looked out over Atlantis for a last time, "you'll continue with my training, won't you?"

"Of course."

"And one day, if I'm patient and work really hard, I'll be just as powerful as you are?"

"Not quite."

She turned her head toward him. "You said I could become a seventh-degree Master wizard," she reminded him.

Merlin smiled suddenly, a gleam of humor in his black eyes. "So I did. And I have every faith in your ability to do just that. But what I didn't tell you is that Nola was wrong about *my* level. I'm a tenth-degree Master."

Serena stared at him for a moment, then laughed. "Then I'll just have to try harder, won't I?"

"Yes—and I'll enjoy it very much." He leaned down

and kissed her, then took her hand and turned toward the shimmering rock face that was their gate. He was carrying the box containing his staff under one arm. "Ready?" he said, halting at the gate to look down at her.

"I suppose." She was almost as nervous as when they had come through the first time. What if they'd failed?

"Serena?"

She looked up at him.

"I love you."

Very slowly she smiled. "I thought I'd have to wait a few millennia to hear you say that."

"It'll be true then, too." His black eyes were tender. "Whatever happens, I want you to know that I love you with everything inside of me."

She caught her breath and said shakily, "If . . . if nothing's changed and the Council orders you . . ."

"We'll find a place for ourselves somewhere," he assured her. "Somehow. I love you, Serena. I'm not going to lose you, no matter what."

She lifted her face for his kiss, virtually certain now that she was lit up like a Christmas tree with happiness. "I love you, Richard. I've always loved you."

They looked at each other for a long moment, black eyes and green bottomless with love, their fingers twining tightly together. And then, with the past spread out behind them, they stepped together into the future.

Varian didn't bother to reconstruct one of the ruined buildings in the Old City; instead, he merely erected a small, plain structure amid the rubble. He gave his creation two rooms that were separated by a closed door, some fragment of shrewdness warning him that Antonia might take offense if she found only a bedchamber awaiting her.

He made the bedchamber inviting, however, with a large and comfortable bed piled high with soft blankets, and a fireplace to provide warmth as well as golden light. In the main room, the one Antonia would first enter, he was more diplomatic, conjuring two comfortable chairs of precisely equal dimensions and setting them across from one another near that room's fire-place. Then he produced a table on which were a number of delicacies, two pretty jeweled goblets, and a generous flagon of wine.

It was far more trouble than he was accustomed to going to in order to set the scene for seduction, but Varian didn't begrudge the effort. Ever since he had been confronted by two pairs of wizards his curiosity—and his arousal—had been growing steadily. He'd found no satisfaction with his concubines; all he could think of was the intelligence, fire, and spirit he had seen in Serena, and the delicate beauty of Tremayne's female. Riding a wizard had become his sole ambition.

He knew himself well enough to be aware that a part of the anticipation he felt lay in the risk: Any woman of power could injure him, and Antonia could quite possibly kill him. But he had thoroughly explored every avenue of sexuality *except* a coupling snatched from the very jaws of death, and the potential danger of such a ride, he had found, was a more potent aphrodisiac than anything else he'd ever known.

In fact, he'd been forced to hide his swollen arousal by making his trousers more baggy than usual and adding a loose tunic over his shirt. He had briefly considered conjuring a far more regal outfit than he normally wore, but in the end decided he had no need of fine trappings in order to impress anyone. So his shirt and trousers were of everyday quality, and the tunic was merely leather.

He stood by the main room's single window, gazing out as he waited impatiently for Antonia to arrive. Like the nearby front door, the window was completely open, without glass or shutters; he'd decided they would both feel more relaxed if they weren't "closed up" during the first tense minutes of their meeting.

It occurred to him that their meeting—most especially if it ended in the bedchamber—could last the remainder of the afternoon and into the night, which meant they'd be caught beneath the Curtain. The whore was accustomed to it, of course, but he wasn't. He had, years before, descended several times into the valley at night merely to experience the effects, and he had once ridden one of his concubines beneath the Curtain to find out what it was like (incredibly exhausting, it turned out; he hadn't been himself for days afterward), but otherwise he'd remained on his mountain.

Still, he reminded himself, if he and Antonia were caught here after the sun went down neither of them would be able to use power. And riding a female wizard beneath the Curtain might, after all, prove a different experience, one well worth attempting. . . .

Antonia arrived nearly an hour later, leaving only a few hours of daylight for their meeting. As agreed, she was alone; if any of her Sentinels had accompanied her, they were to wait at the outskirts of the Old City unless and until they were summoned to attend their Leader. She approached Varian's new building with a brisk and confident step, and he watched from the window as she followed the path among the ruins.

He was pleased by her red hair, having forgotten she was one of the rare redheads of Atlantia, and the graceful vitality of her slender body certainly belied her years; he knew she was roughly his own age, but she certainly didn't look it—at least from a distance. She, too, wore plain clothing, a shapeless robe over a white shift, belted to hint at her slim waist, the colors drab. But that hair . . . Bright red, long, thick, and unbound, it was all the color she required to present a vibrant appearance.

Varian stepped back into the center of the room, his gaze on the wide, open doorway, absently adjusting his tunic to better disguise his arousal. He adopted a relaxed, unthreatening posture, arms hanging loose at his sides as he stood squarely on both feet.

Antonia entered the building, halting several feet from Varian. Her blue eyes studied him, and her expression was somewhat detached without being especially unfriendly. She even smiled slightly when she spoke in a cool but curiously intense voice.

"Hello, Varian. Thank you for agreeing to meet with me. I'm sure neither of us will regret it."

He bowed slightly. "Anything to keep the peace,

Antonia. I have every faith in our ability to come to some understanding. Shall we sit down?"

She went to the chair he indicated while he went to the other, both of them smiling and courteous and guarded. Varian was a bit disappointed to discover she looked nearer her age now that she was closer to him, but that didn't change his state of arousal. He'd been less excited by the thought of riding a beautiful woman than by the thought of riding a female wizard, so a few frown lines and the slight roughening of the skin hardly mattered to him. Besides, her body, though slender, was certainly voluptuous enough to suit him.

He poured wine for both of them (she seemed pleased by the jeweled goblets, just as he'd expected; even the most lofty of females enjoyed pretty things), and for a time they merely sipped the wine, sampled a few of the delicacies, and talked politely about neutral topics—though there were few enough of those once the deplorable condition of Atlantia's groundwater and the upsetting tremors had been discussed.

When the first silence fell, Antonia broke it with a smile and a matter-of-fact statement. "You know, of course, that Atlantia cannot survive under the present conditions."

"I suppose not. But we have attained a kind of harmony, wouldn't you agree?" He returned her smile, leaning back in his chair, with his legs extended and spread apart.

"Not so much harmony as an armed respite," she disagreed in a polite tone. "You males keep to your mountains for the most part, we females cling to our city—and our society grows ever more shattered."

"What do you suggest?" he inquired lazily, only one hand moving as he held his goblet and swirled the red liquid inside around and around rhythmically.

Antonia set her goblet on the table at her elbow and folded her hands in her lap, studying him. She had been a little disappointed at first; he was rougher and coarser than she'd expected, with none of Merlin's grace or elegance—*or* strength. Though Varian was tall and solidly muscled, and his thick hair was the deepest shade of black, he seemed to her like a drawing of beauty and power that had been rubbed and smudged by an unkind hand. Lines of dissipation marked his handsome face, a certain heaviness hung about the jowls, and his black eyes were not liquid but were as hard and dull as two pieces of coal.

Still . . . there *was* something about him she found exciting. Physically, she found him quite compelling. The lacings of his shirt were loosened, revealing a riotously hairy chest that kept drawing her gaze, and his slumped posture was curiously provocative.

Antonia had concealed her own sexuality, wrapping herself in layers of calm, but as she went on talking to him she slowly, carefully, allowed that part of her to surface and begin probing toward him. Wary after the mistake she'd made with Merlin—moving much too quickly and bluntly—she intended this time to take things slowly. After all, it was hours yet until darkness fell.

"I suggest we try working together," she said pleasantly. "It won't be easy at first, but I believe Atlantia can only benefit. I'm sure we can devise a series of laws, for instance, to protect both men and women of power and enable us to live and work together as we did in the old days."

"The other males like living atop the mountains," Varian murmured. "I doubt they'll be easily persuaded to change at this late date." Her eyes, he thought, were lovely. Like the one still-pure lake left in Atlantia, blue and clear and seemingly bottomless.

"I'm sure you could persuade them to at least listen."

"Perhaps—though I'd probably be more successful at using force rather than persuasion." Had he thought her skin rough? Odd. She had the complexion of a much younger woman, he decided, translucent and silky in appearance. Just a touch of color, of inner heat . . .

Antonia smiled. "However you . . . command them . . . the means can be justified if our goal is reached."

"Assuming we agree on the goal." Her mouth was remarkably erotic, Varian thought, watching it move as she spoke and listening to the words with only minimal attention. The lips were red and full and moist, conjuring images in his mind of how they would feel and look touching various parts of his body, trailing across his skin . . .

"We can discuss what we mean to do," Antonia said in a pleasant tone, and smoothly went on doing just that. Advancing suggestions on how they might repair the damages to their society, by either bringing the males down into the valley or allowing the females into the mountains. The latter made more sense as their removal from the valley might well cause the Curtain to disperse once and for all. Putting forth her ideas for new laws, for standards of behavior, for ways in which the men and women of power might work together.

As the sun sank lower and lower in the western sky, Antonia talked softly, explaining her ideas not because she expected him to approve of her plans but simply to fill the silence as she slowly exposed her potent carnality to him in the urgent bid to seduce him. She intended to rule him completely, to chain him and dominate him with silken bonds of lust, and to that end she worked subtly to fill him with a burning desire for her.

Only for her.

Her one experience lay in the brief encounter with Merlin, and from that Antonia had drawn one dangerously false conclusion. She assumed that in order to dominate a male sexually, it was necessary to light the fires of lust as well as provide a steady supply of fuel to maintain the blaze. Because she had found Merlin so cool to her, and because he had been able to resist her, her manipulation of Varian was as intense as it was subtle. She poured everything she had into the attempt, never realizing that all males were different, and that, for this particular male, filling his mind with erotic thoughts and his body with carnal sensations was like pouring oil on an inferno. The result—a conflagration she would have no hope of controlling once it burst its bounds.

Varian responded with nods, grunts, and other signs of agreement and/or interest—and he never took his eyes off her. Antonia was exciting herself as well as him, reveling in her sense of dominance as much as she was anticipating the experience of joining with him. Her body was hot and throbbing, there was an unfamiliar wetness between her thighs, and her nipples had tightened so much in a way that was painful. Exquisitely painful. Even her voice had become husky, the sound of it far more important than the words it spoke.

She didn't know how much time had passed, but the light pouring in the front door had faded quite a bit when she finally allowed her voice to trail into silence. His eyes glittered, his face was sharp and almost hollow-cheeked as if with mortal hunger, and his slow breathing was audible. He was very still.

Enjoying the building of lust, Antonia decided to draw it out even more. She rose languidly from her chair and went to the window. The sun was down, and the first wisps of the Curtain were swirling over the valley.

Sharp disappointment lanced through her. She'd had no intention of remaining here after dark. Once the Curtain fell, she'd be unable to use her powers and he would no longer be under the spell she had so carefully created. She wouldn't be able to control him, to completely dominate him. He might hurt her, and that was a risk she was unwilling to take. Much better to leave now, even if she had to begin all over again tomorrow . . .

"I must go," she murmured. "Perhaps we can meet again tomorrow and continue?"

An odd, hoarse sound came from Varian, and even as she half turned from the window, he was striding across the room toward her. Antonia instinctively lifted a hand, but he was already there, his much larger hands grasping her wrists painfully, and his voice was like a growl.

"Go? What are you talking about, whore? You aren't going anywhere—except to my bed if we make it that far . . ."

Shocked and incensed by the blunt words and rough handling, Antonia found herself hauled against his hard body as he tried to kiss her. His mouth—disgustingly wet—slid over her cheek and sharp teeth nipped at her bottom lip before she could jerk her head to one side.

"Stop that! Let go of me!"

"You want it, whore, you know you do. You've been licking your lips for the last hour," he muttered, trying to hold the back of her head to keep her still.

Neither of them noticed the fine sparks that showered to the floor all around them, signs of building energy escaping its bounds.

Antonia gasped when one of his hands closed over her breast and squeezed roughly, and she struggled to get one hand free to slap him. The blow held her normal physical strength as well as other energy, and more sparks flew.

"No!" She hit him again, this time with pure energy, and though his body flinched his eyes burned hot with intent.

"A whore in my bed, that's what I want," Varian told her with a harsh laugh. "Spread her legs and ride her, haughty bitch. Insolent whore." He was yanking at her robe, trying to pull the skirt up while attempting to get a knee between her legs. "I'll have you—"

She hit him with another bolt of energy and instantly, fiercely, he returned the blow even as he was rubbing himself against her. Antonia staggered, but a snarl, almost a howl, of frustration, rage, and defeat erupted from her mouth. He was utterly, completely out of her control, mad with lust, and she knew she had lost her gamble.

He was bent on taking what she had dangled before him, by force if necessary and no matter how much both of them suffered for it. He would never be swayed by reason, never be turned back by anything she could do or say. Her only choice was to fight him, even though she knew with a hollow certainty how it would end . . .

"I'll have you," he repeated thickly, holding her buttocks to grind himself harder against her.

"*No!*" she shrieked, loosing bolts of her power and not flinching when she felt the heat of them herself.

The jolts pushed him back a bit, but he still had hold of her and his eyes were molten now, blind and inhuman.

"You're mine!" he roared, his power beginning to form an aura that was hot white and shot with streaks of pure black—energy so intense it emitted no light at all.

Antonia shrieked again, this time in pain as well as fury, and her hands were grasping now, clawing at his clothing, raking across skin.

"Never," she panted, her eyes going unfocused as she reached for the farthest limits of her powers . . .

And Varian released another bestial sound, his hands lifting to her throat even as his mouth crushed hers . . .

As a huge full moon rose between two mountain peaks and beamed down on the valley, the Curtain was abruptly disturbed by wild streams of energy lancing upward from the Old City. With a sound like thunder, the Curtain rolled and snapped, and the earth heaved and groaned with a new violence.

Shrieks and a roar of rage erupted from the Old City, where only the stoic night watched as two figures struggled frenziedly in a lighted window while jagged bolts of raw power emanated from them.

Lashed by the effects of a titanic battle, Atlantis broke under the strain.

PART THREE

Seattle

FIFTEEN

Serena had forgotten the unnerving sounds and sensations of time travel. Like stepping into total darkness with no idea if she would find solid ground beneath her feet or only miles of air . . . There was a whistling like wind rushing by, yet no sensation of its passing, and colors she couldn't see and yet sensed were exploding all around her like starbursts. Something yanked at her as powerfully as gravity, but she was weightless, carried along on a raging tide of space and time. What she knew of reality was warped, shaped, and molded into obedience by the skilled and mighty hand of a Master Wizard.

It seemed to last forever, thousands of years . . . or maybe it was only a few seconds. Then, with jarring abruptness, her foot touched something hard and the silence was almost deafening and there was light.

She blinked away the retinal shock of passing from total darkness into the normal illumination of daylight and lamps, and looked around her at the familiar outlines of Merlin's study. And it wasn't until her breath flooded out in a shaky sigh that she realized how afraid she'd been.

"Serena? Are you all right?" His grasp on her hand tightened.

"Fine. I think. We're back, aren't we? We're really back?"

"Yes, we're back. Did you expect the gate to fail?"

"I don't know." Then she shook her head. "No, of course I didn't. You built the gate, and I trusted it to work. It's just that . . ."

Quietly, Merlin said, "You weren't sure what we'd find here."

"No," she confessed. She glanced behind them to find that the gate had vanished; designed for a single trip, its job was done. And she didn't have to touch the base of her throat or look at Merlin's hand to know that the marks had vanished, left in the past where they had belonged.

She looked down at herself a bit warily and then at him, finding them dressed as they had been when they had left the present for the past. Jeans and sweaters. So . . . normal. So modern.

Merlin sent the box containing his staff back to its accustomed place on one of the shelves. Not letting go of Serena's hand, he waited for her to reacquaint herself with their present.

"It looks the same," she murmured, gazing around them. There was the handsome but sparse furniture of the room: a few sturdy chairs and small tables, the desk, a bookstand near the window holding an open, very large, leather-bound manual detailing the abilities of wizards—written entirely in a cryptic language that resembled Latin but wasn't. There were the other heavy dark volumes and neat scrolls on the shelves, a number of them open on his big desk. "Just the same."

"Of course. We've only been gone a few minutes."

Intellectually, Serena knew that, but physically and emotionally she was just as certain that nearly a month had passed. She shook her head. "I guess . . . I expected us to find some kind of visible consequences of the trip here when we came through the gate. I mean, we travelled back in *time*. Way back. Shouldn't our return be greeted by—by something?"

"Like what?" Merlin was amused.

"Bells and whistles. Fireworks. A siren or two. The wizard police charging in ready to punish us for travelling in time without the proper permission. A layer of dust on the furniture. *Something*."

Merlin looked around them at the peaceful study. "No, I don't think so. Like so many things of consequence, our trip is going to pass unheralded by everyone except us."

Serena bit her bottom lip as she gazed up at him. "Well . . . did we do it? Did we change the present for us?"

He answered quietly. "I don't know. I wouldn't expect to see anything changed here in the house—or here in Seattle—whether or not we were successful, since only the society of wizards is likely to be different if we were. To help wizards avoid unnecessary conflict with one another, we live scattered over the globe and gather together as infrequently as possible. When we left, you and I were the only wizards in the Northwest, and that may not have changed."

Serena was a little surprised. She had known they were the only wizards in Seattle, but she hadn't really thought about why that was so. "The decision to live apart from each other—did that come about after Atlantis?"

"Yes, I think so. And even if we *were* successful in changing what went wrong, Atlantis was still destroyed, and given the negative influence of the wizards there, it was undoubtedly taken as a grave warning by the other wizards of the time. It would have been prudent to avoid having too many beings of power together in one place; the society of wizards is still likely to be a scattered one no matter what else changed."

"Then . . . how do we find out if we were successful?"

"We ask," Merlin replied simply. "I can call my father. If we failed, and women are still forbidden to be trained as wizards, I'll know soon enough. He'll want to know how the procedure is going."

"The procedure . . . to render me powerless?"

"Yes."

There was no phone in Merlin's study; Serena glanced toward the door and thought about the one out in the foyer. Such a simple thing, to make a phone call. Such a simple thing to measure success . . . or failure.

"Serena?"

"I'm not so sure I want to know just yet." With effort, she managed to smile up at him.

Merlin leaned down and kissed her, gently but with his strong desire for her unhidden and barely restrained. "Waiting won't change anything," he reminded her.

Serena didn't know how she would have responded to the truth of that, and before she could think about it, the sudden peal of the doorbell nearly made her jump out of her skin. The sound was both alien and familiar, and definitely disconcerting.

"Was it always that shrill?" she muttered.

"You've just forgotten," Merlin replied, gazing thoughtfully toward the front of the house.

Because he was still holding her hand, Serena was immediately aware of his probing, and also of the results. She was pleased that the physical contact enabled her to share a portion of his considerable abilities, but the knowledge of just who had come calling on this already unsettling Friday morning put a damper on her pleasure.

"Kane."

"Mmmm." Merlin looked down at her with a slightly rueful smile. "We didn't have the time to do anything about Mr. Kane before we left—but he does have to be dealt with."

"You don't think he'll stop digging into our lives if we just ignore him?"

"He's here, isn't he?" Merlin squeezed her hand and then released it. "Let him in, Serena. Let's find out what he has on his mind."

Serena was curious herself, so she went out into the foyer and opened the heavy front door. Studying the reporter—who, as usual, looked rumpled and slightly hung-over—she said mildly, "Well, well, if it isn't my favorite former journalist. Good morning, Kane. What can I do for you?"

Jeremy Kane's attempt at a pleasant smile was rather appalling. "Good morning, Serena. What did you think of my article?"

It took Serena a moment to remember—God, had it only been last week?—the details of the malicious article that had proven to be such a powerful catalyst. Gazing at Kane, she wondered if he could possibly imagine what an incredible chain of events he had set into motion.

Still smiling amiably, she said, "I thought the article belonged in a supermarket rag, Kane. It had all the journalistic class of a story about the latest sighting of Bigfoot or Elvis."

Kane flushed an angry red. Harshly, he said, "I went to Merlin's office, but it was closed. Is he here?"

Bring him into the study, Serena.

She stepped back and opened the door wider, thinking how nice it was to hear that calm, resonant voice in her head. She felt very much connected to Merlin, and her awareness of that bond made her certain as his voice. Whether or not they had been successful in changing the society of wizards, together they definitely had found personal triumph.

Kane came into the foyer, looking around and then eyeing her warily as she shut the door behind him. "Where is he?"

"This way." She strolled into Merlin's study and took up a position near the desk as she leaned against the back of a leather wingback chair. She was situated perfectly to watch both men.

Merlin was in front of his desk and leaning back against it, with his arms crossed over his chest. His black eyes fixed on Kane as the older man entered the room—and there was a brilliance in them that Serena had never seen Merlin show to anyone in Seattle. It was the somewhat disconcerting look of a Master wizard: an almost hypnotic, unshuttered power.

Kane jolted to a stop a few feet from the desk, one

hand reaching for his loosened tie in nervous gesture. He wore a slight frown and was clearly unsettled.

"Hello, Kane," Merlin said coolly. Even his voice was subtly different, so deep and vibrant it almost seemed to echo in the quiet room. "Is there something I can do for you?"

After a glance at Serena, the reporter said, "You might want to hear this in private, Merlin." His voice was blustery, the attempt to verbally dominate the younger man completely transparent and hardly successful.

"No, I don't think so. Anything you have to say to me can be said in front of Serena. She knows most of my secrets."

"Most?" Serena queried with interest. "You mean, I don't know them all?"

"Allow me to preserve some hint of mystery," Merlin said, turning his head to look at her. "I don't want to bore you."

"Somehow, I doubt that could ever happen."

"Perhaps not, but I'd rather be cautious."

"Well . . . if you insist. But you know, of course, that now I'm very curious. In spite of myself, I'll have to do my best to uncover your secrets."

Merlin smiled. "I think I'll enjoy that."

"*Excuse* me," Kane sputtered.

Looking back at their guest, Merlin said politely, "Do forgive us. You were saying?"

"I *knew* there was something between you two," Kane said victoriously, allowing himself to be led off on a slight tangent.

Merlin lifted an eyebrow with faint mockery. "Congratulations on your intuition."

"You aren't going to deny it?"

"Why on earth should I? What you see before you, Kane, are two—I believe the phrase is consenting adults—who are breaking no laws and harming no one. If there's a story in that, I'd like to know what it is."

"She was a minor when she came to live with you," Kane pointed out nastily.

"Which was nine years ago. Whatever may have happened between us then is definitely old news. In point of fact, I acted as Serena's guardian until she came of age, and there was nothing sexual between us. If you think you can prove otherwise, go right ahead."

Kane wasn't quite willing to wallow in the gutter to the extent of threatening to ruin Merlin's reputation with veiled accusations of impropriety, and his frustration was as visible as a cloud of steam.

Serena had to hide a smile. She was thoroughly enjoying the little scene, mostly because it was a striking indication of how much Merlin had changed since their trip through time. He was having fun with Kane, and that relaxed, nonchalant attitude was incredibly sexy; it made him seem very human, even as the vivid radiance of his black eyes was a reminder of the vast power under his control.

She didn't know what he had in mind for Kane, but Serena had the distinct impression that Merlin's solution for the problem the inquisitive reporter posed was going to be much more playful than it would have been before their visit to Atlantis.

"I've been digging into your background," Kane told the Master wizard finally in a defiant voice.

"Why?" Merlin inquired, nothing in his tone but courteous interest.

"It's full of weird things, that's why. Name me somebody else who was involved—to put it politely—in half a dozen mysterious cases of fire before he was out of elementary school."

"Richard, you didn't."

"You weren't the only one who had trouble with fire, I'm afraid," Merlin confessed to Serena gravely.

"And you had the nerve to rag me about it!"

"I was much younger at the time than you were, Serena. Much younger. And they were very small fires."

She sniffed disdainfully. "Yeah, sure."

Kane, clearly baffled, was scowling, and his voice broke a bit when he said, "There were other odd things too. I managed to track down a few of your schoolmates—"

"Who remembered me clearly after twenty-five years?" Merlin interrupted sardonically.

"Oh, they remembered you, all right. Most of them just said what they recalled was how incredibly lucky you were."

Serena looked at Kane with lifted brows, and asked in astonishment, "Are you going to hang him for that?"

"No, not for that! But I want to know how he's going to answer questions that have baffled quite a few experts for twenty-five years." Kane glared at Merlin. "Questions like—how was it possible that during the several years you lived in Chicago, three planes that *should* have crashed, didn't? Those planes were mechanically damaged to the point that all the experts agree they should have gone down. Even the pilots didn't know what the hell had saved them. And it's a funny thing. You were there all three times. Twice on field trips with a science class, and the third time about to leave on vacation with your parents."

Serena gazed at Merlin's calm face, thinking of a boy not knowledgeable enough to repair damaged planes in such a way that there would be no mystery for the experts, and yet powerful enough to bring the crippled aircraft down safely. Softly, she said, "So we can't repair the ills of mankind?"

He looked at her and smiled. "No . . . just a few engines here and there."

Kane was more than a little disconcerted by the exchange. He looked from one to the other, then blurted, "There were some other things—"

"Never mind." Merlin studied the visitor briefly, then sighed. "Have a seat, Kane."

Serena had a premonition. "Are you sure this is a good idea?" she asked.

"Why not?" Merlin shrugged. "After all, we really owe him a debt. If it hadn't been for his article . . ."

She agreed with a nod. "Yeah, but that doesn't mean we have to go overboard with gratitude. It wasn't like he had a positive motive for writing that piece."

"It's all right, Serena. Trust me."

She matched his smile, thinking about how both of

them had come to value those two simple words. And since she had utter faith in Merlin's abilities, it was easy to accept his assurances.

"What the hell are you talking about?" Kane demanded, frowning. "I came here for a few answers—"

"You came here," Merlin told him pleasantly, "for a story. I don't know what you expected to find, and I doubt you were very clear on that point, but what you're going to get is the truth."

"Yeah? Let's hear it."

"Seeing it might be more convincing." Smiling, Merlin straightened away from the desk and made a slight, graceful gesture with both hands. Instantly, he was wearing his midnight-blue Master's robe.

Kane's mouth dropped open, and he had to try twice before he could speak. "How'd you do that?"

"I'm a wizard," Merlin replied simply.

"A *Master* wizard," Serena contributed. "That's top of the line, Kane. It means he's the best. Your first clue probably should have been his name."

"Serena."

"Well, it should have."

Gripping with white fingers the arms of his chair he had sat in, Kane muttered, "It's a trick. Just a cheap magician's trick."

Merlin shrugged. "If you think that, then obviously there's no story, is there? You were simply overly suspicious and misinformed. All the experts were wrong, and those planes were quite able to land safely. Those curious little fires in my childhood have a logical and reasonable explanation. And all the other mysteries you've uncovered in my past are really not mysteries at all."

Kane found himself caught in the unenviable position of having been handed a possible answer to all his questions and uneasy suspicions—and finding it so incredible it defied belief. Yet all his instincts were screaming at him, urging him to believe the impossible. He stared at the man before him, at the curiously alien, shimmering robe and that easy, confident smile . . . and those eyes. *Those eyes.*

"And if I believe you?" he asked in a thick voice that was hardly more than a whisper.

Merlin was matter of fact. "Then you have one hell of a story, Kane. Just think of it. There are wizards in modern society, beings of power, something the public is hardly aware of. We can create fire and water and control the weather. We can, for the most part, heal the sick and injured, repair damage to virtually anything, and fly without a plane . . . or a broomstick. We can rearrange matter—meaning that I could turn your chair into a rock or a tiger, and you into a toad if I were so inclined. We can harness and use our own electrical energy as a weapon, precise and deadly as a laser beam. And we can travel through time."

Kane laughed, harshly but shakily. "You expect me to buy all that? Then turn my chair into a tiger, mighty wizard! Show me your power."

With no more than a flick of his fingers, Merlin did, and Kane jerked away from the large, warm, reclining body he found himself sitting on just as it turned its striped face toward him and growled softly.

"Jesus!"

The tiger rose to its feet and snarled again, yellow eyes fierce—and then reformed smoothly into a sturdy, inanimate chair. Kane backed away from it and from Merlin until he was pressed against crowded bookshelves. His face was very pale, but he was managing to control his panic.

"You asked," Merlin reminded him dryly.

"I thought we couldn't do that," Serena said in an aggrieved tone. "Create living beings."

"Some of us can," Merlin told her. "But animals only, and the higher orders are extremely difficult."

"You lied to me!"

"Not at all. I merely withheld the truth. Besides, you won't be able to do it until you're a Master."

"Oh. Well, in that case, you're forgiven."

Ignoring this exchange, the reporter darted his gaze around the room as if looking for an escape, and fixed on Serena. The realization seemed to dismay him almost comically. "You too?"

"Afraid so. I'm Richard's Apprentice. I came to him at sixteen to learn how to be a wizard."

Kane glared at her. "Bigfoot and Elvis sightings, huh?"

A low laugh escaped her. "Touché. But we *are* different, you know. We aren't tacky."

Kane grappled a moment in silence, trying to work things out in his mind, then said, "That announcement about the grant. You did take it from my apartment."

It took Serena a moment to remember, and then she nodded. "Yeah, I did. I wanted to know if Seth got the grant. So I sent for it to come to your pocket. And then I just put you to sleep before you could pass out."

"I don't believe this. Any of it."

Merlin, able to sense as well as see the reporter's rising agitation, spoke calmly. "We're no threat to you, Kane. To any of you. I'll tell you another little secret. Our kind has walked the earth as long as yours has; there have always been beings of power—and there always will be. With very few exceptions, we've learned to pass unnoticed in society."

"Exceptions?"

"Some of us have been careless from time to time, which is why there are stories about witches and sorcerers and the like. And some born wizards don't realize what they are, which is why they make a living performing parlor tricks like bending spoons and taking photographs with their minds."

Kane felt oddly relieved when Merlin—Was he *the* wizard Merlin? But how was that possible?—made another of those supple gestures that apparently caused his blue robe to vanish and leave him dressed normally again in jeans and a thick sweater. Then he leaned back against the desk again while Kane tried to make himself think clearly.

"If you don't want this to get out, then why the hell are you admitting it to me?" he demanded finally.

"Mostly because I knew very well you weren't going to give up." Merlin smiled faintly. "That was obvious. I could have removed any interest in myself and Serena from your mind, but that's an intrusion I'd rather not have to make."

"Is that a threat?"

"No. You see, we don't toy with people, Kane. It's against our laws. At the same time, we have no intention of going public just yet; it's a human trait to always fear what you don't understand, and that could cause us a great deal of unnecessary trouble . . . as it has in the past."

"These are hardly the Dark Ages," Kane scoffed. "We're not afraid of things that go bump in the night."

"Oh? Then why are you backed up against a shelf?"

Embarrassed, the reporter straightened his shoulders and stepped forward toward the desk—and Merlin. But his bravado didn't hide his wariness when he said, "If you're not threatening to do something to my mind, then what makes you think I'm not going to take this story public?"

"They wouldn't believe you," Serena murmured. "You'd sound like a raving lunatic. And in a contest of your word against Richard's, he'd win hands down."

Kane thought she was probably right. Keeping his gaze on the Master wizard, he said, "Maybe that's true, but I wouldn't be the first reporter to face disbelief— and if you yell long enough, people start to listen. And believe."

Merlin looked at him steadily. "I want to make something very clear, Kane. I have the ability to make very sure you never say a word about this to anyone. I can place a spell on you that's rather like a post-hypnotic suggestion, so that all you would have to do is simply *decide* to tell someone—and you'd lose it. You would instantly have no memory of this conversation or any interest in us whatsoever. In other words, you would lose, for all time, a part of your experience. A piece of your being."

Kane found that unexpectedly sobering and not a little chilling. He swallowed hard. "And you don't toy with us, huh?"

"I'm not toying with you, I'm merely telling you what I'm capable of."

"Then we're back to square one," the reporter said. "If you have no intention of going public, why the hell did you tell me about this? To torture me?"

"No. To make a point, I suppose."

"Which is?"

Merlin's wide shoulders lifted and fell in a shrug, and he smiled. "That there are more things in heaven and earth than even a jaded investigative reporter could imagine. You had talent, Kane, and you let it trickle through your fingers; I think that was a shame. I think that, somewhere along the way—and please forgive the maudlin phrase—you gave up on life. It's a waste, and I hate waste."

Kane might have sneered at that, but he didn't. He merely stared at Merlin, unmoved. "So you're gonna save me, huh?"

"I'm not that presumptuous—or that philanthropic. No, your future is yours to shape. I just thought that it might make a difference to a man like you to find out that the world has quite a few mysteries left. I may not allow you to display mine, but I'm sure there are others you would find interesting. If you care to look for them, that is."

Kane didn't know what to make of Merlin, but he knew he had a lot of thinking to do. "Maybe I'll do that," he said, easing toward the door, inwardly furious that he was afraid to turn his back on the wizard. Wizard? God!

"I can be a very good friend to have," Merlin offered, still smiling easily.

"And a bad enemy?"

"Exactly."

Kane found himself in the doorway of the study, and paused there. "So tell me, have you fixed it so I'll lose a piece of my mind if I try to take this story public?"

"No," Merlin replied. "Not yet anyway."

"Don't tell me you trust me?"

"Hardly. I'm just giving you a little rope, Kane. Use it to climb—or knot it into a noose. It's up to you."

The reporter took a step back out into the foyer, but

paused again, this time with a jerk, when Merlin spoke softly.

"By the way . . . the voice-activated tape recorder in your pocket? You'll find the tape blank. Funny thing about wizards; we tend to adversely affect electrical and magnetic fields if we're not careful. I'm afraid I wasn't careful."

Kane looked both furious and nervous, and this time he backed completely out of sight. A moment later, the front door opened and loudly closed.

Serena came out from behind her chair and went to Merlin. "For a nice guy, you can sound a little scary," she told him solemnly.

He put his hands on her waist and drew her closer so that she was standing between his knees. "You don't seem frightened," he observed, smiling.

"No, but Kane was shaking in his shoes, at least for the moment." She leaned even closer and linked her fingers together behind his neck. "Do you think he'll keep quiet?"

"I think . . . life will probably be quite interesting for a while."

Serena eyed him in amusement. "I think you're looking forward to a fight with Kane. Practically every word you uttered to him was like waving a red flag at a bull— and don't tell me you didn't know that."

Merlin shrugged. "I imagine I can handle Kane no matter what he decides to do. And if we didn't change our present after all, we'll be gone and the Council can deal with him."

Her smile faded a little. "I keep forgetting about that."

He bent his head and kissed her, the light touch rapidly becoming more intense, and when Merlin finally drew back a little his black eyes were burning and heavy-lidded. Huskily, he said, "I want to find out if we were successful so we can go forward from here, Serena. Our future is together, remember that."

She nodded. "Then I guess you should go and call your father."

Merlin let her ease back away from him, but took his

hands off her only reluctantly. He wondered if he would ever grow accustomed to the magic of touching her, and knew he wouldn't; it was the only magic in his life that was utterly, wonderfully, beyond his control.

There were some things no man was meant to master.

"Not just yet," he said. "I realized something just before Kane came into the room."

"What?"

He went around the desk and pushed his chair back, looking down at the big book lying open on the blotter. "This. These, really—all the books, Serena. If we changed history, we should find evidence of it in the books."

Serena leaned her hands on the front of the desk and followed his gaze. "Isn't that one the book your father gave you? The one with the procedure to take my powers?"

"Yes."

Uneasily, she said, "Then why is it still here? I mean, if he only gave it to you because of the procedure—?"

"There could have been another reason he gave it to me in this version of the present, Serena. There *must* have been." He turned to a specific section of the book, scanning the text rapidly, then looked across the desk at her and smiled. "Things are looking up. The procedure isn't here."

"Maybe it just moved to a different part of the book," she offered, still apprehensive.

"I don't think so." Merlin turned several pages quickly. "There was a brief section detailing what Tremayne—at least, I hope it was Tremayne—saw from his ship. . . ."

Serena rested a hip on the desk and chewed on her bottom lip, trying not to worry. She was as patient as she could be, her gaze flicking from the open book to Merlin's bent head, then finally said, "I'm going to go nuts if you don't tell me—"

He looked at her, his expression grave. "There's more here than there was before we went back in time. I'll read it out loud."

Serena braced herself.

" 'It happened not long after nightfall,' " he read quietly. " 'Because we had dropped our sails less than a day out for the crew to make minor repairs, Atlantia was still within sight, though barely. We heard the sound first, a rumble such as I have never known. Then the sky over Atlantia was rent by dazzling streams of energy, and the sound grew louder, more terrible. We stood on the deck as if frozen, unable to remove our horrified gazes from the awful sight of the very earth being wrenched apart. It did not take long. The mountains shuddered and heaved, some of them literally exploding, and the sea began to churn and boil. Then there was a last, dreadful convulsion, and the land where I had spent the past months sank without a trace into the sea.' "

Serena drew a deep, slow breath when Merlin paused. "So that didn't change," she murmured.

"No, but the report did. Before we went back to Atlantis, this report was very terse and not a little bitter. And this last part wasn't here. Listen: 'I am convinced that what happened here could have been avoided. The lesson to be learned is twofold. First, no being of power should be allowed to control his or her surroundings to the detriment of others, and should be restrained by reasonable laws from unbridled ambition. And, second, men and women of power must be encouraged to co-exist peacefully, to understand rather than fear or mistrust one another, for neither of us can be whole without the other.' "

"That sounds . . . encouraging," Serena offered.

"Definitely." Merlin's eyes were very bright. He looked through the other books on his desk and then handed her one. "Check this one, Serena—you should be able to read it. Before we left, there were a number of passages that might have dealt with when and how the law against female wizards was created, only they were illegible—deliberately so, I thought. But now there may be nothing they wanted to hide."

She obediently bent over the book, reading more slowly than he would have done but with fair ease. She was aware that he opened another book, but didn't look up until she had found something.

"There's a passage here concerning male and female wizards," she told him. "The gist of it is what we found out ourselves—that the powers of a male and female wizard can combine, making the pair stronger than either alone, but only when there is the kind of deep trust found between mates."

"With that potential dangled enticingly out in front of them," Merlin noted, "I doubt there was much talk of getting rid of the women."

"Umm. Let me keep reading, there might be more."

But it was Merlin who found something less than five minutes later. "Serena."

She looked up. "You found something?"

He was smiling. "Yes. This volume contains a number of family trees. I thought you might like to know that Tremayne and Roxanne had six children—four girls and two boys."

Serena felt herself grinning. "Really? They made it?"

"They made it. And they went on to live long and apparently happy lives."

"And . . . Kerry?"

"She made it as well. There's a note here that Tremayne and Roxanne also raised a foster daughter—who grew up to mate with a man of power." He shook his head slightly. "Two women born in Atlantis, and both of them were able to rise above what they'd been taught, and what they had experienced themselves."

Serena slowly closed the book she had been reading. "You know, I'm not quite so nervous now about that call to Chicago. Why don't you go ahead and make it?"

Merlin came around the desk to her. He framed her face in both his hands, and gazed at her seriously. "No matter what happens," he told her, "no matter what we find out, we're going to be together, Serena. I love you."

"I love you too."

He kissed her. "Thank you."

She was surprised. "For what? For loving you?"

"For that. And for teaching me how to love." He smiled at her, his wonderful black eyes liquid with tenderness. "Come on. Let's go make that call."

EPILOGUE

Chicago, 1993

The late fall day was chilly and blustery, providing a taste of the coming winter, but inside the large study, a blazing fire in the hearth warmed the room.

"We're finally going to meet the Apprentice of Richard's he's talked so much about," Eric Merlin said in a tone of satisfaction as he hung up the phone.

"It's about time."

"I know. Though I suppose it's been for the best, her training taking place out in Seattle without interference or distractions. God knows it's difficult enough for any wizard to learn the art, but it's particularly difficult for someone like Serena."

"Because she was born to powerless parents?"

He nodded. "We lose so many, you know, the ones who have no real understanding of what they are and what they're capable of. It's a genuine tragedy. The Council tries to find the ones with power before they're lost to us, but it's a big world. Thank God a few like Serena have the instincts to go out and find a Master to teach them before their powers are drained or corrupted by the distrust of powerless people or a simple lack of understanding. Richard believes she has the potential to be a seventh-degree Master."

"Good. And . . . what else?"

He smiled. "I've been told by others that she's beautiful. And spirited. I'll bet she's made life very interesting for him. Richard didn't say, but it was fairly obvious from his tone how he feels about her."

"That's even better. He needs a woman who's strong enough to understand him."

"Yes, I agree."

"So they're coming to Chicago?"

"Tonight, in fact, and they'll stay for the weekend." Then he frowned. "It's odd. . . ."

"What?"

"Well, when I reminded Richard that you always kept his room ready for whenever he wanted to visit, he seemed almost surprised to hear it. No, that word isn't strong enough. He seemed . . . almost dazed."

"He was probably pulling your leg, darling."

"Catherine, I know my son."

"Yes, but for all you know, Serena may have come into the room just then wearing nothing but a smile."

He chuckled. "True. Anyway, he said to give you his love, and that he'd see us tonight."

"Wonderful." She smiled at him, then rose from her chair and came to the desk, a beautiful woman who was still slender and graceful and elegant, her face still unlined and her hair still untouched by silver, though she had turned sixty on her last birthday. She bent to kiss him, but he pulled her down into his lap instead, a gleam in his black eyes.

"Eric . . ."

"Catherine?"

"I have to go and check with cook about dinner tonight, and then I have to make sure Richard's room is ready for them—"

"All you *have* to do, sweetheart, is kiss your husband."

"Yes, Your Honor." And she did, delighted by the knowledge that it kept getting better even after forty years. A benefit of loving and being loved by a wizard, she supposed, threading her fingers through his silky black hair. One of the many benefits.

A note from the Publisher

Many of today's most popular and successful writers of women's fiction began their careers writing short contemporary romances. Like Nora Roberts, Sandra Brown, and Iris Johansen, the author of this book made her name and honed her craft on what people in the book trade call "category" romance. The category romance—as published by Bantam's LOVESWEPT—is a wonderful and engaging short contemporary love story. Unlike the old-fashioned, formulaic rich-man-poor-woman romances that dominated the market years ago, today's category romances are timely stories that deal with the very issues that are important to you. The style is captivating, the love is real, and the passion runs deep. Some LOVESWEPTs are more witty, some more sensual, some are laced with humor, some packed with emotion; but they are all well-written stories of true love by talented writers that quickly entrance and entertain you for a few hours.

The author of this book has composed a brief account of her experience with LOVESWEPT, and she invites you to take a dip into the world of category romance. If you have never read a LOVESWEPT novel, the author and her *publisher encourage you to ask for one at your bookstore—and discover a wonderful reading experience.*

As a writer, I was lucky enough to make my first sale both very early in my attempts to do so and at a relatively young age. In other words, I was young enough, and green enough, to have no idea how high the odds were against my success. I was also extremely lucky in that my first sale was for a category—or series—romance.

Why was that lucky, you ask? Because in series romance, I discovered a veritable treasure chest of possibilities. Not only could I hone by abilities as a writer by having to tell a complete story in a limited space, and not only were my storytelling abilities challenged by the fact that I was presented each time with a boy-meets-girl format I *had* to work within, but I was also given a truly liberating amount of encouragement to explore elements hardly usual in the traditional definition of romance.

So if you pick up one of my series novels expecting to find more of the old-style "little romances" of years ago, like doctor-meets-nurse, or boss-meets-secretary, or even boy-next-door-meets-girl-he-abandoned-years-ago, you're in for a shock. Series romance has come a long way, and I'm proud to say I've been a part of the revolution.

So what can I offer you, specifically? Well, I've written stories about ESP and reincarnation, about federal cops and cat burglars, about professional gamblers and computer technicians. I write about characters who interest me, and I drop them into the middle of situations that are rarely as simple as they seem. My heroines have intelligence, spirit, and humor (Serena in THE WIZARD OF SEATTLE is a prime example), and my heroes are strong, intelligent men with the ability to laugh at themselves and the capacity to love as joyously and completely as the depths of the human heart intended (like Merlin, my wizard).

Even more specifically, I've done a series-within-a-series for LOVESWEPT this year, and if you want to know what my books are all about I can't think of a better example. The series is called *Men of Mysteries*

Past, and the titles are: THE TOUCH OF MAX, HUNTING THE WOLFE, THE TROUBLE WITH JARED, and ALL FOR QUINN. The four stories are interconnected by characters and by the setting, which is an exhibit of priceless gems and artworks called *Mysteries Past*.

I don't think you'll be disappointed with series romance. I can promise you, these aren't the stories your mother read years ago; these stories are written for *you* by someone who's struggling with the complexities of today's world just as hard as you are yourself—someone like me.

Happy reading!

ABOUT THE AUTHOR

KAY HOOPER is indisputably one of the top romance writers today. Known for the wit and sensuality of her writing, Kay is beloved by readers and critics alike. She has over 4 million copies of her romances in print.

In her thirties, Kay lives in North Carolina with a menagerie of pets, a huge collection of unicorn drawings and figurines, and within shouting distance of her family who heartily supports her career. Kay is a pioneer in the creation of series-within-series romances and has produced such masterful works as the *Once Upon a Time* ... series, the lauded "Hagan Strikes Again" romances, and the *Men of Mysteries Past* series. She is one of the three authors who created the brilliantly innovative and successful series on the Delaney Dynasty, including THE DELANEY CHRISTMAS CAROL.